ARTHUR SMITH

Kolibri

**Grosvenor House
Publishing Limited**

Arthur Smith is hereby identified as author of this
work in accordance with Section 77 of the Copyright, Designs
and Patents Act 1988

The book cover is copyright to 123RF licensed to Arthur Smith

This book is published by
Grosvenor House Publishing Ltd
28-30 High Street, Guildford, Surrey, GU1 3EL.
www.grosvenorhousepublishing.co.uk

This book is a work of fiction and except in the case of historical fact
any resemblance to actual persons living or dead is purely coincidental.

A CIP record for this book
is available from the British Library

ISBN 978-1-78148-589-7

To my Family

Foreword

"And so, with the Russian forces just a few streets away now, Hitler committed suicide in the bunker, or so the story goes!?"

Introduction

10th May 1945

It was an unusual night for May in Norway. In the cloudless sky, a full moon was visible and if you had been at sea, you would have watched it pass slowly behind the jagged peaks surrounding the fiord.

No wind stirred the surface of the sea, black in its depth supporting a handful of motionless gulls, mere spots of white illuminated by the moon.

Now the birds shifted, swimming around their position, something had disturbed them, by their instinct they were concerned. The water below them moved, at first a slight vibration, now a faint monotonous thud pushed the surface of the sea to where they sat.

It was closer now and louder. The group rose as one, wheeling and calling in protest. Fifty metres away a periscope broke the surface moving towards where they had sat leaving the smear of its wake behind it.

Below, Oberleutnant Schaffer spun around the peak of his cap and pushed his face towards the scope pulling down the side handles of it as he did so. He could see only the outline of the coast against the light of the moon, the craft now some 500 metres from the shore.

The tension inside of him, masked by outward calm, his lips pursed, an indiscernible shake of the head, "Nothing," he whispered. "Take her closer."

As the vessel slowly moved forward he continued to search the shoreline. With each thud of the engine a bead of perspiration lowered itself on his brow leaving a trail as it removed grime collected during the voyage.

Two hundred metres now he pushed harder against the sights. "Stop engines," he ordered scanning the coast from side to side.

"Where is it? Where is it?" his voice betraying some concern.

Five days earlier he had received a message from Admiral Donitz. The war was over all vessels were stood down and should immediately return to their bases. The attack U-boat U977 was outbound north of Scotland.

There was a mixture of joy and anguish among the crew. Joy that they would be returning alive to their families, as not many U-boat crews would, but anguish that the war had been lost. Their personal sacrifices and those of their compatriots, now all for nothing. As Schaffer had ordered their course changed, the crew was silent each member with his own emotions.

Two hours later, the seamen felt the boat turn - changing course again - what was this? Had the signal been an error - the war was not lost? The speaker system crackled.

"We are instructed to proceed to another destination. When we arrive those members of the crew who wish to do so may disembark. There will be no dishonour in doing so, it is your choice, have all your belongings ready. No further information is available at this time."

A murmur passed amongst the crew. What was happening? Where are we going? But they were professional sailors, the elite within the German Navy, used to obeying orders without question, they had a choice, return to their families or stay. Decisions were made quickly, individually. Those with wives and children would be leaving. Those with no wish to live in a defeated Germany possibly under the yoke of the Russians or the Americans would stay, each man silent with his own thoughts.

Schaffer was still at the periscope. "Ah there it is, there it is," he muttered.

A light had appeared ahead on the shore below the cliffs, then another and finally a third, that was the signal.

"Ahead slow to 100 metres from shore," he ordered, the vessel proceeded slowly. "One hundred metres," called the helmsman. "Stop engines – surface."

The periscope lowered, the U-boat broke the still flat calm of the sea, rising like a phantom whale until it became motionless and silent.

Schaffer stood aside, a crewman made for the hatch of the tower and heaving the lever to one side pushed the hatch up and outwards, water cascaded down onto the uniforms of the men but it quickly fell away, weeks of grease and sweat saw to that.

The Captain made the top of the tower in a few steps taking in deep gulps of fresh air in doing so, pushing his head up into the cold of the night. With cap now turned round he scoured the coast with his binoculars focused on the slightest movements, the crew remained silent.

He flashed a torch light towards the shore and rested against the top of the tower. Five minutes passed, the splashing of oars becoming louder each second and then he could see four dinghies approaching, two with people on board the others carrying boxes or crates of some sort.

"Crew who are staying, to your bunks. Those who are leaving, on deck and aft now," he snapped.

The orders were obeyed and the dinghies came alongside. The rowers clambered aboard quickly helping the older and less mobile passengers on to the deck where they moved to the tower and entered the boat.

Schaffer saluted smartly as they left the tower ladder "Please follow me to your cabin. Your belongings will follow shortly and then we can be on our way."

The leavers filled the dinghies which cast off and made for shore. The whole transfer had taken less than fifteen minutes.

The tower hatch closed. The new heading was relayed to the helmsman and the U-boat left the Norwegian coast heading out into the Atlantic. The sea was calm again unmoving, the gulls had returned to resting on the surface until the dawn came and it was as if nothing had happened at this place.

Chapter 1

Tom put down the now empty beer can on to the table after slowly crushing it in his hand and leaned forward once more to look out of the window of the kitchen of the house that had been his home now for more than three years. He stroked the stubble on his chin and frowned into the sun, something had caught his attention.

In the dry red scrub land that surrounded the entire farm where he had made his home, dust clouds were often seen, dry particles of desert soil whipped up by an occasional wind generated by the incessant heat from the summer sun and thirty minutes ago he saw such an event. Usually the clouds were transient, coming and going with the breeze but this time the billowing was still there, closer now, and so he knew that on this occasion it would be no cause of nature. Something or someone was approaching, and the path being taken indicated that his farm was obviously the destination.

It was still too far away for him to make out what was there but on a day such as today he knew from experience that only an object moving at some speed would have stirred up the large volume of dust that could be seen at this distance, he guessed that it must therefore be a vehicle of some type.

Thomas Olive was in his early 40's. A tall muscular man as would befit an ex Special Forces soldier. His fair hair was thinning now but it was kept short, as had been the habit during his service days, revealing a scar picked up in a childhood accident.

Living alone as he did, he would occasionally forego shaving and sport a few days growth of stubble but he looked after himself and with his tanned skin he was always an impressive sight when visiting the nearest town as he did from time to time.

In his days in the SAS he was an expert in unarmed combat and the daily fitness routine that he undertook around the farm preserved strength and sharpness. But it was the eyes that gave him an edge whenever he had been called upon to fight. A light green, friendly enough when in company, but which seemed to alter during combat. Someone once described it as looking into the eyes of a tiger, deep pools of black surrounded by a piercing green, pitiless, fearless and the sudden change from one to the other would give him the edge over an opponent every time and a moment's hesitation by the enemy would give him the chance to strike.

Ever since his arrival in Australia it had been on his mind that sometime he would be visited, most probably unannounced, and now he would be able to see if the preparations that he had made and practiced were good enough.

He had gauged the maximum speed with which a motor could approach on the rough road so that it could be calculated how much time he had available to prepare himself. The track he knew led directly from the town which was North of the farm and went nowhere other than to his property. An all terrain type vehicle would be able to do no more than, say, thirty kph due to the unmade surface, any faster would have made the journey much too uncomfortable for the driver. Along the trail, just about ten kilometres away, was a rocky outcrop and with the dust cloud now at that marker, he had calculated some twenty minutes would see its arrival at the house. However, he was not about to wait to see who was driving and already plans had been made to intercept the approach of any stranger.

One kilometre from his farm stood a bridge over a dry gully. It had been built there by the previous owners of the property as, in winter when the rains came and water filled the gully, the road required a considerable detour to cross the flooded stream at the closest shallow point. Now it would have another use. From there he would be able to watch the visitors as they passed by. Tom knew he could make the bridge without much effort from his cabin in five minutes on foot, having rehearsed it many times in the past and there was cover. The shade afforded by the bridge and the bend in the gully secured a little moisture so that a few hardy shrubs grew on the banks. The cover would be enough to hide him from the view of any passers-by. He had anticipated that no-one would be expecting him to be hiding there and the location on the track gave him enough time to take action, dependent upon who was arriving.

Friend or foe? He needed to know before he could deal with the situation.

Chapter 2

Tom had lived at this cabin, which was part of an old sheep farm - some three hundred kilometres from Alice Springs in the Simpson Desert of Australia for around three years now. His nearest neighbours were on another farm to the South some fifty kilometres away, and the inhabitants of the small settlement of Radinga, north of his property, which he could reach within a few hours' drive. From there he obtained the basics of his everyday life, and it was here that a Post Office box arrangement had been set up for him although little in the way of post ever came his way.

Back home in England he had served with the Special Forces during the gulf war and after leaving the SAS at the end of the war he had remained living in Hereford which was also where he was brought up and where his family now lived.

He had needed to earn a living, of course, to support himself and his wife Tilly and as with many ex-regiment men he knew very little else other than the discipline of service life and so went, as many before him, into the security business. Guarding foreign diplomats on missions or African leaders in their own countries was very lucrative but he decided that there was more money to be made by running his own company and employing others.

The expertise and toughness of these ex-soldiers was highly valued and he had won a lucrative contract to provide security services to an international oil company engaged in exploration in South America. The daily danger to the oil workers at the various sites from the local bandits who made a living from kidnapping or extortion, or the drugs cartels that required the land on which to grow their raw products, ensured that he was paid a small fortune for the protection that he and his team afforded the company.

While the money he earned by putting his life on the line daily was incredible, compared to anything else he could have done, with age his love of danger had begun to diminish and he felt the need to try something else. His wife had continued to live in England during this time and of course he was missing her very much, so after a couple of years he decided to take his money and get out of the danger business.

He had spoken with his wife at least every week whilst he was away, had written regularly and returned home as often as he could and everything seemed to be fine with his marriage although she had, like any service wife might, from some time said that she was concerned at the length of time he spent away, either with the army or with his work in Colombia. They both knew that it was difficult to maintain a working marriage in these circumstances.

He had returned to England expecting to find everything to be as it was when he left or, at least, in a way that enabled them to continue where they had left off, but it quickly became obvious that Tilly had had a change of mind concerning him and in his absence she had started an affair with another man.

This sort of thing was considered an occupational hazard in the army where families are forced to live apart by the very nature of the work and it had happened to a number of his friends. He always thought that his relationship with his wife was strong and had never expected this to happen to him. What was he to do?

With Tilly gone there was no reason to stay in England anymore and because of her betrayal he felt the urgent need to get away. The appeal of solitude in a hot climate led him to Australia where he had bought the farm and 2000 acres of land. There was never any intention of farming, in fact he had been told that the previous owners had found it very difficult to make a living there and the price he paid reflected that. It had some decent accommodation and that, together with the space and desolation, was what was needed at that time.

There were only a few people, family and close friends who knew of his whereabouts and he could not remember when the last neighbour had come to call so he couldn't think who was making their way to him now from the direction of the town. If he had to guess he would put money on it being someone from his past who had tracked him down.

He snatched up his rucksack from off the floor alongside the door and checked that his binoculars were in it. He took his revolver from a drawer in the kitchen, his training and daily practice with the weapon ensured that it was kept loaded. Although close quarters combat was his forte sometimes distance was an issue and it could be on this occasion, learning a long time ago to keep this piece of equipment at the ready in case it was needed quickly. Swinging the rucksack onto his back, his broad shoulders covered by a thin sleeveless shirt, a hat for protection from the sun and clutching his Walther in his hand, he left the cabin and quickly began to make his way towards his rendezvous with the unknown visitors.

He dropped down into the gully which passed close by the house just outside the door. It was around two metres wide; perhaps half as deep at this point and the bottom was flat and sandy. Silently and swiftly jogging along the dry bed he arrived hardly out of breath at the bridge. The depression ran under the track at this point and was just about the only place where there was any vegetation. Rain in the hills to the north caused flash floods to fill it occasionally in the winter and the shade from the bridge helped to preserve some dampness. This allowed a small thicket of thorn bushes to grow providing him with some cover.

The vehicle was closer now and he had enough time to position himself in such a way as to get a view of the occupants as they passed by. It would soon be on the bridge and he tried to work out in his mind just who was coming to his territory. His mind dwelt on the fact that he had made some enemies in the past but he also had a few good friends. Who would go to these lengths to find him?

Putting his pistol down on the ground he took out the binoculars from the ruck-sack. Now he could see the vehicle through the dust, a four-wheel drive, Australian number plates, probably hired, so no real clue there.

The motor was now right by him and he crouched down pushing himself back into the vegetation. It came to a halt, the engine was left running. He had anticipated this. The slight elevation of the bridge afforded a good sight of the cabin and he guessed that a cautious visitor might want to view the lie of the land from this point. As expected the driver stood up on the front seat and with eyes shaded from the glare of the sun, searched the area ahead of him but was clearly most interested in the farm. There would be no movement around the cabin and it would appear deserted but Tom could see him clearly now.

"It's Steve," Tom quietly spoke the name. Steve Olive, his brother.

After a few minutes Steve sat down on the seat of the vehicle and started forward again, slowly, the dust cloud dissipated. He continued as cautiously as possible to the cabin. There was no life to be seen there, having stopped at the bridge but he knew that his approach would not have been invisible to anyone inside any building who might have been on the lookout and he knew his brother to be a cautious man.

As the vehicle left the bridge Tom emerged from cover and began his return to the farm by way of the gully, still un-noticed, always remaining a little way behind. His mind was racing. Why was his brother here? Why had he travelled from England? There was no love lost between the two of them as it was with Steve that Tilly had been unfaithful while Tom had been away in South America.

By the time he arrived back at the cabin Steve had been there for a few minutes, perfect timing if Tom needed the element of surprise. Steve had climbed down from the motor and was making his way to the door. He took out a crumpled packet from his top pocket and shook out a cigarette which he proceeded to light. Taking a deep breath he blew out the smoke which gradually curled around his head and away into the air. Tom decided that he looked harmless enough at this point and that he probably did not need the ambush although, still unsure, he followed noiselessly behind his brother who had now arrived at the front entrance.

Drawing his pistol, he pointed it directly at his brother's head and held it there for a moment. He clicked his fingers and Steve spun round to be faced by the barrel of the Walther, with a finger tensed against the trigger as they looked eye to eye. The finger closed, the gun clicked, Tom smiled. The chamber had been empty.

"You're dead."

"Bastard," snapped Steve.

Chapter 3

Steve was just taller than his brother, also muscular from his army training, his tattooed arms powerful and with large hands. He had grown a beard since they had last met and his hair had a few weeks growth, which suited him outside of the army. His eyes were a light blue and his hair darker than his brothers and, although their colouring was different, there was no doubt that they were related. A small silver cross hung from one ear. Tom considered their Irish heritage had come to the surface in his absence.

He noticed that with his shorts his brother was not as tanned as himself and guessed that he could not have been in Australia for very long or that the regiment had not been to any equatorial regions recently. Maybe he had left the army by now? After all if Tilly had not liked the separation from him, why would she like it any better with Steve.

They stood looking each other up and down for a few minutes and then Steve grinned broadly, breaking the ice and discarding the cigarette, walked towards his brother throwing his arms around him in an embrace.

"Tom, offer me a beer, it's a long way from town to here and I'm parched."

"Sure," replied Tom, "come inside the cabin it'll be cooler in there and I think you've got some explaining to do, why you are here, it's a long way to come for a visit. Is there a problem with Mom or Dad or is it Tilly?"

This was the first time her name had been spoken between them since Tom had returned home from South America and found her gone and there was more than a little sarcasm in the comment. There was a certain look between them at that question but both let it pass. That was now some years ago but the sudden and unexpected sight of his brother brought back some unhappy memories of that time.

They entered the building. Steve looked around interested to see how his brother lived away from home and was surprised to see how tidy it looked considering visitors had not been expected. The main room was large although sparsely furnished. There was no need for much furniture with Tom the only occupant. A large settee covered with red cushions stood in the centre of the room. It faced the French windows which when opened allowed in a cooling breeze. A small table, on which stood an ancient television set together with what looked like a more serviceable radio and a couple of chairs, were placed behind it, a window faced the opposite direction. Two pictures of unrecognizable landscapes and an old clock, ticking softly, hung on the wall, a pile of newspapers resided in one corner. In the other corner was a dark bookcase and on the shelves dozens of well thumbed books. He gazed at the covers and spines. The books had one thing in common, all seemed to concern the Second World War.

'Hm,' he murmured to himself, wiping the sweat and dust from his face and neck with a crumpled handkerchief 'Interesting'.

A door stood in one wall and a presently redundant fireplace took up most of another wall and along the shelf above it stood a number of photographs of the family. Steve noticed that his image was missing although that of Tom and his wife together on their wedding day was on show in pride of place. Below the shelf was the hearth, white ashes surrounded a few pieces of blackened wood with small piles of timber either side waiting for the relative chill of the nights. An old wooden box was placed close by.

Tom disappeared through an open door nearest to the fireplace and a few minutes later returned with a handful of cans of beer a couple of which he handed over. Steve sat down at one end of the settee which was surprisingly comfortable, he thought, especially after the journey from town and Tom took up his Lord of the Manor position, standing with his back to the fireplace.

Steve took a long drink from one of the cans and pushed himself back into the cushions.

"No, Mom and Dad are fine and as for Tilly, well she moved on, you know what I mean." Tom knew what was meant.

Chapter 4

Matilda Mary Regan was considered a beautiful girl by all those who saw her. Her father was an army man and she and Tom had met when both were serving on the base in Hereford although, the family was originally from Waterford in Southern Ireland. Slim and with deep blue eyes she would shake her long blonde hair and anything else that was appropriate at Tom to attract his attention as they passed from time to time, she making sure that their passing was frequent. Occasionally they would speak. He was enthralled by her soft Irish accent and as his grandparents had come over from Ireland in the 1900's she seemed to be someone that he would like to know, he had thought. They started to spend time together and after a while things moved along and they married and settled down to the traditional army life. But circumstances conspired against them and after their enforced separation and her affair with his brother, divorce became inevitable. She was never going to be a loner and in either man's absence, or even their company sometimes, there would always be plenty of admirers.

Steve continued "I work freelance for the government, well whenever they require my services, rather than the army these days, although in a military capacity and I get abroad a lot, Eastern Europe and the like, so I was away from home as much as you were. As far as she is concerned, well what she did to you, she has since done to me. That's life, I'm over it now anyway, I've moved on as well although I have to say I notice the photograph." He nodded in the direction of the display on the shelf. "And you still wear your wedding ring?"

"Why not?"

Tom looked at the picture and smiled at the thought that his brother had suffered in the same way as he had with this woman. When they were young Steve had always complained about receiving the elder's cast offs, so what's new he thought?

"So if there's no problem with the family and Tilly is history why have you spent so much of your valuable time and presumably cash in coming over here and into the middle of nowhere to find me?"

Steve stood up and gazed into the distance through the window.

"There'll be plenty of time for that. I could do with another beer. Tell me what you do here all the day, it seems pretty lonely, no one for miles as far as I can tell, I didn't see a soul on my way down from town."

A couple more beers had relaxed Tom a little and the thought of some company, even that of his brother, was beginning to take on some appeal.

"Well there's no farming here anymore," said Tom waving his arm towards the window and the distance beyond, his tone less aggressive now. "The previous owners of the land decided it was not large enough to make a decent living from sheep farming, they were not getting any younger and they had no children to take over from them and so just wanted out. I heard about the place from some friends and thought it sounded just what I needed at the time, particularly at the price. You know I always liked isolation and there is plenty of that. I was always happy with my own company and I felt pretty pissed off about you and my wife, to say the least. So I decided to get away for a few years. I'm young enough and I came out of the security business with a reasonable kitty. I visit the town once a week, collect post if there is any, stock up and bring back a supply of newspapers and then catch up on world events, all of which pass me by otherwise, but it seems to take ages for any news to filter down here. I have a wireless set for emergencies but I've not needed that yet and in any case how long would it take someone to get here in an emergency. No, whilst I'm still young enough I should be ok."

Steve strolled about the room inspecting his brother's possessions and Tom could see that he was fairly indifferent to this way of life, always after the bright lights he recalled but this was it, this was what he wanted to do and if his brother didn't like the sound of it, well too bad.

He continued. "I've begun to pass the time with a little prospecting. I found some old mine workings about 30 kilometres away to the North and someone I met in a bar in town told me that years ago opals could be found around that area so occasionally I go up there. In fact I've found a few pieces but nothing very big, I doubt I'll become very rich."

"Opals eh."

"Yes, you know, precious stones, gems, actually it is considered as the national gemstone of Australia."

"Really, it sounds pretty hopeless being out here, I know you always liked your own company but don't you get lonely ever?" asked Steve suggestively whilst pulling open another can. Tom detected the suggestion in all its subtlety, but let it pass. He would have plenty of time to think about it and if there was some hidden agenda he knew it would be brought up again soon. His brother couldn't return from wherever he had come until tomorrow at the earliest and he began to feel a little excited at the thought of company and the chance to talk over old times.

It had been late afternoon when Steve had arrived and night was beginning to take over.

"I expect you'll need something to eat?" offered Tom, "and as payment you can tell me what's been happening. How are Mom and Dad, you've said nothing about them yet, and what about my old drinking mates and anyone else who remembers me back home?"

He sat down on the settee next to Steve.

"Well Mom and Dad are ok. Their health is fine, they miss you but then if you were still in the army it would be no different. Of course Dad being in the army as he was, they both know what it's about. I guess they think you should be living back home not out here away from everyone. They say the same sort of things to me because I work away a lot now, but that's parents. I assure them you'll return one day."

Tom decided that again he would ignore the remark and got up and went through into the kitchen to start to prepare a meal. He was more relaxed now in Steve's company but even so kept him in view through the open door.

"I saw Mick Cannon the other day, he sends his regards and Lukey and Jess still spend most of their time at the Cellars, remember that place? Then I go to watch The Bulls occasionally, pity they still struggle but football's still a good game to watch whether you win or lose."

Tom had noted that Mick "Had sent his regards", so Steve had told him he was coming out here he mused. Who else did he tell? What's all this about he wondered?

"So, what is it that has made you come all this way to find me?" he shouted from the kitchen.

"Let's talk about that tomorrow I'll need a fresh head to persuade you to join me, certainly to whet your appetite, ok? Let's just take it easy for tonight, something to eat, a few beers, it's been a long time."

"All right, but I don't expect you're going to have much to say to persuade me to do anything other than to spend my time here until I decide otherwise," replied Tom a little irritated by his brother's obvious confidence in being able to persuade him to join him, did he say? Join him in what, he wondered, a return to England perhaps?

He thought Steve's comment was typical of him, assuming that just by asking, he would change his life, "Typical government," he mumbled, "thinking that all they have to do is ask and we all come running! What a joke."

"I think I fancy a chilli tonight, is that alright with you?"

"Sure that'll be fine do you need any help?"

"No it won't take long but you can make yourself useful. See if you can get the fire going will you? All the bits you need are in the box by the hearth. It turns a bit chilly here at night."

Steve obliged and soon had the start of a blaze going. He had begun to feel the relative night-time cold of the desert compared with the oppressive heat he had experienced driving from town and he rubbed his hands in front of the fire. Picking up a week old newspaper he ambled towards the kitchen just as Tom emerged carrying two plates. Forks protruded from the pocket of his shirt and the pair sat down again to eat the meal and finish the beer.

"I've plenty more beer," Tom insisted. "So why do you want me to return?" His question blunt and to the point, changing the subject so abruptly he felt it might catch the other man off guard.

Steve's time with the government had not been wasted and the question was easily diverted.

"Hey this is a good chilli," he replied changing the subject as quickly as his brother had done. "Look I said we can talk about it tomorrow."

"When you've rehearsed the answers I guess?"

Steve shrugged his shoulders.

"Trust me brother, just let's talk about old times tonight".

The next couple of hours passed quickly. Tom, in spite of Steve's various comments concerning joining him, enjoyed the company and the chance to talk to someone about the past, mutual friends and places and catch up on the gossip from home. The food was eaten, a lot more beer drunk and the conversation, although small talk, was of home, the army, their friends anything that came to mind, just like when they were young.

Finally, Steve stood up. "I think I need some sleep," he said, "the journey, the heat, the beer I feel tired, let's turn in."

"Find somewhere to sleep," mumbled Tom, "I don't get many visitors so I don't have anything made up, even if I had known you were coming I still wouldn't have. I sleep in this room," he nodded in the direction of a closed door, "see you tomorrow get up whenever you feel like it."

Tom disappeared through the door and pulled it behind him.

Steve wandered outside and lit a cigarette. Looking up, the sky looked vast, a million, no ten million stars and the moon provided the only lights he could see away from the glow of his smouldering tobacco and illumination from the house. Through the haze of smoke and sudden fatigue he tried to recognise the constellations but eventually realised that this was the southern hemisphere and as such, things would appear different, still it was the same moon he could see here as back at home. The air was cool and fresh. His ears picked up sounds from the desert creatures and he realized that far from being alone out here, the two of them were outnumbered many millions of times. Not far away an animal howled, a mournful cry. Another answered.

"Perhaps he's right," he muttered to himself. "Perhaps he's right after all."

He finished his cigarette and walked over to the truck, pulling two bags from the back seat he took them into the house placing them on the floor beside the settee that he had chosen to use for the night. Tom had re-emerged from his room hearing the outside door open and then close, he looked at the bags. They don't look much like luggage to me he thought what does he think he's doing here?

"I expect you might be able to use this," and he threw a blanket onto the makeshift bed.

"Bathroom?"

"Through there."

At least Steve had brought some change of clothes, shaver toothbrush and so on, he thought.

Tom went back into his bedroom and closed the door. He couldn't quite put his finger on it but something told him that the casualness was hiding some other motive and he knew his brother well enough. After all, had he not betrayed him once with his wife, had he come all this way to do it again? He checked his revolver.

Chapter 5

Tom woke early the next morning, he found that he always did, something left over from his army training, he would tell himself. The sky was again cloudless and a faint breeze brought the desert heat from the north. This time of year the weather was predictable and it would be another hot day.

As usual, he went outside before doing anything else such as washing or having breakfast. He needed to check his surroundings for anything that might have happened during the night. Dingoes could have been around, digging holes or scavenging around the buildings, apart from that, the animals were never a problem to him.

At the back of the cabin was a pond fed by a spring which trickled over into the gully as it passed by the farm. He considered that the water must have fallen on the distant hills thousands of years ago and finally made its way here. Pure water he thought, no pollution when that fell and it certainly tasted good. A few eucalyptus trees surrounded the pond and a well used wooden seat had been constructed in their shade.

Metal sheep pens spread away from the other side of the pool, unused by Tom and clearly of little use to him but he had no intention of removing them, who knows he had thought, perhaps sheep will become economical again one day and the value of the farm could rise.

Beyond the pens there was just land, sandy, stony and without much vegetation. Dry grass, thorn bushes and very rarely a tree of any size and looking in other directions away from the house the scenery was similar into the distance.

It was only on the far horizon to the north that any change in surroundings could be seen. Hills appearing blue and grey in the morning sun finally broke up the tedious sameness. The occasional shimmering mirage would appear out of nowhere and then disappear just as quickly. When he came to live here first of all he would chase these mirages just for the fact of them being there but, of course, he never caught them.

Tom looked back at the water, still, in the relatively windless early morning. He would sometimes find that a duck or even a couple of them had landed on the pond during the night and this gave him the opportunity to have some target practice and at the same time add wild fowl to his menu.

He was in luck today, four ducks had arrived. Stealthily he approached the pond, crouched down so as to not to be seen and frighten the birds, he raised the pistol which he invariably carried with him when outside, and took aim. A sixth sense told him that he was being watched and the smell of tobacco smoke indicated that Steve had also left the cabin and had made his way around the back of the buildings in search of his brother. Ignoring him he pulled the trigger. His aim was deadly as usual and he took off one bird's head with a single shot. The remaining birds splashed about in panic for a few seconds then took off as one but that did not concern him. He knew that more would come over the next few days but apart from that Steve had been watching. He would have seen the accuracy of the shooting and if there was ever anything sinister in the visit then it would be a reminder that Tom could be a dangerous opponent armed or otherwise.

He stood up and walked around the other side of the pool to recover the bird. Grinning to himself he stepped in up to his knees and hauled it out of the water holding it aloft.

"Nice shooting," said Steve attempting to show little interest in his brother's gun skills other than the spectacle, as he moved away to survey the area.

Immediately around them was a courtyard area and surrounding that were a number of wooden outbuildings, used originally as storage for the farm equipment. The doors to one of them were open. There was little to be seen inside now except for a pile of tangled metal and what appeared to be oil drums. To one side a dirty tarpaulin covered some machinery and just showing below the sheet Steve identified heavily tracked wheels. Making his way over to the building he lifted up the covering to reveal an ex American army jeep and propped up alongside it, an old motor cycle. Back outside and away from the pool there was a maze of sheep pens also unused and just so much scrap metal, he thought to himself.

Steve looked back along the road that he had travelled the previous evening. From that direction many kilometres of wooden posts marched along in line supporting the electricity supply that the farm relied upon.

"What do you think of my farm then?" Tom asked eventually.

"Well you always said that you would be a landowner one day, but two thousand acres here is not the same as in Hereford is it? Where are all your green fields, hills, livestock?" replied Steve sarcastically waving his arms in the direction of nothing in particular.

"It used to be a sheep farm," said Tom refusing to rise to the comment. "It has electricity, you can see the pylons and if there is a problem then I have a generator and a supply of oil in the barn. The water comes from a spring into the pond and it can be pumped into the house. There is a cool room built underneath the cabin just down those stairs over there by the door. I keep my stores there in a decent freezer so I have some way of storing food. I need to go to town maybe once a week, I suppose. I have a jeep and it's a day out."

Tom carried his bird back inside to the kitchen. He would feather and dress it later but in the meantime breakfast was on the agenda. Steve had a beer whilst bacon was being fried, the smell curling out of the kitchen and around the room as he inspected Tom's books. They both ate something although neither was particularly hungry, "Probably too much beer last night" muttered Steve.

"Last night you started to tell me about the old times, and what Hereford is like these days, you mentioned Mick I recall?" Tom had thought it strange that Mick had sent his regards and so the mention of him might encourage some information from his brother.

"Well working away I don't get much chance to be there but, yes, I still see some of the guys from time to time when I'm back home. Mick and Rob are still with the regiment- Mick is with 14 Int at the moment."

"14, I didn't think he had the intelligence for that?"

"Huh, yes the old ones are always the best. Mick's a good guy I think you'll meet him again soon if you are interested in my proposal. I don't see much of Rob these days. He always seems to be on active service, Balkans, Africa, Iraq or wherever, he just likes a good fight."

Breakfast over they sat and chatted over a pretty decent coffee, about the days that each spent with the service and remembering the expeditions with a certain fondness. Steve had always been the one to find a way of making money and he reminded his brother of one of the many the times when he came out with a profit.

"Do you remember that time in the gulf when I got pinned down during some action and more or less taken prisoner by a small patrol of Iraqis? That didn't happen very often but on that occasion I was able to pay my way out. We always carried some dollars or sovereigns to buy ourselves out of trouble if firepower wasn't enough and from experience, the enemy knew it. While the main group sat drinking, the guy in charge took me a little way away, and in his best English said he would shoot me on the spot. These guys are as crafty as a cartload of monkeys. They had already searched me and removed my weapon but found nothing else; I had stashed the money before they got hold of me. So he offered me a way out if I gave him the cash, he would turn his back and I would be away. The stuff was close to where we were and we went over to recover it. I gave him the money which of course he started to count and hide in his uniform, he wasn't about to share it with his mates. I had also buried a blade with the loot which I got at the same time and as he was distracted counting the cash I got hold of him and slit his throat. The others heard him scream and started to come over to me but I got his AK and mowed down the lot of them before they reached me. I got the cash back and six bodies. I told Hereford that I had had to use my reserve and the guy who took it had run away. They couldn't argue with that so I pocketed the money. A good deal that was, especially as I was mentioned for my action."

Tom remembered hearing the tale before and again recalled how this demonstrated his brother's character; he would do anything for money.

Chapter 6

"When you've finished your coffee how about we take a trip over to my mine," he said getting up and making for the door. "You can drive, we'll use your fuel rather than mine although I'll take some spare and we can talk on the way."

"How far is it?"

"You saw the hills in the distance, well it's in that direction but probably only thirty kilometres or so."

"I can't see anything from here. What are you talking about, somewhere underground?"

"Well you could say that I suppose. There is a pile of rocks, a fairly substantial pile I would say but maybe you didn't notice them as they are in direct line with the hills. When I first went there, I found that some excavation had been done and I carried on with it. A couple of hours will see us there so we can return before nightfall. OK?"

Tom collected his rucksack and stuffed a handful of cans of beer into it and they left the house and made for the transport parked outside the front of the house.

Tom threw his rucksack onto the back seat and disappeared into one of the outbuildings and emerged after a few minutes with two cans.

"Fuel and water," he proclaimed placing one can beside the car and walking over to the pond with the other which he filled. He returned and put both into the boot.

"You have to take some precautions in the outback. Take the track out over there and eventually it goes north to the hills, just keep going."

They climbed in the vehicle and Steve started it up. Over night the engine had become very cold and he needed a number of attempts to get it going. Finally it burst into life, sluggishly at first, then building up revs, blue smoke engulfing the two of them. Eventually moving away slowly, picking up speed, he made for the route that had been pointed out to him and was soon on the track and leaving the farm.

"Well," said Tom eventually. "What is it, I think it's time you told me what you want?"

Steve had rehearsed this conversation a few times over the last few days wondering how his brother would react to the proposition, would he go for it or would he have to return home alone?

"OK I'll start at the beginning. Do you remember when we were kids you told me a secret about yourself, and you made me promise never to tell anybody else? How you used to have those bad dreams when you were young and what they meant to you as you got older?" Steve waited for the other's reaction.

"What are you talking about? You don't mean to tell me that it's something concerning that? I remember that you just thought I was crazy when I told you about it at the time and you'll never know how much I hated you for it. To me, at that time, as a young child it was all very real and very important."

"I know and I'm sorry it just seemed incredible to me, an even younger lad at the time. Well just humour me now, tell me the story again and then I'll tell you where I'm going with this."

"I can't believe you've come all this way to ask me to tell you this story. You never believed it then why would you want to hear it again", said Tom impatiently. "If this is a wind-up, if this is a waste of my time......."

"Look, I've said I'm sorry. You don't think I would come all the way over here if there was no good reason. Now just tell me in your own words and I'm sure you'll be interested in what I've got to tell you now."

Tom sat back in his seat blowing air out of his mouth slowly. Although he was irritated, he knew that for Steve to spend some considerable time and money on this visit there must be something very much worth his while in it. It seemed that for him to know what was going on some co-operation would be required. He sat quietly for a few moments composing himself and looking out over the scrub, the wind on his face the warm sweet smell of the desert in his nostrils. He remembered this tale well as in his life it was very significant but how it could be of any relevance to anyone else was another matter. He sat quietly for what seemed like a long time, as if he was considering how best to tell the tale.

"O.K, when I was very young probably four or five I seemed to have been troubled by something. As far as I can remember I would have, what you might call, a recurring dream, a nightmare in fact and I would have it regularly over a long period of time or so it seemed then to a me as a child. I was all alone and it was as if I was walking out onto a platform and it was the walking out that terrified me. Then I would fall and everything would go black and that was it. I had no idea what was going on, what I was imagining, after all I was just a kid, I couldn't understand it. I would wake up but so frightened that I couldn't go back to sleep in case I dreamt it again."

Although it had been a long time ago and Tom had largely got over it, he still went a little cold at the thought of it, his eyes moistened and he clenched his hands together. For a hard man with years of experience as a soldier in some of the toughest areas of the world even he was surprised by his reaction so many years later.

"I had that dream for quite a period of time and on each occasion I would wake up very frightened. Mom and Dad would tell me later that I would be very distressed although they had no idea what was going on and I didn't seem able to describe any of it to them. Well so it went on I guess until I was about nine or ten and then I read something in a book, it was about someone being hanged. I don't know who it was or why I was reading it, even at that age morbid curiosity I suppose, but as soon as I had read it I knew somehow that that was what I had dreamt happening to me. When I realised that, I never had the dream again."

The hills seemed to be still as far away as ever and the track as uneven as usual, but they continued at a pace that the bumps and hollows would allow, the dust streaming behind them.

Steve mumbled some confirmation of what had been related and what he had remembered being told some years earlier.

"Still on the right road?" he enquired releasing his hold on the steering wheel and rummaging in one of the bags. Taking out a can of beer he opened it and took a long drink. With no-one else on the track a slight sway while driving he considered was acceptable.

"I'll join you," Tom replied."Yes keep going another 15 Kilometres or so along this road. You should soon be able to see the rocks that I mentioned."

"Well a few years later I saw a program on T.V about hypnotism and how this guy could take someone back, under hypnosis, to an earlier time in their life by getting them to recall things that apparently were stored in their memories, he called it regression therapy. He reckoned that everything that happens to you is still in the memory, certainly as far as this life is concerned, but he thought that it could be taken further and it would be possible to regress to before the current life, his actual words as I recall were, "the subconscious holds on to trauma from previous lives", we all find it impossible to recall stuff like that but this guy would help it to happen. He said that some hang-ups that we might have could be traced to some event earlier in our lives or even previous lives and that's why he did hypnotism and there was a call for it with some people because it might help their anxiety or whatever. I wasn't sure I really understood it."

"I can't remember his name for sure and it doesn't matter now anyway but he said that there were times when he seemed to be able to take people back to before their present life, before, can you believe that? It really was an incredible idea that you could recall things that happened to you, or whoever you were, sometimes hundreds of years ago. You saw him do it on the television and the person who was being regressed would talk in a different voice or a strange accent and answer questions or tell things about themselves as somebody living years ago. At first I thought the whole thing was a con."

Steve looked over at his brother who seemed to be miles away reliving his memories and totally believing what he was saying. He grunted.

"I wasn't absolutely convinced that this was really happening when I first saw it, I thought it was some sort of stage act but I knew someone, Tony something or other, who worked at the T.V Company and who had been involved with the programme. I asked him what he thought and he said that at first when he had seen it happen, he also thought it was a con. So he said that he was going to ask the guy if he would hypnotise him and take him back just to see what happened. I think he thought he might have been someone important, you know Henry VIII or someone like that. I met up with him a few days after the session he had had with the therapist, or so he called himself, and Tony was something of a changed man. Before the session he had been sceptical, he didn't believe it was possible, treated it as a bit of a joke you know. Now he was full of it, what had happened and particularly to whom he had been regressed. The whole thing was incredible, more so with him as I knew him personally rather than with the subject I had seen on television. Now he was convinced that he was an individual who had lived a couple of hundred years ago. He knew something of the man's life and about the place where he lived, although he swore he had never been there before and he spoke in an odd country dialect. The thing was recorded and Tony was convinced he had lived before and I was allowed to listen to the recording, it was amazing."

Steve had listened intently to the story whilst continuing to drive towards the rocky outcrop which had now become visible to him, occasionally swerving the vehicle as a rock or other obstacle appeared in front of them.

"You know I cleared this route the last time I came over here, shifting stones and so on as I came to them. The track should be pretty clear; I just don't know how stuff finds its way back onto the road."

Eventually the terrain began to alter. There was more of an incline now different to the flat land that they had covered when leaving the farm. The clumps of grass, although still dry and lifeless looking, were more dense now. Small thorn bushes interspersed the tall grass in greater numbers and trees of some height began to appear. Finally almost a small forest came into sight, compared with what had been seen before, as they arrived at the destination. Steve could see that the rocks stretched away in two directions ever higher the further you went.

"Stop here, we walk from here."

The four wheel drive was brought to a halt close to the trees and the engine turned off. Getting down and stretching legs and backs the dust that they had been in their wake whilst travelling to this place was around them now, settling slowly on to the seats that they had just vacated. The sound of the engine was now replaced by the chattering of birds. As they had driven through the grass a flock of birds rose as one and circled the thicket twice before settling into the branches.

"Budgerigars," pronounced Steve, "I've never seen so many together before, but they are all green ones."

"Yeah I think green is natural. The other colours come from deliberate breeding in captivity I'm told, but the Aborigine eat them."

"What?"

"Well why not? I, you even, eat birds don't you? In fact I think the Aborigine word for that bird, translates as 'good to eat'.

Tom collected his rucksack from the back seat and threw it over his shoulders already starting to moisten in the intense heat now that the breeze had ceased having come to a standstill and he gestured the way towards a small path that appeared as an entrance between the two largest boulders. The two of them proceeded to negotiate a slope for several metres and reaching the top they stopped to look around.

"From here you can just see Radinga, I guess from where you arrived yesterday," Tom said pointing into the distance.

Steve could see the faint shimmering outline of the town and an occasional flash of the sun reflected from the windows of some invisible moving car. He nodded wiping sweat from his face. In the heat with no breeze from their travelling they would experience the desert.

"You should be used to this heat," said Tom smiling, "Middle east and so on." His brother grinned, "Carry on."

Chapter 7

The walk continued now with a descent to a hollow within the hills, the greater heights some distance ahead.

"Hey I've seen somewhere like this before. Do you recall those American Westerns, you know, this is just the same as the place where they filmed them. I expect to see a cowboy coming around the corner at any moment."

Tom ignored the comments.

Entering into the depression they arrived at what seemed to be a large excavation to the left and they made their way to the entrance of it. Outside the opening was a pile of rubble and they sat on it shaded by the large boulder behind them.

"Let's have another beer and when I've finished the story we'll go and find a fortune in opals," said Tom with more than a little sarcasm.

A couple of beers appeared from the rucksack.

"So I asked Tony if the guy would regress anybody. You know I began to think that I might like to know about my past and if the dream had anything to do with it. Well he said he would ask him for me. A few days later Tony contacted me and said that he had spoken with him, oh yes, I remember now he was name Joe, and I'll think of his surname in a minute, something like Scratch or Scatch, well whatever, he said he would like to meet me whenever I felt like it, no pressure. However I was keen so I contacted him and made an appointment for the following day."

"I went to his house, which I recall was a big white Victorian property on the outskirts of the City. During the initial interview he asked me some questions, you know, why did I want to do this and of course I told him about the dream. He was really interested in that part especially the bit about hanging. I told him more or less what you know and asked how much he would charge for a session and that was odd, because he said that he would do it for nothing. I asked why and he said he would explain to me later and he eventually did so, although it's not important at this time. I told him my story and he said OK he would do it and did I mind if he recorded my conversation. I thought that was fine, after all I remembered that he had recorded Tony."

"Well we had the session. He seemed to speak to me in what I would describe as a quiet way, very strange, some words I couldn't quite grasp but I know I was relaxed, very peaceful. I recall something about imagining a staircase and going down it. It seemed to take only a few seconds when he got my attention again but he told me that I had been out for about half an hour and even he had been impressed by what I had said whilst I was under. He asked me if I wanted to hear the tape. Of course I said yes and he played back the recording."

"He had regressed me to childhood and I had apparently, under questioning, told my tale of the frightening dream. He had then gone back further and for some time there was silence, this was when I wasn't alive he said, can you believe that?"

"Then he got me again and I couldn't understand what I was hearing. I spoke in a language which he said was German but as he said he couldn't speak the language there seemed to be no reason to carry on and so the session was ended. He said that if he could have spoken German then he could have continued, as it was it was a waste of time going on any longer. I said that he sounded as if he came from there himself with a name like his, Schacht, now I recall, and in any case how could he ask questions in English and have answers in another language. He said that that was just how it was. I still don't understand that bit of it," he shrugged his shoulders.

"However we were both intrigued by the recording and I was asked if he could do it again this time with a German speaking person in attendance so that we would be able to hold a conversation which could be recorded and maybe the regression might be of more value and have some explanation."

"A few days later I returned with Mike, you've already mentioned him, you know 14 Int because he could speak and understand German and we had another session."

"When it was ended we all listened to the tape. Mike and Joe had heard the conversation of course but they couldn't wait to watch me listen to it and give me the translation. After hearing it and the translation, I was literally shocked for a time and they were astonished because of the obvious relevance to me of the dream and the person to whom I was regressed."

Tom stood up from the pile of rubble and walked a little way away. He looked into the distance and finished his beer and returned to where Steve had remained.

"I spoke in German again but couldn't understand what I was saying and that's bad enough. Can you imagine hearing yourself speaking a foreign language fluently and not knowing what the hell you are saying? Well it turns out that I was a German soldier during the last war, but not just an ordinary soldier, an officer in the SS. My name was SS Major Claus Hamann and I was being hanged at the end of the war for crimes against humanity."

"You know the original dream had a really bad effect on me as a child but this was even more distressing. I was being hanged; it was real because suddenly I was silent. As Hamann, I was dead can you imagine it? I have to admit that it reduced me to tears hearing that at the time and it still disturbs me now to remember it. Just think about it, hearing yourself dying, unbelievable".

Five minutes passed while he stood quietly staring past the rocks over the desert into the distance as if the space he was seeing was the space in his mind from now back to 1946. Eventually he motioned Steve to the mine entrance.

"Let's go in, it's cooler in here and perhaps we can find you a souvenir for you to take back with you."

Steve said nothing.

The mine would better have been described as a small cave, although it had clearly been excavated by man, within the boulders and worked slightly downwards, and it was probably no bigger than 10 square metres. Tom worked in the light that came through the entrance so the cave was getting longer but not much wider.

"How are you digging this?" asked Steve examining the wall and the rubble on the floor without much conviction.

"The previous owners did a bit of digging and when they went they left their tools. A bit of pick wielding is good exercise."

"What are we looking for?"

"Well opals are a form of silica and you find them within the rock structure, so you have to smash up pieces of rock to see if there is anything inside. You'll know one when you see one, a bit like those coloured marbles we used to play with, But sometimes you could find a black opal and if it was a decent size and quality that would be great because they are extremely valuable."

Steve seemed suddenly to take an interest in possible rewards for the effort.

"Having said that, it's unlikely we will find one of them in this mine, wrong place, wrong type of rock."

Tom hit the rock face with a small pick he had collected from inside the cave and a chunk of stone fell away.

"I'm told that you find them where there is ironstone so I guess that there must be some of that around here."

"Let's take it outside and see if there's anything in it," he said and the two of them went back outside.

The piece was duly crushed revealing nothing. "Well ninety-nine to go, you might find one jewel in every hundred rocks."

"Seems like a waste of time to me," Steve replied discouragingly.

"Maybe, but one good opal could be worth a few thousand and anyway it's like fishing, you never know when you'll get one, so with me, it's the anticipation that's the pleasure."

An hour passed and all they had to show for their effort was a pile of crushed rock, the novelty was wearing off with Steve who clearly had something more on his mind. He wandered off outside and sat down again on the pile of rubble and lit a cigarette. The heat was tremendous and after only a few minutes he was wiping his face, the sweat came with no effort.

Tom was working hard but still waiting for the reaction to his tale. It was a while now since he had related his story and all Steve seemed to be doing was ignoring it.

He followed him outside irritated with his brother's reticence and with his own inability to find an opal, however small.

"Look I'm losing my patience, Steve, if you don't come clean with me and tell me what the hell you want I'll forget you're my brother and remember you're the guy that stole my wife."

"OK.OK...You're right I'll tell you. You remember that I said Mick was with 14, well you know that anyway. The Det, and I know you recall what they did, they were intelligence, supposed to be ultra secret. They analysed reports received about enemy movements, positions and so on during current operations, but they also reviewed past information obtained from any source from way back in case it has any relevance today and you know that a lot of stuff is being released now fifty years after the end of the war. I suppose the idea is that anyone involved in, how shall I say, anything compromising, is likely to have died by now or probably that none of it matters anymore."

He took a draw on his cigarette.

"Well as you also know Mick was fluent in German and so he was set to work through some of the more background political stuff rather than the actual details of the war. During his research he started to find reports concerning Hitler's plans to build a world class museum and art gallery in Linz in Northern Austria."

"Why Linz?"

"I've no idea really, he was born in a place called Braunau am Inn but he seemed to have an affinity with Linz which was not far away, it was a bigger town so probably it was considered to be the better place. The documents told that the main building was to be called The Fuhrer Museum and Linz was going to be the Capital of the World, a cultural centre with palaces, fountains, squares, parks and so on. It is thought that all this stemmed from the fact that Hitler was something of an artist himself and earlier on in his life he had applied to The Institute of Art, in Austria, for acceptance. He wasn't accepted and Adolf held that decision against the committee, many of whom were Jewish incidentally. Back to Linz, eventually there was to be an opera house, library and even a mausoleum for his tomb. Of course it was at this time that Hitler started to collect works of art, treasures and whatever from the Jewish people. Poles, French and so on and these items would form the stock, if that's the correct word, for these art galleries and museums. Not only was Hitler collecting pieces, many of his officers and so on were doing the same, although mainly for their own personal wealth. Goering for instance was said to have stolen some seven hundred items alone from the Jeu de Paume in Paris when the Germans occupied France. It's not too much of an exaggeration to think that today many rich Germans and others owe their wealth to plunder from the war."

"But wasn't it common knowledge at the time that Hitler had this planned and?"...interrupted Tom.

"Wait a bit, and listen to the rest of it, you may find some of it useful," Steve continued. "The valuables were stored in various places of relative safety such as Berlin while the collection was being built up, sent there from all over the place by senior officers who looted wherever and whatever and who wanted to ingratiate themselves with Hitler. He had let it be known that he wanted works of art and those who looted for him would get a good position in the army or government after Germany had won the war."

"Hitler had the plans for the art gallery building drawn up by Albert Speer along the lines of the Great Hall that he had built for Hitler in 1936 and he had entrusted the logistics of collecting the treasures with one of his favourite officers who seemed to have found a niche for himself for the duration. We know a little about him, he seemed to be well connected, related to a first world war general, a good family and this, as well as Hitler's patronage, kept him from being sent to the Russian front."

"Actually he turned out to be pretty good at his job and as well as persuading officers to hand over the stuff, or Hitler would know about it, he looted for Hitler himself. Anyway, having got the idea going, Hitler let others get on with it while he fought the war, hoping that at the end of the war, the collections would have been set up and he would have a ready made monument to himself in the form of the galleries containing the finest displays of works of art in the world."

Steve wasn't sure that Tom was too interested in this part of the story but he had to give it to him as this was what made sense of Mick's discovery.

He continued "Now some of this is guesswork as the released documents give mainly the allies side of the story, together with reports collected from the victims who were still alive after the war and Germans who may or may not have been telling the truth to save their skins, but the theory is that when the war effort started to go badly wrong, and you know the ending to that, the plans were put on hold. We know where the building was going to be but there was no trace that it was ever started."

"So what happened to the valuables?" said Tom who had begun to find that he did have an interest in the story.

"Well no-one knows for sure, because no-one has ever found any such cache, as might be expected, as far as we know. We certainly know that some of the paintings, for example, are identified from time to time and the current owners, very often world famous galleries for instance are encouraged to return them to the rightful original owners or their descendants. However we don't know where the bulk of them were in Berlin and so on at the end of the war. If they were there they may have been destroyed during the Russian advance or taken by the Russians themselves. If either of these are the case then that's probably the end of it, but there were some other possibilities. One such was Lake Toplitz. There is an account of Serbian gold, valuables, secret plans and so on being dumped in Lake Toplitz during and at the end of the war, you may have heard of it?"

Tom nodded.

"In 1960 a long retired SS officer died during a dive in that lake. It is thought that he may have been involved in putting stuff in there in the first place otherwise it would have been too much of a coincidence, you know valuables in the lake, an SS officer and so on. Well it seems that a number of dives were undertaken in the lake during the 60's and in 1970 a casket was found. They raised it off the bottom but it only contained a rock, God knows what that was about. Then there was Operation Bernhard.

"I think I've heard of that," Tom interjected."Wasn't that Bernhard Kruger, the forger? Didn't he produce millions of fake £5 notes with which the Jerrys planned to flood the country? I seem to remember reading a book about it. I heard that the notes are still there in the lake and in good nick, it sounds like that might be the place wouldn't you think?"

Steve was encouraged that Tom was now taking a serious interest in the tale it looked as though his skills of persuasion were paying off.

"Maybe," mused Steve," but that story is pretty well known and you may well have read a book about it, there have been a few written. Operation Bernhard was the name given to a German plan during the war to destabilize the British economy by sending in to the country forged bank notes just as you say. The plan was set up by SS Major Kruger who got inmates of concentration camps to engrave plates for printing notes. This was done mainly at Sachsenhausen and by the end of the war a colossal amount had been produced, I think I read somewhere nearly £135m and that was some money in the forties. They even started counterfeiting US $ at the end of the war and it seems that most of the notes ended up in Lake Toplitz where some were recovered in 1959 but examples kept turning up in circulation and so The Bank of England withdrew all notes over £5 and didn't reintroduce them until later on in the 1960's."

"All this is in released documents?"

"Absolutely right it's incredible isn't it but Mick and I don't think that Toplitz is where all this stuff went" Steve continued, "It's unlikely that so much freight could have been transferred out of Berlin at that time without the allies seeing it and can you imagine vast quantities of works of art being dumped in a lake? Even if the war was lost I can't believe anyone would just destroy so much wealth. So, ignoring Toplitz, where even if there were forged bank notes still about, what could you do with them if you found them? We think that any great quantity of stuff must have been got out earlier when there was less urgency over a period of time, under the control of the officer and maybe without Hitler's knowledge. You can draw your own conclusions as to why the man removed the cache from Berlin without telling Adolf."

"Mick and you don't think so eh, so what is it that Mick and you know that the rest of the world doesn't?" Tom interjected.

Steve picked up another rock and hit it with the pickaxe, smashing it into a hundred pieces. He smoothed the pieces over in his hands and his eyes caught the glint of something among the rubble. He picked it out and smoothed away the dust. Wiping his fingers across his brow, the sweat moistened the fingers and he used the wetness to clean the find. The dust was removed and it glinted, holding it up to the sky revealed the colours. A milky white, pastel yellow a distant blue and green, he held it in the palm of his hand towards Tom.

"An opal?" he asked triumphantly.

"Yes you've got your souvenir."

He put the piece in his pocket and his hand on Tom's shoulder.

"Well, what Mick and I know involves you, which is the bit that no-one else knows. The name of the officer that Hitler trusted with his plans was, Sturmbannfuhrer Claus Hamann."

Tom took an involuntary step backwards and for a moment there was silence. A look between the two of them indicated no emotion although he felt as if the blood was draining from his body. His stomach churned and the sweat from the heat of the day seemed to disappear. Outwardly he was controlling his feelings, this was not the time to show emotion, but inwardly his body was suddenly not his own and his mind was racing.

Chapter 8

Tom walked a little way away from Steve, who stood there watching his reaction, and he looked up to the sky. It was clear, nothing broke the blue and there was silence as if the whole world were waiting for him to speak. Even the birds that they had seen earlier had gone away or had fallen silent and he gazed up for several minutes as if he was looking for something or someone to give him an explanation. He took a deep breath.

"What are you suggesting?" he asked, anticipating the answer but needing to hear someone else give it to him.

Steve saw that he had already had the thought so there was no problem in confirming it.

"That the Major Hamann in your regression and the Sturmbannfuhrer Hamann in Mick's reports is the same guy".

"Hamann is not an unusual German name, is it?" said Tom seemingly in an effort to have this potential burden taken from him. "I mean there could be several people, you know, officers in the army and the like, named Hamann. I understand that during the war there were half a dozen guys named Josef Mengele listed as soldiers in the German army."

"Yeah, no doubt, but how many with that name were in the Waffen SS as was your man? Sturmbannfuhrer was the SS equivalent rank to Major. How many had the first name Claus and how many were hanged at the end of the war? I bet that cuts down the number a bit".

"But there's no certainty they're the same man, it could be a coincidence, you can't prove it for sure."

"I know that at the moment, but probably it could be proven if you came back to England and we explored the possibilities."

"How would that help?"

"Well, we know something of the history of one of them and we could ask you questions relative to him if we had another session with your man Joe. I expect that there is every chance that he would still be around even though it was some time ago when you had your sessions with him, but if not him then someone else. If you gave the right answers then, ten to one, we are dealing with the same man."

Tom sat down on the rubble. The sun had moved around since they had arrived at the mine and now it was beating down on him as he sat there. He took a beer from the rucksack and downed it in one go and threw the empty can back into the entrance of the mine.

"So this is what you think, you have to persuade me to come back? You think that I'll be interested to know more about this guy and what he did. Well, look I'm not really concerned with it these days; I got over the dream and the therapy sessions a long time ago. What's the point anyway? What good is it if I knew anything more? It's not going to change anything is it?"

Steve was surprised that Tom hadn't spotted the point in all of this. He was a sharp individual usually, perhaps the years had changed him or perhaps he had understood it and was waiting for Steve to play his hand first. Whichever way it was it was now necessary to play along with him.

"Well, look, if it can be proven that the two Hamanns are the same person, that is the man in the reports and your regressed guy, then it might be possible to get you, or whoever you were, to talk about this Linz business. You might be able to talk about the plans as you knew them to be, you know who else was involved, that sort of thing."

"Who else was involved? What were the plans? Don't tell me all of this is so that any old SS officers who might still be around and who I might talk about under hypnosis, could be found. What would be the point in that?" Tom asked, his voice trailing away as he began to ask himself the question.

Asking himself the question began to give him the answer.

"Wait a minute, I must be losing it. I get it now. You're not in this for any social motive are you? You're not expecting to search out any people, Weisenthal fashion, you're hoping that if I can come up with anything then it would be...where did the valuables go?"

Steve said nothing. Tom had hit on to the other's motive. Knowing where the disappeared works of art and valuables had gone in his role as Hitler's man and then being able to recover them, would make anyone concerned with the find extremely wealthy, but his face gave nothing away.

"I'm going back to the cabin now," said Tom. "Get in the car and let's go."

Steve didn't push it, the journey back would take some time and he knew his brother would be thinking as they went.

No words were exchanged as they drove back. The track was of course poor and the journey was not fast. This suited both of them as it gave more thinking time.

As they drove, Tom looked with intensity over the land, looking at nothing in particular, just taking in the beauty of the desert and its natural innocence compared with the times more than fifty years ago when the world was in complete turmoil. The sun had moved around now and the blues and greys had turned to gold and reds. A bit like parts of Iraq, he mused, and his thoughts now went back to that war, when the two of them had been more like brothers, before his brother had killed off their relationship through his affair with Tilly.

They eventually arrived back at the farm. No word had been exchanged for the entire trip.

"Well we're back," said Steve in a redundant fashion. "What do you think?"

They both remained seated in the car. Tom turned towards his brother, his green eyes taking on their menacing look.

"You're a wheeler and dealer aren't you Steve? You know what I'm going to say. I saw you looking around the cabin, at my book collection particularly, and you said nothing."

"Concerning what exactly?"

"Please don't pretend you don't know what I'm talking about. Credit me with a little native cunning."

"You saw that the vast majority of my books related to WW2, you would surely have seen my book about Toplitz, after all you have already referred to it. Not a coincidence I would say and my books about Hitler and his Generals, his henchmen and supporters. You know why I read all that sort of thing, don't you?"

"I came to some sort of conclusion I suppose. Yes you are most likely correct but I need you to tell me."

"Yes I read them just in case there is any reference to me, Hamann."

"And have you found any?" said Steve with a curious interest.

"No," replied Tom seemingly disappointed, "I haven't. It appears that lower ranks are not that noteworthy. Oberstgruppenfuhrers or Reichsfuhrers on the make are much more interesting to the reader."

"Or it could be that Sturmbannfuhrer Hamann was particularly important and making him some sort of figurehead, such as Goering, Himmler and so on, was not on the agenda?"

"Yes I saw your books and came to that conclusion. You have an interest because of what you might discover about yourself, nothing more I guess, so you will have to expect me to play my strongest card. I will have to play on that, like it or not. So this is a chance for you to discover more concerning Hamann....or you if you prefer it, and if anything else comes to the fore, well so be it. What do you say? You've spent a lot of time reading and finding nothing. I'm offering you the chance to know something of yourself."

Tom climbed down from the vehicle and Steve followed watching him intently. He looked around about him at the farm and then out over the desert, his land, two thousand acres stretching away to places he had not yet visited.

The sky was darkening and, as he looked up, stars were beginning to show amongst the purple. It had been a hot day as usual but the cool fingers of the night were starting to make themselves felt. Slowly he walked towards the bench at the side of the pond and sat down. The land was silent, only the rustling of leaves from the trees above him broke into his consciousness. He shuffled his feet in the dust which rose up and encouraged by the faint breeze settled on the water framing the reflection of the moon. Tilly came unexpectedly into his mind. He looked at Steve.

"OK," he said.

"OK I'll do it. I'll come back with you."

Chapter 9

It was eight days later. Tom had packed a change of clothes, appropriate for the summer in Australia but most unsuitable for winter in England, still he thought, I don't expect to be away for long. They had left the farm and made their way to Radinga in the hire car and then taken a bus to Alice Springs, the closest large town. It was yet another very hot day but the air conditioning on the transport was a welcome relief over a journey of several hours. 'The Alice' as it is known locally is situated more or less at the geographic centre of Australia near the southern border of The Northern Territory. Although it has a good population and every necessary facility for a town in such a position and is within a day's journey of Radinga, Tom had never had the need to venture there during his time spent in Australia.

From the Town airport a direct flight took them to Brisbane and then on to London where they hired a car for the journey back to Hereford. The overall journey was long and tiring and throughout the pair of them seemed deliberately to avoid any talk of the future and how they would have to play out the various scenarios that would now have to be faced. Only once did Tom refer to the whole episode in which he unexpectedly now found himself.

"This must have cost a few quid," said Tom as they made their way from the air terminal to the hire car depot. "Who's paying for it all Steve?"

He received no answer just a casual shrug of the shoulders.

Several hours later, the car started to descend Callow Hill a few miles from Hereford.

"Stop just along here," instructed Tom, "from what I remember there's a lay-by just ahead on this side of the road."

A couple of hundred metres further the parking place came into view and the car came to a halt just off the road.

"What's this stop for?" enquired Steve. "We are almost back, why do you need to stop here?"

"This is going to be my first sight of home in nearly three years. Tilly and I used to come out here sometimes and just sit in the car and look out over the City. I won't be very long."

Tom reached into the back of the car to where he had placed his travelling bag and eventually pulled from it a coat. Steve had brought some warmer clothes for Tom to wear, clearly anticipating a successful outcome to his trip over to Australia and this had not gone unnoticed. A pair of trousers and a warm sweater had also been made available and worn since arriving back at the airport. England in February was a much different proposition to the Simpson Desert in summer. If he was going to be outside the car for any length of time a little more protection would be required after the shorts he had been wearing for most of the time whilst away.

Getting out of the car he made his way across the road to where a drive-in led to a wooden gate at the entrance to a field. He leant against the barrier and gazed across the fields to the City in the distance. To his right was a higher part of the hill surmounted by tall trees leafless at this time of the year but festooned with rooks investigating last season's nests. Some birds would rise in a small group calling in unison to their comrades still sitting on the bare branches of the trees, urging them to take flight and join in the melee.

To his left the road continued towards the City and following its line took his sight directly to the Cathedral, Hereford's tallest building. From this distance the buildings of the City appeared to merge into one great amalgamation but the height of the Cathedral and the spires of the half dozen or so other churches interspersed within enabled him to determine his bearings. Although he been away just three years, suddenly it seemed as if it was thirty years and the only thoughts in his head now were of times past.

Looking out over the City he recalled the times when, to earn a little extra cash, he worked as a walking guide around Hereford. The house which was the birthplace of Nell Gwynne, and the plaque on the ground on the river bank for Dan the dog that fell into the river, inspiring a variation by Elgar. Moving on he would arrive at the castle green where the bowlers in summer rarely knew that the green, so lovingly tended for their enjoyment, covered the last resting place of hundreds of people killed during ancient conflicts. Then to the column on which Nelson's statue is supposed to have taken pride of place, only for it to have been diverted to London and finally the cannonball in the City wall. His father had told him that it was most likely cemented in there by some locals one Saturday night after closing time, but it was always a good story to tell to the punters. The horn from the car sounded bringing him back to the present. He looked over at Steve who was gesturing impatiently for him to return.

"So what happens now?" he mused to himself.

The February day was clear but he could feel moisture on the wind and soon it would become dark. He made his way back across the road to the waiting car and got in. The two continued with their journey. The view over the City was just as Tom had remembered it from when he was last here, except for a few years growth of trees. Why should it have changed he thought? It was only a few years ago that I left. The City has been here for hundreds of years, it's only people who change that quickly and he started to think about the people to be met again now that he had returned.

A couple of miles on and they passed the City boundary and the car was travelling along the Ross Road in an area well known to both of them.

On either side of the road there was ordinary and unspectacular residential development and anyone travelling along, just using the road to pass through Hereford on their way to the north or to the south of the county, would assume that that was all there was here. The locals knew different of course and looking carefully you could see the tell tale signs. To the right between the houses tall masts were to be seen and occasionally a green metal fence. The street names reflected, if anyone bothered to notice or understand, the military presence here. Within the housing area was the regiment site, the headquarters of one of the best known and least known divisions of the British army.

"Anything happened here since I've been away?" asked Tom as they passed along the road.

"Well, I'm told that everything is moving soon to the old RAF base at Credenhill. You remember it? Better communications, more room away from these houses, some new buildings, much better all round," replied Steve.

"And about time too. You know if this was America then this site would have been top secret, miles from anywhere in the Arizona desert, somewhere like area 51, not here right in the middle of a housing estate. No-one would know where it was, but here, everyone knows. They even play football matches with local teams coming on to the base, but that's the British army for you."

The car continued along the road. Office workers, shoppers, school children carried on about their own business. Conversations on street corners, assignations planned, places to be visited. They arrived at the new bridge, held up by the usual evening traffic. The last mile had been long, especially as their destination was so close, anticipation was supposed to be half the pleasure, he recalled his father saying many times, but not just at this moment he thought. Now they were crossing the bridge. Tom tried to look over the side into the river and then across to the old bridge its stone arches still able to support a single line of vehicles heading in or out of the

City as the traffic signals would allow, and the pedestrian passing places ensuring that there would be no collision of people rushing to and fro.

Leaving the bridge now, the car turned left and stopped outside a small terraced house. Tom sat back and looked. Just over a week ago he had been in the wilds of Australia, on his own with no real plans to change his way of life. His brother's tale had intrigued him he had to admit to himself and although he would not say anything, so had the thought of seeing his family and possibly Tilly again and he had agreed to return home, but only for a while on his terms, he had told himself. The journey from Australia had been long, via Japan into London. An overnight stay and leaving the following day saw them back in Hereford that afternoon. A lot had happened to him in the last week and he felt like he wanted to take a break before getting involved in anyone else's plans, but that was to be seen.

Chapter 10

The car had pulled up to a halt at their parent's house, a neat terraced property in a road just outside the City walls. On the opposite side of the road was a black recently painted metal fence and behind the fence a neatly trimmed hedge around the same height. Tall plane trees had been planted at intervals within the hedge, but this still afforded a good view over the field to the river and Tom recalled the times, when as youngsters, he and Steve had found their way, much against their parent's permission, into the field and down to the riverbank. There they played soldiers and once, he remembered, Steve had fallen into the river. Mom and Dad were not well pleased with him, although Tom, who had pulled him out, was considered something of a family hero, which the younger brother had always seemed to resent. Now they were back at home.

Steve had told him that he would be able to stay there whilst back in Hereford and Tom now realised that he was looking forward to seeing his family again.

He started to get out of the car.

"Oh I should have told you, Mom and Dad have gone away for a few days," Steve mumbled with some obvious discomfort.

Tom got back into the car, slamming the door and glaring at Steve.

"What did you say, gone away, to where? Why would they do that if they knew that I was coming back?" demanded Tom.

"Well, you know, I didn't tell them, I wasn't sure if you would come back and I thought there's no point in building up their hopes and after all, I didn't say they would be here, just that you could stay at the house."

"That's bullshit. Mom and Dad would never go away anywhere if they knew that there was the slightest chance that I was coming home and you expect me to believe that the only time they do coincides with my visit. Look, you have arranged this haven't you? You wanted them out of the way so that you can push this plan along unhindered. There's no real concern here for them or me, is there? You just want to go ahead with your own agenda. Look you'd better level with me now or I'm out of here. I must have been crazy to have agreed to this. You pay for me to come back from Oz, when did you ever do anything for me without there being something in it for you?"

"Come on mate. Look I needed some time to organise things and, yes I needed to push this along. I thought that you were interested in this idea, otherwise why did you agree to come back? Let's go inside and we'll discuss it off the street."

Steve got the bags out of the car and had crossed the road. He opened the front door and motioned his brother to go in.

Tom although appearing to have little choice, reluctantly followed and entered the house.

Immediately inside was what they called the front room. A polished wooden floor with a large red rug covering most of it, and on top of it a heavy table with four matching chairs stood in the middle of the room. A couple of comfortable two-seaters around the walls with a gas fire filling the original open fire-place. Against one wall stood a glass-fronted cabinet filled with drinking glasses and a green and white dinner set. Two old vases stood on the fire-place mantle and a gilt clock in the centre was about to chime the hour. A dark sideboard stood to one side and on it photographs pictured the family in days gone by. Tom walked over to the photographs and picked up one of himself and his wife on their wedding day and after running his finger across the top replaced it with care in a gesture that his brother could not fail to notice. A large mirror hung from the wall above the fireplace.

He recalled that this was never his style but was probably the best his father could afford and he understood this. Steve on the other hand never had and had always wanted to better himself financially. To their parents, life was comfortable with what they had, to Steve it was always bigger and better and the need to finance it whatever it took.

He wandered around the house All the other rooms were very familiar hardly anything had changed and in spite of his parent's absence, he began to feel glad that he had returned to the warmth of the family home. Although his life had taken some strange paths and turns he felt that he had never really left this place and he began to look forward to his time back here in Hereford.

"Let's call a truce on this for the time being there's no point in arguing. You said you'd come back and its better if we work together. Mom and Dad will be back in a few days anyway. Look its three o'clock, I've arranged to meet Mick in The Cellars pub at around eight so I'm going up to my room to unpack, have a cup of coffee and relax. What about you?" asked Steve.

"So you are living here as well these days?" Tom queried.

"Well just while you are over here and we deal with all this business and also I can look after the house whilst Mom and Dad are away."

"Yeah, OK. Well I feel a bit tired after the journey, but you know I'm not one for resting too long, so I'll unpack have a coffee and then go out for a while get some fresh air after the journey. Quite honestly I need to think about all this and you know that the way I can think about things clearly is to walk and talk to myself. You used to laugh at that, seeing me walking around and talking to myself, but it was always the way I worked things out. I'll go along the river for a while. You know if you want my co-operation you'd better let me deal with this in my own way."

Steve nodded and went upstairs and Tom wandered back into the kitchen. Everything still as he remembered it. He opened a few cupboards, finding what was needed to make coffee and soon two cups were made and placed on the table. He sat down and looked around him, sipping the hot drink and peering through the window into the deserted street and away towards the river bank. Finishing his coffee he rose and went upstairs to what had become his bedroom after having departed the marital home and before leaving for Australia. He opened a wardrobe to unpack his few clothes and found that many of his own things, left here when he went away were still as they had been, at least there would be a warm coat he thought.

He sat on the bed; 'Tom, I hope you know what you're doing,' came the thought in his head. "Still if not you can always get out of it easily enough."

"Steve I'm going out now," he called. "There's a coffee on the kitchen table. I'll see you later."

There was no answer from his brother.

"Gone to sleep I expect," he muttered.

Tom left the house, pulling the door quietly behind him he walked back along the street towards the main road and crossed at the traffic lights. He walked through the old gate in the City walls and down past the shops and houses. Little had changed in the years he had been away, a new restaurant perhaps, a new estate agent maybe and soon he had reached the old bridge, a place that he loved dearly for all the memories it brought back to him, just standing there looking into the endless flow of the water. How it swirled under the arches creating backwaters, two different rivers in different seasons. In the summer, the water low, exposing the arch foundations of the bridge, a resting place for ducks, fish on the surface out of the current facing upstream. In winter many feet higher, brown with carried mud and branches of trees from well upstream, broken off during bad weather. No ducks or fish today but a wheeling, squealing flock of gulls scavenging off the surface risking their lives with each dive.

It was not yet spring and the river was up, high against the arches and well onto the banks. He always would look at the flow of the river some fifty metres below the bridge. Here it was never smooth, even in summer. It marked the spot on the river where the ancient crossing had been constructed by whoever lived there at the time. Then there was no bridge only a ford, from which the City got its name, made by placing hundreds, even thousands of stones across the shallowest point, thereby enabling travellers wishing to cross from one side to the other, perhaps visiting the cathedral, to do so with relative ease. The winter was a different matter. Then the bridge was built and the crossing was no longer used and therefore not repaired. Floods washed away the stones over time but during low water summer months the path could still be seen. He walked across the old bridge and turned left onto the path to walk towards the more modern Victoria Bridge. He noticed a boat moored to the wall, moving in the rapid current. It was strewn with leaves and water slopped about in the well. A sign proclaimed 'River Tours'. Not now he thought maybe in summer, will I still be here? The walk along the tarmac path, between the huge beech trees brought back more memories of his time with Tilly, walking in autumn kicking up leaves, sitting on benches, laughing. He sat on a bench facing the river. It made him think of what he had made of his life. He was now 40 years old. Most people at this age had made inroads into their careers, put down roots, started families, but he had done none of this. He had moved around, seen the world, lost his wife, made some money and probably lost that now because he knew he could not stay in Australia forever and who would buy the farm. Perhaps it was time to take stock, think of his future, get some money, maybe move back to Hereford, find a wife again? Where was Tilly these days?

The river bank was very nearly deserted. February; misty chilly, no fishermen, no walkers, no lines of escorted four year olds walking from the nursery school with their blue and yellow caps, just two lads on bicycles and a mother and child crossing over the meadow to the houses on the other side, but Tom was a loner and he needed to think. He caught a glimpse of movement back along the path. Perhaps it was a squirrel or a blackbird turning over leaves to find a meal. The path was dark now, the lights already dim were lost among the branches and trunks of the trees, maybe it was imagination. He moved on and arrived at the foot bridge, a relatively new structure painted white, bearing a coat of arms and two large lights at either end, he turned left onto it. He walked to the middle of it deliberately with a heavy tread, remembering that the relatively flimsy construction bounced when more than one person walked on it in unison.

He stood there for some time, pulling the collar of the coat tight around his neck against the wind in his face, beginning to feel the cold, looking into the water watching patches of vegetation racing underneath, remembering summer evenings here watching the fish moving upstream hiding amongst the shadows by the banks. This idea of Steve's, just maybe there's something in it, perhaps this is the chance I need, let me sort things out, he thought and the more he did so, the more interesting became the plan.

Deep in thought he had not noticed the two walkers approaching the bridge from the same direction that he had come. The motion of the walkway under his feet and the sudden heavy scent of Cologne in his nostrils restored his focus on his surroundings but not swiftly enough to anticipate the attack. The men were on to him, lifting him off his feet and pushing him up and against the metal rails in an effort to get him over the bridge and into the water. Twisting, using his strength, he grabbed at the collar on the coat of one of the men and the force from the other propelled him and the assailant over the parapet.

As they fell he loosed his grip on the garment, wanting to land in the river on his own, but in the process of letting go he swung a foot in the direction of the attacker. He hit the man's stomach and heard a gasp. The man was winded and this gave him the vital seconds he needed to get his bearings on hitting the water. He was up first and on to the man, head butting, hair pulling, gouging eyes not giving him any space to think. Then hands pushed down on his head as the attacker fought back and they both went under.

The water raced them along, feet sometimes dragging on the bottom catching the submerged rocks. Breaking the surface the current moved them towards the bank, Tom got the other's head underwater again and into the rocks that were closer now that they were in the shallows. He tugged violently at his hair, and as knees touched the river bottom, he gouged at the man's eyes drawing blood, this was not a pretty fight but few contests to the end ever were.

They hit a tree that had fallen and was lying in the torrent; Tom lost his grip and found himself slammed into the bank by the flow but at last away from the power of the water. The other man was in trouble now, his arms flailing as he was dragged down. He hit another tree and became stuck to it by the force of the river. The undercurrent and his weight were pulling him under the tree. Trapped under the branches and unable to free himself, he would not last long and now the odds were even, one on one.

They had travelled perhaps fifty yards in the water and were now out of sight of the bridge as the course of the river bent round. Tom hung on to tufts of grass and gradually pulled himself out onto the bank keeping below the remaining tangle of last year's thick vegetation. He needed some time to recover before the second man found him as would surely happen. It was only necessary to come along the water's edge and if armed, he would have the advantage. It was dark along the river bank, no light from the nearby roads reached here and five minutes passed, then ten, nobody came. Tom put his head up, there was no-one to be seen. In the blackness it was possible to crawl away unseen from the river on to the path between the trees. He had regained his breath now and was able to stand up. Still no-one, he moved silently between the trees. Gradually making his way back to the bridge and passing it by along the way he had come earlier.

Back now to the old bridge his pace increasing. He was wet of course now getting colder he started to run. In the dark a few people looked at him, a bedraggled individual travelling the roads. A mile to the house and soon he was there. The light was on in the front room, but he stopped just short of the house, something was wrong, he sensed it. Crossing the road to approach from the other side there was a better view. The door was open and he could see the lace curtain hanging down from one side of the window. No movement from the door or the upstairs rooms all of which were lit. He waited five minutes, nothing happened, and slowly made his way across the road. He could see through the window, no Steve, no other person; he moved silently through the doorway into the room. The furniture had been flung about, there had been a violent struggle or search that was obvious, but there was no-one here.

The rooms upstairs had been searched, wardrobes opened, doors left open, but no-one. He looked for any clue. His mind racing, what the hell was going on? Someone had just tried to kill him. One person was still out there. Where was Steve? Who was after him, both of them? He had to think. His clothes were still wet and collecting a few things, quickly he ran back downstairs. The hire car was still outside, but where was the key? No, leave the car, walking or running was better, narrow alleyways to use, easier to hide. Where to go? Leaving the house away from the City sometimes running, sometimes walking, he soon found himself travelling along another street that he seemed to recognise. It was as if something, some unseen force was drawing him in a particular direction, although he had no idea why.

Several minutes passed as he ran, stopping at street corners when changing direction, looking back, no-one following and meeting no-one on the way.

The house on the corner in front of him was now in sight. He stopped in his tracks his mind flooded now with other thoughts. This was the house where Tilly lived before they married. Could she still be here? Is this what he was being drawn towards? It was a long time ago. It was worth a try, nothing to lose. The light was on, the bell was rung.

It seemed to take an age but it must have been just a few minutes. Through the glass in the door a figure appeared, the door was finally opened, it was Matilda Mary.

Chapter 11

She stood at the open door looking out into the street lit by the dim lights from the lamps. She hesitated, seeming scarcely to believe what or who was there in front of her.

"Tom, is that you?" she said with some incredulity. "What on earth are you doing here?" There was no answer, seeing her again, so suddenly and without warning was a shock even to him. She noticed the condition of his clothes and the mud and straw in his hair and on his shoes.

"Christ, Tom what's been going on?"

"Nice to see you Tils," he replied half casually regaining some composure. "Are you going to invite me in?"

There was a moment's hesitation, a questioning look on her face which quickly softened into a smile.

"Of course, come in but why are you in this condition, what's happened?"

Tom entered the house, it had been a number of years since he was here or in the company of his ex-wife, but he quickly gauged his surroundings as the door closed behind him into the warmth of the room. He turned around and peered through the curtains into the street, a couple walked by arm in arm passing the window as he looked out, surprised to see someone at the window just at that moment, but there was no-one else outside, and then again back towards Tilly.

She stood expectantly in front of him. She had changed little from when they last met. Ten years younger than Tom, a few years maturity since their divorce had improved her he thought. Tall for a woman, around five feet nine inches, and still wearing her blonde hair long. The loose clothing she wore hid her figure, but her smell brought back to him a vision of the body beneath and he remembered why he had been crazy about her.

"Tils, can I have a shower and then change into something dry please. Give me half an hour to clean up then I'll tell you what I know, just trust me?"

"O.K I guess you remember where to go, but I've nothing to fit you."

"I've got some clothes here," he replied, waving the bag in her general direction and at the same time making his way upstairs to the bathroom.

She walked about the room, looked out of the window, sat down. Rising from the seat another look into the street, what has been happening out there? The noise of the shower coming from the room above caused her to look upwards. It had been some time since a man had been in the house and took a shower, she thought. What will be the outcome of this?

Thirty minutes later Tom returned. The shorts and shirt did not suit the occasion but at least they were dry and a coffee had been made for him which was welcomed.

He sat down in a chair near to the window, close enough to see into the street through the gap in the curtains and Tilly sat opposite him. With Tom now refreshed and with his tan and clothes revealing his fit body it was remembered in return why she had been in love with him.

The two of them sat quietly for a few moments, each wondering what to say, where to start a conversation, what they had to talk about.

"It's really good to see you again" she said finally, breaking the silence.

Tom knew from the way it was said, the tone of her voice that it was meant and said with some feeling but this was not the time to pursue that or any sort of a relationship again, he thought, more important things to consider.

He sat back on the chair holding the coffee mug firmly in both hands, extracting some warmth from it.

"And it's good to see you also, very good," he replied finally hoping that his voice betrayed some feeling that she would notice in return.

"I bet you wonder why I'm here and what's this all about?"

Tilly nodded rapidly. "Yes of course, but why are you in this state? What's happened to you? What sort of trouble are you in? While you were upstairs I was worried sick, could I expect a knock on the door or what?"

"Well I think that at the moment I also wonder why I'm here and what's going on. Where shall I start?" he paused considering what was needed to be said and what was not relevant to the conversation.

"Look I'm fine just a bit of local difficulty I guess. The shower has calmed me down so I'll start at the beginning."

This was typical of the man, recently in mortal danger he was well able to think clearly. "I'll get to the aggravation eventually."

This attitude had always infuriated his wife, but that was Tom, he'd get to the point in due course.

He continued. "You know that after our breakup I went over to Australia. I bought a property and I thought that I'd just stay over there for however long it took to get my mind straight again. There was no intention of returning yet, everything was fine. I wouldn't say that all of it was completely enjoyable, but it was the best for me at the time, comfortable would be the word I guess."

"Yes I know."

"Well, after three years of no contact at all, out of the blue, Steve came over. I thought it strange that he would go to all that trouble and expense just to find out my whereabouts and pay a visit, not his usual style at all."

She nodded knowingly.

"Eventually he told me why he had come over and later about his attempt to persuade me to come back to England. I wasn't really bothered at first but, you know, after a while, thinking about it and so on, I thought well, why not? What he had to say was mildly interesting to some extent, but as much as anything I began to think of you." He gave a half smile reflecting some embarrassment and perhaps a little anticipation.

She smiled, her head lilting to one side, appreciating his comments.

"So here we are back in Hereford only just a couple of hours ago, I'm at Mom and Dad's house, Steve made all the arrangements. We planned to go to The Cellars tonight and so while he had a rest I went out for a walk. You know along the river and over Victoria Bridge?"

Tilly nodded. "I know."

"Well I stood on the bridge looking into the water, I suppose just reminiscing, thinking of the past, when suddenly a couple of guys came on to the bridge and got at me, you know attacked me. I thought what the bloody hell's going on? The next thing, we were in the river. I got rid of one of them but the other must have thought better of it and just legged it. I made my way back to the house, soaking wet as you can guess, the locals who saw me must have wondered what I'd been doing, some crazy bloke swimming, fully clothed this time of the year. I arrived back at the house to find Steve had gone and the place ransacked…and here I am."

He shook his head slowly, looking again out of the window.

There were a few moments of silence.

"How much of this do you know about already?" he asked in a mildly accusing way, wondering if she had any idea of his brother's movements.

"Hey, nothing with regard to Steve, we've been apart for some time, but then I expect you know that. I had no idea that he'd gone after you, how would I?"

She hesitated for a moment.

"Look I know that this will be a bit redundant now, but God I'm so sorry that we ended up how we did."

Tom looked deep into her face. She might be telling the truth he thought to himself, or she might not, but at this time there were bigger problems he had to think about.

"OK about us I can't forgive you, to forgive is to condone and I'm not the sort of person to do that, some can but not me but for now, something serious is going on here. I don't know what but it's heavy, will you help me?"

Although her father had been in the regiment, she had never had much involvement in the daily life around the base, except for the social aspect of it all, but with the family connections all round some of the spirit of it had naturally rubbed off and a tinge of excitement seemed to begin to creep over her. She had only had a little while to comprehend Tom's return and now he was asking for help with some serious deal, she seemed to like the idea.

"What do you want me to do?"

"Have you got any transport?"

"Sure, I've a car parked just outside".

"OK, take your car and drive along past my Dad's house, you remember where it is, see if you can spot anything unusual. Anybody in the house or something suspicious in the street, and then come straight back here, it'll only take a few minutes."

Tom peered again between the curtains.

"It's all clear as far as I can see."

There was no hesitation, picking up her keys the front door was quickly opened. Leaving the house she made for the car parked a few metres along the road under the nearest lamp-post. The light rain went unnoticed.

Moving away with some obvious urgency, she was soon turning the corner at the end of the road and off towards her former in-law's property.

Tom walked around the lounge of the house. His thoughts had returned to Steve and he had begun to be curious to see if anything in it reflected her life after him and with his brother, but there was nothing, no photographs or mementos of their life together after she had left Tom. He was encouraged by that and also by her reaction to seeing him and the immediate response to his request for help. This thing in Hereford, whatever it was, could well be difficult but at the end of it, who knows, perhaps there was something again for the two of them, he thought.

Suddenly there was a movement at the door, bringing him back to attention. He heard a key inserted in a lock and the door opened and rapidly closed again.

"That didn't take long," he said as she came into the room, throwing the car keys onto a side table.

"Well?"

"Just as you said, lights on, door open, but nothing else, no-one in the street that I could see, nothing unusual, a few cars parked, that's all."

"Look, we'll have to deal with the folk's house, I can't let it remain wide open like that, anyone can get inside, real thieves maybe, so phone the police. Will you, tell them that you've just driven past the address and that the place looks like they've had a burglary. No better still, tell them there's a burglary in progress, you never know, they might deal with it a little more quickly. Don't tell them who you are, just let them deal with it, I've got something else to do."

"Yes I'll phone them of course, but I think that when you say that you've got something else to do you really mean that we've got something else to do, you asked for my help remember?" Her support was comforting to some degree and Tom could see the advantage of her company in more ways than one, but for the time being, he would make do with only part of it.

Chapter 12

The two of them spent the next hour, drinking coffee and talking over the last three years, when they had gone their separate ways. Tom described his farm and daily routine, the opals that he had prospected and eventually the loneliness of the evenings without company. He had not really appreciated that part or, perhaps, had ignored it at the time, but now with some female company, it was taking on a different emphasis.

"The farm sounds a lovely place," she said encouragingly, "you always wanted something like that, I recall, but yes, I know about loneliness as well. Still I have a job these days and it gives me an interest at the very least, oh and some income of course. The regiment is in the process of moving the base and Dad works for the army still, nothing energetic these days but he says he has a skill that they still require."

"Intelligence?"

"Yes well you would remember I guess that that was his interest, so he asked if I would be interested in earning some money. I said I would and so he found me this little job as an administrator at Credenhill, helping with the move and so on."

"An administrator eh, I recall that covered a dozen or more things generally not talked about."

"Well whatever, I took the job. It's flexible, more or less I work when they need me, but it pays some bills and I bought a new car last year, so it's fine for the time being."

She talked frankly of her feelings having her husband away for so long in the past and of her life without him. This was the first time they had spoken in this way and he began to feel differently about her now, of how she had come to leave him and the affair with Steve. It was good to talk, and the more they did so, the more comfortable they were with each other in spite of what had happened in the past.

It was now early evening and the events of the day were settling down in the mind of Tom and he was beginning to plan his next moves. His attire was very inappropriate for a visit to town and although he had managed to retrieve some clothes from his parent's house they were nowhere near enough for his immediate needs.

"Tilly," he said, "clearly I can't go back to Dad's house at the moment and I need something more to wear, any chance of some clothing do you think. I want to get into town but really I can't go looking like this. I can buy some stuff tomorrow, but I need things now."

"Well there's nothing I'm afraid, everything Steve left here was thrown away some time ago, but I'll tell you what. My Dad is about your size and he and Mom live pretty close. I'll give him a try if you like; he may have some stuff, nothing to lose. OK?"

Tom was unsure at first, someone else to be involved he thought, but there was no choice. It seemed to be the only way, he needed some more clothes and there was nowhere else to try at that moment.

"Sure that'll be fine," he said finally. "Look while you're away I'll see if I can get some food together, then if you are able to borrow some clothes I'll change and we can go into Town, what do you think?"

"Sounds good," she replied with some obvious enthusiasm. She was warming to Tom's presence.

Her father was indeed around the same height and build as Tom and a trip to his home had produced enough clothing, particularly a good overcoat to enable them to leave the house later that evening.

The older man or his wife had not asked too many questions when their daughter had arrived asking for clothes, although naturally they were curious to know why Tom was in the picture again and why the clothes were needed.

"If there's any help you need you just have to ask," her father said, knowing that his daughter had always retained strong feelings for Tom and amongst all of her male friends he was the one that he had got on with best in the past, "but for Christ's sake take care, just watch you are doing."

"Thanks," she replied getting into the car and starting the engine. "You know I will, we may need some support later, we'll be in touch." The car accelerated from the house along the side roads and back around the corner to where Tom was waiting. The street was quiet; a neighbour was arriving home from work. A passing "Good evening" as she left the car and made for her door with her father's suitcase.

At the house Tom had produced a half decent meal with what was found in the fridge, from his time in the forces and living alone he had become a reasonable cook.

Tilly was impressed with the meal that had been prepared and the production of a bottle of wine discovered in a cupboard, made it something of an event, a reunion dinner. No perhaps not quite that she thought, just an unexpected meal with her ex-husband, nothing more.

Throughout the time they indulged in small talk concerning friends, family and whatever else came to mind, the wine encouraging conversation, although both remained reserved in relation to their own personal situations. Eventually the meal was over and Tom finally brought the subject back to the matter in hand. He had to go into Hereford, to The Cellars perhaps to meet up with Mick and if he could, to find out what had happened earlier at his parent's house and with Steve.

"I got you some clothes from my Dad. I think they will fit you, maybe not your style, but with an overcoat against the cold, I think you'll do. By the way Dad sends his regards."

"Yeah I bet he wonders what the hell is going on. What did you tell him?"

"Nothing, he trusts me to know my own mind. I said if it were to be necessary to have some future support was that alright? You can guess what he said."

"Yes, I always liked your Mom and Dad. That's good of him but let's hope we can deal with this without having to involve too many others."

"Get changed while I clear the table and then I'll put something on and we can go," said Tilly.

"Don't go to any great trouble, it's only a pub."

She laughed.

Thirty minutes later the two of them were ready to leave the house.

Tom had found something reasonable to wear from the borrowed items and, in spite of his comments Tilly had dressed up for the night out.

"I know you said it's only a pub, but I don't have much of a social life these days so this is a bit of a treat. Anyway, if I look good then perhaps no-one will notice you, unless of course you want to be noticed?"

"No not really, I suppose," he mumbled. "Come on, let's go. Let's see if any of the old crew are about. If Mick's there he might be prepared to say something or have some idea about this. From what I was told, I think he was involved with Steve in this deal anyway."

"I'm beginning to wonder who is in with all this based on what you've told me. At least I can watch your back," she replied.

Tom looked out through the window. The street was quiet and a light wind had helped clear the mist and rain away.

"Let's walk". He said, "It will only take fifteen minutes or so and we can think about how we should handle Mick if he's there."

The door clicked behind them as they stepped into the evening, the street was still quiet and they began the walk along the roads towards the City and the pub. Tilly took Tom's arm and held him close against the cold.

Chapter 13

"You know," he said as they walked, "I've been thinking, if this thing is just so my brother can get rich, why have I had this trouble already, within a few hours of getting back. What do you think? Is there another reason?"

"Well, that story about your dream and so on, I recall you telling me about it when we were together, and this idea about regressing to this guy Hamann so you could find the looted works of art? Yes why not, you could become very rich that way so I guess it could be that, but perhaps there is another reason."

"Yes, what are you thinking?"

"Well Steve has encouraged you to consider that that was the plan, you know, to find these things, get rich perhaps, but you may be right suppose it was for something else, suppose that there was another reason."

"Well, yes, the idea was formed largely as a result of Steve, but not only works of art, remember the Nazis stole anything of value they could find. Tons of gold from teeth were known to have been collected from the camps, was that ever discovered? I don't know. It was just that from my knowledge of my brother it seemed unlikely that there was an interest in anything else. Do you have another theory?"

Tilly thought for a while, "Well possibly. I was reading a magazine article recently about the United Nations. Do you remember that a few years ago they appointed a new Secretary General, the position at the top of the organization, very influential throughout the world? The guy's name was Kurt Waldheim. He seemed to be a professional diplomat and the story went on to say that he sought election as The President of Austria later on as far as I can recall."

Tom nodded. They stopped at the main road, waiting for a gap in the traffic.

"Apparently there was some controversy concerning his appointment to Secretary General and the rest of his political career, when it appeared to have been discovered that during the war he was an SS officer. He denied any wrongdoing whilst he was serving in the war, as I guess they all did, and also there was some suggestion that this could have been a false slur against him for political purposes. But mud sticks and eventually someone produced an incriminating photograph of him in an SS uniform. There was a considerable outcry concerning this and what he might have done during the war, as I remember, and eventually, of course, he had to retire from political life."

She looked at Tom.

"I'm listening."

"OK, so there is much more to his life than that and it's not the issue now I know but, just think, if this was remotely true look at the implications. He must have thought that after all this time he was in the clear and his past wouldn't catch up with him and so, if he thought that then I bet there would be many others who thought the same. People with a Nazi past that they wouldn't want revealed. Well just think about it for a moment, if you could recall the whereabouts of paintings or gold and so on might you not also recall people from that time, from your past and as with this U.N man there might be plenty of people in high ranking jobs around the world who wouldn't want their past to come out. Who knows both ideas are equally believable as they are unbelievable."

Tom looked up. A few spots of rain began to fall as they crossed the main road and on through the City walls. They quickened their steps.

"That's an interesting idea, what made you think of that. I don't recall you ever being seriously involved in world affairs of that sort?"

"I'm not involved, as you call it, it was just that I read about it and actually, when I did so, it reminded me of my grandfather."

"Your Grandfather? He wasn't an old Nazi, was he?"

"Of course not, but I recall him telling me about when he lived back in Ireland. You remember that our family came over from Waterford and he used to talk about the time that a Nazi, as he described, him lived there."

"A Nazi, who the hell was that?"

"Well from memory, his name was Menten, Peter Menten I think and he apparently came over to Ireland at some time after the war. He had a mansion there so I guess that he must have got in somehow, with a purpose, certainly with some money, probably unofficially, and the story goes that as recently as the mid 1960's he lived in Waterford. He had a big house there and the locals knew him as an escaped Nazi, although not as a wanted war criminal at that time. There was some suggestion that his wealth came from his personal business dealings, but he also had an extensive art collection, anything to do with you or rather Hamann do you suppose?"

Tom shook his head.

"How would I know, anyway if he was a war criminal do you know what he was supposed to have done?"

"Well as I recall, it was something to do with killing Polish Jews."

"What happened to him?"

"Well eventually he was handed over to the authorities, the Dutch I think, he went to trial and was given a prison sentence and then banned from going back to his house in Ireland by the government."

"So why is this important to anyone?"

"Well you have to wonder how he came to be there, did someone in authority allow him to come to Ireland in the first place and keep his identity secret? If so that would be embarrassing to anyone still around now wouldn't it, and while we are talking about my old country, what about America? They were possibly the worst offenders. When I read this article concerning Waldheim it also named many ex-Nazis who went to The States and they were actively encouraged to do so. You know rocket experts, scientists, such as Von Braun, Rudolph and others. Now, of course, these people are in the public domain, but was that the right thing to do, do you suppose? Who is to say after all this time but names like that would be just the sort of thing that Hamann might be able to recall."

"It's unlikely that the Yanks are very worried, that was never a secret, you know what they're like."

"Sure, but these are the names we know about and I guess that deliberate war crimes were not at the top of the agenda of those individuals but perhaps there were others who should really have been in the dock, who knows?"

He thought for a while.

"Steve's a man for material things, he's after wealth not protecting some old guy who has risen to some important position somewhere, although I can see there could be a financial angle in that, no it's money."

"Are you certain?"

"Well I guess it's possible that he's not the key here. I could believe it if that's true. He's a bloody good liar if that's the case, but then who else could it be. The only other name mentioned to me has been Mick. You don't think it could be him do you?"

There was no answer.

They stopped walking for a moment. Tom thought he felt her loosen her grip of his arm. He looked at her, the grip tightened again.

"Suppose it's someone else who has been using him to get to me. The only other person in the frame would be Mick."

"Or Joe", Tilly quickly reminded him.

"Joe?" he replied surprised at the suggestion. "What do you know about him?"

"You said that the only other name mentioned was Mick, but the two of you also spoke of Joe, remember?"

This was true, he recalled, Joe had been mentioned, but this man was the therapist, what had he got to do with this?

They passed the Cathedral in silence. Tom was thinking that this was becoming much more complicated.

They walked on, the bright lights of the main street distracting him for a few moments. Traffic passed them by and a few couples hurried along hugging the tall buildings as a shelter from the rain which had begun to fall again.

They turned into Behyndthewall Lane. Tom suddenly grabbed Tilly and pulled her behind a wall by a small car park. She knew to be silent as they melted into the dark. Footsteps approached at a brisk pace. A man walked by on the opposite side and continued along the road. They watched him disappear into the distance. His demeanour showed that he was no threat.

"Can't be too careful," he whispered.

This was the first close contact he had made with his ex-wife since they had met again and in the dark and the quietness their lips met and lingered. A car drove by and snapped his attention back as it sounded its horn at a cat crossing the road too slowly for its own good.

"The Cellars," he murmured. "Just along here."

Chapter 14

In a few strides they had arrived at the corner. The pub was less than 50 metres along on the other side of the narrow medieval street, these days pedestrianised. They waited a few seconds; the street was quiet, just a few people taking the shortcut to or from the Cathedral gardens and the cold and damp encouraging all but the hardiest of drinkers to stay at home. The lights of several premises, still open for business, shone out.

The window and door of the public house took up the whole of the frontage along the street enabling them to see right inside and anyone inside to see out. However they reasoned that they were not expected by anyone other than Steve or Mick if they had indeed arrived and so they approached the place and entered.

The pub was an old building probably in the same business for centuries and thankfully it maintained its ancient charm. Well beamed, with a stone floor and a series of corners and alcoves giving patrons a feeling of relative obscurity at their own tables. A long bar flanked one side and this extended to the back of the building which opened onto a small courtyard well used in the summer months. Entering they found a table giving a view through the window and Tom sat with his back to the door with Tilly facing it. She would know anyone with whom they had an interest and Tom would not be recognized immediately.

The place was popular with men from the regiment and sooner or later someone would show. Tom started to relax and after a couple of minutes made his way to the bar. The mirror on the wall behind the bar enabled him to see much of the rest of the room and he searched for a familiar face as he bought some drinks. He recognized the barman from previous visits but the recognition was not reciprocated and apart from the usual polite greeting no real conversation ensued. He returned to Tilly at their table.

"Why did you kiss me?" she asked quietly.

"It just seemed the right thing to do," Tom replied looking deep into her eyes, "Is that a problem?"

She moved her face closer to his. "No problem at all," she said and softly kissed his lips.

This conversation was going somewhere, they both knew it, but before they could explore the possibilities Tilly pulled back, "Mick," she whispered.

Mick Cannon was a pretty incongruous individual as far as the army was concerned. About a foot shorter than Tom and with long fair hair his stature belied his strength. The T-shirt that was invariably his dress, even at this time of the year, revealed powerful arms, bearing tattoos showing mythical creatures of his own imagination. Here was a man confident in his ability to look after himself, that appearing as he did, wherever he went, no-one would dare to question his choice of apparel, a man who looked every bit as tough as he was. Entering the room he made straight for the bar.

He stood there for a moment, looking around the room reflected through the mirror. Tilly knew that he had seen her and she guessed that Tom would have been recognised also, but no obvious acknowledgment was made. Then as quickly as he had arrived he left, casting a glance in their direction, a slight movement of the head indicating that they were to follow.

In a second the two of them were out in the street again following after Mick and in a few strides were at the road where a black saloon car had stopped, its engine running and doors open. Mick had got in the passenger seat and was urgently signaling the others to get into the back. Tom hesitated a moment. Was he going to be an issue? His recent conversation with Tilly had not been conclusive on the subject and here they both were now expected to trust and follow him. Holding back his companion, he looked into the vehicle to see who was driving. The open door permitted the courtesy light to illuminate the inside. It was his brother.

"Steve, I thought"…

"Let's get away from here," Steve interrupted, "I'll explain in a minute."

The car door slammed and he accelerated the engine. The wheels screamed and slipped on the wet road surface but finally achieving some traction they moved away from the vicinity at speed.

The car was driven quickly through the streets barely stopping at any junction, and certainly not for anyone crossing the road, and turned right onto the main route out of the City.

There was little traffic at this time, but Tom could see that the driver was intent in looking at what was around them and through the driving mirror. What was to be seen? Was someone following?

Coming on to a straight piece of road the car gained speed. The roadside trees, bare of leaves, were just a blur. Tom knew this road and realised that just up ahead was a sharp turn. At this speed and with the road wet from the continuing rain this was just too fast. Approaching the bend with its warning black and white chevrons Steve braked heavily. The car slewed to the left as the forward motion suddenly reduced, the rear of the car sliding around the bend as they slowed. Steve skidded into a gateway mercifully wide enough to take the almost sideways on vehicle and they came to a halt on the deep gravel drive. He switched off the lights, a few minutes later a motorcycle raced by and off along the road, now absent of houses.

"That's the guy," Steve muttered, "O.K let's get out of here."

He reversed onto the road and drove back towards the City turning onto the ring road at the next junction. In a few minutes they were on the other side of the City and Tom realised that the car was heading towards where Mick used to live and presumably still did. He squeezed Tilly's hand and she nodded confirming that she was alright after the hectic journey. The car continued.

Within a few minutes they had arrived at the house. Steve drove into the drive at the side and straight round to the back of the property leaving the car out of sight from the road. Mick was the first to exit the vehicle and quickly he made for the door at the rear of the house gesturing for the others to follow.

Throughout the journey Tom had remained silent. He knew that they had been making an escape from someone and that was the priority at the time but from whom and why he would find out soon enough.

"Everything alright?" asked Mick as the other three entered the house.

"What's going on?" demanded Tom, "You bloody fool, you nearly got us killed back there."

"Saved your life, more like," mumbled Steve turning around and peering through the windows. "Enjoy the white knuckle ride did you? I think we lost the guy."

"Yeah looks like it," added Mick closing the curtains and switching on the lights.

It had been a long time since Tom had been in Mick's house and he remembered very little of it, but he noticed that Tilly seemed to be more aware of the surroundings, perhaps she had been here more recently, he mused.

Mick walked over to the cupboard in the corner and got out a bottle of Paddy Irish Whiskey and some glasses which he put on the table.

"Help yourselves, I'll be back in a minute," he said leaving the room.

Tom poured himself a glass and one for Tilly remembering that they had finished off many a bottle in their younger days together, Steve helped himself but said nothing and continued his vigil at the window waiting for Mick to return.

Chapter 15

The three of them remained in silence in the small sparsely furnished living room of Mick's house. He was upstairs and they could hear the sound of opening and closing drawers. Tom and Tilly glanced at each other; the message between them was that they needed to get away from here as soon as possible.

Tom stood up.

"Look I'm leaving. No-one is telling me anything and..."

At that moment Mick returned from his expedition upstairs with some large brown envelopes which by their thickness clearly contained a quantity of papers and, sitting down, proceeded to untie the thin red ribbon that secured the contents.

"Should you have those?" Tom asked glancing at the parcel and seeing the words Top Secret on the front. Mick shrugged his shoulders and started to remove some paper from the largest envelope at the top of the pile.

"These are the documents that I told you about," said Steve, hoping that the sight of them would encourage his brother to remain at the house.

"You know the ones that Mick was looking at when he spotted your name."

"Not my name," replied Tom tersely, "but I suppose you mean Hamann. Look you blokes I think it's time that you were straight with me. I've had a rough day. I've driven from London, had my parents house broken into, been attacked on the bridge, been chased by some unknown guy on a bike, come straight here from The Cellars and now you think it's time to talk World War II," he walked to the door, "maybe tomorrow I'll contact you."

He pulled Tilly up by her hand and opened the door.

Steve knew that at this time it was best not to push the matter. Tom would come round in due course. "Where are going to stay?" Steve enquired.

Tom looked at Tilly and she returned his silent question.

"Mick, open the front door and run down the street. If a vehicle or anybody follows we have a problem. Return through the back door," Tom suggested.

Mick was clearly not happy with being given the instruction but he knew it was right and he had to keep him onside. Opening the door he started out, first walking then running. The others kept watch through the windows, there was no-one else outside and within a few minutes he had returned.

"There's no one about as far as I can see, but you've no transport. Where are you going and how are you getting there?"

Tom ignored the question and opened the front door. Looking out into the street and judging that it was all clear, he and Tilly left the house.

The rain and mist had gone with the rising breeze and now it was the sort of night that Tom liked best. He and his wife used to walk for miles on such an occasion and it seemed just the sort of thing to do now.

"Do you know the way back to your place?" he asked quietly.

"Yes I think so," she replied casually.

"Tils, what am I missing here? Steve, after years of no contact, finds his way over to Australia and tracks me down. He persuades me to come back to England and spends a lot of money in the process. We arrive back, presumably no-one else is aware of any of this. As soon as we are back, the house in which I am to stay is ransacked, I get into something on the bridge and later on some guy chases us from one side of Hereford to the other. All the time this is on the basis that I might know something that will make a fortune for Steve."

"A fortune for Steve?" she asked in a puzzled tone. "What makes you think that?"

"Well he told me about stolen and hidden works of art. He spoke about Lake Toplitz, something I had read about in a book and I know my brother. Why else?"

She let the question lie. Just up ahead she had spotted a dark form against the glow of the lights from the main road.

"Down here," she whispered pulling Tom into an alleyway as they reached it a few metres further along the street. Walking more quickly now along the narrow unlit path, and passing by the rear gardens of the houses either side, they soon arrived at the other end. Tilly stopped and looked back along the alley. A lamp shone out on the other side of the road, illuminating the entrance. A person passed by and stopped, looking along to where they stood at the other end and then moved off again. They crossed over to the other side of the next street and were soon away from whatever or whoever she had seen. Looking back it seemed clear. Their walking speed greater now as it had again started to rain. Turning left at the next junction, Tom recognised Tilly's street and soon they were at the front door.

"Glad you knew the quickest way home," he said questioningly.

"Well it's just the neighbourhood. I live in this area or had you forgotten?" she replied.

"It's raining Tom, you've nowhere to go, may I offer you a bed for the night?" she continued as if in an attempt to justify what seemed to have been on both of their minds for the last few minutes.

"Well a sofa perhaps."

Chapter 16

Tom woke late the next day. The remains of the long journey from Australia and the events of the day had fatigued him, even Tilly's presence had not on this occasion been enough to keep him awake. She had been up much earlier and had made a few phone calls. The sound of her voice had woken him and he made his way to where she was. "Have a cup of coffee I've got some news," she said. They both walked into the kitchen. The coffee on the breakfast bar smelled good and Tom sat down on a stool to savour the first cup of the day, Tilly joined him.

"I've spoken to the police and they say they found nothing at your parent's house last night. They sealed the door and now it's back to whoever to deal with it, although of course they have no idea that you are in the country. I guess that they will try to contact your parents, if they know where they might be."

"Mick phoned and asked when you can meet again, he seems pretty anxious to get things going. I said that's all up to you and I'll pass on the message. What are you going to do?"

"Nothing at the moment, let him wait until I'm ready, maybe tomorrow," he replied. "Perhaps there's something else I need to do now, who knows?"

Placing his now empty cup back on the bar he made for the stairs.

"OK if I take a shower and freshen up. I think I want to read the paper for a while afterwards. Is that alright? Unless you've anything better to do."

"No not really," she said, "let's just see what happens, the rest can wait."

The late morning moved on. Tom read the newspaper, catching up on some world events that had passed him by over the last few weeks. Tilly had spent the last hour or so in the kitchen and Tom had begun to anticipate a late lunch. Catching up on the news while his wife made a meal, just like old times he thought.

It was 3 o'clock, they had just started a meal. Ignoring his own efforts the previous evening, this was the first real food Tom had had since arriving in Hereford yesterday, when the phone rang. Tilly got up from the table to answer it.

"It's Steve he wants to know if we can meet at Mick's tonight."

Tom thought for a while and eventually nodded slowly in reply.

"We'll be over later," she said and replaced the handset.

"He's keen," she continued, "what time do you want to go?"

"You know I don't really want to go at all," he replied, "but this is just not going to go away is it? After this meal I'm going out to have a look around. The folks house, the Cellars, Mick's house -see what's about O.K?"

"Do you need me to come?"

"No let me have a look around on my own for a while, get my bearings. I'll be back later. I just need to think about things, you know, see what's around."

Chapter 17

It was 4.30 as Tom left the house and it was already dark with the clouded sky. He made his way along the streets he had used the day before, casually to his parents house. There was no hurry. Arriving at the top of the street, he paused and could see the house was in darkness and there was little activity along the road. A boy delivering the local free newspapers was making his way slowly along the properties in the direction of the house. Tom watched. The boy arrived eventually at the house, negotiated his way around the police tapes and posted a wrinkled copy through the letterbox. No light came on. The place must still be deserted. Tom walked down the opposite side of the street keeping close to the hedge and the trees which kept him in the shadows. He had taken in all he wanted to see by the time he arrived at the house. The hire car was still parked where it had been left the day before and none of the other vehicles in the line had anyone sitting in them.

The house had indeed been sealed by the police and it seemed deserted.

Continuing towards the main road he stood by the crossing, looking back. Still just the delivery boy made any movement along the street.

The traffic was heavy at this time. Workers returning home, a bus filled with passengers, faces pressed up against the condensation on the windows. Hereford was still a rural area. A slow tractor pulling a trailer, pieces of farm debris occasionally being thrown clear unerringly attaching to the pedestrians in the smartest clothes. A transporter carrying dull eyed sheep, as if they knew their fate, stopped in front of him as he waited for a chance to cross over into the City. The sheep moved away each one seeming to stare at Tom as they passed by where he stood. A gap in the traffic and he sprinted across the road and quickly hid along the wall by the City gate. No-one had followed, so far so good. He continued along the street towards the City centre arriving at the Cathedral gardens and, passing through them on this occasion, he turned left and made his way along the lane to the pub, arriving from the opposite direction to yesterday's visit. The first few customers were already in there, mostly office workers at this time relaxing before leaving for home, chewing over the events of the day. Their insular office intrigues and problems insignificant in relation to what appeared to be surrounding Tom at this time. There was no-one except for the barman that he could recognize and shaking his head as if to answer his own silent question he walked off towards Mick's house.

His inbuilt navigation system worked well and remembering the route that the car had taken the previous evening soon he was making his way to the house. There was no activity there that he could see. The curtains were drawn and a yellowish glow through them showed that someone was probably at home but now was not the time to visit. He stood at the street corner and watched the house for a while wondering what Mick would have to say when they met up later that evening. The walk back to Tilly's house gave him more time to think and although his round trip had taken more than an hour there was still no resolution in his mind. For once his walk about had come up with no answers. What is this all about? Where do I go with my ex-wife? Shall I stay in England or return to Australia? Maybe all these questions will be answered by a resolution of the first.

Tilly opened the door as he approached. During his absence she had scanned the road a number of times and the relief in her voice at his return was evident.

"Did you find anything of interest on your walk?" she asked as if expecting him to have solved all of his problems in that short time.

"No. I don't know what I might have seen but it was all just as you would expect. Nothing sinister, nothing unusual."

Steve's been on the phone again, can we make 8.30 at Mick's?"

Tom nodded a reply, "I guess so, by the way where is Steve living, I never asked?"

"He lives on the base," she replied, "I thought he might have told you, he is still active."

"The bastard," he whispered to himself, Staying at the folk's house is he?"

They sat down facing the window the curtain still open from Tilly's watching episode and gazed out on to the street. Winter evenings are miserable he mused dark early, long cold nights, Oz sounds much better. What about Tils, would she go back with him would he want her to? He smiled to himself, maybe, maybe not, time would tell.

Chapter 18

It was 8.30 they had arrived at Mick's door, the lights were on and pressing close to the door they could hear voices. Tilly knocked, clearly anxious to move things along. Tom liked the idea of her involvement.

The curtain moved, the occupier clearly checking who was likely to be there and quickly the door opened. Mick stood in the doorway and cast a glance along the street in both directions. Satisfied that the visitors were Tom and Tilly and that no-one else was about, he ushered them inside and closed the door.

"Good to see you again you pair. Come in I've got something to show you."

"Coffee everyone?" shouted Steve from the kitchen as they sat down at the table.

"OK," said Tom "Let's get on with it."

Mick produced the folder that had been seen briefly the previous evening and removing a bunch of papers laid several sheets on the table. He was careful with the unfolding of the browning paper. Tom could see that the documents were Type written, he looked carefully. His suspicions were high, were these papers genuine or made up recently by Mick, Steve or someone else? It looked to him as if an old machine of some sort had been used in their production but even from upside down he could see that some pages were not typed in the English language.

He nodded.

"I know Steve told you about this," said Mick," but let me explain further."

Steve appeared with the drinks and sat down next to Mick.

"I was sent to work in records some time ago, you already know I was in intelligence and I was given a desk on which these envelopes had been piled. I can speak German as you also know and so I was told to start translating the papers which had come from captured documents or Army records made at the end of WW11. I think you are aware that records kept secret for, say, 50 years are eventually read and revealed if there is any national interest in them and that was my job. I had to decide which could be made public and which should remain undisclosed. The majority of the papers were notes of interrogations undertaken by the British Army of captured Staff officers from the German Army including some Schutzstaffl, you know SS? Most of these guys came into our hands from the Russians who had taken them in Berlin in the final days of the war. The Russians had obviously questioned them but got nothing. I guess these advance troops didn't have the technique for interrogation, just hard fighters mainly, and were more interested in advancing on Hitler's bunker. I think we were lucky in a way because the Germans were probably happier to be in our hands than they would have been in the hands of the Bolsheviks, at least when we executed captives it was relatively quick."

Tom looked at Tilly, she smiled.

"The regular army guys were fairly compliant, whether they liked it or not they were just doing their job and only did what they were ordered to do and knew what they were told, but the SS officers acted differently, you know, superior and cunning I suppose and the papers show that. Whenever there was a chance to lie, they would do so. Whenever there was a chance to implicate a fellow German or anyone else for that matter and shift the blame from themselves, they would do so."

Steve nodded as if in confirmation.

"As I was working through them I came across a name that I recognised, a guy named Claus Hamann with the rank of Sturmbannfuhrer. He seemed a bit different to the others from what I could read, keeping his answers to the point and without any elaboration. What I mean is that, the others seemed to be fairly garrulous, you know tell you everything as long as it implicated someone else, but Hamann didn't do that. It was as if he was only saying what he had to and nothing more. The interviewer at the time wrote 'interesting' against the report which meant that Hamann would be escalated to more intensive interrogation later."

Tom took a drink from the coffee mug and sat back in his chair.

Mick continued.

"Now this brought back memories of some translation that I did for you when you were seeing that therapist. I recalled the name and rank of the officer and so on and also from the session I remembered that the conclusion was that you, or he, if you prefer, was hanged. So I researched this guy and guess what? I found he had been hanged after the end of the war; apparently he turned out to be very interesting indeed."

Tom remained silent. It was obvious he was considering what Mick had related and personal feelings were beginning to come to the fore.

Tilly broke the silence.

"OK," she said. "There must have been others with that name, what makes you think it was our man?"

"Well," replied Mick, "I did a lot more checking after I found this and actually there was no-one else of that rank, with that first name in the SS who was hanged, so I guess that he had to be the same man."

Tom shook his head, although he had heard this before when he was regressed it seemed to be becoming more real to him as Mick told his story.

"What did he say under interrogation Mick?" he asked in a quiet fashion. He seemed to have lost some of his aggression now that he had some-one else on his side and he moved closer to Tilly as if to get her support.

Mick continued, "Hamann was captured by the Russians when they got to Hitler's bunker and at first he said he was just a valet to the Fuhrer. Heinz Linge was captured at the same time. He was certainly Hitler's valet and protocol officer and initially Hamann thought he had got away with it insisting he was the same, but the soldiers found some photos and identified Hamann in his uniform, not the clothes of a valet. He was taken away and questioned by the Reds for a couple of days but in the end they considered he was just an acolyte, you know hanger-on I suppose and they handed him over the

Yanks. The Russians were not going to spend time on a guy like that, they had bigger fish to fry and they didn't even wish to waste a bullet, so he came into our hands." Mick stopped for a minute "O.K Tom?" he asked.

Tom nodded and he felt his ex wife squeeze his hand.

Mick continued.

"We had also taken some lesser mortals and in return for a promise that they would live they squealed on anybody and we soon started to get more information concerning this man and what had been his real role. Initially it was thought that he was just a competent officer from a good family who was doing a special job for Adolf, receiving and cataloging looted treasure, paintings, works of art and so on but as time went by his name appeared in other areas of investigation and he started to take on a much more compelling identity. Eventually I began to find intelligence that there had been a Major Hamann at Mauthausen concentration camp, could it be the same man? The investigators at the time clearly wondered and they started to look closer because that camp was one of the most infamous. It transpired that Hamann's job there had been to collect gold from the teeth of the dead inmates and send it to the central bank where they melted it down and turned it into ingots. To speed up the process he decided that he would prefer to remove the teeth before the bodies were burnt so as to maximise the haul and avoid any loss during the burning. Sometimes it was done even before the victims were actually dead, and he set up a squad to do that. Inmates who resisted, and that would be more or less everyone, were shot, many by Hamann, and it was his personal involvement with the actions of his squad and what he himself did that that got him convicted of war crimes and ultimately hanged."

There was no sound from the others as Mick continued his story although from time to time Tom was aware of one of the group glancing in his direction. Hell this isn't me, Tom Olive, he thought to himself but he was becoming very uncomfortable with Mick's tale.

"I remember reading about Mauthausen," said Tilly in an attempt to divert some attention from Tom. "That was where Aribert Heim worked wasn't it, you know the man they called Doctor Death? He was the one who experimented on the inmates by injecting poison into their hearts to see what happened, I don't think he was ever caught, that seems a lot worse than what Hamann did."

"Agreed", replied Mick, "and look, no one is pointing any fingers especially at Tom. I'm just saying what I know so we can see where we go with this."

Steve stood up. "Well I guess that's where I come into it," he continued. "Cards on the table, we all know what sort of guy I am, always after the main chance and to be fair I should think we all have that same inclination to some degree so let's not get too hung up with my motives. When I heard how this story went I thought that there must be some way to benefit from it, after all it's not every day that a chance like this comes from beyond the grave. Sorry Tom I don't mean it to sound so callous but I always believe that things happen for a reason and this was so incredible that we had to make something of it. Well I've got you back from Oz and I've got you to hear the story and I think we can all get something out of this. Tom what do you think so far?"

Tom had said very little all evening, it was taking some getting used to hearing what he had been nearly 60 years ago. Part of him didn't want to believe it but secretly part of him was fascinated by the idea and he had certainly got something from the episode with the few hours he had had to spend with his ex-wife. It was the thought of where they could both go in the future that had encouraged him, not necessarily the possibility of becoming wealthy.

"Steve," he responded, "I hear what you say and perhaps there is an opportunity for something here but I'm not certain what you are after and the big deal to me, now that I am back from Oz, seems to be who else is interested. The house has been trashed, I've been attacked on the bridge and we got away from someone last night, who else has an interest in this?"

"Sorry I just don't know that. It is as much a mystery to me as it is you but it shows that we could be on to something doesn't it?" Steve replied hopefully looking at Mick for support.

Tom moved forward in his chair. He had come to understand that he was the main man in this venture, without him nothing was going to happen. He could call all the shots and now was the time to do so.

"Mick let's have a real drink shall we, how about a whiskey?"

"Sure I'll get a bottle, Irish alright?"

"You know it is. It was always my choice and Tilly's, come to think of it."

Yes, coincidence that Mick produced her favourite brand? He wondered to himself. Yes of course it is just a coincidence.

The bottle was produced and generous glasses were filled. Tom considered the position while savouring the drink.

To be a member of the Special Forces, you had to be a particular kind of person. It was unlikely that the quiet life was on your agenda but that had been the way of it for him over the last few years. This new situation was beginning to appeal to him, some excitement, certainly some danger already experienced and perhaps the promise of some reward, financial and maybe, probably more importantly, Tilly.

"Once a blade always a blade," he muttered to himself. A nod of his head was all the encouragement that Mick and Steve needed.

Chapter 19

Steve had disappeared into the next room and quickly returned with a well thumbed magazine which he placed in front of Tom.

"This thing works if we assume that the two Hamanns are the same," he said now with more confidence that his brother was on side. "So let's say that they are. The guy in Mick's papers was in charge of collecting the art works from wherever he could and they would be stored until the war was won and Hitler's galleries were built in Linz. I've already told you that the best guess for his birthplace is Braunau, in Austria but Linz was chosen as capital of the world with Hitler as ruler because it was something like his adopted City. The stuff had to be stored safely and probably not all in the same place in case it was looted or bombed or whatever, eggs in the same basket and so on. Now apart from the things that came to light after the war, and of course they are still being discovered now, and the pieces that ended up in the families of the leaders at the time, from what we know only a small part of the total has been accounted for. Tom, as Hamann you must have known where it was stored and logically if it never came to light then it must still be there. This magazine," he continued pointing at the open publication in front of him, "tells the story, factual I understand about the Yanks finding thousands of pictures and so on in a mine in 1945. Patton's third army captured the village of Merkers in 1945 and following interrogation of some of the locals a member of MI attached to 358th infantry in Bad Salzungen found some French people who had worked in the mine. They said that gold and art works had been stored there and that they had been used to unload the stuff as it arrived. There's a lot more to it than that but to get to the punch line the mine was searched and tons of gold, jewellery, statues and pictures and so on were recovered. For example nearly 9000 bars of gold were found, but the mine was so vast that to this day the Yanks are still looking, they reckon they haven't found all of it yet. If this was part of Adolf's stash and Hamann was the organizer then he must have had some responsibility for putting it there".

"O.K," said Tom, pouring out another drink, "but if the Americans are still looking for the rest of it how would we get to it even if I did know". He realized immediately what had been said. I not Hamann, but he decided not to correct the remark that would only highlight the comment.

"Yes you're right," Steve replied, "but if as I have said there was so much and Hamann hid it in a number of places then Merkers was not the only place, and in fact it's not the only place where such a large amount has been found to date.

After the war German soldiers, then POW's, were obviously being interrogated. One such guy let slip during a conversation with a US officer, that he knew of hidden treasure underneath Nuremberg Castle. He gave details of the stuff and the officer recognised what was being described, the cache was valuables looted from all over Europe, items from museums mainly, but really important pieces, you know, and I mean important, not just things personal to individuals but world class treasures. Eventually when it was discovered some of the pieces proved to be jewels, if that is the way to describe them, that belonged to Charlemagne, the Holy Roman emperor and included in the stuff was what is known as the Spear of Destiny, the spear that was supposed to have pierced Jesus' side when he was being cruxified. We are talking of things that are literally priceless. So there must be more and the only person to know that would be Hamann, and so we need you, as him, to tell us. Remember also what Mick found out concerning the concentration camp. Hamann in his position there was collecting gold, he was executed for it and 9000 bars of the stuff were found at Merkers. Think about that. Another report tells of a disused coal mine close to a town named Bytom. The individual who was given control of occupied Poland was Hans Frank and he forced prisoners of war to carry crates of stuff into that mine. It was believed to be looted artwork and treasure, just what we are talking about. Having stored it all down there, the POW's were shot presumably so as to ensure that no-one talked about it, many were British."

"So is that still down there? And in any case if all the prisoners were killed how does anyone know about it?"

"Well there would be so many people in the know and not just prisoners, that it just needs one to be around to talk and to know whether the stuff remains in the mine, I don't know. Is that not what Hamann could tell us? Now what we need to do if our assumptions are anywhere near correct is to ask you the questions. I guess you will accept that that is the only way we can go forward on this and that means Joe I suppose."

Tom nodded slowly finishing off the whiskey.

"I think we've had enough tonight," Tilly interjected. "Tom needs to consider this."

"Yes I suppose I do" Tom added, pleased with Tillys support and now her protection of his position. "Let's think about it, I know what you want and what has to be done. I'll phone you tomorrow Mick, what's your number?" He and Tilly stood up. The room was warm and the drink was having a soporific affect on them all, not the best of conditions to make important decisions he thought.

Mick scribbled his phone number on a scrap of paper and handed it to Tom.

"See you tomorrow then?" he said as if it was a hopeful question. Steve opened the door as Tom and Tilly crossed the room. The cold and damp of the night hit the pair of them as they stepped out into the street and coats were pulled around shoulders as they started back for Tilly's house.

Mick closed the door after watching them turn the corner at the end of the road.

"Well Steve what do you reckon?" he asked.

"Well, for one thing, I think Tom is expecting that the two of them are going to be an item again, which suits us doesn't it?"

"What do you mean by that comment?

"Well Tilly left me for you, didn't she and I thought that the two of you were still together or am I wrong there? If that's the case, wouldn't she be a great help in this enterprise, you know, bringing him over to the plan?"

"You don't miss much do you Steve? Yeah I guess it does I'm going to have to live with it for the time being."

"But I also think he will phone, certainly she will encourage him, so why don't you get hold of Joe? We are going to need him soon."

Chapter 20

Tom woke early the next day, it was still dark, the illumination on his watch showing 7 o'clock. He glanced sideways, Tilly was still asleep and he smiled to himself. Maybe coming back wasn't such a bad thing after all he mused. I still fancy her after all this time and judging by last night she still fancies me, where do we go from here? Well I've got nothing to lose so let's see where this goes. He wasn't sure whether his interest in Steve's story was due to Tilly or his spirit of adventure, but probably it didn't matter. If none of it worked out he could always go back to his farm.

"But I've got to clear up where Mom and Dad are" he muttered to himself getting up slowly so as not to disturb her. She stirred.

"What's the time" she mumbled, "You getting up, wait a minute" Tom sat on the edge of the bed.

"Love you Tom" she continued. "I think I always did, even when we broke up." Tom turned around, he wasn't expecting that, even after last night, but suddenly he knew what he was doing and why he was here. He lay back on the bed and put his arms around her. He knew he had missed her over the years and now he felt that there was a future, his life was going nowhere in Australia, he knew that now, and suddenly it seemed turned on again, with her and the machinations of his brother.

Tom got out of bed and after a shower he dressed and went downstairs. The morning was a little misty but already it was brighter than yesterday, it seemed like an omen and with his ex-wife now back beside him he was looking forward to what the day would bring. Mick and Steve could wait. The phone call would be made later in the day, his immediate future was more important at this time.

"After breakfast, let's go for a drive to the mountains," he said as Tilly came downstairs.

"I see I'm expected to do the wifely thing and make breakfast am I? Yes O.K," she grinned, walking into the kitchen. "Anything you say, but I know you want to sort out your parents as well. Let's do both, the other business can wait a day."

"Yeah I've already made that decision. I'm in no hurry."

"Fine," she called over the sound of cups and plates being moved around.

Tom knew that his parents had a caravan near Hay, some way away from Hereford, but also near the Black mountains. He remembered that they rarely went anywhere else and it was a place to start without having to speak to Steve.

Breakfast was a leisurely event and by the time they had finished the day was clear and bright. A light wind had cleared away the early morning mist. This was just the day to walk the hills.

Eventually they left the house and made their way to the nearby transport.

"Do you want to drive?" she asked as they reached the vehicle. It was a blue VW convertible.

"Hey nice, must have cost a few quid, do you trust me with your new car? If you're certain, sure, let's have a go. I haven't driven in Britain for a while but in Oz it's still on the left so it should be no problem in getting used to the roads. The volume of traffic, even in Hereford will be a bit different I guess. Can we call in at the police before we go?" he said getting into the driver's seat, "I just want to see what has happened to Mom and Dad's house."

The car stuttered into life, being damp having stood outside in the rain over night, eventually pulling smoothly away from the house.

The police station was not very far away, just off the ring road around the City and within a few minutes Tom was parking the car on the road just outside the building.

They climbed a few steps and went inside and Tom approached the reception desk.

"This must be my lucky day," he said glancing at Tilly. "Look who's here."

"Tom?" enquired the desk sergeant.

"Andy how the hell are you? Tils you remember Andy? We were on the base together, How long ago Andy?"

Andy was a short man and he had put on a lot of weight since Tom had last seen him. His face was red and he had lost most of his hair, probably not much activity in the police compared to the army thought Tom.

"Oh probably 10 years ago, bloody hell, maybe more than that. You'd just got married hadn't you?" said Andy.

"Christ that is some time back, I think you're right, do you remember Andy Tils?" asked Tom.

"Only vaguely," she replied shaking hands across the counter with Tom's friend.

"Tom what are you doing here? The last I heard you were on the other side of the world after you broke up with your wife. Is that why you've come back?" he enquired glancing inquisitively at his companion.

"No," Tom replied, "but it may be the reason I stay."

Tom noticed that Tilly looked a little embarrassed, not something he had seen in her too often before.

"Andy we will have to have a pint sometime," he continued, "but I just need some info now. I guess you don't give out stuff to too many strangers so a good job we know each other, I hope?"

"Let's see what you want eh, we do try to help the public if we can," said Andy with a semi sarcastic grin.

"Well I got back to the country just a short while ago and I went round to my folk's house, it was taped off like something had happened."

Tom was being sparing with what he knew."Well I spoke to Steve, you know, brother Steve, and he said that the house had been burgled while Mom and Dad were away."

"What's the address?" asked Andy turning the pages of the incident ledger.

The address was given.

"Yeah I've found it. Seems like it, yesterday I think or was it the day before? Whatever. When our blokes arrived it just looked like it was trashed rather than burgled, you know stuff thrown about, but we need to get hold of the occupiers, your parents, before we can be sure. They will need to have a look to see if anything is missing. Funny thing is that we had no name for whoever reported it, just some passer-by I think, so we checked up on the telephone number of the caller and found it was a Miss Regan."

"Why did you do that?" asked Tom concerned that Tilly might now be implicated.

"Well we have to check all calls like this in case some-one is just fooling about, but as it was obviously genuine, in that the house had been the subject of a break-in, at this time we take no action. We can always get hold of the caller later if necessary. Anyway we got it boarded up and taped off but that's about it. The sooner we can contact the owners, the sooner we can move on, although what can be done now is anyone's guess."

Tom considered this for a moment looking at his companion.

"OK mate, thanks for that. So on the basis that they were not at the house at the time, I'm now just going to drive over to Hay. They have a caravan over there; presumably that's where they are. I'll have a word with them and then they can come and see you, get it sorted. Anyway, nice to see you again I'll be in touch with you for that pint." He shook hands with his friend and the two of them turned to the door of the station.

"Cheers Tom," called Andy, "see you soon and you Miss Regan."

The two of them continued out through the door, not wishing to turn back and give away anything concerning the officer's last comment.

"Well what do you think of that?" Tom said shaking his head as he opened the car door, "do you think he said that because he knows something or was it just a slip of the tongue?"

"How would he know my maiden name?"

"No idea, he met you first as far as I know after we were married."

"I find that very strange. Does he know Steve or Mick?"

"Steve, but so what. Do Steve or Mick know anything about your phone call to the police?"

"How do I know that?"

"Well it's very odd that he should say that if he knows nothing," said Tom earnestly.

"Who knows, if they did have anything to do with it I doubt they're going to say and that last remark by your friend, what do I know? At least, there's no suggestion that the folks are in trouble as far as the police are concerned and you think you know where they are, so let's go over to Hay and see if we can find them alright?"

The pair got into the vehicle and as they did so Tom looked back to the police station door unsure if anyone was watching them leave. They started off, driving back onto the ring-road and before many minutes they were heading out of the City towards the Black mountains.

Leaving Hereford, the road with its terraced properties widened, trees lined the more verdant neighbourhood and residences became larger. Soon the number of houses diminished and fields and hedges lined the route as they turned towards the Welsh border. On the way they talked small talk with Tilly filling in the details about their joint friends and her relatives, weddings, divorces, babies the sort of things that couples talk about in their relaxed times together and Tom wasn't too upset about it, he was getting to like even more the idea of the two of them back together.

Chapter 21

The car drove down the long incline into the town and then left up the hill towards the castle. Passing it by on the right they continued to the other side of the town and as soon as they arrived in Hay they were leaving it again.

Just out of town they turned left and after a short distance the car started to climb. The road was narrow with a drop on the right where a stream ran off the hills and before long a cattle grid heralded the fact that they were nearing the highest point on the road. The trees and hedges gave way to wide grassed areas, cropped short by the sheep and rabbits. In a short time they were at the car park conveniently placed for walkers, people just viewing over the Wye valley and kite flyers during the daytime but couples at night and Tom remembered the number of times that the two of them had visited the spot before they were married, maybe they could do so again he thought.

He stopped the car and after a few minutes got out. The wind was always a problem here and at this time in the year it was more so, chilly as well. Tom locked the car and they both wrapped up against the cold and holding hands they strode out.

"Up to the top we go," said Tom. Tilly said nothing she seemed to be happy to be with her ex husband. In spite of what might lie ahead Tom thought that she was beginning to feel that he was back to stay.

It took half an hour of walking along a narrow dirt track. Withered bracken and brambles along the path slowed their progress and occasionally a grazing sheep would burst across in front of them. Eventually reaching the top of the hill they stopped and looked around them. From here the view over the valley was breathtaking. The river in the distance sparkling in the early spring sun was as a diamond necklace tossed carelessly into a lawn. Hills on the other side of the valley blurred into the blue sky. The wheeling jackdaws climbing into the wind and then down again. Then the return, dawdling on the way, stopping to view the valley talking of the past and occasionally considering the future and when they returned to the car their faces ached because of the constant chill wind. They got back into the car and immediately felt warmer just for being out of the wind.

"Let's drive over to the caravan now," said Tom, "I need to sort out a few things with the folks, find out what they know about any of this, although I expect they will know nothing if Steve has had anything to do about it."

He started the car and reversed it off the car park, the wheels crunching on the gravel, the car headed back down the hill. They were now driving alongside the ditch as the track reached the cattle grid. Here the road was wide enough for only one vehicle and around the side of the gate, a dirt path permitted the passage of horses with their riders. This path extended away to the right along a wire fence which kept the roaming sheep within the confines of the grazing area. The car slowed to cross the grid and Tom caught sight of something along the path by the fence. A motorcycle was parked. Its rider sitting astride the machine, hands on the bars the engine ticking over.

Tom's eyes narrowed, immediately concerned as he recognised that this was the same bike that had chased the four of them through Hereford the day before. His hand went to his inside coat pocket and he withdrew the gun and offered it to Tilly. She drew back at the sight of it, not knowing that he had been armed in this way. He shook the weapon at her.

"Take this," he snapped.

She took the gun as Tom accelerated the car over the grid and away, along and down the road. The motorcycle took off from the path, wheels squealing on the dirt as it gained traction onto the road. Within seconds it was close up to the less manoeuverable car but at this speed, along this narrow road, the ditch dropping away to one side, nothing could happen just here. Up ahead was a slight bend to the right away from the drop by the road and as the car turned, Tom braked hard and spun the back wheels across the road. There was only one way for the pursuer to go and he veered left to avoid a collision which would have had him over the top of the car and defenceless on the road. Now he was off the main track and on the verge. Dirt and stones shot from beneath the wheels. There was no grip as he attempted to regain the metalled road surface. The machine toppled over throwing the rider into the ditch and slamming his flailing body into a pile of large rocks. He lay there motionless. Tom stopped the car and got out taking the gun from his shocked passenger. He stood at the top of the bank, the weapon pointing at the leather clad man.

"No," shouted Tilly from the car, "a guy with a bullet in his head is a problem, a guy with a burst tyre is not a problem. Go down and look at him, and burst the tyre.

He clambered urgently down to the bottom of the ditch, the man was lying awkwardly against a rock and Tom put his fingers against the assailant's throat to check for a pulse. Close up to him he detected the Cologne scent that he had noticed on the bridge. "This is the same bloke" he muttered "third time now, I've had enough." Tom ensured that his body was within the line of sight from the car. He removed the crash helmet and placed an arm against the side of the man's neck. With the other hand pushing the top of the head, his powerful arms quickly exerting pressure on the spinal cord and the neck snapped with a dull crack.

"How is he?" called his companion from the car, "what's happening?"

"He's dead, neck broken, nothing I can do."

Back along the road, in the distance they could hear another vehicle approaching. Firing the gun the tyre burst open and gasped empty as he regained the car back on the road. Driving off, Tom watched in the mirror as the other car arrived at the scene and braked to a halt.

"Hold on Tils", he shouted, "we're getting out of here, let them sort out the trouble," and he pushed down his foot to the floor.

Racing along the now wider track they soon reached the main road and turned left away from town towards the caravan park where he had hoped to find his parents.

"Just up ahead," he called as they passed by a sign declaring the site 200 metres further on and driving onto the field as they reached the site, he brought the car to a halt, behind a hedge which shielded them from the road and any passing traffic. Tom sat back, arms outstretched on the wheel, he looked over at Tilly.

"The gun?" she asked accusingly.

"Hell I didn't use it on the guy. Look I take it with me wherever I go, it might come in handy, what's the big deal? That's the fourth possible attempt on my life. I'm glad I've got it. I want no aggravation from you OK?"

Tilly knew he meant it. She would not question him like that again.

"Have you got a pencil and paper?" he demanded. His passenger opened the glove compartment and found what he required.

"Write down this number" he said, "it's the registration of the bike, maybe we can trace the owner sometime."

Chapter 22

He had recognised the site as soon as he had driven on to it. He knew exactly where his parents' van was parked and was quite relieved to see a light on as he pulled up alongside. The two of them got out of the car, Tilly walking around it, inspecting, removing the marks from adhered soil as she did so.

"I thought there might be some damage," said Tilly, running her hand along the nearside wing, "but I expect that I'll just need some tyres a bit sooner. Nothing that money can't put right, how much have you got Tom?"

He looked at her disparagingly. Having probably just saved her life she was worried about the car's tyres, was she joking?

Tom was already at the caravan door. Remembering that he hadn't seen his parents for a number of years he wondered how they would be and what would be their reaction to what he believed would be a surprise visit from their prodigal son.

Tom knocked on the door, he heard movement behind and the door swung open.

"Hi Dad," Tom said cheerily. The man was around 65 years old but looked younger. He was ex-army and it showed in his upright stance. Toned and tanned he looked facially very like Tom and therefore his other son Steve, but now balding and with a moustache and, since Tom had last seen him, a pair of spectacles. Although he was always an alert man, the sight of Tom caught him unawares and the sight of Tilly alongside him caused a serious double take.

"Bloody hell," he gasped. "Mary look who's here, come inside boy and you Matilda," he always preferred the use of her full name, "well I'll be buggered." He took hold of Tom's hand and hauled him up the steps. Mary appeared at the door.

"Who's there Len?" she asked. Her eyes widened and immediately moistened, "God it's our Tom and what, Tilly as well, I don't believe it. What's going on, come in?"

"Hi Mom," said Tom hugging his mother, a tall woman whose dark hair and classic features still reflected her position as a base sweetheart many years earlier.

They entered the van. No-one sat down, the parents were still shocked. Tom grinned and his companion just smiled. Len broke the silence.

"Sit down, sit down both of you, when did you get back? Why didn't you let us know? Are you alright? What's with Matilda?" The questions just flowed.

"Take it easy," Tom replied, one thing at a time, how about a cup of tea?"

For the next hour Tom related his time in Australia, certainly the most interesting parts and the four of them laughed and drank tea and enjoyed each other's company. Eventually Tom had to come to the part where Steve had travelled over to persuade him to return and, at this time, without implicating his parents, he merely indicated that Steve had persuaded him to return for a while, not knowing what they knew of it.

After some time of general conversation it became obvious to Tom that they knew nothing concerning his return to Hereford and so now he had to broach the subject of his proposed stay at their house and the subsequent break-in. His parents were strong individuals and he felt that there was no point in holding back. He told them of the arrival at the house, the attack on the bridge and the break-in at their home and as he told the story he found that he needed to relate some of Steve's plan, again not knowing if they had any knowledge of it. Of course they knew of Tom's childhood dream and were not too surprised to hear of their younger son's plan to find Nazi treasure. Len and Mary just listened, they knew of Steve's vivid imagination and a lot of what was said did not surprise them, but they could never have dreamed of what was happening or involved in the idea and it was a lot to take in all at once. Their absence from the house was no mystery. They visited the caravan often during the year but Tom wouldn't have known that as his contact with his parents was irregular, living as he did on the other side of the world.

"The police are up to speed with the break-in, we've just been to see them, but as the event was reported to them by some neighbour, I believe," he glanced at Tilly, "they need you to say what is missing, if anything. You can do that when you get back, but I have to say that I think it has more to do with me than just a straightforward break in."

"From what you have said I guess that you are probably correct, we don't have much to steal. Look whilst all this is going on, I think more so for your mothers piece of mind, we should stay here, you know away from the house. I'll go to see the police and give them some vague information so that they are out of the frame with regard to your situation. I'm not worried about the house, I can drive by from time to time, see what it looks like but it might only complicate things if I become involved any more than that. So what happens now?" said Len.

"Well there is still something going on Dad," he said cautiously. "We went for a drive over the mountains this afternoon and got attacked up there. The motorcyclist took a bad fall and we got away," he continued, deliberately omitting the fact that the rider was dead. "We're alright but it's getting a bit of a nuisance," he added with somewhat of an understatement.

"Do you think you were followed here?" asked his mother.

"I didn't see anyone behind us on the road and really I think it's unlikely there's more than one of them" said Tom thoughtfully. "I guess he would still be in the ditch, although just as we got away another vehicle came along and I would expect them to have told the police."

"Unless they were in on it."

"Yes, possibly, the road from Hay to here is fairly straight so I think I would have spotted a tail, what about you Tils?"

"Well I didn't see anyone and I've been looking out of the window here for a while now and no-one's about, but who knows, these guys seem to be pretty sharp up to now but if we were followed then your Mom and Dad could be in danger."

"Look you two stay here for the night," offered Mary. "It's getting dark and we haven't seen you for ages and the two of you together, well that calls for a celebration and I'm prepared to risk it, what about you Len?"

"Certainly."

Tom kissed his mother.

Chapter 23

The night passed without incident and the following day, after a good breakfast, Tom and Tilly departed, promising to keep the older couple informed of any developments. Len and Mary would return to their house in Hereford and then contact the police as requested.

The immediate plan was to seek out Steve and Mick and to see about arranging a meeting with Joe.

"This may take some time," mused Tilly as they drove through the Welsh and English countryside back to Hereford.

"You know, somehow I don't think so," replied Tom. "I've been thinking about Joe's involvement in all of this and although he is just the conduit, if you like, there could be more to him than we have considered so far."

"Yeah I said that the other day if you recall. The four of us seem to be the only ones that know you have returned from Australia and so If you exclude us, then there has to be another person or persons unknown that have some interest in your being back. Steve, well, you know him and I think the adventurer in him has got hold of his imagination this time. Mick maybe a bit like Steve, I wouldn't know what could be his motive but Joe is different. I don't know what to say, he may be interested but why? What you have told me concerning the previous times when you have met gives me the impression of indifference to it all, other than his professional connection. I think his family might have been German in the past, although he told you that he didn't speak the language, and so maybe that alone could have sparked some interest in him. Let's see how quickly a meeting can be arranged and that might give us an idea as to what he is about."

The trip back to Hereford was uneventful and soon the car pulled up outside the house and the pair got out. Tom knocked on the door and Mick rapidly appeared.

"Where have you been," he questioned, "I thought we were meeting yesterday?"

"Well we had a day off," replied Tom lightheartedly. "But we are here now so let's get on with it. How quickly can we get to see Joe?"

Chapter 24

The Golden Eagle was little changed since the last time Tom had been there and at a time when old public houses were ripe for a renovating theme, that was an achievement. A black and white pub in the shade of the Cathedral and just along from the lane in which had once stood the home of The Duchess of St Albans, better known as Nell Gwynn.

Tom and Tilly sat at the far end of the low ceilinged room that served as the main bar so that they could see the entrance but also in the proximity of a side door that could serve as a quick exit if necessary. Tom didn't know why that might be a requirement but the longer this episode went on the more he wondered what was anyone's involvement and how cautious he needed to be. After a while in which the two of them had indulged in small talk and relaxed with the aid of alcohol, Mick's unmistakable form appeared in the doorway closely followed by a smaller man.

Tom immediately recognized the man, although he had not seen him for some considerable time, noticing that the years had not necessarily been kind. His hair had turned grey and he seemed more round shouldered than Tom recalled. He wore an old black mackintosh which he had wrapped tightly around himself against the cool February weather. A trilby hat completed the outfit and Tom considered that there was perhaps an eastern European look about him. Maybe it was that Joe did not think it necessary to consider his appearance much these days as he might have done when he was on television or maybe it was just that he had grown older. Joe held out a hand to Tom as he and Mick approached. His handshake was firm and seemed friendly as if the pair had been close for years. That was true to some extent as although it was some years since they had first met Tom considered the friendliness was because Joe had some special knowledge of him through the sessions of regression therapy, something that not even Tilly could claim. He acknowledged Tom's companion as he sat down and Mick soon joined them having collected a couple of pints of cider from the bar.

"How have you been since we last met?" enquired Joe in a faintly discernable accent. "I understand you've been in Australia away from the rest of the world."

"Yes," replied Tom. "I felt like getting away from it all and that was about as far as I could get, but being back here at this time, well I never guessed that. Who told you I had been in Oz?"

"Mr Cannon."

"I see. So how are you?"

"Well, you know, I'm fine. I do a bit of this and a bit of that but generally you could say that I've retired.

Given up the stage work and also the private stuff but now the chance to meet you again, my most interesting client, well that made me think, that was something I had to have another go at and with Mr Cannon saying that you were also interested in seeing me well, yes let's have a look at it I thought."

"Have a look at what?" replied Tom looking Joe straight in the eyes.

"Well, you know, this regression thing, what we looked at before, what you want to find out. Mick, Oh is it alright to call you that?" Mick nodded.

"O.K. well he said you wanted to have another go but he didn't say why."

Tom felt that Joe did have some understanding as to what this was all about, more than he was prepared to admit, but he decided he would tell him as much as he thought appropriate and no more at this time. Just enough so that he could gauge Joe's reaction because he did think that there was more to him than just a hypnotist, what was his background, his family history? Was this German connection just a coincidence? Or perhaps he was just being over cautious, still with all that had gone on over the last few days or so maybe caution was a good thing. This was developing in a way Tom would never have guessed a week ago, trust no one seemed a good plan of action for the time being except possibly his ex wife he thought.

"You will remember our sessions at your place?" Tom commenced, "the regression, what you said about me, what I had said under hypnosis. Over the years I had thought about this although only insofar as I could relate it to those dreams I had as a child. Then after I'd been in OZ, minding my own business, Steve comes all the way over to the other side of the world" his sarcasm noted by Tilly, "and tells me about Mick and what he found when working through the released records. I guess that you are aware of all of this?"

Tom declined to let Joe know that, in fact, he had been more than just a little interested in Hamann and had built up a substantial library of books relating to The Second World War in the hope of coming across the name.

"No not really," the old man replied, "my interest is that, as I said before, you were my most interesting subject. I never forgot my own personal surprise and feelings when it seemed that I had regressed some-one who could be real, some-one about whom there may be records."

"Nothing more than that?" Tom pressed on, although he felt that Joe was going to give nothing away at this time.

"Nothing more than that."

"OK, well I suppose that I was interested in what Steve had to say, you know a bit of excitement, but also perhaps an excuse to return to England for a bit, see the family and some old friends." He glanced at Tilly. "Then when I came back and got involved in this aggravation over the last few days, you know about that I hope? Well, I wondered what's it all about, what's going on, who are all these guys causing me grief? It must be something relative to my past."

"Yes I was told about some trouble. So is that why you want another session, to see if we can find out what's been going on?"

"It might help. So I consider the possibilities with Steve, Mick and of course Tils and I suppose I just now need to know. I'm still in the dark and I might not like it when I see the light. There are so many thoughts going through my head, what can it be? I just don't know. Between us we have thought of many possibilities."

"Tell me about those possibilities, which one of them in particular concerns you?"

"You know so much intrigue stemmed from the war and in particular the end of it. Works of art missing, people disappearing, lives changing so much that half the time you wouldn't know who was who."

He felt that at this time talking in any detail about stolen works of art at the Merkers mine or Lake Toplitz wasn't appropriate as Joe was only ever involved in his regression, the rest had come from supposition between others and even Tilly at one stage suggested he might have some knowledge of important people who were once SS or whatever. "What do you think I could find at another session Joe, after all your family are German aren't they?

"German? Why do you say that?"

I seem to recall I was told so."

"By whom?"

"I'm afraid I can't remember. Is it not true?"

"Well not exactly. I was born in Poland but then Germany invaded Poland as you probably know and so I suppose that you could say that I was living in Germany at that time. I did learn to speak the language of course so I don't know anything about what you are saying. I am just the way back to the past and the fact of being German or Polish well that's just an irrelevance," the older man replied, but less firmly than he had been a few moments earlier.

Tom had thrown that question in not knowing what would be the answer. He had felt that there might be more to Joe than at first thought and the answer was certainly interesting. He recalled that during the first regression, Joe had indicated that his German was not that good, Mick had been used to interpret, but now he said that he could speak the language. Was there something he had heard said during the sessions that he hadn't passed on, did he recognize the name Hamann? There was certainly some connection he thought and now he knew Joe's family was from German occupied Poland he was even more curious.

The conversation between them was general for the rest of that afternoon, the weather, Australia, the economy, just simple chit-chat, but all the time Tom was looking for clues. They never came and as it began to show dusk outside the meeting came to an end.

"So when do we have a look at this?" said Mick breaking his silence on what, after all, they had come to talk about. "Joe's free tomorrow and we may as well make a start if we want to find out what's going on."

"Well yes" Tom replied "I certainly do want to know some more, I seem to have had a fair amount of trouble recently and I'd like to get to the bottom of it all and this has got to be the first step I suppose. Where would we meet?"

"Well my place I suppose," said Joe. "I live out on the Tenbury side of the City, but you have been there before haven't you?"

"Don't worry about the address," Mick interjected. I know where he lives and I'll pick you up in plenty of time. Where will you be in the meantime?"

"At Tilly's house I guess. What time are we talking about?"

"Eleven o'clock suit you?"

Tom nodded "OK see you then."

The meeting broke up. Mick and Joe left first and Tom and Tilly finished their drinks and walked out into the chilly evening.

"Mick was keen to get a move on with this meeting I thought," said Tom as the two of them walked towards the main road.

"Well I suppose that's right really. If you want it sorted then it must be right, and you do don't you?" she asked.

"Tils, throughout this I get the feeling that you are encouraging me, you know pushing it along." His voice had an accusing sound to it.

"Tom, look you have a problem? I feel that it is getting in the way."

"In the way of what exactly?"

"Our future, perhaps?"

"We have a future?"

"Maybe, but this has to be sorted first of all. You know, if there is trouble here then we have to sort it out, we can't go through our lives looking over shoulders all the time. If there is no problem in that way then you just have to get it, whatever it is, out of your system, put it to rest, move on or you will always be wondering what if? I know you remember."

I can't argue with that, he thought to himself, if that's why she is doing it, well fine. But still there was a doubt, just one or two things that had been said or done he couldn't quite put a finger on it.

Chapter 25

It was 9.30 the following day, Tom and Tilly were having a late breakfast, sitting watching the news on T.V when the phone rang.

Tilly answered it and after a brief conversation put down the receiver.

"That was Mick, he's on his way over. He'll be here in 30 minutes, we'd better get ready."

"He's early isn't he, didn't he say eleven last night? What do you think about all this Tils," said Tom switching off the TV. "I really haven't a clue what's going on. The only good thing so far is meeting you again."

"Look let's just take it as it comes," she replied "What's the worst thing that can happen?"

"Well we could have got killed coming off the mountains," Tom answered "and then there was that ruck on the bridge the other day, so I guess that some-one getting killed would be the answer to your question."

She shook her head. It wasn't what she wanted to hear but it was probably true.

"You know someone's playing rough here and it's beginning to wind me up a tad. Joe had better come up with an answer although I've even got my doubts about his motives. It's like I thought the other day, trust no one."

"Not even me?"

"I have to trust you," his reply was ambiguous.

"I know I let you down with our marriage but I won't let you down again I...." A loud knock at the door interrupted the conversation. Tom looked around the curtain into the street.

"Mick," he said moving to the door and opening it.

"You're early Mick."

"Not much mate and by the time we get over there..."

"I guess so OK. Tilly are you ready, come on get your coat let's go and see Joe."

Thirty minutes later the three of them pulled up outside a large white house partly hidden from the road behind an expanse of Rhododendron shrubs. The Victorian building was considerably larger than Tom had remembered it to be, and from the number of stone framed windows he could see, both on the ground floor and the first floor, it seemed a substantial dwelling. Joe must have made some money from his stage work, he thought.

"Stop on the road a moment, will you. I want to walk up to the house, you drive on afterwards," Tom said.

Mick shrugged his shoulders.

Leaving the car, he and Tilly walked on to the gravel drive and towards the entrance. A large metal trellis around the front door supported an unrecognizable climber that itself, was surrounding the whole entrance; with the double front door up three steps the façade was quite impressive. The plant itself had been cut away over the years so that the name of the property could be seen. Tom whispered to himself 'Kolibri?' That's a strange name but what a property, this guy must be well off, you'd never know just looking at him."

After a few moments, Mick drove the car onto the gravel drive and the sound of the wheels crunching on the surface must have alerted the occupant and Joe appeared at the door before the car had come to a halt. Clearly he had been waiting for their arrival, his keenness noted by Tom.

Joe appeared less disheveled than the day before, as if he was about to do his stage act which perhaps was true to some extent and he welcomed them all into his house. A large hallway greeted them as they stepped inside. The wood paneling and a wooden floor reminded Tom of some of those old houses he had seen in American films. The soft, warm smell of the polished wood, somehow comforting.

A wide staircase led up to the first floor and as they passed by it into a room beyond Tom glanced up the stairs. A few pictures caught his eye, they seemed like family portraits. Not many of Tom's acquaintances had family portraits he thought; I wonder what Joe's background is? Moving away from the foot of the stairs a sound caught Tom's attention. A just discernible low continuous humming seemed to emanate from somewhere above, probably from the top of the stairs and as he looked up another smell seemed to drift lightly into the nostrils. Mildly antiseptic and stale was perhaps how he would describe it, maybe no more than might be expected in the house of a single old gentleman. The group moved on into a room which did nothing to change Tom's first opinion of the house. More paneling, some large leather armchairs and a big open fire, more pictures and a grandfather clock ticking soporifically in the corner. Tom thought he recognized some of the people, but probably not.

"I didn't know houses like this still existed in the Hereford area," he said to no one in particular, and no one in particular answered, they were all thinking the same.

"Do you live here alone?" asked Mick.

"More or less," Joe replied. "I have a housekeeper and she comes and goes. She knows what I require and it is done. She's probably here around the house somewhere."

That seemed to satisfy Mick, whose question Tom guessed, stemmed from the fact that he had heard the humming noise also.

"Sit down all of you," Joe instructed in a businesslike manner, clearly wishing to move quickly on to the matter in hand. "We have some work to do, so tell me what you have in mind."

He took out from a bureau drawer a pen and paper and waited for the conversation to begin.

"Well as I seem to be the subject or even object of the exercise I'll start," said Tom.

"You remember some time ago I had a session with you at your clinic, would you call it?"

"Yes that was here."

"I think that it most likely was. Well you recall that I appeared to regress to a previous time and you told me that I had gone back to a time when I was a soldier."

Joe nodded.

"You said I was a German soldier named Hamann and that I was living during the Second World War. Well I think I want to know more about this guy and his life in the German army and so another session might be appropriate. So that I can fully benefit from the session, I have written down the questions that I would like you to ask." He handed a folded paper to him.

Joe sat back in his chair and read what had been written down. Tom detected a raised eyebrow. A knowing facial gesture he thought, which he took to be the older man only half believing that the one reason for all the group being there was a mild curiosity of Tom's past. After all over the last few days missing and valuable works of art, important people and war criminals, had been discussed. Joe shrugged his shoulders. Tom continued.

"I have in my mind a number of things that I think I want to have explained to me, so if you ask the questions I might understand the answers. I promise you that there is a reason for these questions and if you will bear with me I'll explain why I need to know these things after the session O.K?"

Tom had considered that he had to get this information to go forward with all of the thoughts that he and the others had had. He knew it was a risk because Joe would then be involved with the ideas but there was no choice, perhaps, after all, it would mean nothing to him, but he had to chance it.

Joe replied half-heartedly.

"Let's go into my studio and see what we can see, but you are not all wanting to listen in are you?" he asked in a rhetorical way.

"No of course not," replied Tom. "I'd just like to have Tilly with me if that's alright?"

"Whatever you want just follow me through," Joe concurred and he led the way through the large double doors at the back of the room. As Joe went ahead Tom held back a little to talk to his companion.

"Everything alright?" he said to her.

"I've got everything I need," she whispered and followed the two men into the next room.

The studio was much like the room they had just left, "Just a little less crowded," murmured Joe as he gestured to Tom to sit with his back to the window. He noticed that a large table was in the centre of the room, solid oak just as would be expected in a house such as this and on the table a collection of objects which he took to be related to Joe's occupation. A lamp, a number of old looking leather bound books and a large white china hand, the fingers of which stretched upwards to the ceiling. The old man closed the curtains and the room was immediately darker and quieter, the noise from the world outside, such as it was, was no more. Automatically a dull reddish light came on behind Joe's chair and the whole room took on an ethereal hue. Tilly sat to one side out of Tom's direct line of sight but close enough to be able to hear what was being said by both the therapist and his client.

Joe began to speak, his voice had changed to one of confidence, control and in quiet tones reminiscent of a priest in the confessional he explained to Tom what he was going to feel and sense during the regression. Then he approached him and for a few moments whispered something to him that Tilly was unable to hear clearly. Joe regained his chair and she could see that Tom's eyes were half shut and fluttering gently as if in a dream.

"I have to do that," he explained, "it is necessary to speak in that way to my subject without anyone else hearing the words of suggestion or it could have the same effect on them and that would not be very professional, I think you will agree?"

"I guess so," she answered with some suspicion of his motives but without any alternative had to accept what she was being told.

Guided and encouraged by Joe, Tom started speaking and Tilly was immediately enthralled by what she could hear. The softness of the voice, the intonation, and the inflection of how the questions were answered fascinated her. To hear Tom replying to the questions sometimes in German, sometimes in a heavily accented English was incredible to her and the time passed so quickly that she wondered if she had not also been hypnotized.

Eventually the voices ceased and Joe sat back in his chair.

"Well I've asked him all of the things that he wanted to know and I think that he has given relevant answers to the questions. As there is nothing else I can say to him shall I bring him back?" he asked.

Tilly nodded. She had noticed that Joe had remained silent on the subject of what questions were required to be asked or even the reason for them. Throughout the session however she had observed him carefully to note his reaction to the questions and answers and she considered that there had been times when he appeared particularly interested in some of the answers. During the time she observed that he had made notes prolifically although clearly it was a requirement, there were many responses and some in German. Tom was awakened but appeared to remain drowsy for a while.

"You will see that it is very much like waking up in the morning," commented Joe, "after a while he will be wide awake but unable to recall anything. I think that went well," he continued, "I asked everything he wanted to know and I made all the notes I could which you can have. Sometimes, as you could hear, he spoke in German and I wrote down the English translation as best I could. Occasionally where the word was colloquial for example, you will have to make of it what you can. Yes if you are wondering I can speak the language. Living in occupied Poland for many years it was necessary to learn to speak German. I have to say that some of what was said was very intriguing to me and I hope that one day you might be prepared to let me know why you are all concerned with this man Hamann, perhaps I can help you more than you realize." They ignored the comment.

He held out his hand to Tom, who by now was fully awake and had risen from the chair and he guided him with a firm grip towards the double doors. Opening them they returned to where Steve and Mick had waited.

"Thank you Joe," said Tom "I am very grateful to you for your help at this time. I will need to consider what you have written down and see how any of it relates to what I wish to find out. Can I see you again if I need to?"

"Certainly you may, I hope that I will have the chance to meet with you again. Good luck."

The group made their way to the front door which Joe opened and they passed out onto the drive and towards the car.

"Well I think that went well," said Tom, "but we can see what we have got when we get back to the house. Tilly taped the whole thing so we can get Mick to hear it and see what he thinks. Tom looked pleased with himself although his companion's smile indicated that it might have been her idea in the first place.

"Not only the tape," she replied, "but Joe was writing all the time and he handed his notes over to me at the end. He said that some of it was translation as well as answers to your questions so we can look at everything when we get back. I wasn't sure Tom but I thought that I saw him keep some of the notes that he made, that's odd isn't it?" She handed the paper to Tom.

"Well possibly, but if we have the tape then we have everything and if we find items are missing from the notes that are on the tapes, then we may know what he is interested in."

The car doors slammed shut, Mick glanced back at the house.

"Interesting place, must have cost him a fortune, housekeeper as well. Hmm."

Chapter 26

The drive back to Hereford was uneventful and silent, each with their own thoughts of what they had just seen and done and soon the car was pulling up outside Mick's house.

"We seem to come here to discuss everything," commented Tom as they got out of the car, "seems as if it's the headquarters of our little enterprise, whatever the enterprise is."

The comment was ignored by the others as they all went into the house.

"I could do with a coffee," Tilly said taking off her coat as though at home and putting it across the sideboard. She made her way directly to the kitchen, "anyone else?"

"Yes," was the omnibus reply.

"Coffees all round and let's start to think what we do now," said Steve.

After a few minutes Tilly brought in the drinks and laid them down on the table and then returned to where she had placed her coat on the sideboard. Bringing it to the table she took out of the pocket a tape recorder.

"No time to waste," she said, "let's get on with it and see what we have. Mick you are the linguist can you write down what was said please?"

"And especially what was asked," interjected Tom, "I would have no idea what I was saying to whatever was being asked and that is as important as anything in my view." "O.K," replied Mick, "Just as you wish," and he activated the machine and sat down pen in hand and prepared to write.

The listening and writing went on for an hour or so, Mick occasionally stopping the tape to rewind, perhaps to listen more closely, sometimes working out the interpretation, many of his facial expressions indicating surprise at the question or the answer. He stopped the tape for a final time and threw the pencil on to the table. He sat back and gave a low whistle through his teeth.

"Bloody hell," he exclaimed, "there's some stuff there and it's going to take some thinking about I reckon. Let's have something to drink, more substantial than coffee, we've got to consider this very carefully."

Tilly went back into the kitchen with Tom to fetch the refreshment, nothing was said. Tom knew that he was about to have some part of his life exposed to the others, would he be embarrassed? Would he find the answers to his questions? They all knew each other well enough, but he also knew that this was going to be revealing and where would they go from here? Steve maybe was after some financial gain, maybe also Mick perhaps. Tom thought about that part of it and it was certainly a consideration but he wanted more from it. Tilly was supporting him whatever happened so he had, he considered, already made a profit from his return to England and was now more intrigued than anything. What about Joe, he was the unknown, what was he after, perhaps the tape would show something. Well we will soon know Tom thought to himself and the pair returned to the lounge with four large tumblers of whiskey, Mick was ready with his notes, Steve sat quietly and Tom and Tilly sat together. Mick took a drink and began.

Chapter 27

"I'll read all that I wrote to start with and then compare some of that with the notes Joe made. You remember he said that there were some German words and some figures of speech perhaps. I have to say that most of the recording is in English. Presumably because he asked the questions in English but what is interesting is that some questions were asked in German. I don't know why except that you may draw some conclusion from the answers and I guess that he didn't know that Tilly was recording.

Tom, it seems that your family, the Hamann family that is, came from Linz originally and they were a military family, you had relatives in the first war. That gives you a couple of connections with Hitler, if that is anything to be proud of. He was in The Great War and Linz became his adopted place of birth but whether that is just a coincidence I have no idea."

Mick ticked off what he had just written.

"I'm giving you this stuff in the order it was requested by Tom, so you can guess the question most of the time based on the reply," he continued. "You joined the SS and after having seen service in Poland you were promoted to Major and given a desk job as it seems your forte was administration. You were then sent to Mauthausen."

"Mauthausen?" interjected Steve, "that was the concentration camp wasn't it? I remember you saying about that the first time and having heard about it, I read a book about it. It described it as the most notorious Nazi camp in Austria. God Tom you weren't one of those....?" his voice trailed away.

"Murderers?" asked Tom. "Look if I was then I probably paid for it at the end of the war, you remember what I told you?" There was a few minutes silence between them Tilly shook her head despairingly

Mick continued.

"Not everyone in the camps killed you know. I heard nothing in the tape to suggest you did, although the question may not have been asked or any answer given."

"But that was certainly something that I wished to know, as it could give the reason why I was hanged, wouldn't it?"

"All I can say is that the question was not asked"

"So Joe didn't ask the question then, why not?"

"I've no idea, perhaps he missed it, or maybe an answer would reveal more about Hamann than Joe wanted you to know."

"So there is something going on with him," said Steve.

"Could be," replied Mick "but you may remember what I said I had discovered concerning Hamann from the records, the gold from the camp inmates? Those reports show that the Major, if that was you, was responsible for collecting it, gold teeth and so on and the shootings as well, that was the reason for his demise, for his execution after the war's end. I can say no more on that subject from the recording, but here is an interesting thing. At this point Joe spoke to you in German. I couldn't catch your answer, it was mumbled. It's not recorded, but at this time he wrote AH on a piece of paper, the one given to Tilly. I don't know what this means but we can think about it later OK....AH... Adolf Hitler?"

"Well we shall just have to ask him" Tom said.

"He did this again a bit later on when you spoke of the bunker, only this time he wrote HS I've no idea about that one. You wanted to know about Hamann's military service and what you have said in reply to Joe shows that you, or he if you prefer, had a considerable knowledge of the Fuhrer's plans. In 1943 Hamann was transferred to Hitler's personal staff, which you must have considered as a good move, and it seems that you got a very special job. At the time Hitler, who you recall had this connection with Linz, was planning for the end of the war. He wanted to make the place a monument to the third Reich and of course himself. He would name the place Welhaupstadt, that translates as World Capital. You said that he would have statues of German heroes erected on Niebelungen Bridge. He had donated a statue to the Bergbaupark in 1942 and it was intended to turn Linz into an artistic centre to rival Vienna and Berlin. A world class museum was to be built which would have been filled with some of the most important paintings and works of art in the world, all looted from the defeated enemy. This was your task, to have the museum constructed and filled with the treasures. He gave you authority, in this respect over all of his other senior people, even Himmler, Goering etc., so you would get the pick of the stuff that was coming their way. You were a very important Nazi my boy."

"Did I say that to Joe, that I was a very important Nazi?"

"Well no, not that particularly, but as you said that the task for the construction after the war was to build a museum and you were the guy to stock it, then you had to be."

Tom half smiled, although in the circumstances he knew it was inappropriate.

Mick continued,

"Of course we all know which way the war went and Hitler ended up in the bunker in Berlin when the Russians were approaching the City. It seems that you were there also. He really must have thought a lot of you to have you with him at the end."

"Or I thought a lot about him to want to be there?"

"Sure that could be the case. You and all the other survivors were arrested by the Russians when they got to the bunker, although Hitler was supposed to be dead at that time. You and others were questioned but the Soviets never found the body proper and no amount of interrogation revealed the story of the end. You were eventually handed over to the authorities, Americans, British and so on, tried and sentenced to hang for your efforts whilst at the camp....you understand the rest of it?"

Tom sat quietly for a while and the others knew better than to interrupt him. He thought of many things during this time but in the end at least it was understood how he came to be hanged and that was as much as anything what he had always wished to find out.

"You know," he said eventually, "the main questions I needed answered were concerning my military career. Joe has covered the whole of that time up to the end and that's fine as far as it goes. Clearly I was involved in the museum and gallery business and so I have to accept that I would have knowledge as to the whereabouts of pictures or whatever that remain unaccounted for. So now that we know this much then, Steve you are right, I guess that I can be taken back and asked to divulge the places where the stuff was stored and if it is still there and we can recover it then we are rich."

Steve stood up and walked across the room to his brother, putting both of his hands on the other's shoulders and shaking them back and forth.

"Yes, I knew that it was possible. Tom, Mick we're going to do it, we're going to be millionaires, I told you so."

"Now hang on a bit," said Mick, "knowing the military record of this man is a long way from finding any valuables. We would need more time with Joe, some information will be available to him, and what will he do about that?"

"We can eliminate him when he is no longer any use to us."

"Steve you bastard," shouted Tilly. "You'll do anything, won't you, anything to get rich. We are nowhere near that stage yet and already you're getting rid of people. For Christ's sake use your head, think about it."

"I've thought about it for long enough. We're as close as we ever were to the bonanza; no creepy old guy is going to get in my way."

"OK, OK you pair pack it in," interjected Tom. "I'm the main man here. I'll make the decisions. Steve if that's not good enough for you then get out now." He approached his brother and stared directly into his eyes, deep, soulless. Steve blinked and said no more.

"There is a lot to think about in what you say Mick, and some of it throws up more questions. I think we should spend some time analyzing it all and if necessary speak to Joe again, you remember as we left he said he might be able to help us more."

"Yes but he's just after whatever's going," Steve blurted, "I always said he knew more than he was letting on."

"You may be right," replied Mick in a considered tone. "Having just regressed Tom and listened to the answers, Joe now knows quite a lot that he didn't know before. What will he do with the information; will he do anything with it? That's another question entirely, but think about this. I've just listened to the tape and read the notes Joe made and there doesn't seem to be much discrepancy apart from how Hamann came to be hanged and that may mean something or nothing. Most of it is in English and you must have heard the same words as any of us, so where is the problem?"

"Well there's AH for a start," Steve said "and now Joe's aware of what we have been considering, you know the valuables, Toplitz, Merkers and so on. OK he never mentioned those places specifically but he's a shrewd guy, he'll put two and two together and he can always look up about what happened to the stuff in the same way that we did."

"I'm not so sure that he is interested in paintings and so on," Tilly added. "I was with Tom during the session and as a woman I think I can understand what men say and what they mean by how they say it. I noticed a couple of times when the tone of his voice changed. His voice was very distinctive and it wasn't difficult to spot the change. Once was certainly when you talked about the concentration camp and another was when you spoke of your arrest in the bunker."

"But he is my only way to the past," said Tom, "I've used him to discover what I needed to know. How can he be interested in Hamann on his own account? What is the connection? *Is* there a connection, Mick?"

"Well, perhaps, he has translated for you, asked the questions and found the answers, so on the face of it that's his only involvement. He did write down AH and HS relative to the camp and the bunker but apart from that, nothing. If Steve is concerned, then at some time I think we have to discover his past, his history, or at least what writing down the initials meant to him."

Tom shrugged his shoulders. "Who knows"? He sighed. "I'm going back to Tilly's house. I'm going to think long and hard about this, you know, do I want to find out more? What's it leading to? When will we know that we've come to the end of it? I'll get back to you guys when I'm ready. O.K see you later, come on Tils let's go, have you got the tape?"

Chapter 28

The door closed quickly behind them as they left Mick's house and out into the chill of the evening. The dampness of the footpath sparkled with the reflected light from the streetlamps and their breath was illuminated by each one as they passed it by. February was cold and damp and Tom was thinking about his place on the other side of the world. The information Joe had provided was as much as Tom had ever wanted and yet now was this enough? Could he return to Australia and leave it at that? The two of them continued the walk to what Tom was now considering to be home and it would not take them long to reach Tilly's house.

Steve and Mick had finished off the bottle of whiskey and Steve had lit up a cigarette, much to Mick's annoyance, but clearly the thoughts concerning Tom or Hamann were taking precedence.

Steve broke the silence, "You know we could make a fortune out of this if we go about it in the right way. I'm sure Tom could give us the info if Joe asked the questions. That stuff is just out there waiting for someone to come along who has the key and we've got the key – Tom."

"I'm not so sure," replied Mick. "There's something here I think we're missing. Yes I think Joe can help but there's something else. You see if it was just Hamann's life that was the subject of the session, why did Joe need to question him about other things up to and after the death of Adolf?"

"But didn't he just ask what Tom wanted to know? Are you saying that he asked some other questions?"

"Yes, you recall I said that sometimes he spoke German and I couldn't quite get it, well that's when he asked questions not on the list."

"And he received answers?"

"Sure."

"And you haven't told Tom?"

"No I haven't I'm just thinking about that for the time being."

"You crafty sod."

"OK, OK. Look the war was over at that time, there was no more stealing being done, certainly on the industrial scale that happened during the war. The top guys were getting out and taking things with them, but not the real wealth. Hamann had already got it locked away. I know Tom wanted to find out about his hanging - fair enough but it wasn't that. Joe seemed more interested in the camp bit - the initials you remember. But AH - Adolf Hitler? Maybe there's something more valuable than paintings behind all of this."

"Of course it's Adolf Hitler," said Steve impatiently, "he lived in Linz, the camp was near to Linz. What's the big deal? Hitler, concentration camps, they go together don't they? Hamann was a favourite of his, so why wouldn't it be him?"

"Well strictly speaking Hitler had little to do with the camps, even one near his home town wouldn't have been much of an interest to him," said Mick. "The camps were for extermination and Hitler left that to others, he was more interested in winning a war. Yes alright the camp would be used to get rid of what he considered to be degenerates but the glory was winning the war. There's something else here that we haven't seen. I don't know...Look, Tom will see us when he's ready. It's got to be down to him now, I'm calling it a day."

Tom and Tilly had arrived back at her house. The journey had been in silence and the silence continued at the house.

They entered the front room and felt the warmth. The central heating had been left on and after their walk back in the cold, it was very welcoming. Tom slumped down on the settee and wiped the moisture from his face. "Bloody English weather," he called as Tilly disappeared into the kitchen.

She reappeared with two glasses filled with golden liquid and handed one to Tom.

"Christ girl, you've got me drinking again by the looks of it," he said putting it away in one and handing back the empty glass, gesturing for another. A full glass was returned and Tilly sat down on the settee next to Tom.

"What's your Jimmy doing these days Tils?" Tom asked eventually.

The question seemed to surprise her. James was her elder brother and during their marriage she had never considered that he was of any interest to Tom With him away on army duty or in South America and James living a busy life away from Hereford, they had been no more than acquaintances throughout. What had Tom been mulling over during the silent walk back?

"Why?" she enquired. "What would you want with him?"

"Well what is he doing these days?" Tom insisted.

"OK I suppose that you've got your mind on something. Err, well if you recall he was a history professor based in Oxford. He's not at university these days, left that role some time ago. He seems to be some kind of consultant, writes books, that sort of thing. We only see him rarely now when he comes to visit Mom and Dad, otherwise he's abroad mostly."

"What sort of history?"

"Come on, history is history isn't it? I don't know."

"No it isn't. There's the sort that you get at school, William the Conqueror, Henry the Eighth, dates and all that and then there is the specialist sort, concentrating on one particular event, writing books about it, exploring it in depth giving lectures. I seem to recall him lecturing me on warfare and whether it has any benefit to anyone. I used to think, why me, why not your Dad, he was in the forces. Look I need to talk to him. Can we go down this weekend? Can you contact him tell him it's really important?"

"Wait a minute, we can't just get hold of him like that," she replied.

"OK OK I'll try," she could see Tom was getting frustrated. "I'll try to contact him and see if he's free anytime. But you'll need to tell me why. What will I say to him?"

"Tell him I need a history lesson. If he bullied me about warfare when you and I were married then I bet he would know something concerning World War Two. Tell him I need his help. I'm going to bed, don't wake me up early." With that he left the room.

She sighed "Just as bloody obstreperous."

Chapter 29

Tilly was fortunate, the telephone call to her brother got through quickly.

"Hi Jim here," came the brusque reply.

"Hello James," Tilly replied, "it's your sister here, how are you going?"

"Christ Tils what are you wanting at this time of night?" he snapped, not standing on ceremony.

"I asked how you were James."

"Yes fine but it's the middle of the night, is something wrong?"

"Just bear with me, will you?" she asked. "No there's nothing wrong in the way you mean, all the family are fine. Tom's back from Oz, it's a long story so please don't make any comments about the past as you do usually. I want to know if we can meet, that's the three of us?"

"What, Tom's back, what's going on, I thought he'd gone to the Antipodes forever? Well I'll be damned;

I never expected to hear of him again. Are you back together or what?"

"You most likely will be damned. Look, James can you see us please?"

"Well I'm busy at the moment sis. The best I can say is that, by coincidence, I'm coming over to Hereford at the weekend to see Mom and Dad, I suppose I could spare some time," he answered grudgingly.

"OK, that's great," she replied. "Actually I saw them both just recently and they said that they hadn't had any contact with you for a while and they hoped you'd be in touch, so perhaps we can meet you when you do come up?"

"OK that's fine, but what does your ex want with me?"

"Tom needs some information about the second world war."

"What?" replied James in his familiar impatient way.

"Just listen and help if you can. I promise you that it's very important."

She sat down on the settee and began to relate an abridged version of Tom's regression with Joe and the connection with Hamann.

"Tom thinks that he was this German officer during the war and he needs some confirmation of the fact," she continued.

"What? He's crazy."

"Please listen. He's not crazy, I promise you. The reason at this point is not important. What is important is that if Tom was this German then he needs to know what Hamann did in the war."

"Are you serious? Look I'm sorry; I'm too busy for this nonsense at the moment."

"James I'm deadly serious and anyway isn't this the sort of thing that you like to dig up with your historical investigations and so on?"

"I dig up facts, not stories such as this. I've never heard of anything like this before."

"But look James," she persisted, "if you find stuff about Major Hamann and Tom can confirm it against his information of the man, which he got from his sessions with Joe, then wouldn't it be possible that they are one and the same person?"

There was silence at the end of the phone.

"James are you still there?"

"Yes I'm here. I can't think of an objection to your logic at the moment. If what you say is correct, you know that they are one and the same, then at any other time it could be mildly interesting, but I'm not sure about it at the moment."

"Interesting, look brother, just consider for a second, that's all you'll need, I know you only too well, if this was remotely true this could be another good book for you to write."

Again there was silence. Tilly's remark had hit her brother where it mattered.

"Maybe, Alright, I'll see you at the folk's place this weekend. If I can find anything about this guy, Hamann did you say….?" The voice trailed off. Clearly James had begun to realize the potential in this small piece of research and had replaced the receiver.

Tilly put down her receiver and returned to the kitchen with the empty glasses. Her brother was a difficult man probably, she assumed, in direct proportion to his relative importance at Oxford, but he was always thorough in his research and she knew that if anyone could get to the bottom of this conundrum, then it was James. She silently congratulated herself on knowing which button to press to gain his attention.

She had many thoughts in her head at this time, all of them relating to her ex-husband and the immediate future. Where would they all be in a week's time, two week's time? 'Who knows,' she whispered to no-one, walking back into the lounge and switching on the television for the late night local news.

The picture showed a police vehicle, lights flashing, parked outside a house that she vaguely recognised.

"The body of a man has been found on the drive of a house in the Hereford area. It is believed to be that of Joseph Schacht. As we get more news we will of course bring it to you."

Tilly went cold and the room seemed to take on a chill. For a moment she was silent even her breathing appeared to be non-existent. Although not entirely sure of Joseph's last name, some sixth sense and her recognition of the property told her that the man with whom they had spent the afternoon was one and the same.

She raced upstairs to where the sleeping Tom was laid out on the top of the covers, still fully dressed.

"Tom," she shouted, "get up quickly. Something has happened."

The almost lifeless body moved and groaned and returned to its previous position.

Shaking him now produced more movement and finally an possible appreciation of the urgency with which he was being awakened.

"Come and see this," she shouted, making her way back down the stairs.

Tom staggered down holding the banister and appeared in the lounge as the newscaster was repeating the headlines.

"Joseph? Hereford?" he mumbled, "what's this all about?"

More alert now as if the story had thrown cold water over his face he blinked his eyes and rubbed the stubble on his chin.

"Is it the same man?" she whispered after the newsreader had finished the story, "found on the drive, is he dead?"

"How do I know if he's dead? It might not be the same bloke, although I think he was named something like that," replied Tom, now fully regaining his wits.

"But listen, they said he had been taken to hospital, perhaps he's not dead, let me think for a moment."

Tom sat down.

"I've got it," he finally said. "You remember that guy, Andy, at the police station when we went to find out about the break in at Mom and Dad's house, well I'll phone him. Let's hope he's still on duty at this time of night. He gave us his number if we needed anything else. Have you got the number?"

Within a few minutes Tilly had found the telephone number from a draw in the sideboard where she had put the piece of paper for safe keeping. Tom snatched it from her and quickly dialed the number. A few seconds later Tom was speaking with his friend.

Tilly could hear some of the conversation, but after several minutes Tom put down the phone.

"Well?" she demanded.

"Ok," replied Tom, "we're in luck, Andy was on duty and you know he owes me a few favours from the old days and so he told me what he could. The guy, Joseph, was found on his drive by a neighbour who had come outside his own house after hearing some altercation and the wheels of a car screeching on the road outside. Apparently, so Andy says, the neighbour has complained to the police in the past about the number of late evening visitors that come to Joe's house in their big cars. The police watched but they decided that, as the visitors were causing no trouble or unnecessary noise, there was nothing they could do except ask the guy next door to keep an eye on things. If it became worse or there was any trouble then contact the police again and on this occasion he did so. Good thing too as the victim was found lying on his drive. He's not dead but in a bad way, you know beat up and so on. But because they found him tonight and not say in the morning by the postman, frozen to death or whatever, he's in Hereford hospital. I had to tell Andy something of my interest but he's a good bloke and he's taken me on trust at this time. Let's get over to the hospital right away, too much alcohol or not, this is an emergency."

Less than half an hour later the pair had arrived at the hospital and were making their way to the ward, having told the receptionist that they were relatives and had seen the news on Television. Within a few minutes they were at the ward, a private room just off the main area, an armed officer stood outside barring the entry of anyone who should not have been there.

"Who are you?" demanded the officer as they approached.

"Relatives," Tom replied in a confident manner hoping that would be good enough. "Eh my name is Tom and this is Matilda."

The policeman spoke into a mobile phone and after a short while he ushered them into the room.

"I didn't think it would be that easy," whispered Tilly as they passed through a small lobby towards the main part of the suite.

"Only because I want it to be," came a voice from within as they came face to face with Joe.

"What the hell is this?" Tom spluttered. "We've just seen the news, you're supposed to be dead or beat up or something, what is this?"

"Sit down," replied Joe, "let me see if I can offer you an explanation"

Chapter 30

The pair sat by a window and they looked around the room. It was certainly a hospital ward with all the usual equipment available and Joe was lying on a bed. Clearly he had had some injury with bandages covering his arms and body but he looked pretty well for a man who was only a short while ago reported to be dead.

"Look I'm feeling OK, a bit off after the beating happened, but as I have been expecting something like this for a long while now I've kept a record of what I've been doing so if I did get done over then at least the authorities would have something to go on." "Authorities?" questioned Tom. "When I hear that word then I know it's usually more than a local matter, you know, the police or whatever."

"You're quite right," replied Joe. "I think that it is time I told you what's going on. I'll tell you what I can, what I am allowed to say and then you can take the report with you to read later.

"You'll let me see the report?" questioned Tom. "What have I done to deserve treatment that seems to be reserved for the authorities?"

"It's not what you've done but how you relate to what I've been doing that involves you. I think you'll understand more when I've explained what I can, although it may take some time," answered Joe getting down slowly from the bed and sitting in a chair by the side of it.

Tom and Tilly looked at each other questioningly. This was going to be interesting and could answer many questions.

"Just talk on and we'll try not to interrupt," said Tom. Joe moved the chair around so that he could see both of them face to face.

"My real name is Joseph Ciemny and I was born in Poland. I think I told you that much, when we had our session earlier today. That is why I can speak German; I needed to learn the language during the occupation. When Germany occupied Poland, my family was taken into a concentration camp and I never saw any of them again. You will understand that that was the fate of many millions of people. I had escaped that fate so at the end of the war I was determined to find the madmen responsible for the murders of my family and those of thousands more Polish people. I started an organization similar to Weisenthal, you've probably heard of him, although I think he followed through with Jewish persecutors mainly, where I searched for Polish persecutors. So like his organization and with some joint cooperation, I must admit, we set out to try to track down Nazis, SS war criminals and so on and particularly, as far as I was concerned, those in charge at the camp where my family died. I am a trained psychologist and I came to Britain around 30 years ago when reports of war criminals started to surface here. Whilst running my group I spent three years at University where I did some research in Hypnotism and during that time my research seemed to go off in a different direction. Something happened during a session with a patient, if you call them that, that made me wonder if it might be possible to hypnotise people to remember their past. I quickly realised that this would have been useful if we ever caught a suspect and needed to find out about them, because in the normal state they could lie or have a good story and we would never identify them as a war criminal, but under hypnosis they would be unable to lie. Are you with me so far?"

Tom nodded.

"As I developed this theory it seemed that I might also be able to encourage subjects to remember times in a previous life. People at University thought I was mad but you know some people seem to have memories of things that happened to them even before they were born; it's like Déjà Vue, when you see or do something that has happened to you before. So I continued with the research and I used students as guinea pigs and found that in some cases it did appear to work and we could confirm some of the information that we got from known history. When my university work became more widely known I started receiving some interest from the police who thought it might work with criminal interviews or even finding missing persons. There were some legal problems there but nevertheless they looked at it for some time. Then I came within the government's radar or more properly the secret service. I couldn't believe they were interested, my work was in its early stages and only worked in certain circumstances but they were serious. It seems that they knew of my background, well I was a foreigner after all and I had this connection to Weisenthal, but do you know what they were really after?"

"No idea," replied Tom. "But I can see that you are going to tell me, although is it not official secrets time?"

"Maybe," continued Joe, "but you've signed the papers haven't you and anyway I've cleared it already because your case is special as you will see later. Ten years ago the government started to consider releasing papers and records from the war and some of them concerned the connection of British Royalty with the German Government. I still have no idea what was in the papers, they wouldn't tell me that, but I do know there was some concern about The Duke of Windsor and Mrs Simpson over their visits to Germany and their meetings with officials at the top of the German hierarchy, including Hitler himself. The authorities were worried that if my work as a psychologist and with my group, threw up a war criminal, as was the intention after all, and he or she could be regressed then there might be something to say about the English future King. Now I know that there is a long leap between one and the other but with Royalty, well you know how much scandal that could produce if there was any connection whatsoever so they wanted to be sure nothing came about. I think the secret service only partly believed what I was doing but they couldn't take a chance and so kept close to me and I have to say I got some funding from them, against a promise to let them know if anything occurred"

"So that's why they are involved at this time with the attack and so on?" queried Tom. "I quickly worked out that it wasn't the local police who you have here."

"Well yes to some extent," Joe continued, "but I finally got a breakthrough when my group caught up with someone whose name was on our list. I was given permission to interrogate him and during a regression he revealed that he was a guard at Mathausen. You can imagine how I felt, my theory was proven to work and we were able to prove some of what he said from records kept at the time. At last I had someone from the very camp where my family died and I thought I was going to find something very close and relevant to me. He was only a minor figure in the scheme of things as it turned out but it was the fact that I could prove regression worked that switched everyone on to what I had developed. The importance of this man however, was that he gave us names. Some were already on our list, some were not but one of the names that we already knew about was Claus Hamann."

Joe stopped his story at this point he felt sure that Tom would need to think about what he had just said. The younger man had stood up from his seat and walked towards the windows. He hadn't realised how long they had been at the hospital and how the time had passed by. The low early morning sun glinted through the blinds, traffic was passing by on the road and people were making their way around the City. Outside, the world was carrying on in the twenty first century. Inside the room a time sixty years earlier was the issue, a time of utter madness, a time of unbelievable inhumanity but at the same instant a time when people went about their business whatever it was. Did they ever conceive what future generations might think of what they were doing, of what they had done then? Tom slowly shook his head. Tilly just watched, she knew Tom was taking this hard but he was a strong character and would get through it. She remained silent as did the others in the room. Tom returned to his seat his look at Joe indicating that he should continue and he did so.

"We knew Hamann to be some sort of administrator, definitely someone I would wish to find as much as anyone else because, on a personal level I might find something concerning my family. However Hamann had been executed at the end of the war and that was the finish of that trail."

"Then I came along," suggested Tom.

"Yes," replied Joe. "At first I could not believe my luck. I knew that this could be the big one, the one I had been waiting for all my life. At last I had someone of importance. Not merely a camp guard, but a real senior officer, someone executed after the war and perhaps someone with whom I could make some progress with Mathausen, and Heim, who was the camp doctor there, you may recall they called him, Doctor Death.

However, after the first session, of course you went away. I was desperate but I couldn't do anything about it. If I had pressed you I might have ruined the whole possibility, I just had to wait, to be patient and hope you would come back. I had some contact with Steve, just out of interest you know and he told me where you had gone and what you were doing so I knew what was happening."

"Did Steve have any interest in this?" queried Tom. "I had a theory that he might have been interested in pushing something forward with works of art, you know looted valuables, because he told me about Hamann's job with Hitler and the museums and so on."

"Well who knows? That only came about when your other friend Mick Cannon was put to translating some released papers and he also found the connection with the SS Major. So I expect your brother did find his interest in the connection at that time."

"How do you know about that?" Tom asked cautiously.

"Cannon works for the Government, in a way I work for the Government. I suppose they thought it was right to tell me because of my research, in case it was of any interest to me and certainly it was, and so I guess I let your brother do the spade-work for me. I reasoned that if he was going to do anything about the gold, paintings or whatever, he would get you to come back to Britain and then I could get involved again and that's what happened obviously."

Tom was not sure that he fully believed this story, although it was certainly feasible, he thought, as special branch officers were affording Joe protection at this time. He knew that it was necessary to carry on with this for the time being and he was happy to let Joe tell him more, after all what he was being told could possibly be checked out when he saw Tilly's brother James later in the week.

"Ok Joe tell me more if you are up to it," said Tom.

"I'm definitely up to it," replied Joe, "this is what I have been waiting for, a chance to get to the bottom of my family's fate, perhaps find those responsible and bring them to justice."

"But Hamann's dead."

"Yes but it's what he might know about others who are not dead that I need to find out. Let me explain some more. Hamann was an official at Mathausen, I know that you know something about that from your regression. I realised when we had the last session your lady was recording it and no doubt you've had the chance to listen to it by now. Well if Hamann, or you if you like, was an official at Mathausen then you may know what happened to the main war criminal who came out of there...Aribert Heim. Doctor Death."

"Doctor Death?" said Tilly, "surely there cannot be an individual named that can there? What on earth did he do to earn such a title?"

"Ah so that's it. I've heard of him," said Tom, "perhaps if I say what I know that will give you a bit of a rest although I assume you can correct me if I'm wrong anywhere in the story. Any chance of a glass of water before I start?" he asked looking over at the guard who seemed to have begun to doze off. The man straightened up and moved away from the wall against which he had been leaning and opening the door called to his colleague in to next room. Almost immediately a jug of iced water and glasses were delivered.

"That's service," grinned Tom. "Joe you must be an important guy."

Joe shrugged his shoulders.

Chapter 31

"Before I start let me tell you that I know something about this because when I was in Oz I spent a lot of time reading and the Second World War always fascinated me. You may be able to guess why that is. As you were talking, Joe, I was wondering if my interest in it was merely curiosity or due to the fact that I was, apparently, involved. Perhaps that's something that you will need to investigate with me at another time. Aribert Ferdinand Heim was born in Bad Radkersberg in Austria Hungary 1914. He was the son of a policeman and he studied medicine in Vienna before joining the Waffen-SS as a volunteer in 1940. In 1941 he was sent to Mauthausen-Gusen concentration camp where he was able to carry out 'experiments' on prisoners. He earned the nickname Doctor Death," he continued looking over at Tilly, "because he carried out lethal injection experiments on inmates. He injected petrol or other liquids into their hearts to see which killed them quickest. According to witnesses in 1941 he was treating a Jewish athlete who had a foot infection. He anaesthetized him, cut him open, took one kidney apart, removed the other and also castrated the man. He then removed the head and boiled off the flesh and used the skull as a paperweight."

Tom stopped talking for a moment and looked at Tilly. "Are you O.K Tils?" he asked. "You know if this is upsetting for you, you can go outside."

"No I'll be alright," she replied. "At least I now know how he got that name but just carry on and try not to be so gratuitous."

Tom nodded and continued.

"After the war he, of course, disappeared but in 1962 he was discovered in Baden-Baden working as a gynaecologist. Before he could be arrested, he disappeared again. For the next few years he was 'spotted' on a number of occasions around the world, from South America to the Balkans and the Middle East but the most interesting report came from his son who said that Heim led a secret life in Cairo under the name Tarek Farid. He was reported to have died from cancer in 1992. The son said he was with him when he died and he had known of his location in Egypt for a long time. Apparently German law allows him to avoid prosecution for sheltering his father. They even know the name of the Hotel where he spent his last years."

Tom looked at Joe who had been listening intently to what he had to say. "Is that about all that is known concerning Heim?" Tom asked.

"That's very impressive young man obviously your time away wasn't wasted," Joe answered, "but his death just encourages everyone to think that there is nothing more to be done. It's very convenient, is it not, but ask yourself, where is the body, where is the grave and of course there is the question of around £1m sitting in his bank account in Berlin. There has been an attempt to have him declared dead legally so the family could get control over the money but there is no death certificate so perhaps he isn't dead at all. I accept that he would be very old by now but I have a feeling he is still with us and still to be caught, perhaps with your help Tom."

"Well don't forget everything I just said is in the public domain and some of it happened after Hamann was executed, perhaps I don't know any more than that," said Tom, "but if it helps then I will regress again. I think a guy like that deserves to be caught after all this time and shown for what he is and perhaps made to suffer even at his age."

"Well Hamann may have been a devoted Nazi but there is no doubt that you are not," said Joe in a way that Tom considered as being curious to say the least.

"Joe," said Tilly, "is that all you have with Tom, you know, the question of whether he could recall what he knew about Heim?"

Joe looked quizzically at her, wondering what she had in mind.

"Well you've told us that you are aware that I recorded the last session you had with Tom, obviously I wasn't surreptitious enough but I got from it two sets of initials AH and HS. Well we guessed that AH was Adolf Hitler and that seems as if it may have been incorrect as we have just had a discussion about Heim, so who was HS?"

"HS?" questioned Joe, "did I write down HS?"

"Yes," she said firmly, "I didn't make a mistake, I have the paper at home and I remember it."

"Perhaps I am a little tired after all," Joe said his voice less confident now, less triumphant than before. "I'm afraid that I can't recall it."

"OK let's have a time out," said Tom.

"No," said Joe quickly regaining some composure. "I think it best if we call it a day now, rather than just a break. I am supposed to be at deaths door and if the guys who attacked me are around I don't want them to get any thoughts other than that I am seriously ill, otherwise the MI people who are in the background here might miss a chance."

The group indulged in small talk for the next few minutes as the meeting drew to a close. Tom still had many questions to ask and he could see that he was going to have to wait for another time. Many of his thoughts would have to be left in abeyance. After all he still had to speak to Tilly's brother and he might get something from that before he asked Joe any more.

"How are you feeling now?" Tom asked vainly hoping to get back to the point at issue.

"Tired," replied Joe, "but however well or unwell I feel at any time is not the big issue here. I just have to know what we are dealing with for the sake of my family and the other millions of Polish, Jews or whoever were caught up in that awful period of history. There may be nothing that can be done so long after the war but that is not the important thing, what is important is that the world knows. Do you know that many people these days believe that nothing at all ever happened, that it is all a fabrication, that millions didn't die in the camps and the graphic films we can see were Hollywood produced. I may not have many years to go but I cannot waste any time now we have got to this stage."

Joe's speech, for it appeared to be such, seemed to revive him or, as Tilly later observed, gave him time to think and he continued to talk, his voice much stronger now and the end of the meeting some little way off.

"I told you earlier that my real name was Ciemny but I have used the name Schacht." Tilly nodded, "I said I thought your name was something like that."

"Well I used that name," Joe continued, "because at the end of the war there was a report that Hitler was not dead."

Tom looked at Tilly in a quizzical fashion and the room fell silent. The longer the silence went on the more fantastic that thought became and their frowns of disbelief were noticed by Joe who quickly continued to speak.

"Of course there were dozens of conspiracy theories from all sides but a man described as Germany's Financial Wizard, possibly a very important individual in the running of the state from the monetary point of view, suggested that Hitler was not dead. This was Hjalmar Schacht and after the war he was captured close to the Italian border presumably trying to make his escape from retribution or whatever might follow. To say Hitler wasn't dead was just about the last thing anyone like him would have said, so it might have had some truth in it. Anyway I decided to use the name in the hope that it may just flush out someone over the years. So far, no luck but I always kept the thought with me, what if Hitler didn't die in the bunker?"

"OK," said Tom. "We've heard about Heim and now Hitler, coincidence about the same initial letters, and now you've answered our question with regard to HS, so who is it that you are really after?"

Joe shrugged his shoulders, "I don't really know but probably I don't really care, either will do or perhaps both who knows?" he replied asking the question of no-one in particular.

"Look," Tilly murmured, "all this is very complicated for the likes of me. I've heard a lot of things this evening and I think I would like to consider them. Tom would also I guess as you are going to need him again very soon I've no doubt. Let's finish now and meet again perhaps in a couple of days? I know this is very important to you, but I think Tom will be of more use to you one step at a time."

"OK," replied Joe. "You are right I'm going on a bit when I do need to take it more slowly. After all it's taken years to get this far so a day or so will not matter much and don't forget we have now flushed out someone. I didn't get this beating for nothing and if it hadn't been for a bit of luck I assume the intention was to kill me."

"Yes, and the same with me," replied Tom. "I've had an attack at the footbridge, the folk's house was done over, Tils and I were nearly driven off the road in the mountains and I had this feeling that we were trailed during the journey back from Oz. This is not just a local matter, someone is taking this very seriously. I wouldn't be surprised to find a tail waiting outside the hospital when we leave. Hey any chance of a way out of the back door?" he added looking at the man who he had been led to believe was an agent of the state.

"I'll arrange that for you," said Joe summoning the man over to the bed. "You can leave your car here and have it collected at a later time."

Chapter 32

The ambulance drove away from the hospital. Crouching down in the back even though the windows were opaque the pair considered the story told to them by the older man.

"You know, I think we should get to speak with James as soon as possible," Tom broke the ice, "you said his forte was World War Two so I guess he would know as much as anyone about Hitler. This thing about Schacht was intriguing I have always thought that if Adolf was as powerful as he was supposed to be he would never have let himself get trapped in that bunker with no plan of escape, but where on earth did Joe get the idea? You know some of what he said had, how can I describe it? A strange feel to it as if it was not really meant, just something he was saying for our benefit. What did you think?" She shook her head holding on to the seat as the ambulance turned a corner.

"When do you think we can speak with your brother?"

"When we get back home, I'll phone him and see if we can make a firm date. He said he would come over at the weekend, well it's Saturday tomorrow but I'll try to firm that up. Well I'll do it later on at least, have you seen the time?" she replied wearily.

The ambulance pulled up outside the door to Tilly's house. The driver had been introduced to them as a friend of Joe's. A silent man with powerful arms they noticed and both guessed that he was a Government agent of some sort.

"I'll drive around a while to make sure that no-one's about," he said as the truck pulled away from the front of the house.

"Let's get inside," said Tom. "If that guy thinks there's trouble about he might well be correct." The door slammed behind them and even though the daylight had arrived Tilly kept the curtains closed.

"What do you think about Joe's story?" she asked quietly.

"I'm not sure I believe everything he was saying."

"No, that bit about HS, some quick thinking there. Could you make up a tale like that? Hitler still alive after the war?"

"Well, military intelligence must believe some of what he says," Tom said, "they are clearly looking after him. All that stuff at the hospital, agents around him, a private room and I'm not really sure that he was hurt as much as they made out and, if that is so, then the news broadcast was, well would I be wrong to say, encouraged? Look if I'm correct and there is some involvement with MI then I think we should be very careful. We already know that someone has been following us about, maybe spooks or maybe the other side, whoever they may be, and they will have some clout. Telephones could be tapped into, the post intercepted or anything else that seems worthwhile, so let's imagine that we are being listened to. I think that for the future we should connect with each other by cell phone, what do you think?"

"Sure, good idea. I think that I still have Steve's number and Mick's also, so yes, let's do it that way in future. Look we've been up all night and I feel like getting some sleep, I'm going upstairs what about you?"

"Yes, I'm with you. Let's get an hour or two."

It was early afternoon when they woke up and the remainder of the day was spent reading the newspaper or watching television. It passed quietly, without any incident although from time to time one of the occupants of the house would peer around the curtains just as a nosey neighbour might, although there was of course, more of a motive on this occasion. A proposed visit to the pub in the evening, the sort of life that they led from time to time when previously married.

No-one made any effort to contact them that day but Tilly had spoken with James who had promised to give his thoughts on the demise of the German leader.

Saturday arrived, the day promised by James as the day of contact and around ten o'clock a loud rapping on the front door surprised Tom who was relaxing with the aid of the morning newspaper. Quickly throwing it down on to the floor he made for the window and peered around the edge of the curtain.

"Who's this guy?" he called to Tilly who was in the kitchen. She hurried into the lounge and joined him at the window. The young man in a semi official uniform suddenly looked to the side as if by a sixth sense and clearly realised that he was being watched. He gave a smile towards the half invisible watchers and waved a small parcel in their direction.

"It's just a delivery guy," whispered Tom, spotting a blue courier van parked across the road.

His companion opened the door, tightly drawing the dressing gown around her.

The man looked at her face directly and then made an assessment of the rest of her with a slow downwards and upwards gaze handing the parcel to her as he regained the face.

She took the package and with a slight nod of the head, closed the door returning to the warmth of the room.

"That'll teach you to open the door, half dressed, to a stranger," he teased pushing back the curtain.

"Yeah OK," she said turning over the brown envelope and reading the sender's name on the other side. "It's from Jim."

Tom stood by her side as the paper was pulled apart revealing a book bearing a cover showing a rust coloured Uboat hull complete with rivets and a German military black and white cross on the front. Coming from within various pages were markers and a number was written on each piece. The envelope also contained a covering letter.

Tilly commenced to read the correspondence.

'Dear all,' it read, 'I'm sorry that I cannot undertake a visit to you at this time as, following our telephone conversation, I received a telegram asking me to fly to Paris for a meeting. Paris is marginally a better bet than Hereford at this time of the year, so by the time you read this, providing the courier service is efficient, I will be halfway across the channel.'

'I have enclosed a book that I wrote some years ago and have marked the pages with references that may be of some use to you. Perhaps we can meet when I return later next week. Best wishes James'.

"Just like your brother," said Tom, "I had it in my mind that he would not be able to come for some reason or another, but I suppose that at least we have something to read."

"James has written a few books to my knowledge. As a history professor I suppose that he is obliged to. As I recall he always had this streak of controversy in his writings, so they would sell I guess, and the theories used to stir up the establishment."

"Well let's hope that they stir us," Tom replied sitting back down on the settee and flicking open the pages at the first marker. "Is there a note in the letter as to what each reference relates?"

"Yes, note one refers to the possibility that Hitler escaped Berlin before the end of the war."

"Good, then he must have listened to what you said and our time is not going to be totally wasted. Let's see what the oracle reveals."

"Don't be facetious. Just read it, it might be what you want."

Tilly went into the kitchen to make coffee while Tom started to scan the pages.

"Hey this is an interesting read," he called out after a few moments." There is certainly a style to this. No wonder the books sell, come and listen to this." Tom began to read picking out the relevant parts.

"In April 1945 as the battle for Berlin raged in the streets above the Fuhrerbunker. The occupants of the bunker in the garden of the Reichskanzlei in Wilhelmstrasse prepared for the worst. Above them the Russian army was no more than a dozen yards from the building and those down below were expecting, at any minute, to hear the thunder of explosives as they attempted to blast their way into the last hiding place of The Fuhrer and his entourage. The soldiers had been promised rewards to whoever captured the German leader and those rewards would be greatly increased if he could be taken alive. The last few feet were soon breached and half a dozen grimy Russian faces appeared at the gap in the wall leading to the underground sanctuary. 'Schicklegruber' they shouted as they climbed over the debris and stared into the huddle of the bunker's inhabitants. No one answered. The officer in charge pulled out a tattered photograph, spat on it and wiped it on his trousers in an attempt to clean the image, then waved it at the group. He studied it and the faces before him, but there was no recognition. The troops entered the rooms of the bunker one by one but in none of them could Hitler be identified. This was hardly surprising as Hitler was not in the bunker anywhere and he had not been in there for some time."

Tilly moved closer to Tom entwining her arm with his as the story continued."This will be interesting," she murmured, "how can this man get away when he is entirely surrounded by thousands or even millions of enemy troops?"

He continued reading. "A few days earlier, as news of the Russian advance on the position was passed to him Adolf decided to make a break for it. Like many of his senior generals who had already made their escapes he was not going to wait to be captured, least of all by the

Soviets... and the German people?, well they could fend for themselves. Their leader, the Fuhrer, had long ago decided to escape if he could and his plans were now put into action. He was helped inadvertently by Goering who had just been dismissed as head of the Luftwaffe for his alleged attempt at a coup d'état. Having dismissed him, Hitler needed to appoint another head and he decided on Robert von Griem.

Throughout his time as leader of the German nation, Hitler had followed the career of Hanna Reitsch, who was an incredible woman aviator. She held many records for her flying feats and was asked to test many experimental craft on behalf of the Luftwaffe, included in these were the rocket propelled Me163. She became a favourite of Hitler who awarded her the Iron Cross first class, the only woman ever to receive the award.

Von Griem needed to meet with the Fuhrer to receive his appointment and he had to get into the City. Hitler would not be pleased if Von Griem failed to arrive and retribution would surely follow if the war eventually went the way of the Germans. He couldn't risk it and so he asked Reitsch, who was his lover, to fly him into Berlin, an impossible task in the circumstances you might think, but he thought well within the capabilities of this daring, fearless, record breaking woman from Silesia. An incomparable German heroine.

Late one evening two nondescript individuals made their way out of the bunker towards the end of Wilhelmstrasser which had not yet been shelled and where the road had been previously cleared. Above the clamour of the exploding shells and cracking gun-fire an approaching drone could be detected. They switched on their torches, aiming for the sound of the aircraft, guiding it towards the clear landing strip. Through the darkness of the night and the smoke of the Battle a light aircraft dipped out of the sky onto the clear road and landed, wheels screeching, close to the waiting party.

The small group quickly made their way back to the bunker and were rapidly ushered inside by the guards.

Von Griem and Hanna Reitsch were led into a small stuffy room two floors below the general business floor of the bunker. As they entered, a short disheveled man stood up from a chair by a table, one hand trembling, not from any nervousness but from the beginnings of what was believed to be Parkinson's Disease. The pair recognised Adolf Hitler immediately and his companion Eva Braun. Hitler held out a hand to Von Griem and within a few moments had conferred upon him the status of Head of the Luftwaffe.

It was now that Hitler revealed his plan of escape. There was an aircraft within a few hundred metres of the bunker and the best woman pilot that Germany could produce. The four of them would now make their way to the aircraft and take off leaving the desolation and destruction of the German capital and the fate of the German people to the Russian army.

Within a short space of time the four had arrived, through the continuing bombardment of the City, at the plane and boarded it. Adolf and Eva sat behind the pilot's seat on a blanket which covered the dusty floor and Hanna Reitsch took over the controls. Within minutes the aircraft took off gaining height as quickly as possible and immediately changing direction so as to fly away from the advancing enemy. Thus Adolf Hitler made his escape from the Bunker."

Chapter 33

Tilly took a slow drink from the coffee cup, so enthralled had she been with the story that the contents had gone cold. "I had always believed that he died in the Bunker, they found his body with a bullet hole through the head, the Russians have his skull, how can this be right?" she queried.

Tom continued with her brother's story.

"History tells that Hitler and Eva committed suicide in the bunker, but did they? The Russian officer would have received a considerable financial reward for the capture of the German leader, even more if he was taken alive, but if the Fuhrer had escaped there was every possibility that the Russian officer would be held responsible for the escape and a summary execution would have taken place. Failure with such high stakes at issue could not be tolerated, and so with something being better than nothing and finding no sign of the Fuhrer within the bunker, he faked the death. Adolf had left some time earlier in disguise, leaving his uniform behind. So the officer dressed up one of the remaining Germans in Hitler's discarded clothing and killed him together with one of the women secretaries to represent Eva. He then burnt the bodies so identification would be difficult and when his superiors arrived he claimed the reward, showing the charred remains and passing them off as the leader and his mistress.

The Russians were ecstatic, they had Hitler's body, a great coup at the war's end and something that no-one else, and the Americans in particular, had. They would be in a position to make considerable political capital out of this.

However, rumours began to circulate that the remains were not The Fuhrer's and so in an attempt to prove that they were, the Soviets questioned his personal dentist who they had captured some time earlier. They reasoned that he could identify the remains from dental records and he obliged."

"But if he escaped the bunker then the skull wasn't his, so how did he do that?" questioned Tilly.

Tom continued adding his own knowledge to what James had written.

"The doctor immediately spotted the discrepancy with the remains and must have realised that Hitler wasn't dead and must therefore have escaped, but to save his own skin, and also that of his leader, he gave a positive identification. If he was dead no-one would be looking for him and obviously the positive ID was what the Russians wanted to hear anyway."

"Russia you know is a very political country, certainly now, but at the end of the war, even more so. It meant a great deal to them to be first in Berlin, first at the bunker and first to find Hitler. There were no DNA techniques such as we have today and the confirmation of the identity of the skull by the dentist was about as good as it got. They believed it and after that, when tests became available they could not admit to making a mistake and so no-one else is allowed to have access to the remains. So it continues to be what is left of The German Leader."

"Back to the escape, the plane flew away from Berlin and the continuing battle until eventually the party landed just over the Italian border. The passengers disembarked disappearing into the countryside with the assistance of supporters, after all the Italians were still friendly at this time. Reitsch refueled the aircraft and returned to Berlin ensuring that she and Von Griem were captured and soon after the two were interviewed by American Intelligence. The Americans were by this time aware that an aircraft had been seen in Berlin. A report by advancing Russian troops said that a group of soldiers had come across a road that was clear of any debris or rubble. At a time when the whole of Berlin had been battered and shelled and there was barely a building left untouched this was incomprehensible and as they crept cautiously along the side of that road a sudden roaring noise caused them to dive to the ground. Looking up they were astonished to see a light aircraft taxiing along, gaining speed and taking to the air, their collective amazement ensured that no-one fired on the craft and they just watched it climb into the night and away from the City. Adolf had disappeared."

"The Americans guessed that the plane must have been flown by this woman. When they were asked why they had been in Berlin in the craft and why they had left, and presumably returned, they repeated the same answer, 'It was our blackest day when we could not die at our Fuhrer's side'."

"This convinced the interrogators that Hitler had died in the bunker and so the Russian account was confirmed."

"Over the next few months stories came in to the British and Americans, and probably also the Russians, of sightings of Hitler in various places in Europe but nothing was ever proven when the reports were investigated. Some were accounts of people being seen, who looked similar to the pair. Other accounts were probably from Nazi supporters whose reports were deliberately misleading to throw pursuers of the trail, and some would have come from the obligatory crank. As time wore on he was supposed to have been seen in other countries, and interestingly one sighting was in Egypt where Heim was also seen. Mainly however a South American connection became the best guess and over time some escapees were in fact discovered over there. It is reported that Mossad, spent much time and effort in different countries on that continent in chasing Nazis and certainly were successful when they captured Eichman, but there is possibly more to it than that. My thoughts on the amount of time spent over there are that it could only really be justified if it was believed that they could find Hitler there. Also the only the only known execution of a Nazi occurred in Montevideo, that of Herbert Curkrs, the Hangman of Riga. So there can be little doubt as to the amount of work undertaken in South America over the years, by the Jewish Intelligence Service."

Tom closed the pages of the book and put it down on the table.

"Your brother tells a good story and he must have done a lot of research. I have no idea how much of it is correct but I expect that most of the book is right and his way of telling the facts sells."

Tilly nodded, silently turning over James' words in her mind.

He continued.

"So the deal is this I guess, Hitler escaped and Heim escaped. Hamann was the common denominator and Joe and his organization must have thought they had cracked it when I was regressed and found to be the officer. They just had to get me to tell them what I knew and something was bound to come out or give them a clue and eventually lead to either of them."

"One complication might have been that they did not know which one, as both had the initials A.H and if I said anything based on that, well it would be a lucky dip but nowhere along the line as far as I can see are we dealing with works of art. I think you can see that Joe confirmed that."

"How do you think he knew about Hitler, he seemed fairly confident about telling us that he had not died in the bunker?"

"Well, Joe has the background to find out that sort of thing I expect. What did he say? Born in Poland and lived under the occupation, family killed in the camp, operates some organization along the same lines as Weisenthal. He has to be in a position to find out anything that may be current thinking with regard to Hitler and, of course, don't forget that there are probably thousands of publications, pamphlets and so on that produce all types of theory concerning his demise. Your brother had written a number of books, also we have just read one of them, and when we were at Joe's house did you not see the size of the library that he had in the waiting room? No, I'm not surprised that he could have a view like that."

"So if Joe or even James is correct to any degree then that is probably the issue and not valuables and my brother was just chasing rainbows again?"

"As usual, but somehow Joe must have got him to think along those lines in order to encourage him to bring me back from Australia."

"So you are convinced that Joe encouraged Steve. You know," replied Tilly, "that transcript of your last regression might be worth looking at again. I recall Joe wrote down the letters A.H so maybe you did say something and he certainly wrote down HS but then denied it which was strange. But we've got to trust him haven't we, that stuff about his organization can be checked can't it? You know I remember reading about Weisenthal in the past and that his family was at Mathausen as well as Joe's. After the war he started his organization in Linz so that's very similar to Joe and he said he knew him. He wouldn't have said something that could be checked on so easily if it wasn't true. I think he's OK after all he found Hamann some years ago with his first session with you and was prepared to wait all this time to follow it through. No I think we can trust him."

"Maybe," Tom mused, "but who or what the devil are we after and how do we find them or it, what if we find nothing, after all either person must be very old by now and that itself would be ironic wouldn't it? The guys who cut short the lives of millions live to a great age themselves."

"How old would they be now?"

"Well, Hitler was born 1889 and Heim in 1914 so they would be 111 and 86. Tom sat back in his chair. You know Tils, I don't think they are still alive when you think about it and if they aren't alive what is all this about? Who are we looking for or what are we looking for? Are we back to the treasure or other Nazis in the public domain or what? But you know that there must be something out there and because of the trouble we've had there must be someone interested in all of this. I think another conversation with Joe has got to be on the cards."

"James may have something to add when I think about it." said Tilly. "He knows a lot about this period in time and what he has told us through the book, is only in reply to what we asked him. Perhaps we are asking the wrong question or perhaps we need to expand the question we have asked."

"Expand?" queried Tom. "How do you mean?"

"Well all we have asked is how Hitler might have got away from Berlin in 1945 but we haven't asked where he might have gone or more particularly which route did he take and who helped him? I know he said in his book that there were some sightings but was there any evidence, how good was the intelligence, you know that sort of thing?" she stopped talking, her eyes began to close as if she had come to a conclusion.

"How about this?" she continued, "you could well be correct when you say that these guys are no longer here, that they must have died over the years, but one thing that doesn't die is a country's government and such like. They must have had help. The individuals who helped them are possibly also gone but the authority, the government or organization that was represented must still be here. How embarrassing could it be for an organization that espouses a certain virtue, these days, to be found as responsible for enabling war criminals to escape, even if it was sixty years ago and more to the point, what would they do to prevent it coming out?"

"You have already reminded me of the situation with Waldheim and so this must be similar, I would think. We need to speak with James again. Can you contact him and see when he is finished in France, then ask him to come up for a visit?"

"Look, he said he would come up to see the folks one weekend, let's see if we can make it soon. I'll speak to him. You know if he could make something out of this just think how it would look for him. The man who solved the mystery of Hitler's disappearance, or even Heim's."

"Tils you are as crafty as they come," said Tom, "even James wouldn't pass up on the chance to solve that conundrum. Contact him and tell him what we are after and when he comes up for the weekend we can meet and I bet he's found a clue or something that he has written in some other best seller. He's a sharp bloke even if I say so myself."

Chapter 34

Over the next few days Tom and Tilly spent all of their time together, visiting old haunts, pubs in local villages and talking about their respective times apart and wondering how their breakup had ever happened, as in each other's company they appeared never to have felt happier than at this time. No contact had been made with any of the other individuals involved and Tom was happy with that. He felt the need for more information from Tilly's brother and with James away in Paris on some conference, it would take time for a further discussion to take place.

The weekend arrived. Saturday dawned bright but chilly and Tom had decided to go to a local football game. Tilly had been invited to a shopping trip in Worcester with a life-long school friend and was getting ready upstairs.

She had managed to speak with James two days before to let him know what they hoped he would be able tell them and what information they needed and he confirmed that he would be able to visit on Sunday.

Tom had just made coffee and was preparing to sit down to read the morning newspaper when the usual peace and quietness of the small street was shattered by a sudden unexpected noise. He threw down the newspaper onto the floor and jumped up out of the chair and made for the window, the noise emanating from outside. Looking through the window he saw a large and powerful motorcycle had pulled up just outside the house and the rider had opened the throttle as if to grab the attention of anyone who might be around. A large cat which had been sitting on the step of a house opposite looked over in disdain and walked casually away down a nearby alley.

The bike was black and Tom's first thought was that the rider who had chased them through the streets of Hereford and who had ambushed them on the mountains had returned, but that rider had been eliminated hadn't he?

He ran into the kitchen to retrieve his weapon from a drawer, take no chances he thought and returned to the front room window. But this machine was different, larger and more powerful looking; a Harley Fat Boy, if he knew his bikes, no ambush would come from that, he reasoned.

"It's Jimmy," Tilly shouted from upstairs. She had heard the commotion outside and had looked out of the window. "Tom will you open the door please?"

"Why can't he just knock on the door like anyone else?" he muttered as he opened the door to be greeted by Tilly's brother.

James was as tall as Tom. With his hair cut short and dressed in his leathers he seemed to have a bigger build than him, a beard and moustache gave him an interesting appearance. Tom hadn't seen him for many years since before he and Tilly had separated but he could remember him, largely through his demeanour and he quickly recognised the grin.

James was a history professor, an academic, but at the same time an engaging individual ready to join in any opportunity for a bit of fun and his 'street cred', as he called it, came from such things as owning this flamboyant motor cycle.

Tilly had run down the stairs as Tom was letting him into the house. She came to the door to greet him and they hugged."Hey that's a tan," she exclaimed, "been somewhere where it's hot and sunny recently?"

"Only Nice, a conference," he replied.

"Not Paris?"

"No the venue was changed at the last minute and that suited me, I much prefer the Med."

They had always been close. It was good to see him again and both Tom and James at the same occasion, well it had been a long time since that had happened.

"I'll have a tea if there's any going," said James, "the usual, you know Earl Grey with a few grains of sugar." He entered the house and proceeded to make himself at home by sitting on the sofa and removing his boots.

"I'll fetch the tea," said Tom, "you pair must have more than me to talk about at this time," and he disappeared into the kitchen.

Tom eventually re-appeared and James had removed his leathers.

" Tea," he announced, "and a coffee for you Tils."

"Thanks broth," said James.

They chatted over the drinks. Just general small talk and Tilly enjoyed that. Lately she considered life had become a little fraught and serious with what was happening around them.

"How's the love life?" asked Tom, always wanting to know that sort of thing and wishing to join in the conversation.

"Well it's fine thank you. No-one particularly in tow at the moment," replied James somewhat wistfully, "but I'm so busy at the moment, another book you know, I guess relationships will have to wait. Still it gives me some time to consider your problem without any other distractions," he added, finishing off the drink and placing the cup on the table. Getting down to business was typical of him.

Chapter 35

"Tils said that you needed to know what the thinking was with regard to Hitler or Heim after the war. My work, well you know the book I sent you, was done ten years ago and since then, as you can imagine, other stuff has come to the surface. What with official papers being released and so on, I've collated that which might relate to what you are after. I have to say that some of it has even surprised me on occasions, not having looked at the situation for some time, and it's made me think that I might need to update my book."

"*You're* surprised? What about us?"

"Before I start I just need to give you a sort of warning, a disclaimer if you like concerning what I can tell you. I do a lot of research, as you can imagine, and what I glean comes from many different sources. There is nothing secret about these sources and I expect you know some of them yourself. I research books, film, television documentaries, contemporary reports and so on. Now many of these have to be taken with a pinch of salt. Authors and film producers need to sell their productions, so a slant, perhaps something salacious, will always help."

"A bit like your own case?" said Tom.

"Well why not? If it is no more than a certain way of telling a story, providing it is factually correct, what's the problem?"

"Nothing I guess."

"It's the same with media reports and of course statements taken at the time, say the end of the war. Remember whoever is giving the statement may have a vested interest, the need to protect someone or themselves, the wish to implicate another individual. There will be different reasons for what they may say."

"The point I am making here is that what I know comes from this sort of environment, but it is as clear and accurate as I can make it, therefore, for your purposes it is just that, as accurate as I can be. OK?"

Tom nodded his confirmation.

"Right you remember from what I sent to you, that it was thought Hitler escaped from Berlin before the Russians got to the bunker. I found a report by a Soviet soldier that Berlin Boulevard, as he called it, had been cleared of rubbish at some time before his group arrived there and this guy and his comrades had seen a light aircraft take off from it. So surprised was he and the group at seeing this that they just let it happen, no firing or anything to try to bring it down, it just flew off!"

"Yes we got that from what you sent. Are you now of a different opinion?" asked Tom.

"No as far as I am concerned that is still relevant and highly probable. The guy would not have known about

Hitler's visitors, you recall Von Griem and Reitsch, so if you put both reports together then the aircraft leaving in that way is, in my humble opinion, pretty accurate."

"Now if you consider that it did happen in that way, as I said originally, and by what this witness saw, Adolf was well away before the bunker was stormed and there were only a few officers and secretaries left there including one who was probably a double used by Hitler. It was known that he had a number of lookalikes, throughout his time in office, for security purposes."

"Many such leaders still do," added Tom.

James continued. "Hitler, or perhaps even his double, although my own belief is the former, was known to have greeted a troop of young boy soldiers, on his birthday, in Berlin and so maybe assuming that report to be genuine he was in situ on 20th April. This must have given the thought that he was still around when Zhukov's men arrived some time later, but I suggest that he had gone by that stage, but to where? I think, as I said before, that he had flown to Italy. The aircraft was then flown back to Berlin to throw any searchers off the trail. Reitsch was such a fanatical individual that I have no doubt whatsoever that she would have been prepared to risk her life returning to Berlin to do that and ensure that Hitler was well away and his path covered up. I believe that Adolf and Eva were then smuggled, I guess you could use that word, out of Italy, either by a friendly government or a compliant and supportive organization, to a neutral country."

"Any idea where?" queried Tilly.

"Of course I have, what do you think?" replied James with a little impatience.

"I subsequently found a report that he had been seen in Sweden together with Eva Braun and that they had gone there because that was where their two children had been sent," he added triumphantly.

"Two children?" questioned Tom. "I never heard of him having kids."

"That's right, why would you?" James replied. "That certainly was news to me but not a shock. Remember the two of them had been together for a long while and pregnancy happens. The authorities would probably wish to keep something like that quiet for political purposes, you know, a father of children responsible for the deaths of millions of children? Not good," he continued, "a boy and a girl I understand, so just hold that thought for a while and I'll come back to it later. Right, let's assume he was in Scandinavia not Egypt or Italy or wherever, another tea sis?"

"OK. But don't you continue until I return," Tilly said making for the kitchen.

"Sure I'll wait. So are you two back together again or is this just a holiday?" his typically abrupt question catching Tom off guard.

"Well who knows?" he replied after a brief pause.

"Only you I expect."

"What are you pair saying?" demanded Tilly returning to the room.

"Just passing the time of day," said James winking at his sister.

He continued with his tale.

"I then made an interesting discovery from a US source; you know I have some American friends that I met when I was over there for a holiday? You remember

I had some time biking across the country, Route 66 and all that? Well a curious thing occurred at the end of the war. Obviously when the hostilities were declared to be over, some troops and ships and so on were still out there on duty or whatever, men still on the front line, not yet surrendered, you get the picture."

"Well one of those assets was a U-boat. Number U-977. Now dates are important here so if you let me finish the story then I'll answer questions later."

"Sounds like you're delivering a presentation at one of your meetings Jimmy," interjected Tom.

"Well do you want the story or not?" he replied impatiently.

Tom just shrugged his shoulders and sat back to listen.

"Now it is generally accepted that the war officially ended on May 8th, but before that date on May 2nd U-977 was sent out on patrol and was therefore still at sea on May 5th when Admiral Donitz, knowing that the war was in reality over and finished, ordered all surface ships and submarines to stand down. This particular vessel was north of Scotland at the time. The captain, a man named Schaffer, decided for some unknown reason to ignore Donitz' orders and not stand down by returning to Germany, but instead put into port on Holsenoy Island, near Bergen in Norway, which, of course is not far away from Sweden. When the boat arrived there, so he said later, he offered married men the choice of going on shore if they wished to, the rest of the crew would remain on board. A number apparently did take up that offer, or was it an order? We may never know, and after their disembarkation the Captain ordered the craft to sea once again, continuing to disobey orders."

"Disobeying orders eh?" Tom laughed, "that's got to be a first for any German officer."

"My point exactly. Why would the man do that? The war was over, every serving person would have one thing in mind, relief that they had survived, the wish to return home to their wives and families, certainly not the thought of travelling around five thousand miles away."

"Five thousand miles," said Tilly, "to where?"

"Listen and I'll tell you. Donitz was a very senior man to Schaffer, not the sort of guy that would take kindly to being ignored even if it was the end of the war. So how about this idea, that Schaffer was given other orders, this time from someone more senior to Donitz?"

"Who?"

"Your guess is as good as mine. My own conclusion is that he was ordered to port there and some sailors disembarked so that there was room to take on another cargo."

"What was that?" enquired Tilly, who was beginning to find the whole tale fascinating.

"Well isn't it obvious? It had to be Hitler, Eva, possibly the children, some of their aides and probably some wealth, looted gold or something like that. Then the U-boat sailed, it could have gone anywhere. And so it did and that was probably to a friendly South American state where the Hitler family disembarked. After leaving Norway, nothing more was heard until 17th August when the boat arrived at Mar del Plata in Argentina."

"Argentina," whistled Tom, "that's some idea. Where did that come from?"

"That's no idea," continued James, "American naval records show that it actually happened and having arrived in South America Schaffer surrendered to the Argentine navy who handed him, his crew and the boat over to the Yanks. The crew was sent to the US for interrogation on 22nd August and the craft was finally scuppered on 13th November. His story was that he didn't think that after the war German officers and members of the armed forces could expect to be well treated and so they wanted to escape. the flaw in that argument is obvious, why then did they surrender to the allies, albeit by way of the Argentine authorities."

"Again my thought is that the journey had achieved its purpose of spiriting away the Fuhrer and his family to a place well away from Europe and to where there was a well established German community within which they could hide. Don't forget some sightings of top Nazis had been made in South America and of course Eichmann was found there by the Israelis some years later as well as Cukrs."

"Yes I read that in your book, but Argentina specifically, alright I understand that there was some support for the Nazis over there, but that much support?"

"Certainly. In 1939, at the start of the hostilities, a German pocket battleship, The Graf Spee, was engaged in the South Atlantic. I expect you've heard of this, a film was made and many stories told of the event?"

"Yes."

"Well the sinking, or rather the scuttling of the vessel, is irrelevant to my point here, but after it went down the Captain, name of Langsdorff, committed suicide, military honour and all that and he was buried in La Chacarita cemetery in Buenos Aires. His funeral was a huge event with thousands of mourners, mostly from the German community, all giving Nazi salutes as the cortege went by. This was 1939, the war had barely started. Just think of the support given later, during and after the war, this was serious stuff."

"Well it certainly sounds as if he would be welcomed over there. So that's where he went, Argentina?" said Tom. "No wonder no-one could find him in Germany or Europe generally and it answers the queries you posed about the remains in the bunker. Jim this a good job you've done here."

"Thanks," replied James. "But the more I investigated the more I was personally intrigued by it all and so there is much more to consider."

"Look, can I just stop you for a moment?" Tilly ventured. "What you are telling us is the story about what happened to Hitler, right?"

"Sure," he replied, "isn't that what you want?"

"Well yes, but also we would like to get closer to the reason, if there is one, as to why Tom appears to be in some sort of danger. You know, why attempts have been made on his life and possibly in the long term what Joe has got to do with any of this?"

"Well if this isn't good enough for you..," he retorted.

"No, no it's great. Everything you've said so far is great. Please don't get the wrong idea, we are both very grateful for all your help but will there be a conclusion to all this that we can act upon?"

Tom looked over at Tilly. Why has she asked that? What is she after? he thought to himself. Or perhaps I'm becoming a little frustrated by all this, maybe she is right?

For the first time Tom thought that he had seen something different in Tilly's attitude to the problem. Some self interest, maybe? Another agenda, who knows?

"Look, let's have some lunch can we?" His comment designed to defuse what he thought was a developing hiatus between brother and sister.

"Good idea," replied James.

"OK," said Tilly not wishing to upset her brother at this point. I'll do some sandwiches and I guess that means this afternoon's plans are on hold?" she looked at Tom.

"I expect they are," he replied.

Chapter 36

Lunch seemed to placate James and the occasional glass of wine completed the restoration of tolerance between the three of them. The conversation moved from matters relative to the war and to a more general family involvement and James told them of his intention to visit their parents the next day and then to return to Oxford. He seemed interested in the situation as it was with the other two and Tom was surprised that he appeared genuinely pleased with a possible reconciliation.

Lunch finished but a bottle of wine left on the table heralded the next episode in James' tale and his next probable best seller. The more he revealed his findings the more certain he was of that.

'It's as if I'm bouncing ideas off an audience,' he thought to himself in a business like way.

"All right, back to the plot. I've thought about what you said earlier Tom, you know coming back from Australia, people following you, the attempts on both of your lives and so on and you may be pleased to know that I have drawn some conclusions. So before I continue let's deal with that as it is clear you have some concerns. For a start I think we can forget that it might be about finding some amount of treasure or whatever you wish to call it."

"A considerable amount was discovered after the war and in any case why would your life be threatened over something such as that? Think about it. If you know where anything is hidden and you are killed, then it will remain hidden, no use to anyone who has a plan to get rich. The only possible reason, if it is treasure, has to be if someone knew of your supposed connection with Hamann as Hitler's collector of valuables. Joe is the only one who knows of that."

"Plus Tilly, Steve and Mick," Tom added, "and of course you."

"Family?" he questioned. "Maybe, but works of art it is not and I also think we can forget the possibility of finding Hitler or Heim. Both of them would be very old by now and I guess would have died some time ago, although I can well understand the wish to take them if they are still here, especially with the likes of Weisenthal and Joe."

"Yes," replied Tom, "I think we had come to a similar conclusion as well, so what's left? There must be something very important to a lot of people to have this amount of aggravation?"

"Yes," continued James. "Let's see what we have left. I understand about finding Nazis in today's society and I have not yet discounted that and to some extent it may well relate to the existence of Nazi sympathizers or supporters, think about Josef Mengele for a moment.

He escaped to South America and lived there for many years apparently undetected, can that be possible? He was in contact with friends and family throughout this time, even making trips back to Europe occasionally. He was funded from Germany and wrote many letters. Is it possible that no-one could find him with all this activity going on? I can only surmise that little effort was put in to finding him and that must be down to the authorities, both German and Argentinian at the time, and remember he did not die until 1979, so we can guess that someone was protecting him for all that time and they are probably still around now either in person or by way of the organization of which they were a part. There are still a few of what I would call originals left alive and I understand that the right wing movement in Germany and other places is growing. It is known that they celebrate Hitler's birthday each year for instance and the anniversaries of other events important to them. More importantly there are supporters of the cause of a much younger age these days who join societies to keep the old beliefs going and they all need one very important commodity, a figurehead, you know someone or something to rally around. If there was such a figurehead they would go to great lengths to protect it, especially if it was really of profound value to their cause."

James stopped talking and looked at both of the members of his audience, a ploy he used many times in his professional life. Gauge the audience, are they with you? Do they want more? The answer was not long in coming.

"You have something in mind, haven't you?" said Tom. "I can tell by the way you're building this up, what is it?"

James stood up a satisfied look on his face, the audience was his. He walked across the room as if searching for something. Pouring another glass of wine he sniffed the liquid and tasted it, building up the tension and then placing the glass carefully back on the table he turned towards the others.

"You remember that I said before that there had been reports of Hitler being seen in Sweden with Eva and...."

"The children," interrupted Tom. "That's it isn't it, it's the children. They would still be alive, bloody hell that would be a rallying point for Nazis, wouldn't it? And well worth protecting at all costs. Jesus if that's what it is no wonder we've had all this, and Joe, I bet he came to that conclusion as well. He might think Hamann would know about that, he didn't tell us that did he?"

"I haven't finished yet," James continued, "and you are going off ahead, although you may be right in parts, just hang in there a while."

"You've got something else haven't you Jim?" Tilly said knowingly, "look whatever's the time let's get it all out so we can have a day or so to think about it obviously what's left must also be very interesting."

"It certainly is," replied James. "Let's do the rest of it."

"I wondered about the children and that angle may be part of it, but there was only ever one report of the existence of children that I could find. Having said that, I mentioned earlier that the State might well have been concerned at any publicity attached to the Fuhrer's children far more so than any other leading Nazi, because of course many of them did have families and children anyway. I thought that if they had had kids then earlier on the world might have known about it.

You know Hitler and Braun were often pictured together, seen on film that sort of stuff and if Adolf was convinced that he could win the war why would he not show off his children, the heirs to his future Germany, Aryan descendants of the master race? I'm not entirely sure about that one just yet, but let's not dismiss it either at this time." "I need to go off at a bit of a tangent for the next episode so bear with me."

Tom had quickly learnt that James was very thorough in his research and for anything that he might ask there would likely be an answer.

James continued. "At some stage you thought that perhaps the whole deal concerned Aribert Heim, didn't you? I can well understand that. Joe said his family died in Mathausen and we all know that Heim was a doctor at that camp. I looked at this angle, Doctor Death and all that, but came up with an interesting connection that expanded the thought of it and it seemed to take Heim out of the picture but brought into the picture someone else of a not dissimilar name, or at least a nickname. The Angel of Death. Now if Heim is not the issue, what is Joe's interest? And didn't you tell me that he wrote AH following one session that you had with him?"

"Yes he did and he also talked about his organization, one similar to that of Weisenthal indicating that Heim might have been a target," confirmed Tom.

"OK back to The Angel of Death. Josef Mengele was also a concentration camp doctor but he was at Auschwitz. Again a properly qualified medical man who became something else because of the war."

"Can I just say?" interjected Tom, "that Heim was only in the frame, as far as I can tell, because Joe's family was at Mathausen and Heim was, as you say, the medical man there. I know he disappeared and that Joe would have a good reason for hunting him down, but the more I spoke to Joe the more I thought he had another agenda in all of this, mmm interesting, sorry carry on Jim."

"The Mengele family were well known business people in Germany and in fact they still are and their son, Josef, was a doctor. It is believed by some people, and maybe correctly, that during his disappearance he was supported by the family who always knew where he was, again South America. During the war he worked as a doctor at Auschwitz-Birkenau, which was in Poland. Joe is Polish I believe, but as with Heim his main interest was the opportunity that the camp inmates gave him to work on his own experiments without sanction. The inmates were eventually to be exterminated so they were dispensable and he used them. His particular interest was with identical twins because he could test two different theories at the same time. Are you all right if I talk about this Tilly," he asked, obviously sensing his sister's growing discomfort.

"Fine," was the unconvincing reply.

He nodded.

"Mengele would inject eyes, for example, to see if he could reproduce the colour blue which is what the Ayran race that Hitler wanted would have. I won't go into the detail any further of what he did as it is not particularly relevant to this story, but you just need to know that he was a terrible man and someone else who disappeared and was hunted after the war. At the end of the war he was captured along with thousands of others, soldiers and so on, but bluffed his way out in spite of having an SS identification mark under his arm. He escaped through Bolzano in Italy and with the probably innocent assistance of the Red Cross he left Europe at Genoa taking a boat to Argentina."

James was now well into his presentation, walking around the room, animated as if he was at one of his conferences. He knew that the trick to keeping your audience with you and not dozing away was this constant movement, but there was no chance that the listeners on this occasion would be lost, they were clearly enthralled by his story. His continual emphasis that what he was saying was fact, or at least, based on reliable reports produced around the time, seemed to be involving Tom in the history of the events. He and Tilly shifting in their seats as another revelation was delivered, looking at each other, occasional head movements as they gauged the others reaction. No this audience was there to the end.

He poured some wine from the bottle and took a drink from his glass, licked his lips and continued.

"Argentina was led at the time by Juan Peron who was a very right wing leader and as such supported the SS and anything relative to Germany and, as I said before, there was a large German presence tolerated in his country for that very reason. The tolerance was not only political but financial as the guests in his country were of some substance, supported by their families back in Germany or even the recipients of looted works of art. Whilst in Argentina Mengele started a medical business with the financial support of his family and led a reasonably untroubled life in the community. In fact in the 50's he started to use his own name again so sure was he that he would not be caught and some people believe that he might have had help from the German embassy.

We know that the Jewish intelligence was covertly looking for him over there."

"Do we know what became of him?" queried Tilly.

"Well," replied James, "there was, as you might guess, speculation throughout the time, sightings and the like. Then there came a report that he had died in South America, Brazil to be exact, in 1979 but there was no evidence at the time. However investigations continued and finally a body was discovered. Some said it was him and others said that it wasn't but eventually, as time went on, it became possible to undertake DNA tests and lo and behold they proved that the body was in fact Mengele. His family seemed to have known about it all the time as it was they who later confirmed that he had died from a stroke."

"Well he can't be what Joe is after then," interrupted Tom. "So what's the deal then with Mengele, however terrible he might have been?"

"Let me continue," said James, "all will become clear in a minute."

My investigation shows that other doctors escaped to Argentina with Mengele, many of them known to him through his work as a medical man back in Germany and they again worked with him in the medical business which he started over there.

This time there were no live guinea pigs as you might say, to enable there to be any experimentation, although you may have heard that a number of children were produced in Brazil that could have been the end result of some breeding program, who knows. However there was always going to be one group of people who would volunteer for medical research and they may well have made their way to the doctor and his colleagues only too willing and prepared to pay for him to practice on them."

Tom and Tilly cast a glance to each other.

"Have you ever heard of cryonics?" James continued but now at a slightly slower more deliberate pace, clearly he was coming to the climax of all this work and research.

"Yes I think I have," replied Tom. "It's some sort of medical procedure relative to freezing isn't it?"

"Well, something of that sort," James conceded turning another page in his notes, "but today in simple terms it means, and I quote 'the preservation of legally dead humans at a very low temperature in the hope that, at sometime in the future, there can be found a cure for whatever incurable disease they might have had and so they can be restored to life and health,' end quote. These days the ideas are possibly no more than interesting and any activity in the practice is very severely controlled, hence the words 'legally dead in the first place'. No-one really knows whether the procedure works and certainly as far as I know no one has been frozen, if I can use the word, and restored to life or health with some cure being available for their illness. Apparently, so I am told, there are actually quite a number of people in this frozen state as we speak presumably waiting for their cure and the restoration to the living."

"Anyone that I might have heard of?"

"Well, rumour has it that Walt Disney undertook the procedure. I've no idea if his body is still in this state as he was supposed to have died in 1966."

"So how did this sort of thing come to the fore at that time?" queried Tilly, "it seems a modern concept, are you saying that it was known about then?"

"Well yes of course. Remember the concentration camps, and what went on in them? There were opportunities to experiment and freezing was just such an experiment."

"Why?"

James blew out through his pursed lips, he couldn't understand why it was not obvious.

"The German armed forces would be fighting on many fronts and in many different parts of the world. The army would be at the Russian front, soldiers fighting in very cold conditions, the navy would be in the north Atlantic, sailors might at some time be in the freezing ocean and the Luftwaffe, well they were always trying to fly higher, above the enemy undetected and it is certainly cold up there. Now if any man succumbed to the cold, in any one of these arenas he might die without the enemies assistance and that would be a waste of manpower, so they thought that if it was possible to restore to life people who had frozen to death, then they needed to be able to do that."

"So in the camps they would freeze prisoners and then see if they could unfreeze them?"

"Sis you've got it. When the various camps were opened up, equipment, baths and so on were discovered and camp inmates who had survived reported such activities. People placed in baths of cold, iced water, left to suffer hypothermia until dead and then restored to life, as it were."

"And that's where this, cryonics, did you call it, came from?"

"Exactly. Now back to Mengele in Argentina. It is thought that one of his partners in the business brought with him from the camps ideas along these lines. I've not been able to find his name for sure at this time, although I have a thought and I'll tell you that shortly, but suppose that this procedure was being tried. Anyone would want it to work and if you had an incurable ailment you'd want it to be tried on you wouldn't you? I certainly would if there was any chance to live longer and there wouldn't be many who would turn down the opportunity. So what are we talking about here? Bearing in mind that this is a theory as far as I am concerned but with the big thought in the background that as Joe has been cultivating you over the years, and you have had serious aggravation from unknown potential murderers recently, I might actually be not far away from the truth, my guess is this."

"Mengele's partner developed, from the freezing idea, some real advances in cryonics during the 50's and he would have experimented on willing individuals in Argentina at that time. I know, and the world knows, that a number of senior Nazis were there then. Remember Eichman was captured by Mossad, Mengele himself was there and maybe the big one...Did Hitler get there on U977?"

"Now some of my research involved looking at photographs or even film taken during the war, newsreels as I suppose they would be then, and I found one that was very interesting. You recall I said earlier that Hitler had met with some boy troops on the occasion of his birthday? Well there is film of the event and he can be seen shaking hands with the boys. I know that the films were doctored for propaganda purposes but unfortunately for the censors they missed cutting out one vital and very important piece of information that was seen on the film. As the Fuhrer was greeting the lads and shaking hands, his left hand was held behind his back and it was shaking, the tremors? I believe he had Parkinson's, an incurable illness, certainly at that time. And if he did have it and he eventually became very ill, did he submit to freezing awaiting a cure? And if so, is he still lying frozen somewhere awaiting his rebirth?"

James sat down, his presentation finished for the moment. The punch-line had been delivered and it was now for the audience to make the next move, finishing off the wine he placed his wad of notes on the table.

There was silence in the house. Both Tom and Tilly felt at that moment as if *they* were frozen. They held each other's hands. This couldn't be right, could it? They seemed to know what the other was thinking, is this thing possible, James was known for his fantastic plans and ideas, but could he really be serious, joking, no this was so no joke, he wouldn't joke about something like this, he meant it. They could see in his face that this was serious.

Five or so minutes passed without a word, without the need to say a word. each within their own thoughts of what this meant, what were the implications and what was going to happen now or indeed what was happening now, in Germany, in England or Argentina, was Hitler's body waiting to be found.

"You said you had an idea of the doctor's name," Tilly said finally. "Are you going to let us know?"

"I already know," whispered Tom before her brother could answer and anticipating the next few words he remained silent allowing him to continue if he wished.

"You know, what do you mean, how could you possibly know?" replied Tilly.

The words came from Tom in a way that he could not believe. It was so strange that he knew he would never say anything as profound ever again.

His voice was hesitant and weak, unusual for such a strong willed and powerful man. "When I was regressed by Joe for the first time he asked me some background questions, probably so any facts could be checked with known history and I asked him to let me know if I had said anything that would involve me, my life or my family as it might have been before. I must have given him the names of my parents as after the session he told me what I had said."

"He told me my father's name Artur. Artur Hamann…AH… that was what Joe wrote down wasn't it? Not Hitler or Heim. The AH was my father, and by profession he was a doctor."

He looked at James. "That's the guy isn't it, AH, that's the man who undertook this freezing experiment? That's my father. That's the doctor who froze Hitler!"

James nodded as he placed his notes on the table, his presentation finished.

Chapter 37

It was Monday; James had visited his family over the weekend and had returned to Oxford. Tom and Tilly had spent the Sunday in contemplative mood. James' suspicions and conclusions needed some serious consideration and a walk over the hills might help Tom thought. Tilly had learnt from their previous relationship that silence was his preferred way of dealing with situations like this and so accompanying him on his walk was all she could do at this time, that and hope a conclusion would be reached soon. They would be expected to contact Steve and Mick in order to progress any proposed plan of action, except that Tom appeared to have no plan. He remained quiet, shocked to some degree by James revelations, unable to quite come to terms with the belief that it was none other than his father who had ministered to Hitler at the end and that somewhere in the world the body still lay frozen. The thinking time had however produced an unexpected thought in his head.

What James had told them seemed very comprehensive, very exact and definite. How had he produced such an expansive report in such a short time, after all, Tilly had only telephoned him a couple of days earlier and here he was with such a detailed report. Had he, by coincidence, been researching this very subject recently? He had mentioned a book, but this was too much to accept. He considered that James had all this information on hand, just waiting for a call from his sister.

"Tilly," he ventured, "how do you think your brother had all this stuff on Hitler and my father and so on just at the time when we needed it?"

"What do you mean?"

"Well you phoned him and he appeared within a day armed with everything we ever wanted to know. How did he have all the research? It was as if he expected us to call him."

"I told you he was writing a book."

"No I think the implication was that the information might help him to write a book in the future, not just at this time."

"Well I don't know, maybe it was a coincidence, he's always researching something. Look all I did was telephone him, what's the problem?"

Tom was surprised by Tilly's response. Since the two of them had met again, she had seemed happy with his company; pleased to be back together, what was this reaction all about? He let it ride.

"No problem," he murmured and returned to his thoughtful state, but not completely satisfied with her answer and less so with her attitude.

Chapter 38

Joe had left hospital by now although he had not made any contact with them. Many of Tom's thoughts and deliberations had centered on him, his real motives and connection in all of this and he knew that it would be necessary to make contact with him again as time went on. Was the fact that Joe had made no contact himself a sign of being disinterested, or a double bluff? He was beginning to suspect everyone, even Tilly.

They were sitting in the Golden Eagle, conversation was light, and clearly the report that James had given to them a few days before was still at the forefront of the minds of them both. Tilly decided to progress the matter.

"You know Tom, I think that Joe is the key to all this."

"How come?"

"Well, Steve is your brother, do you really think he intends you any harm? Isn't it always with Steve what can he get out of it, he would never cause you any serious grief would he?"

"He had an affair with you, it cost me my marriage, isn't that serious grief enough?"

"OK, I accept that and I know that you were hurt, although it was as much my fault as his, but I mean there was no intention to harm you physically then and through all this latest stuff, has there been a time when you were worried for your safety?"

Tom nodded. "Presumably you are accepting the fact that the attacks on me and you, don't forget, had nothing to do with him?"

"Yes I am," she continued finishing off her drink.

"Mick is a good friend to both of you and apart from being efficient at his job as well as a tough soldier I think he's a decent bloke. Also what would either of them have to gain from what happened sixty years ago, neither was alive then, all they know is what you or Joe has said or what was found in the records. No it's got to be Joe that has some involvement here that we haven't seen yet."

"OK let's explore that angle," said Tom finally coming into Tilly's one way conversation. "What do we know about him?" he stood up and made for the bar, "same again?"

She nodded.

Tom went to the bar; he could see Tilly through the mirror behind the counter. It was as if she was looking around expecting someone to join them. He took his time, watching her, wondering if their relationship was going anywhere, he found himself thinking about that very often.

She caught sight of him in the mirror looking at her and smiled, at the same time smoothing back her hair and crossing her legs in a provocative fashion. He smiled back. 'I know why I fancied that girl' he thought returning to the table. 'I'm just becoming too suspicious of everyone'. He sat down and took a long drink of his pint at the same time placing his hand on her knee. "What were we saying?"

"What do we know about Joe?" she replied quickly returning to the subject. "Look only what he has told us, let's look at that first. He said his name was Ciemny although I seem to remember he called himself Schacht as a professional name, so for a start we can look up the records, get Mick to help, that's his forte, looking up records. If the names are not too common we may find someone with either name from back then who may be connected to him or his family. He said that he was from Linz and also had a connection with Mathausen so we can check up on that, and I bet that if he was running an organization along the lines of Weisenthal then there has to be something concerning that on record. I also recall when we went to the hospital that he said that he had some sort of clearance with the authorities, perhaps that's worth a look. My Dad used to say that he found those spooks to be pretty sloppy on some occasions it would be good to confirm what they think they know about this guy."

"That's right your Dad was in intelligence at some time wasn't he? Hey he may be able to help. I bet he still has some connections, you know. He knows where the bodies are buried and so on, and might be able to call in a favour or two."

"Let's get a meeting with Steve and Mick as soon as possible and I'll speak to the old man, we'll keep Joe out of this for the time."

She finished her drink quickly.

"I'll have another if you don't mind," she concluded.

Tom walked to the bar. "Same again," he ordered.

He waited for the drinks at the bar looking through the mirror again.

'I think that when this is all over, whatever it is, I'm not returning to Oz, I'm staying here with her' he mused.

Chapter 39

A couple of days more passed by and during the time Tilly had spoken with her father and Tom had had a chance to contact Steve and Mick. They had arranged a meet well away from Hereford and Tom had suggested that each arrive separately at the appointed time and place. He had a feeling that they may still be under surveillance, even though he had removed the motorcyclist from the equation, and this arrangement could be monitored with a lookout just away from the meeting place and with someone watching the arrival of each of them from a distance.

A pub was chosen up on the Clee Hills, one that they had often visited in the past. It was at the top of the hills just through the small village and was approached by turning left before the cattle grid. A parking space for cars had been provided along the main road near the turning and stopping there would leave a hundred metre walk along the lane. This public car park afforded spectacular views over the valley and was well used by walkers to the area during the day and, as Tom recalled, couples during the evening. It was arranged that each would arrive from a different direction and they would drive directly to this spot. Tom and Tilly would be there first and with Tom walking along to the venue, the other could hide within the scrub just along the lane, keeping the car park in sight. If they were all being watched whilst in Hereford, this plan would also help to split up the watchers, who might, as a result be more easily recognised. The day was set for midweek when trade at the pub might be lighter.

On the morning of the meet Tilly had spoken with her father who had managed to collate some information for them so that their conversations could be full and with all the possible known facts. On leaving the house they drove towards the main road and turned left in the direction of Ludlow. Just outside the town they would turn right, the road taking them directly to the planned rendezvous. They arrived at the car park. The view was beautiful especially on a day such as this, no breeze and clear skies. The air was fresh and Tom got out of the car took a deep breath and looked around the valley. After a few minutes they made their way to the meeting place, a small country public house, little changed for over a hundred years. Tom entered the front door directly into the lounge, it was empty.

'Good', he thought to himself.

Tilly, as planned, walked a little way further along the road and then turned right onto a sheep trail towards a small clump of vegetation. This would offer a sight of the car park and hide her from view at the same time.

Steve and Mick would leave Hereford in separate vehicles; each taking a separate route so as to arrive from different directions. By the time they reached the place, Tilly would be well hidden and able to observe their movements and those of any possible followers.

Steve was the first to arrive. Tom could see him walking along the road, smoking a cigarette as usual, the smoke following on behind in the still air. He arrived at the venue and stood outside the door for a few minutes, taking in the view over the valley and also ensuring that no-one had followed him. Flicking the cigarette end on to the gravel path and grinding his heel into it, he went inside.

"Morning brother," he said casually, "nice day for it, whatever it is. I see I'm the first to arrive."

"Well after us actually," Tom replied tersely, "let's hope Mick isn't too long in coming."

"Here he is now," said Steve looking through the window at his friend strolling along towards them.

Mick walked straight into the pub where the others were waiting, no glance back in case he was being followed, always less cautious than his companions and somewhat conspicuous in his shorts and tee shirt.

"Glad you dressed for the occasion," said Tom.

"Well you know me, nice day, SAS casual uniform."

"What are you guys having?" asked Tom.

"The usual for me," replied Mick looking around the lounge, which was empty of any other drinkers.

"Where's Tilly?" he questioned, surprised that she seemed not to be there.

"Mine's a pint please," added Steve.

"OK, she'll be here in a moment," replied Tom ordering the drinks and gesturing for the others to sit down. He then brought the drinks over to the table, looking out of the window as he did so and seeing Tilly coming along the road.

"Here she is now," he said as the door opened and she entered.

"Everything alright?"

"Yeah, all seems to be OK," she replied. "I reckon I would have seen any other people over the period when you got here, so I guess that our meeting should be secret enough."

The others looked at each other with curiosity.

"What's that all about?" queried Mick.

"I was just keeping a look out to see if you were followed, but nothing seems to have parked up down there and no-one has walked along the road after you, so I should think that we are alone for the moment. Which way did you come here?"

"I came through Cleobury," said Steve.

"And I came through Caynham."

"OK you blokes," commenced Tom, "now that we are all here and seem to be away from the unwanted, let's get on with the meeting. I just want you to listen to what I have to say, with questions at the end if you don't mind."

The others nodded.

"You know that something strange has been going on since I was visited by Steve when I was in Australia and persuaded by him to return to Hereford, and from what I can see, we all seem to be involved in some way in whatever is happening. Clearly you will be aware that Tilly and I have got back together and so are spending much of our time with each other and are therefore talking about this matter more or less on a constant basis. As we talked we looked at the position of everyone connected and finally, you Steve and Mick. I'm glad to say that we have probably eliminated you both from our considerations concerning who are the bad guys although your motives are still not certain as far as I am concerned."

Both shuffled in their seats at Tom's blunt assessment of their involvement and they looked quizzically at each other.

"By that I mean that I was greatly puzzled as to the reason Steve came all the way across the world, probably at great expense, to find me and bring me back. I know Steve was and probably still is a bit of a lad, you know after the main chance. I've known him all of my life. No problem with that really but I didn't know what he was after here, he wasn't telling me and it irritated me. Eventually I guessed that it was probably the looted wealth and I bet it still is if there is any to be had at the end of it all."

Steve grunted.

"Mick had me even more puzzled. I know how he came to the conclusion about my regression and with what he found from the released archives he could have had a great find and that would have helped his career, but why. We only ever sign on to the forces for a limited period so what is this, with the career? I probably still don't know for certain. However what I do know is that whatever the reasons, selfish or otherwise, you most likely had nothing to do with the attacks on me or Tilly and so I have dismissed any serious intent from you both and I know therefore that it must be someone or something else."

"Well, thanks for the vote of confidence," Mick replied glancing at Tilly who was peering out of the window.

"What I am going to tell you now will be like something of a story, but I am trusting you to keep quiet because it may not be anything but speculation, but if it is what's behind all of this then we are going to blow history open. Someone may not wish for that to happen, it could be very dangerous and I mean *very* dangerous for all concerned."

"Hang on some-one's coming," warned Tilly, still looking out of the window, as the lounge door opened.

"Morning blokes," said the visitor, "oh and lady."

"Morning they replied in unison.

The man was in his thirties with dishevelled sandy hair; his jeans were old and his jumper torn.

"Just time for a pint before I fetch a few sheep off the hills," he added, "you people on a day trip or something?"

"Something," replied Tom.

"Ah," said the man realizing that his presence was not welcomed and he retreated to the bar leaving the group alone again.

Tom proceeded.

"As I said I, or we, have not been able to square the circle here. What is it that I have, or know, that is so important for others in this country or even the wider world, excluding you pair? I may know the whereabouts of looted works of art which could make some people very wealthy indeed and it may be that I would be able to give names and whereabouts of people wanted for war crimes or even have information that could seriously embarrass governments that might have, at the time, been responsible for ensuring the safe passage of criminals out of Germany and so on. Some of those individuals may still be alive, but reputations of important organizations could be sullied, such as the Red Cross or the Catholic Church."

"The Catholic Church?" asked Mike, a devout Catholic himself.

"Absolutely, it is reported that one of the worst officials of the Church, was Bishop Hudal. He gave absolute support to Hitler and the Nazis and during his life, helped German officers, including war criminals, escape the justice that was due to them by getting them out of Europe to places with no extradition arrangements. I found this information in one of my books."

Tom continued.

"Tilly contacted her brother, James and he paid us a visit last weekend. Apparently he is writing some sort of book about the Second World War and she thought that he might have some useful information. As we are talking frankly here, I have to add that I thought it a serious coincidence that he could have some facts or whatever that relate to what is going on with me at this time. However I don't suggest that he is involved, but you know me, I don't think that there ever was such a thing as a coincidence. Things happen for a reason although we probably won't know what that is at the time, only later. They call it hindsight and maybe one day I'll know why he had the information so readily at hand. His book research, I'll call it that for the moment, seems to link me with some well known names from the war. Steve, before I go on how, about another round?"

"Sure," said Steve, getting up and making his way to the counter.

"Nice place up here," said Mick during the interlude.

"Eh, you said you'd never been here before," queried Tom.

"Did I? Well I guess I must have forgotten."

"Hmm," Tom uttered.

Steve returned with the drinks.

For the next half an hour Tom related the story which James had told him a few days before. How Hamann seemed to have been connected with Hitler, how Hitler escaped the Berlin bunker and made his way to South America and how Artur Hamann had most likely been the doctor to perform Cryonics on the terminally ill German leader.

Steve and Mick remained silent, hypnotised by the tale and how it seemed to be feasible.

"Well," Tom said finally, "that's where we are. My question to you is what do we do about it?"

"If any of this is remotely true, then you are correct, Tom, world history is going to change and if Adolf's body is still somewhere in the world today, then God only knows what could happen," said Steve solemnly but with a gravity that impressed even his brother.

"So you've given up on the treasure hunt?" asked Tom.

"Well for the time being I can't see us getting very far in that direction so, yes, I suppose I have, it seems to be a non starter at the moment," he replied somewhat dejectedly.

"I've spoken to my Dad about Joe," added Tilly, "and as soon as he is able to come up with anything then I'll tell all of you what he has discovered. I had hoped that he might have had something to say for us today, but Joe seems to be a more interesting character than any of us thought, so it's taking a little more time to get to the bottom of it. As I've already said, I reckon that the solution may lie in that direction and there's nothing that my father has said so far that has made me think any differently."

"Ok," said Mick finally. "Let's assume that he is the man. How did he come to get beat up the other day, you visited him in hospital didn't you, did he look like he had had a beating?"

"Well possibly," replied Tom. "In any case he had some guys with him, he said they were security and I have to say that, at the time, they seemed like they were."

Tom thought for a while.

"Could that have all been fixed, I wonder? You know, to make us think that it was all genuine. Come to think about it now I look back, it did seem a bit too easy. They were too relaxed for spooks. Government intelligence usually acts tough, thinking that they are, but they didn't do that did they Tils?"

"No I think you could be right, I noticed that as well," she replied. "OK let's assume he is involved in something somehow, we've got to get closer to what it is. Like I said, I've asked my Dad to look up some things for me. As soon as I get anything back from him I'll let you all know and we can take it from there. I can see that we are going to need another meeting with Joe so that Tom can have another regression where he asks about his family, his father and what in particular, he did in the war. See how Joe deals with that, because if AH is Hamann's father and he showed a particular interest in that when you saw him last time, then we may find out something more during another session. If you are in on it Mick you can hear the words, you know translate the

German and so on. If Joe does have an interest we could get a line from the answers. What do you think?"

"Good plan, he's going to be careful how his question and answer session goes even if he doesn't suspect anything with regard to us. Tom, can you pretend to be under the hypnotic influence? Because if you can then we could get more from the session," said Mick.

"I'm not sure if I can. I occasionally speak in German and I can't do that unless I'm hypnotized."

"Alright back to square one. I'll be there and I'll have to get the conversation. OK when are we going to do this?"

"I'll speak with him tomorrow. Tils should have the info from her old man and I'll tell Joe I've got some interest in my family as was. He shouldn't think that too surprising. I would guess after all he knows my feelings about this regression, how it made me feel about things. I'll be as normal as possible and see how it goes. Right that's got to be it for now. I'll let you know when we are on for the session next time, so let's get going."

Chapter 40

The group dispersed each with their own thoughts on the day, what they would be looking at as time went by and what was left in it for each of them? As Tom had said, what was it that each individual was after, would it be the same having heard James' tale?

The following day Steve's phone rang, it was Tom." Hi brother any news?" he asked.

"Yes I've spoken with Tils' Dad and he gave me some good info and so I've contacted Joe and arranged for another session with him."

"What had he got to say?"

"Well, he asked me why and what more I was after. I have to say I noticed a bit of surprise in his voice. I said that I had had a thought that I, as Hamann, would like more information about my personal life during the war, you know, who was my mother and father, where did they come from and what did they do during the war and so on?"

"Did he go for it?"

"Well as I said he sounded surprised but he said that was no problem. After all Steve, if he was in on this then he would want to have another go wouldn't he, he'd want to know what I might say and probably more importantly what I might know. I doubt that he would wish to encourage our interest in other things by refusing."

"When is the session, I'll need to contact Mick?"

"Next Wednesday. I'll contact you just before and I will bring Tils, you bring Mick. It shouldn't raise any suspicions with Joe if everyone's there; after all we've been at his place all together before."

"OK, I'll wait for your call."

Tom put the phone down and turned to Tilly.

"Right that's all arranged, now we just need to think about what your Dad said so we will know how to play it. I want to try to get Joe to give something away although he has seemed pretty cool in the past and he's never let anything slip as far as I have noticed."

Chapter 41

Wednesday arrived. Tom had given Steve the time of arrival at the house and it was confirmed that Mick was available also. Tom and Tilly would arrive separately.

They had had plenty of time to discuss what her father had found out concerning Joe either as Ciemny or Schacht or as principal of an organization similar to that operated by Weisenthal.

He had in fact found nothing that could confirm or deny the claims made and that could be taken two ways. If as Joe had said, his family had been exterminated at the camp it would always be difficult to prove. Little or no records were ever kept. The comments relating to Heim were a matter of historical record and so it was information available to anyone. The name Schacht had been found as being that of an individual described as 'Germany's Financial Wizard'. He was captured by the Fifth Army close to the Italian border in 1945. Under interrogation he had said that he could not believe Hitler was dead, either that was the ranting of a Nazi who thought the Fuhrer indestructible or a man who knew something else concerning an escape plan perhaps? Tilly's father had discovered some information relating to a parallel organisation to that operated by Simon Weisenthal. It appeared to be a poorly run group, a collection of Polish nationals supposedly concerned with bringing to justice Nazis who operated in Poland during the occupation. It was not clear from where it received its funding, who its principals were, or what success they may have had. No mention of Joseph Ciemny or Schacht was found. In spite of a number of attempts through the calling in of favours, the British Military Intelligence was conspicuous by its lack of help. Joe had said that he was under their protection and receiving support when in hospital and earlier during the alleged tracking down of Nazis, but they were singularly unhelpful when it came to giving information as to what was their role in all this. Tilly's Dad took this as some sort of success as it could be interpreted that here was something of such note that no-one could be encouraged to speak out. Only a matter of the gravest importance would warrant such silence or there was nothing at all in it and so nothing to say. Who could tell?

"Well your Dad was not able to come up with anything definite about Joe so I guess we are going to have to encourage him out into the open," said Tom finally. "If he is the key to this then we have to force his hand."

"I agree. He must be the main man, nothing else fits," she replied.

The group arrived at Joe's house and they were ushered in by him in his usual affable way.

"Hi Joe," said Tom. "How are you? You're looking OK after your incident. Now the blood has been cleared away you look pretty clear of damage."

"Guess I was lucky," he replied. "If my neighbour had not come out of the house at that very minute it could have been much worse." Tom and Steve exchanged glances.

"Does anyone know what it was all about?" enquired Steve.

"No. The police can only assume that I disturbed an intruder when I went outside that evening."

"But an intruder would just wish to get away, wouldn't he, not spend time giving you a beating?"

"I'm sorry, I can tell you no more than that," replied Joe quietly, but in a way that indicated that he would answer nothing more on the matter. "Let's go inside."

They made their way through the hallway towards the consulting room, as it was called. Tom at the rear lingered for a few seconds looking up the stairs as he passed. The same odour greeted his nostrils and the faint humming which he had detected before was still there. Moving through to the next room Joe closed the door firmly behind them.

Tom explained Mick's role in the session that he would record much of the German dialogue concerning Hamann's family tree so that they could know of it afterwards.

"Out of interest why this concern about your family?" queried Joe. "In the past I remember you have mentioned the name of your father, Artur wasn't it?"

"Well no great concern really," replied Tom shrugging his shoulders, "it's just that I discussed with Tilly recently the things that you have told me I said under regression.

Now I appreciate the importance of discovering Nazis, especially to your goodself, and of course I don't want to ignore that part of it, but that is for you to follow up, through your organization, and I am quite happy to be regressed however many times you wish, if it will help you. It's just that I have started to think about my own past and my life outside of being Hamann the Nazi. What was I like earlier? What were my grand-parent's names? Did I have a wife, children, brothers or sisters, that sort of thing, you know where was I born? Where did I live and so on? Yes I have said my father's name although it means little to me, and even then I don't know what specifically did he do for a living. Where is he buried, personal stuff such as that I guess. But wait a moment; it's very thoughtless of me. Joe I'm sorry. These are things are for me and here I am asking you to spend your valuable time on it. Look if it's not convenient."

"Thomas it is not a problem I am more than happy to help you if I can. I told you that I obtained information from you concerning my own particular interest. You recall my family and Aribert Heim, so the least I can do is to repay you in some way and if knowledge of your family is important to you at this time then fine."

Joe seemed prepared to help, based on what Tom had said and so the regression would again be undertaken. The room was just as before but as Tom made his way to the chair passing by the large table, he noticed that another item had been placed on it since the previous visit. He paused whilst passing the table and glanced at the extra book, a large leather bound and gold tooled volume. He touched the cover gently with his fingers and ran his palm across the sumptuous tactile leather, turning the book towards him as he did so. He read the title. 'Mein Kampf von Adolf Hitler'. A surprised expression crossed his face and he glanced at Joe who had been watching him with interest. He nodded at Tom.

"Know your enemy," he commented. There was no reply. Tom sat down and waited for the session to begin. Mick sat to one side of the pair and as the session progressed and the questioning and answering continued, he made notes for future reference.

As usual the subject was allowed to recover over a few minutes and the three of them returned to where the others had waited.

"I hope you got what you wanted from that," said Joe, "any other time just call on me. Tom you've been a great help to me in my research so if there is anything more that I can do for you just ask. It will be my pleasure to assist."

"No problem," he replied. "I'm just sorry we haven't helped to find any Nazis for you, but there's still time I guess."

"Well time runs out, people grow old and die and the secrets remain buried," replied Joe. "Who knows what we might yet find between us."

They left the house and Joe closed the front door, leaving them standing together on the drive.

"What did you make of that last comment?" asked Mick to no-one in particular.

"Interesting," said Steve. "It was as if there was something to know and he was challenging us to find it or am I being too suspicious of the guy?"

"No I don't think you are," said Tilly.

"You're pretty sure that there's something here, aren't you?" Tom added.

"Yes," she replied.

Chapter 42

It was early evening, nearly dark and the still air of the last few days remained with them. A light precipitation had started as they made their way to The Cellars for something of a debrief of the morning session with Joe. During the day they had had all time to think it over, consider what could come of it, in particular with regard to his attitude in dealing with the request to explore Hamann's family. If what James had said concerning Artur Hamann, the medical man, had any truth or significance and Joe knew of the connection, then surely he would give something away. Mick had made copious notes of Tom's conversation under Hypnosis and he was studying them with some serious intent. The group had all noted Joe's last comment and as they had been looking for something that he might have said that would go along with their current thinking on the matter, there was no doubt that it seemed significant.

"Well it may have meant something or nothing at this stage," commented Tom, "but at this point I want to know what I said in my regression."

"OK," said Mick, "let's go through my notes. You asked me to give Joe some questions to ask and I gave them to him on the basis that any answers given would be relevant to the information that you wanted to have in order to identify your family, or at least the family of Hamann. He seemed OK with that, you know, nothing was queried and he just seemed to ask the questions in the usual way. I'll give you the answers that you gave and then I'll make a couple of observations that I noticed, you may feel they are significant. Are you alright with that?"

"Sure."

"The first question concerned your family. Your father, although you already know this, was Artur Hamann and your mother was Freda, you had two siblings. Heinrich was the eldest and he was killed at the Russian front in forty three, he had no children. You were the next and then you had another brother also named Artur presumably after your father, again a soldier. At the time of your death, it seems odd to say that phrase, your death; he was not married and had no children. Finally you're also not married and no children.

So that means that in total there were four from your family in the military. You already know something of your own career, your elder brother died earlier on in the war as I have said. Your father was interesting and if anything caused Joe to, how shall I say, show a reaction, when he was talking about him. Apparently your father was a medical doctor before the war and he volunteered to work for the army in the field as such. This meant that he was involved in many conflicts, you know as one of the usual medics, patching up wounded in the field and so on. He himself got wounded, withdrawn and sent back behind the lines. When he recovered after some months back in Germany, he was discharged as unfit. He joined a medical laboratory and started some research, although when Joe progressed the subject, you didn't seem to know exactly what that was."

"If James' investigations are anything like accurate, then he thought it was Cryonics." Tom commented. "Could it have been that, what do you think Mick?"

"Well, my thought here is that if it was and the answer was significant, then Joe might not have wanted that known and I have to say that some questions did seem to be asked in such a way that a particular answer would be given, I noticed that on a number of occasions, or at least so it seemed to me, I could be wrong though. Anyway let me continue as the next bit is particularly important.

Your father was a Medical Doctor, he had the same name as your younger brother so let's not get confused with the two. If we assume Jim to be correct I guess he would have identified the right Artur by age, so we must believe at this stage that the man mentioned by him was the father and not the brother. Now here we have another possible significance. You wanted to know where your father worked but Joe did not get you to say where that was, only that it was an internment camp, for that I interpret a concentration camp. That's of interest because earlier we found out that he was discharged from the army and so must have been working in a civilian establishment. Now again, if James is correct then he must have returned to Government employment and a good bet would be Auschwitz where we find Mengele. If so they would certainly know each other and you recall that James said Mengele encouraged other medical men that he knew to work with him in Argentina."

"How do you come to that conclusion? It could have been any camp, Joe's Mathausen for instance."

"Let me continue. Your family grew up in Gunzburg, Bavaria. Now that might have some significance as again the question was asked in an odd way and I thought he looked a bit disappointed at your answer, but it is significant as far as our business is concerned, as I happen to know that Mengele was born in Gunzburg, his family is well known and so there is every chance that the Hamanns were acquainted with the Mengeles. I accept the Auschwitz connection might be tenuous but are we not thinking the unthinkable every time now? Tom that was all you seemed to be able to recall but there is some interesting stuff there and in particular the Mengele connection both in Germany and, if James was anywhere near the mark, in South America also."

Tom sat a while; clearly he was digesting this information.

"I need to think about this in regard to what Tils' brother said," he finally commented. "With all this information I think I am beginning to get a picture and if we assume Joe to be more involved in my personal situation, rather than as a Nazi hunter, then that picture is becoming clearer now than ever."

"Well it's all got to be down to you Tom," said Tilly. "You're the main player in whatever we have here, you're the one that has to go with it or call a halt. What are you going to do? Mick would you mind getting in the next round?"

"No problem," he replied, handing his notes over and moving to the bar.

Tom frowned, giving a quizzical look towards her as she picked up the papers. She saw the gesture and smiled back at him, clearly understanding the meaning, Mick doing her bidding?

"Well Mick's been talking for a while, I thought he could do with a break, so fetching the drinks, you know I just thought…," her voice tailed away, she shrugged her shoulders.

Tom was searching for an answer, something appropriate at that moment but with Steve and Mick present he seemed unable to formulate the words.

"Hey Tom is that you?" A voice he just recognised broke the silence. "When did you get back mate?"

Tom glanced up from his drink. It was an old army pal.

"Hi Kaz, how are you?"

"Fine thanks."

"Kaz I'm just a bit busy at the moment let me get back to you."

"Sure," he replied looking around the table. Tom, his ex-wife, her second husband, maybe some serious discussion was the conclusion.

"See you soon," and the friend returned to the bar. The interruption gave Tom a little time to think and the reply to Tilly became redundant at that point.

"Right let's just clarify where we are then," he continued. "If I go over a bit of old ground then I'm sorry but talking about it helps me to think and to see more clearly so please just bear with me. You know this could be momentous and we've got to get it right. Firstly, based on what you all know are you all with me? Tils said about calling a halt, which goes for you lot as well, if you want out tell me now, or are you with me to the end of this saga?"

Mick returned to the meeting and together with the other two answered Tom's question positively.

"OK. Let's go. I'm fetched back from Oz by Steve. Why? What did he want? Initially I thought that money was involved, knowing my brother as I do. He told me that he was some sort of Government advisor, working freelance and therefore probably having plenty of spare time to fill and a bit of treasure hunting, if that's how you could describe it, could suit him well. I still think in the first instance that that was his plan," he looked over at Steve who was gazing into his drink.

"So I returned to England. Was it the thought of making some money with him or something else? I'm not really sure but I came anyway.

"From the beginning of my return to Hereford, things have been happening, attacks on me and my family so someone didn't want me getting involved in whatever it was. At this point it could still have been Steve's pipe dream that was causing the problem although gradually I started to understand that there were many other possibilities. Tilly has offered some suggestions and with what Mick has discovered, either through his research with old records or what has been recalled through my regression with Joe nothing, it seems, could be ruled out."

"We have analysed various situations that could be at issue and discussed them with various people and my conclusion is that it's a pretty important deal. Jim's report was quite fantastical when I first heard it, but the more I consider it and what we now think of Joe and the additional stuff I have about the Hamann connection, makes me think that there may be some truth in it, after all nothing else seems to fit at this time, so I guess I have to believe that the main deal is with my family, you know my father in particular, but as I appear to be the conduit to the past then obviously I have to be considered as the threat to those parties who are involved in it whatever it is we are beginning to uncover. Now if it is my father, according to James he most likely went over to South America with all the other escaped Nazis, including Adolf, so it is coming around to the possibility of the solution being over the Atlantic."

"If we assume that all parties and I mean all parties went to South America eventually then that is where we find the answer."

"Hang on," interrupted Steve. "You really believe this then and are you saying that you are considering going over there?"

"Sure, why not I've been over there before it's not another planet and hey Steve just think this might be the most valuable find ever made."

Steve thought about it, he shrugged his shoulders. "How can we do this? Where would we begin?" he asked.

"OK it's going to take some organizing, but I've got to get to the bottom of this however dangerous it is I can't stop now I've come too far and I am too close to the problem, I could never live comfortably again if I didn't have a resolution and I would always think that, as with now, someone could wish me out of the way, I can't live like that."

"Tilly I think we need another talk with your brother James. We need to get closer to the South American connection. Ask him what he knows of Mengele, the German enclave in Argentina such as it was, even Eichman, didn't the Israelis catch him over there. There were some big names about at that time. Ask him to think about something unusual that could go along with what I've just said, anything however impossible it seems."

"Sure, you know my brother, the more impossible the better as far as he is concerned. He'll come up with something."

Chapter 43

A few days later the doorbell rang, Tilly answered and the smiling face of James appeared around the opening door. "Hi sis I wondered how long it would be before you asked for some more help."

"Well I'm glad you could make it but I have to say that you are showing some enthusiasm for this research, why is that? Normally you're a bit cool when it comes to driving around the country in this way, what's got you interested in this?"

"You know the more I look at the situation the more I think of how important it could be and if it was solved, well, I'd like to be in on that. I don't expect to get rich over it but who knows, name down in history perhaps that might look good on a CV."

"Sit down I'll get Tom."

"A cup of tea, the usual please, would be good."

Tom had heard the conversation and was already on his way down the stairs.

"Hi James thanks for finding the time I really appreciate it. How are things with you?" he said entering the sitting room.

"Oh fine thanks yes, you know always busy in this job."

"But not too busy to help us out again."

"Look Tils has already made some facetious comment, just accept me and what I am, if not then you can sort it out yourself. If it helps, let me put my cards on the table. As I told you previously I am writing a book and believe it or not it concerns the end of the war, the period about which you need information. I do research as you are aware, but that research is available to anyone else who might just be writing a book at the same time and so I need an edge. If it is remotely possible that I could obtain information from someone who lived at the time, who might have personal knowledge that is unknown elsewhere, then I must have it. With what my sister tells me about you, it could just possibly be the case here or, at least, the next best thing."

"So she told you about my regression?"

"Of course, she had to. If she required my help there had to be something in it for me, she's not daft, she knows me well enough. That's just how I am."

"OK Jim point taken. I suppose that I have to say how grateful I am for your help. Well did you find any more stuff relative to South America?"

"Tea," said Tilly coming back into the room.

"Thanks," said James taking a few sheets of paper from his bag. "I think I've found what you may be interested in but I'm not sure how you will be able to deal with it, certainly not on this side of the Atlantic."

"Yes," said Tom, "I have already given some thought to how we progress any further investigation and I think a trip back to South America may be on the cards." He glanced at Tilly and he knew what she was thinking. The last time he had gone over there was for work and whilst he was away Steve had moved in on his marriage.

"You'll come over this time won't you Tils," he added.

She nodded and sat down next to her brother.

"Ok," said James, "let's get on with it I've got to get back tonight, busy day tomorrow. I've looked further based on what we discussed last time. You remember that I suggested that Adolf had been frozen on death, you know cryonics, but this was always on the basis that he had gone over there on that U-boat in the first place. Don't ask me how but I've seen some reports via Mossad, the Israeli secret service, covering the time that they went to Argentina to bring back Eichmann."

"He, as you recall, was captured by Mossad in 1960 and by coincidence at the same time Mengele was discovered over there. Apparently Mossad were concerned that it could be too difficult to get both of them at the same time so they just made do with the one, after all they could always go back again if necessary."

"Well they did go back I believe but Mengele had moved on to Paraguay and it seemed a bit more of a problem to get him out of there compared to Eichmann out of Argentina. Nevertheless they did follow him over time and saw various people, Germans in particular with whom he had contact, Klaus Barbie was one of the most famous ones, but some reports started to come in concerning a contact whose name they could not discover and who seemed to be treated with considerable deference by the German community. This was unusual as the Germans were then and probably still are not noted for that national trait. Mossad trailed this individual for a good while but got serious aggravation when getting close to him. The communities ranks closed, the Government of the day became obstructive and even a couple of their agents disappeared. This was difficult stuff operating so far from home and without any cooperation even with the obligatory greasing of palms, threats of violence hampered any progress it seemed that they felt that the enclave was doing all it could to protect this guy against any discovery. One agent said it seemed as if they would die for him if it came to that."

"You think that that may have Hitler?" queried Tom.

"Who knows? But they certainly thought a lot of this man to react in that way, there was no such resistance with Eichmann was there? Mengele and Barbie were not as revered apparently as the agents thought they could still get them but by now they had become distracted with this other man who seemed a much higher value target based on the protection he was getting. My conclusion has to be that, yes there is every chance Mossad were on the trail of Adolf Hitler at this time."

"Then he just seemed to disappear from their radar, No sightings, no information, no nothing even the locals seemed to have changed. The obvious theory has to be that the individual had gone. So if that is correct where had he gone? Let's speculate."

"If he had left for another area there would most likely be a trail, no trail was found according to the reports. So was he still there? Well if it was Hitler he would have been in his eighties and remember, I told you before that I had this information that he was ill when he left Europe, you recall the film showing a trembling hand, the tremors, Parkinson's? And so when I say still there, then I mean his remains, his body, he had probably died."

"And he was still being protected even though he was dead?"

"Of course, why not he was revered dead or alive and don't forget, did he have children?"

"Now remember Mengele was around at the time although he had gone to Brazil. It was known that he lived in Nova Europa just outside Sao Paulo. In 1979 as we now know he died in Bertioga from a stroke probably and he was buried in Embu des Artes under the name Wolgang Gerhard. Mossad searched that area but couldn't find the other man so I guess he hadn't gone along with Mengele, probably because, as I say, he had died."

"However Mengele wasn't the clue really although the medical profession was and that's when we move, with even more speculation to Artur Hamann, your father."

The clock on the mantelpiece chimed twelve.

"Fancy some lunch," asked Tilly.

"Certainly, with all this talking time flies and a sandwich or so would be very welcome."

"The same with all this listening," added Tom, "let's take a break."

Lunch was forthcoming and Tom relaxed a little. Hearing all of this speculation concerning his Hamann family was tiring, physically and certainly mentally and it required some serious thought and consideration as the story was told.

"So what are your plans for the future James?" he asked during a lull in the proceedings.

"Well, I have to say that with your help, with what we are doing now, I expect a best seller," he replied finishing off a jar of olives that he found in the fridge.

"I like olives, perhaps that's why I like you Tom," he laughed.

"You like me because I might help you make a great deal of money," was the sarcastic answer.

"Don't you pair start, just finish lunch so we can get on with this, there's a long way to go."

"OK sis, what's the hurry?"

Tom wondered that also.

Chapter 44

James continued, "Artur Hamann, now I am surmising here but from what I have been told about your latest regression it appears he worked in a concentration camp, let's for the sake of intelligence say Auschwitz Birkenau, so if that is correct then he would have known Mengele and of course the two of them were known to be interested in research. The whole world knows about the Angel of Death and his experiments, they are well documented but actually a lot more experiments were undertaken by his assistants and it isn't much of a leap to place Hamann in that category."

"One of the items in a report on Nazi Human Experimentation that I found concerned freezing." James stopped at this point. He had spoken at length and recalled that he had broached this subject with the others during his first visit. He expected that this would be of special interest to Tom and guessed that he had considered the implications since it was discussed the last time. The conclusion from before had been that Hamann may have been the doctor who had taken care of the Fuhrer's body by way of freezing or cryonics. The problem was that cryonics seemed to be something that was not available at the end of the war but this information showed that it was in its infancy and maybe the circle was complete."

"Well what do think?" James asked, clearly wanting a quick answer so that he could continue.

"Well first of all I must say that you need not tell me this story again. My father, South America, Adolf Hitler, freezing, I've heard it before. Do you tell it to me to make me feel bad, guilty or what?"

"No, I tell it because it is of such importance, so that the magnitude of it is understood, so that the implications of it to you are appreciated," replied James annoyed with Tom's attitude at this time. "OK, I'll try not to mention it again, as long as you understand."

"I do, I do," snapped Tom.

"Alright, I asked you before, what do you think?"

"Christ I don't know," said Tom. "Just tell me what you have and then leave me to consider it."

"Right," continued James. "What I have discovered is that during 1941 or so the Luftwaffe started to conduct experiments to find ways to prevent and treat hypothermia. This was done to see what the effect was of cold on soldiers on the eastern front against the Russians. Many of the tests were carried out on captured Russian soldiers. It was also of interest with regard to flying at great heights, you know above the enemy or for the navy when sailors might spend time in the cold seas during battle, all aspects of German warfare had an interest in this as you can see. Any advantage they could get over the enemy would be invaluable, but I've told you this much before."

"Yeah you have, just carry on will you?"

"Fine, one study involved placing subjects in tanks of ice water for up to five hours at a time and another had prisoners placed in the open air for hours whilst naked. As well as studying the effects on people of exposure to cold, they also tested various methods of reheating anyone that was fortunate to survive."

"So my theory is that Hamann helped with these experiments whilst working with Mengele and later when they both got to South America he developed it further into what we now call cryonics, the deliberate freezing of a body. Having also done work on rewarming or reheating, having undertaken one process then the other naturally follows on."

"But there were no prisoners of war to use at that time, where did the patients come from?" said Tilly.

"Well as I, we, discussed before there were no prisoners, so I believe that we are looking at volunteers and these people have to be desperate and they have to be individuals for whom there was no alternative - terminally ill patients. Freezing now and restored to life when a cure was found for the illness or whatever they had, that is exactly what cryonics is about. Who would most favour something like that and who would want someone to be treated in this way. Well I guess no one would be a better candidate at that time than Hitler, of course with the help of his supporters."

"OK, Jim let's assume that some of this is true and that Adolf was frozen in South America some time ago.

Let's assume that this is the 'Treasure'. What's this got to do with me and why the aggravation?"

"Well look at it this way. If Hitler is frozen somewhere, the plan must be to bring him back to life at some time, that's always going to be the end product of this process. His remains are there somewhere, they are being cared for, protected and if your father was the medic involved and if you can be regressed then you might know where all this is being hidden."

"But I died at the end of the war, executed, I'm sure Tilly has told you that. If that is the case and Hitler did not die until much later, how is it possible that I, regressed to Hamann, could know of the whereabouts?"

"Absolutely correct, you couldn't possibly know, but we are talking about a unique situation here. Adolf Hitler's body is somewhere in the world in suspended animation, waiting for the time when it can be restored to life, reborn if you will. There must be people supporting that idea, guardians protecting him, living for the day he returns, for him to commence the rebuild of The Third Reich or even the building of The Fourth Reich, spending considerable sums of money on the enterprise and then you appear. That throws the entire organization into confusion, doubt, danger. Here is man who can be regressed to the son of the doctor at the centre of the whole thing. What does he know? What can he say? Will he endanger the plans? They can take no risks too much has been invested in time and money. He must be eliminated. If he knows anything then that would be gone with his removal from the scene, if he knows nothing, so what?"

"Tom stood up and walked to the window and looked out on to the world, his thoughts anywhere but in

Hereford England at that moment. Who wanted him out of the way? Where would he need to go in the world to end this episode in his life? James had put the scenario into graphic reality. This was no enterprise of curiosity this was now a matter of life or death. He felt, for the first time in his life as far as he could recall, an element of foreboding, even fear, but this was not the time or place to show that.

"So no paintings then just the possibility of finding the Fuhrers body lying in state somewhere?" The attempted humour falling flat.

"Exactly."

"And someone is out there trying to stop me finding it or telling the world about it?"

"Yes."

"So it has to be a person who knows all about you and us. A person who knows and understands what you can do, who knows that you can be regressed to Hamann's son," insisted Tilly.

"Do you think that Joe is the man then?" asked Tom now resigned to what he has to do eventually.

"Who knows, but if you are asking my opinion then I would have to say yes. From what you have told me about what has happened here, then I think he has been around from the beginning. You said that Steve had discussed your return to England with him before he came out to Oz after you. OK perhaps your brother was on a treasure hunt at the time and knew that some more regression might help, but that tipped off Joe to your return."

"So that explains how we seemed to have had trouble from the start."

"I guess so," replied James, "and so from there Joe just had to keep close to you and be a friend, I suppose you could call it. Each time you had a session with him he would know what was going on and how far you were getting towards the eventual truth. It seems to me that he has a considerable part to play in this although Tils told me that Dad had found little of interest when he looked at the guy's background, but that means nothing."

"You know what I have to do now, don't you?"

"I think so, you've got to find out where the body is and to do that you need regression? That's going to be interesting if you need Joe to do it."

"Yes, well I have no doubt that that would be a problem so I think that we are going to have to see if we can work it out without Joe. There's plenty of recorded evidence of Mengele's travels around Argentina, Brazil and so on we just need to solve the clues."

"Always assuming that following Mengele's trail is the same as following Artur Hamann's trail and that if you are able to do so, that it will lead to where Hitler's body is hidden," said Tilly, her comments always succinct and to the point thought Tom.

"Jim you have been a great help so far, I am truly grateful, but could I ask you to help me further with this. Your problem solving has been first rate and I wouldn't be where I am now with this investigation without you."

"Are you excluding Steve and Mick from now on?"

"I think so. Look will you help?"

"Yes OK. I've got some leave coming up and I have to say that I have become quite intrigued with all this, not to say involved as the success of my next book may depend on it, but why leave out Steve and Mick?"

"Well I've got nothing to worry about with them being involved but I can see what has to be done next and that has to be trip to South America."

"If we are being watched and I suspect that we must be, then all of us going over there would be a giveaway wouldn't it? However if Tils and I went on our own, we could make it seem like a holiday. After all whoever is watching must know that we've become an item once more and a holiday to the sun, away from a wet and cold England in the early spring wouldn't be too surprising."

"How do I become involved?"

"You probably aren't suspected at this time I guess. The four of us have been seen together over a period and of course we've been to Joe's place together but you have only just come on the scene and after all you are Tils's brother. If you returned to Oxford and then travelled from there we could meet up and hopefully avoid too much attention, what do you think?"

"Sounds like the best idea if we have got to do it then that should be the way, what about you Tilly?"

"Fine," she replied. "You know that I've got to be in on it, let's do it."

Chapter 45

That evening James returned to Oxford to confirm his leave and begin to make his arrangements for travel to Buenos Aires, where he would meet up with the others. It seemed reasonable to him to commence their search there as it was the Argentine capital and of course research showed that U977 had travelled to that country at the end of the war, maybe there would be a trail of some sort even after fifty five years. From Buenos Aires the group would move to Mar del Plata where the vessel had surrendered to the American navy. He reasoned that although it was unlikely that any physical evidence could be discovered there, stories, apocryphal or otherwise might still be in the public domain and, with his years of experience of research, he might well be the best placed to find the information they required.

Tom and Tilly met with their friends the following day and told them of the plan, and they concurred without any disagreement. They understood that a trip taken by all four of them might be of more interest to any observers, than if it appeared to be no more than a holiday for two.

"We shall have to plan this carefully," said Tom later that day. He and Tilly had decided to review the research. If it was necessary to go to South America they had to consider the best course of action. There was a limited time, especially with James' unplanned leave and they wondered how much dust would be thrown up by their visit and any subsequent investigations. Although it was now many years after the end of the war they reasoned that Argentina would still have a substantial German population and with many of those people being there at the time or at least now first generation families it could be expected that their presence would be noted. No time must be wasted in the search, whatever could be done before the trip would be time saved over there.

"What we know of any of this is what we are being told," continued Tom. "I have been collecting as much info as I could over these last few weeks. I've got newspaper cuttings, stuff from Mick from his released documents, things from books I have read and of course all the copies of the reports that Jim has given to us in the last few days. It is all complicated by the fact that these items are historical, possibly from someone's memory and remember the story about Hitler's dentist, if whatever he said was a deliberate ploy to confuse the authorities then how much more could be deliberate lying to hide the truth."

"Some of it I think is probably correct and we can be happy with much of what we have. For instance the story about U977, the yanks will undoubtedly have proper and correct reports of the boat's journey, surrender, destruction and what happened to the crew but things such as Hitler and Braun in Sweden, well I just don't know. I can see the possibility of the escape from Berlin and going to a neutral country, but they had two kids, isn't that what Jim said? How is it possible for such a high profile man, and woman for that matter, to have a family and for it not to be known? Whilst the boat did sail across the Atlantic is there any real proof that they were on it? What about Mengele and Hamann in South America? Well that must be right as Mengele's family have confirmed that he died there and DNA proved the remains to be his. But you see any of it could be correct or not, fact or fiction, truth or confusion, who knows. Let's have a look at what we have and then see if we can come to some conclusion, OK?"

"Sure, tell me what you think first and I'll act as devil's advocate."

"Let's start with the assumption that if Hamann was a colleague of Mengele as we suspect, then the tracks of one might be the tracks of the other. This is what I think from the various reports I have seen myself and from what James has indicated to us. Mengele was around in Argentina in the early 1950's."

"How did he get over there and stay hidden for so long?"

"Well it is thought that having been taken as a prisoner of war by the Americans, and surprisingly under his real name, he was released in June 1945 with papers showing his name to be Hollman. Until 1949 he lived in Bavaria but as Nazis begun to be chased down by the various organizations and governments, he escaped Europe via Innsbruck and Genoa probably with the help of the Odessa network, an organization that helped many Nazis at the time."

"In Buenos Aires he lived around many other wealthy Germans, some of whom had also most likely escaped the war as potential criminals and knowing who he was they supported him in the early years there, it was at this time that he met Eichman. In 1955 he bought a share in a local pharmaceutical company and the perceived information was that the purchase was funded by his family back in Germany who must therefore have known his whereabouts all the time, but unsurprisingly denied any knowledge of him."

"The family are still around aren't they?"

"Yes I believe so, but I doubt I would get any help from them even if I asked."

"I'm not suggesting that you do ask, just interested."

"He divorced his wife and then married Martha the widow of his brother Karl and she moved to Argentina with her son Dieter. For the marriage he must have returned to Germany as I don't expect they could have gone through a ceremony with one of them in Europe and the other in South America. They lived in the suburb of Vicente Lopez practicing medicine, but after the capture of Eichmann in 1960 by Mossad agents he must have thought that he was next and so left the area and moved to Paraguay."

"You said Mossad nearly caught him at the same time as Eichmann?"

"Yes, that's right, but I think the number of agents that they had over there at the time was fairly small and they could only manage to kidnap one at a time. By the time they could return for the other, he had gone."

"The dictator of Paraguay at the time was Alfredo Stroessner who himself was of German descent and who recruited former Nazis to help the countries' development, so he would be sympathetic to Mengele."

"So what did the world community think about that?"

"Well I expect they weren't very happy with it but what could they do? Paraguay was an independent country. We have the same problems today, countries with leaders that the rest of the world might not like. You can't just move in and get rid of them however much you would like to."

Tilly nodded.

"After a time in Paraguay he moved to Nova Europa just outside Sao Paulo in Brazil, living with some Hungarian refugees and working for them as a farm manager."

"There was some talk of a move to Bolivia but Mengele was comfortable where he was and so he stayed in Brazil where in 1979 he died at a place called Bertioga."

"That's fine as far as it goes, but you have not mentioned your Father, as he was. What evidence is there that he was in the company of Mengele and in any case, how does this help in finding Hitler, he wasn't travelling around with them and at that time he had most probably died anyway. Tom where do we begin? We are talking about a number of different countries, thousands of miles away and as all this happened forty or fifty years ago, from reports that may or may not be accurate. It's like looking for the proverbial. I wouldn't know where to start, and just think about it if what we are looking for is in fact Hitler's frozen body, then those who are hiding it will have covered every possible track. I can't see how we have the slightest chance to know where we start to look and with all due respect to my brother, the same would apply to him."

Tom shrugged his shoulders. He knew Tilly was right as usual. They knew what they were after but there was no way of knowing where to look or even begin to look.

"There is one way," Tilly finally said, "and I know that we've to some extent removed Joe from the equation but he has to be the clue and also it has to be through Hamann."

"But if we involve him any further and he is the clue as you describe it, won't we be giving away what we are doing, what we are after?"

"What choice do we have? South America is probably out, we both agree. If we are going to progress this then all we have is Joe and you, we shall just have to play it softly. You know I don't think he suspects anything at the moment. The last time you spoke with him he was OK, wasn't he?"

"Yes, I guess he was, we were talking about another session I recall?"

"Yes, but I think we should look at him again. You know my Dad didn't come up with anything the first time although he said he was working in another direction, something about his name I think."

"Yes that always made me wonder, why did he use two names? He said it was for his research, you know to flush out any hidden Nazis. Well you may be right that has to be the way to go, another session but let's hear from your Dad first of all OK?"

"Sure, you know I was beginning to look forward to a trip abroad, now it looks like Hereford in the spring."

"I'll phone James and tell him to hold off for a day or two."

Chapter 46

The following day the telephone rang at the house, Tom answered and called to Tilly, "It's your Dad."

She ran down the stairs to take the call.

"It sounds urgent."

She grabbed the handset from the table. "Make a coffee will you?"

Hi Dad, you OK?"

Tom could hear only a murmur over the other end of the phone, so he would have to wait to know what was being discussed. He went into the kitchen as instructed.

After a few minutes he heard the ring of the telephone as the handset was replaced on the receiver, forgetting the boiling kettle he returned to where Tilly was reading some notes that she had made.

"Well I don't know whether we have made any progress with this yet," she sighed, "I'm afraid that that was not much help, Dad still can't find out anything about Joe. If this guy is hiding something then he's doing it pretty well and Dad says he must be hiding something. After all if British intelligence is unable to identify a foreigner, someone who has lived in this country for years, then either he has an unbreakable story or, Dad says, he has a first class network around him that keeps it all quiet, that would take a pretty impressive organisation. The only thing Dad did say as positive is that with the two names he uses, did you know that the name Ciemny is Polish for dark or more possibly Brown?"

"Of course I didn't. I don't speak the language what does your Dad think of the significance of that?"

"I'm afraid that I've no idea but maybe it means something."

"Well I'll thank your Dad next time I see him, but I think we've got to move forward now. If we have decided that we are not going over to South America, then we have to tell Steve and Mick that we need them again over the next few days and you've already put Jim on standby."

The coffee was finally made and the two sat down at the kitchen table.

"You know Tils, coming back to England wasn't such a bad decision after all. OK we have a problem here but I know that it will all work out in the end and then I'd like to think that perhaps we could make the move permanent."

"That would be good," she whispered and kissed his cheek, "but let's get this thing sorted first eh?"

"Always the practical sort," he murmured, "but you're right as usual. We can't do or plan anything while this is going on."

He finished his drink.

"Look, what I want to do is have a reccy at Joe's house. You know that was a particularly impressive property for a man who doesn't really work. I know he would say that at his age he has retired, but even when he was working what did he do and where did he make his cash?"

"What would generate the income to pay for a residence such as that. It wasn't likely to have been inherited wealth because he told us that his family died in a concentration camp so if that was true where did he get his money?"

"I think that we need to do a bit of reconnaissance. Tell you what, I'll get Steve to spend a night over by the house to see if anything goes on. He'll like that, he was always good at that sort of thing. Let's see if he's at home now."

Tilly took the cups over to the kitchen sink and Tom sat down by the telephone to contact Steve.

The bell rang once and was quickly answered.

"Hi, it's me, you OK?"

"Sure," replied Steve surprised to hear from his brother. "Hey I thought that you were off shortly, any problem?"

Tom explained his concerns about going to South America.

"Yes I can see that," said Steve eventually. "I was always unsure as to whether all of the information that we got was accurate. You know anyone could put out stories like that to hide the truth especially in circumstances like this."

"Well, I think that most of it is probably reasonably accurate, it's just that after all these years the trail must be cold. Where would we begin and if you think about it, why have I had all this trouble here in England? You could say that if I returned from Australia then whoever is behind this might be alerted, I understand that and if I'm a danger then getting rid of me here is as good as anywhere else. I just have this feeling that South America is not where it's at. Don't ask me why, I can't really give you an answer. Maybe it's the whole thing about me. If I can be regressed then also perhaps I have a sixth or even a seventh sense."

"Seventh sense, what's that?"

"Well I don't know, maybe there is no such thing but perhaps it's the ability to feel things around me, like an animal maybe."

"It sounds extraordinary to me but knowing you, yes it could be. You have this regression business which I also find strange so why wouldn't you have other powers that the rest of us haven't. So are you saying that what we are looking for is here in England?"

"Possibly although I don't really know what I am looking for, but, yes it's possible and that's where I need your help again brother. What I need is some watching of Joe's house, can you give it a couple of days?"

"Watching Joe's house? What are you after?"

"Well I don't know, anything that looks out of the ordinary. We haven't had the chance to have a good look at the place even when we've been there and I just wonder if we might find some clue if we gave it a viewing from a distance and then who knows, maybe a closer inspection."

Steve was silent at the other end of the phone for a while.

"So you think that he's involved in this do you?"

"Possibly."

Another silence.

"You still there?" enquired Tom.

"Yeah sure," came back his brother, "yes OK I'll give it a go over the next couple of nights and let you know what I find."

Tom replaced the receiver. "He'll do it Tils," he shouted into the kitchen, "but God knows what he'll find, if anything at all."

Chapter 47

Steve set out from his home at 23.00 hours. When the group had visited Joe's house previously they had passed under a railway bridge just before turning into his road. Steve had checked a local street map and realised that from the rail track, which ran over the bridge he would have sight of Joe's house and garden. He had decided that this was the best vantage point for any viewing of the property and so that would be his first call. He had checked the timetable at the local railway station and knew that at that time no traffic would be running along the line, the last service being thirty minutes earlier. There would be good height and cover especially in the dark and he also knew that if for some reason he was seen from the house or by any passerby and needed to get away quickly, then there was a good escape route along the track, over the river and away along the path on the other side.

He drove his car towards the target, across the main road and along the City walls out towards the route for Ledbury. This was a good area of Hereford from the point of view of the quality of the properties. A quiet neighbourhood, large Victorian houses with private, laurel hedged gardens and substantial areas of ground surrounding them. Tree lined streets, parks and the proximity of the river added to the value of each residence and Steve knew what his brother had meant about Joe's house. How could he afford to live here?

Just before the bridge was a small public garden and in front, set back from the road, a small lay-by. Steve drove his car onto it and parked. He would walk from this spot approximately fifty metres along the road and around the bend to where the bridge was situated. Leaving his vehicle, he looked around, all was quiet, his dark clothes and the dim street lamps ensuring his near invisibility as he made his way to the bridge. On one side of the bridge was a flight of stone steps, blocked by a locked wooden gate a metre high. He looked about, no-one to be seen and an athletic leap over the barrier saw him onto and away up the steps to the top. Crouching down so as to be shielded by the parapet, he made his way along the track to a clump of shrubs, half way across the span. Gaining the cover in a few strides he stopped to survey the area.

He was now above the street lights and standing alongside the shrubs gave him a decent view into Joe's garden, which sloped down to the river, three houses distant along the road. He moved back towards the top of the steps, still above the lights and covered by the wall, he could see the front of the house, onto the drive and more importantly the road in front of the house and he settled down to keep watch.

There was no moon that evening and Steve felt a little rain start to fall, this was good cover he thought to himself.

"I could do with a smoke," he considered, "better not though, a flame, smoke could be seen."

The house was along a road which joined one of the main exits from the City, not much traffic passed this way, mainly the vehicles owned by the residents, so any activity would be seen easily and at this time of night more noticeable.

Steve saw that a light was on in one of the upstairs bedrooms of Joe's house. Glancing at his watch, the illuminated dial showed 23.40. "Staying up to watch the late news I expect," he mused.

He looked up to the black cloud laden sky, the rain had become heavier now and with nothing happening around the property at the time he considered how this episode had developed and that in the end he was unlikely to find any hidden works of art by way of Tom's recall of his past life.

A scuffling noise along the track to his left brought his attention back and he pressed himself into the wall. A cat appeared through the darkness and stopped, staring at Steve as he stared back. The animal soon assessed the danger in what was to be seen and considering there was none, nonchalantly glided down the steps from the bridge and away along the footpath.

He looked at his watch again the luminous dial showing that midnight had passed.

The sound of a car caught his attention. It was becoming louder and seemed to come from the City.

It approached from the direction that he had taken earlier, the first vehicle in a period of twenty minutes. It turned the corner and passed under the bridge slowing down as it arrived level with the house and stopped. Steve brought his binoculars up to his eyes and wiped the water from the lens and shielded them from the falling rain. After a few minutes the car started off again and disappeared along the road away from Hereford and around the bend some 200 metres away. Steve dropped down again behind the parapet. What was he expected to see, what was Tom expecting him to find out. "I could be here all night, see nothing and get soaked," he whispered to himself, "still I did volunteer."

Another car, this time coming from the other direction, again approached and slowed down outside the house. He looked through his binoculars. "Hang on it's the same car, what's going on?"

The vehicle turned onto the drive the lights were turned off and he saw two tall figures get out, the door closed quietly and they went towards the front of the house. As they got to the door it opened and they entered. Steve couldn't see who had let them in as, the greeting was hidden by the trellis and the ivy growing over it. He continued to peer onto the drive but could see nothing more, it was dark and the rain was hampering his vision.

Five minutes passed by, he heard the sound of another vehicle coming from the City direction.

"Nothing for twenty minutes," he muttered, "now two come at once," allowing himself a wry smile at the joke that only he could hear.

Another car arrived and the same procedure took place. It drove away from the house and then reappeared from the opposite direction a little while later. It too turned onto the drive and a single shape emerged from the vehicle and made its way to the front door and was let inside. "They're coming to the house, seeing if the coast is clear and returning," he thought.

There was no more activity for some time. The rain had ceased and although it was the month of February it was not too cold. Steve waited. He heard the front door open and two men left the house and got into the first car that had arrived. The engine started, gravel crunched under the wheels as it moved away onto the road and sped off towards the City.

Yet another car arrived, performing the same actions as the previous vehicles, eventually parking on Joe's drive and with the occupants entering the house.

"Busy night at Joe's, what are these guys doing?" he wondered. "I need to get closer." He made his way back to the steps and walked slowly down on to the road. There was a dirt path beside the bridge along the steps and moving down it he saw that it went to the river bank.

"I should be able to reach the bottom of his garden along the river and see into the house from the back," he considered and within a few minutes he was crouching down behind the low fence at the end of the garden. The light that had been seen earlier was at the front on the ground floor, but from here there was a different source of illumination, a sliver of light showed below a window on the first floor. He shook his head, rain water dripped from his hood.

Returning to the path and back to the bridge, he began to walk along the road towards the house. Just before reaching it he crossed over and crept along the dark drive of an opposite property and the two cars were now in view, still parked at Joe's house. He moved forward a couple of paces down the drive towards the road and taking a piece of paper and a pencil from his pocket he wrote down the registration numbers, just discernible with the dim illumination of the street lights, returning the paper to inside his coat.

"Well I guess that's enough for now," he mumbled, "let's get back home, out of this rain."

Chapter 48

It was midmorning the following day when Tilly's phone rang, Tom answered.

"Hi Steve here, you'll never guess the fun I had last night."

"Tell me then I'm all ears," came the reply.

"Well apart from the rain it wasn't a bad nights fishing. I got up onto the railway bridge around a quarter to twelve, after the trains had stopped running and I could see the house pretty well from there, front and back. You were dead right; from the elevation of the bridge the property was substantial and in a nice area, must be worth a few quid I reckon. Anyway I saw five vehicles arrive throughout the time I was looking and the people in each one did the same thing. Drive up, stop, look around and drive off again then come back a few minutes later, presumably so long as the coast was clear. Considering that Joe is just an ordinary guy that seems unusual to say the least."

"Yeah but the more I hear of him the less ordinary he becomes."

"I had a look from the back of the house, along the river and then managed to see the front of it from a drive of a house opposite. Well I got a couple of registration numbers of the cars and this morning before phoning you I got on to a mate on the base and called in a favour. I asked him to let me know who owned the vehicles. I guess that you could have asked your pal Andy at the local police, but I know the regiment can find out these things with a certain amount of urgency, more so than the official way and probably with less red tape and my man got back to me just before I phoned you."

"And?"

"Wait for this, the cars belong to hire firms and it seems that in each case the vehicle was hired from a depot at a port of entry to the UK. They were from different ports, Dover and Felixstowe, you know ports from Europe and the interesting thing is that I was able to get to find out who hired the transport. They were different people, of course, but one was German and the other Austrian according to the passports."

"And the other three?"

"Sorry I didn't get the numbers of those, but I wouldn't mind betting that the same result would apply."

"Your contact is a useful guy."

"He owes me from some time ago, I thought it was a good call this time."

"Look thanks Steve this is excellent stuff and as I said before the more I hear about Joe the more I think he's the clue to all this. Any chance of persuading you to have another look at the house tonight do you think?"

"No much chance brother, anyway you've probably got enough for the moment to be getting on with. I've been up all night, I'm wet and I need a cigarette, then I'm going to get some sleep, see how I feel about tonight later, who knows, see you."

Tom put down the telephone.

"Anything interesting?" said Tilly who had come into the room while he was speaking.

"You bet, you know that Joe is the answer to all this," and he related Steve's story to her.

"I think I need another meeting with your brother. He's been a great help so far and I want him to see if he can help unravel this Joe thing, no-one else seems to be able to. Something is going on at that house and before I have a look I need to hear what Jim has to say. He said to call on him if we need anything more, obviously he wants to stay close so that nothing is missed for that book of his. Fine, let's take advantage of the offer."

"Before you have a look did you say? What are you going to do now then?"

"I want to get all the stuff I can from Jim. I need to know about the house and the possibilities of what is happening there, then I'm keen to have a look. I know Steve will be with me he's always good for a bit of breaking and entering. That was he forte with the regiment, remember the Iranian embassy, twenty years ago? He was only a lad then but now he's the man."

Tilly did not argue with Tom or try to persuade him to do otherwise. He, in fact the both of them, had come a long way with this investigation and even Tilly had begun to feel she had to know what would be the outcome, whatever the dangers.

"I'll speak to my brother," she said, "he'll help. He was a bit cheesed off when the South America plan went pear shaped, so you'll find that he will be more than willing."

Chapter 49

A telephone call saw James arrive that afternoon, even he had not spared his valuable cruising motorcycle in getting to Hereford from Bath where he was visiting friends. Tilly was right, he was very keen.

"What can I do?" he said taking off his leathers.

"I need some help with Joe and this house business," Tom replied and he related what had been found out over the previous night.

"Sounds like something is definitely going on there, what else do you need to know, what do you want me to tell you?"

Tom related all the information he had about the property. He and the others had been there on a number of occasions and he described the place as best as he could recall.

"Well I don't know what I can make of that," said James finally, "you've just given me an Estate Agent's description. How do I tell anything from that description? Or even the fact that the property has a certain smell and the sound of machinery comes from one of the rooms. I'm an historian not someone in the market for a house, however wonderful it sounds."

Tilly interrupted the conversation. "The only other thing I can remember that you haven't said, Tom, is that you noticed the name by the front door, what did you say it was?"

"Oh yes I did notice a name. I'm not sure if I can recall it though….. It was a word that I didn't recognize… it began with a K I think…I'm not sure, something like Kolibri? And don't forget your father said he thought Ciemny was Polish for brown."

"OK, well actually that word Kolibri sounds familiar. I think I've come across the name before, let's use my laptop see if it comes up with anything, together with what we already have we may get lucky. It doesn't sound like a German word, or Polish for that matter, but Joe says that he is Polish and he can speak German so let's see why his house might be named, what did you say Kolibri with a K?"

James typed in the word to a site that he used a lot in his job. Many of the papers that were used for his research and some of his books, needed some form of translation and he was soon into a program that was regularly used by him when required. The German and Polish pages flashed into view.

"Well for the Polish it just comes up with the same word, so no help there, but the German, well, that's a surprise, there is a direct translation, but what it means as an English word I can't recall. The word is Hummingbird."

"Hummingbird, you don't know what it means?" queried Tilly.

"Well yes, of course I know what a Hummingbird is, but for the name of a house? What's that all about?"

"Just a nice name for a house," she replied, "what's wrong with that in any case, the previous owners may have used the name and Joe just kept it."

"Maybe," he answered slowly, clearly something was stirring in his mind. "Wait a minute, the word has rung a bell. I seem to recall the word from some previous research I did when I produced my dissertation for my degree."

"You've got a good memory," said Tilly, "that was ages ago."

"Yes but you know that I have a good memory, it's a requirement of the job but in any case I enjoyed doing that work, so in those circumstances, you do remember," he replied. "It was very interesting and I have looked up some stuff recently when I've been doing other work for Tom. You know the things I did about Hitler and so on."

James returned to his PC and started to press buttons. Tom stood at his shoulder. He had never become as computer literate as James and he watched with some admiration as the screens flashed and changed. Tilly made some coffee.

"Wow I've got it, why didn't I remember that?" he shouted eventually. "Let me think about this because it may be significant taking into account everything else that I've researched for you."

He started recalling his previous work from the laptop and continued for nearly half an hour before he surfaced. He had clearly found what he was looking for. The expression on his face was triumphant and at the same time he was clearly considering the implications. The drink was cold by now, but he downed it anyway, a long draft and he pushed himself back into the chair as if savouring the moment.

"Come on," said Tilly, "don't keep us waiting whatever it is tell us."

"You'd better listen to this very carefully because if this theory is correct then it's what you've been after all along but, if it's not too theatrical it's earth shattering." His voice hushed as if he didn't believe what he had discovered or what connection he had made.

He continued. "Now look this is just a theory, but you know I'm good at theories and generally they are correct. This one might be different however, I just don't know, it's just too fantastic."

"I've looked at the stuff I did for you before. You remember Hitler maybe going to Argentina and so on and possibly ending up as a patient of your fathers. I'll call him your father as I can't think of anything better at the moment. The deal was that as Argentina or South America in general seemed to be the end of the trail, then we would then go over there to find out whatever we could."

"I accept that it would be like looking for a needle in a haystack although knowing you if it came to it then you would go."

"Please get on with it."

"OK, OK I just want you to recall some of what I said previously, but if you believe that it's all nonsense then fine, suit yourself but I'll just say what I see."

"When I went through the reports and stories, and bear in mind some of them could have been put about by Nazis hiding their tracks or those of their Fuhrer or there could even have been genuine mistakes, I told you all about Sweden and South America, probably with Eva and maybe children."

"Let's suppose that it was correct, but just going back a moment, if Hitler was seen with his children at that time they must have been born before the marriage because that was alleged to have happened in the bunker."

"Ok so far?"

"Carry on."

"Well if the Sweden sighting was correct and they were not married when the kids were born, then as their mother was named Braun they themselves could have been named Braun and not Hitler or whatever else he might have called himself. Do you recall that we said it seemed odd that no-one knew about them? Maybe the authorities kept it quiet and using her name was a good way of doing that. If so, they could have grown to adulthood across the Atlantic as Braun."

"Yessss?" said Tom trying to make the connection.

"Well the point is that you should consider that their names remained as such. After all, that name didn't necessarily connect them with Hitler, it was fairly common within the German community, and anonymity was paramount. But look, you told me that Joe's surname was Ciemny."

"Yes and…?"

"Roughly translated from German into English Braun is Brown."

"Yes…?"

"Roughly translated from English into Polish Brown is Ciemny."

James sat back in the chair with a jubilant expression on his face, waiting for a comment from the others.

"How about something stronger to drink?" he enquired as if expecting a reward for his efforts.

Tom and Tilly looked at each other making the connection and wondering if it could possibly be just James vivid imagination that had got them this far.

She walked to the kitchen in silence and returned a few moments later still in silence with a glass of Gin, James favourite drink. She handed it to him.

"Are you asking us to believe that Joe might be one of Hitler's children?" she asked half expecting her brother to say he was just joking.

"Believe what you wish," he replied. "I just come up with solutions to problems, they may not be correct solutions but with the information that I have it is a possibility isn't it?"

He stood up and walked around the room, deep in thought, sipping the gin. Then the glass was emptied in one draft and placed noisily on the table. He sat down and returned to his PC pressing furiously at keys, the screen flashed again.

"If you think that's incredible then listen to the next bit."

"Incredible, fantastic, unbelievable, save all your metaphors for the book will you," said Tom beginning to get annoyed by James' constant exuberance whenever he found another clue.

"Tilly put her hand on Tom's arm and they looked at each other.

"Be patient please," she said in a soft calm voice, "let's just go along with it, my brother will never be any different. Please Jim carry on."

His enthusiasm unabated, he continued

"Tilly said that Joe's house was called Kolibri and in particular spelled with a K. The word Kolibri is a

German word meaning Hummingbird. Odd that a Pole whose family were exterminated in a concentration camp, who says he spent his time tracking down Nazis, should name his house using a German word, don't you think? Unless as you say, it was named that before he moved in, but somehow I don't think so, because I expect in those circumstances he would have changed the name when he bought the place wouldn't he? You know Polish, German. Well Kolibri was something more than just the name of a bird. Have you ever heard of The Night of the Long Knives?"

"Possibly," replied Tom hesitantly, "but if you asked me for any details then I wouldn't be much help."

"Well that event happened in 1934. I'll précis what I've got here because it's complicated and in any case most of it, although extremely important at the time and factually, can be ignored as far as we are concerned."

"Hitler was Chancellor at the time and felt that he needed to strengthen his position within the government such as it was, as the Sturmabteilung, or the SA, the Brownshirts, led by a guy named Ernst Rohm seemed to be running the country. Hitler saw him as a political opponent and decided that he wanted him out of the way so he could run the show unopposed. In those days it was felt that the quickest way to get control was to eliminate the opposition, no democracy then, why waste time with an election? So at the end of June and the beginning of July his own forces, the SS and the Gestapo, moved against Rohm and the SA. Over those few days and nights his enemies, as he felt them to be, were arrested and summarily executed leaving the country under the control of Adolf and his supporters. He also took the opportunity to get rid of critics of his regime, individuals who had offended him personally and anyone else, who had crossed his path on his way to Chancellor, or just during his life and at the end of the purge he was left in control of the country and the rest, as they say, is history."

"Now if you consider that this operation was the start of Hitler's reign or his birth, shall I say, then that could be good description of the events."

"Now the leap."

James waited for a reaction. He was a master of political timing.

The others remained silent.

"Although what I have just said, what I have described was known as The Night of The Long Knives as with most of these things there was a code name for it and the code name for this event?...Kolibri...."

The others glanced at each other. Tom shook his head.

"If we assume that Hitler was frozen, and who am I to say that that is not correct and of course by your father, Tom, then if he were to be unfrozen at some time in the future, or bought back to life, or reborn shall we say, then Kolibri would be a word from the past that would have some great significance to him or his supporters."

Tom mumbled to himself.

"Say it louder," insisted James.

"You heard..... bloody hell....What have we got here?"

"If it's possible," added Tilly

The three of them drifted into silence.

"Look," Tom said eventually, "this is too much, I just can't believe that what you are saying could possibly make sense. You say that Joe, by virtue of his name, is one of Hitler's children. He lives in a house in Hereford, a house that has some mystery to it I accept, visitors at night that sort of thing and he's called it after an event that saw his father come to power. No it can't be possible because what you are leading up to is that Hitler's body is probably at the house. Rubbish. I'm not listening to anymore of this."

Tom got up from the chair and walked quickly to the door, pulling it open and slamming it behind him. They heard him run up the stairs and the bedroom door bang shut.

"Well that's up to you," James replied annoyed at Tom's reticence and calling after him through the closed door.

"Jimmy I'm sorry he's gone off like that, I know you're doing what we asked. It's just that, well imagine if it was you that had had to listen to it."

"All I'm doing here is dealing with what you tell me. To that I'm adding what is known about this time in history from reports and whatever else is available to anyone doing research on the subject and then I make an assessment of that information much as I do every day in my work. There may be other conclusions to be reached if someone else was doing the same, but as you know I am one of the best there is at this sort of thing and however unbelievable it might turn out to be then that's what I offer as a conclusion."

"I know I'm sorry," she said.

"I think I know what one of his objections to this could be and I guess that he can't get his head around the fact that if I am correct then here in Hereford of all the places in the world is the body of Hitler. Why here?"

"Yes that is something which even I have difficulty understanding," she added. "I never imagined that this could be the outcome, Tom certainly didn't, I know."

"If I offered an explanation would that help?" he replied.

"Well possibly, but it should be to Tom really. Look I'll go up and see if I can placate him. I know that this whole thing has been building up on him over time. A week or so ago he was in Australia, no worries, living his own life, doing whatever he wanted and now his world has changed and still it could change further if what you say is correct."

"Sis, it is correct."

"You said it could be."

"Yes I know but also I know I'm right, I've researched it, everything fits, it's too much of a coincidence, you know I don't believe in coincidences."

"OK let me go and see him. Stay here, have a drink or two, watch the television, whatever, just let me have some time with him."

James stood up and opened the front door. "I'm going for a walk I'll be back in an hour. If you haven't got him on side in that time, then I'm away and you can tell him I'm still going to write my book. I'm not letting this go."

James closed the door behind him.

Chapter 50

Tom, from upstairs, heard the front door open and then close again; he looked out of the window and saw James walking along the road away from the house.

"Where's he going now?" he said to himself.

The door to the bedroom opened.

"Tom please just take it easy will you? I know that all this is a shock, but Jimmy's only doing what we wanted. He's good at what he does, dispassionate, analytical and if that's what he sees or works out, then that's what we get like it or not."

"Tils, this whole thing, I've had enough and it can only get worse. Suppose he's right, Hitler's body just here where we live, in a house that we have visited, awaiting rebirth did he say? What if it's true, what is going to happen if it is true? Hitler's resting place, here? Hess, you remember him? When he had died in Spandau he was buried in his home town, the grave is a shrine, they consider him to be a martyr and he was just one of

Hitler's men and not the most senior. Think of the impact if it was the main man, all of the world's crazy people coming to Hereford? Right wing, National Socialists and left wing whatever, we have got another world war on our hands? What does anyone do? What does the government do?"

"Tom we've got to see it through. It may not be true but even if it is, the body may not be 'reborn' or we may be able to stop any 'rebirth' call it what you will."

"Stop it, bloody hell Tils only a third world war can stop it."

"Look let's see what Jimmy says, we can take it a step at a time and if push comes to shove, well we've got some powerful people behind us."

"Powerful people? Who are you talking about, powerful people?"

"Well you know I mean the authorities, the Government, Military Intelligence. Don't forget Mick works for them, Steve's in the forces. With something like this, it won't be a problem getting help."

"If anyone believes us."

"They'll believe us. Just listen to James. He'll be back soon. Trust him. I do. Let's go and have a drink he won't be long away."

Tilly took his hand and lead Tom out of the bedroom and down the stairs.

Chapter 51

The two sat quietly in the living room waiting for James' return, no words were exchanged. Tom was beginning to understand and accept the conclusions made by Tilly's brother earlier and he began mulling over in his mind where they would go from here. If the Fuhrer's frozen body was in the house that Joe called home, why was it there? How was it being preserved and what had to be done to prevent it becoming the focal point for all the world's worst intentions? He could see what would happen if it all came out into the open and soon it became clear that, if it was indeed at Kolibri then it must never become public knowledge and Tilly's comments concerning the powerful people upon whom they could call might be of some use. But her comments, how could she make such a statement, he thought. What does she know about any of this? And the more he considered this the more confusion came into his head.

He looked over to where she was sitting. His ex-wife, a beautiful woman, he had begun to consider that they had a future together. She caught his glance and smiled. He smiled back and returned to his deliberations. Thinking of Tilly again, a number of things passed through his mind. She had been quick to accept his presence when he knocked on her door unexpectedly some time ago, but was it unexpected? She clearly had some knowledge of Mick, he recalled, who was involved with Steve's original visit and without any real employment that she could talk about, she had a nice house and a new car, where did the money come from? Was she forcing the issue with Joe from time to time? The more he thought about the whole episode, the more he began to have feelings of unease concerning her.

"No, I must stop this," he mumbled, "this is Tilly, she can't be involved. This is nonsense, no."

"Tom are you OK?" she said hearing his low mutterings.

"Just thinking."

"About what?"

"Look, I've got all this mess around me at the moment, but it's not just that, it's you as well."

"Me, how so?"

OK when I knocked on your door you let me in without any trouble, you know it was as if you expected me."

"Expected you? Hey come on, you were my husband once upon a time, you were in a state, just come out of the river, you said. Why wouldn't I help you?"

"And you seem to have been forcing the issue with Joe and so on."

"Christ Tom. It was bothering you to a great degree, the whole thing, I just wanted to help you get it all cleared up. I was only trying to help, offer advice, support."

"And you seemed to know Mick. Coming from his house I thought you knew the area, why would you?"

"Bloody hell. Of course I know the place; he is a mate of Steve's. Remember Steve, your brother, didn't we break up over him? Tom you've got a problem if you are suspicious of me. Get a grip I'm only trying to help. Jesus, you are in a mess."

"Maybe."

"Yes my friend, maybe or even definitely. Look if it helps, leave me out of whatever you have to do. Go and find somewhere else to live. I don't need this aggravation. Just make...."

There was a knock on the door, she stopped mid-sentence and looked around the curtain.

"It's James back. Well shall I let him in, or are you leaving or what?"

"Let him in."

She opened the door and James entered taking off his jacket and throwing it over the back of a chair. He looked at Tom and then at his sister.

"Blimey you two had words?" he asked cautiously, sensing the atmosphere in the room between them. "It won't be the first time, will it?"

"Right Jim," said Tom brusquely, "what's next?"

Tilly sat down, arms folded, body language speaking volumes.

"Well I enjoyed my stroll around the roads," he replied, "gave you some time to consider what I've said already. So shall I continue?"

"I said so didn't I?" Tom snapped. "Just get on with it."

"OK, you recall I touched on the whereabouts of Hitler or at least his body and maybe there was some evidence that it was where your friend Joe lives. Now the house name and also his surname were two pieces of information to consider, but why Hereford? If Joe is the guardian, shall I call him that? Then why here? Why not in South America or even back in Germany or Austria? Now Tom, have you ever heard of Operation Sea lion?"

"Not another bloody operation. Does anybody do anything without having to call it operation something?"

"That's the military, German or British, whatever," James replied with some restraint to the comment, realizing that Tom's demeanour was disturbed at this time.

"I know you will have heard of it," he continued.

Tom nodded.

"Fine. Operation Sea lion was the German plans for the invasion of Britain. Basically it started in May/June 1940 and led up to the Battle of Britain day in September. You recall 'The Few' and so on. It was thought that Adolf shelved the plans when that went wrong and perhaps he did, who knows? Whatever, the plans had been written before then and included every aspect of the invasion even going on to deal with the logistics of running the country afterwards. For instance, what would happen to the population? Who would support the Nazi regime? Who would be in charge? Prisons for those who refused to accept the new government and so on, everything, execution of political and military leaders, very comprehensive. Nothing was left to chance, you know the German efficiency."

He continued, "well the plans also covered where the centres of government would be when the Nazis took over. Hitler was actually quite fond of Britain. Our language has the same roots, he had many friends over here, a similar country in many ways and we can tell this by what he said about us at the time. He had a great deal of respect for British people and the monarchy and nothing gave him more pleasure than to think he would own the British Isles. Look at his delight when the Germans took over the Channel Islands, not simply a military success, at last he was in possession of a part of Britain. Any chance of another drink this is thirsty work?"

"Yeah," said Tilly, "I'll get a coffee, at least I'll be fine doing that." She glared at Tom and went into the kitchen.

James continued. He was clearly enjoying this and Tom understood that he was good at his job and that he had to be taken seriously.

"Within the invasion plans, as I said earlier, the Nazi future government had decided more or less where they wanted to be located and in particular this was Hitler's wish."

"He wanted somewhere away from the industrial centres, somewhere away from areas of high population, in short somewhere rural. He liked the thought of a river close by and places where he could walk with his family and his dog when he was in the country, a bit like his place in Germany I suppose. He felt he needed a place of historical importance yet a place with an airstrip close by and the operation plans actually named towns that had been identified as possibilities."

"Well London I would have said, but your description of the place sounds anything like the capital?" asked Tom.

"You are correct, surprisingly not London. Remember this is the 1940's the communications that we have today, motorways and so on were not available then, so anywhere near an airstrip, some height to receive radio messages was going to good enough."

"Now I've read these plans and you may be surprised to learn that Bridgnorth in Shropshire was considered as his first choice. I had never ever considered a place such as that and if you asked anyone in this country or another country, Germany for example, where is Bridgnorth I doubt that one percent of the population would have heard of it, but that was his choice. But more importantly for our purposes, was the suggestion that an alternative town or City was actually here at Hereford, the same reasons as his first choice I guess. It had everything he thought he needed at that time, so why not?"

"So let's suppose that he had eventually settled on Hereford, does that make the present situation as to where his remains are stored more or less plausible?"

Tom shook his head. He had to admit to himself that it seemed that James had thought of everything and the more he heard what was said the more he came to accept the circumstances surrounding Joe, his house and what had happened to him over the last few weeks since his return from Australia.

Silence descended on the three of them. James was waiting for a response from Tom. He was considering this latest information in the light of what had already been discussed and Tilly was trying to make a point.

They drank their coffee and he looked out of the window and up to the sky. Placing his now empty cup on the table he walked over to the door, which he proceeded to open. Standing on the step he took in a deep breath. The air was cool, the sun was attempting to shine through the clouds as if, Tom thought, to provide some hope, some inspiration. He closed the door and returned to the centre of the room.

"OK, so what do we do now?"

Chapter 52

It was the following day, James had returned to Oxford, Steve and Mick had been contacted and were due to arrive at Tilly's house. Since he had left there had been little or no conversation around the house and Tom had slept downstairs on the settee. If Tilly was to play a part in the action, Tom knew he would have to break the ice and he did consider that she could be of some use to the group effort.

"Look about yesterday;" said Tom, "I'm sorry I went on like that. I've been under pressure, you know that and I guess that I was thinking all sorts of things around what's happening."

Tilly nodded and went over to the window she had heard a car engine outside and guessed that the other two had arrived.

She opened the door just as Steve threw away the remains of his cigarette into the road and was about to knock, she ushered him inside with Mick close behind.

"Morning blokes," said Tom.

"Morning," came the reply, "what have you got for us?"

"Well I've not been in touch for a day or so, while James has been up here. I felt that I had to find out more about this, about Joe and what's surrounding us at this time."

"And," replied Mick, "did he come up with anything?"

"I would have to say yes to that, but if he is anywhere near the truth of it all then we have got to give some serious thought as to where we go from here."

Tom relayed James' findings to them whilst Tilly went into the kitchen to make coffee.

"Steve, Mick," she acknowledged as she returned to the living room and placed the cups on the table in front of them.

They both nodded in her direction at the same time continuing to absorb what they were being told, frowning, shaking heads looking at each other from time to time as another important point was covered.

Tom finished speaking, he stood up in front of the others and held open his arms waiting for a reply.

"Bloody hell," Steve was the first to speak, "is he serious, is this guy really serious? Hitler's body is at Joe's house. We've been there, we didn't see anything, I don't believe it."

"Remember what you saw when you staked out the place," replied Mick, "visitors late at night and don't forget where they came from, your mate said German, Austrian passports? Who would you expect to visit Hitler's body? Joe's a German not a Pole, his name, the name of the house? It all adds up."

"Mind if I say something?" asked Tilly.

"Go on," said Tom.

"Joe knew about you or Hamann, if you prefer it. He must have got wind of the fact that you were coming back, well he was told wasn't he I seem to recall?" she looked at Steve. "But whilst you were over in Australia and out of the way, then there was no need for him to worry about anything, you were not a threat on the other side of the world, but coming back, then that would be a problem a risk he, or whatever he represents, couldn't afford to take, so you had trouble, people trying to get you out of the way, to kill you and anyone with you."

"But Joe was always ready to help with further sessions when I wanted them."

"Of course he was. Would you expect him to refuse your requests, that would probably raise some suspicion, wouldn't it? And in any case with your regression he might find out more of what you know which could be of importance to him. OK, so what do we do now? We can't just allow the body to exist; you know remain there forever and what about if someone comes up with a way to unfreeze it?"

"Well we do nothing," replied Tom. "I think it's going to be up to the three of us to find out if what Jim says about the house and Joe has any truth, and it may mean that we have to get into the house."

"The three of you, what about me? You are not going without me and I'll tell you that," she protested.

"Look," Tom replied firmly, "this is going to dangerous. We've already had trouble and then we were nowhere near the truth, think of what we could face this time. I think this is a situation where the three men, and can I remind you, men trained for just such an occasion have the experience to handle physical problems and that is what we shall face without any doubt."

"Yes, but perhaps I can help in some way."

"You can help by keeping out of the way when the shooting starts."

"Please Tom let me help," she pleaded and caught hold of his arm pulling him away from the others so they would not hear the conversation.

"Tom, since you have returned and we have been involved with all of this, you know that I have grown closer to you, Christ, we have been living under the same roof for some time now. I can't let you go again. Please let me help, there must be something I can do."

Tom hesitated. Normally he would have stayed firm with his decision but he knew what she meant and what he really hoped for the future.

"Tils we will have to see. I've got to discuss this with the others."

He returned to Steve and Mick.

"Look guys we need to have a plan, think about how we proceed and what equipment we might need if this is going to be like some military operation. Let me think about it for a while. This is going to be big, it needs some thought. Can you both come back this evening when I've had a chance to consider all the options and problems? We should meet here I think because we can't risk someone overhearing what we say, if we're in the pub for instance."

"Sure," replied Mick, "sounds good. I'll be back around six o'clock, will that do? Steve?"

"Fine by me. I'll see you then."

Chapter 53

It was now early afternoon and there continued an awkward truce between Tom and Tilly, neither felt that there was very much to say, better leave it, time might help to heal the rift, however small it might be.

"I'm going for a walk, think about what to do, what to say to the guys when they come back later," Tom called out as he opened the door and walked out onto the street.

The thin sunlight struggled between the darkening clouds, a couple of hours would see night time he thought. A slight breeze confirmed his decision to put on a jacket for his walk.

He turned right from the house and made his way towards the end of the road, turning left towards the river. He was in no hurry. He kicked at a few leaves that had congregated around the foot of a lamppost and looked upwards at the branches of trees, still bare now but with the promise of life in the spring, not far away.

A dog barked and sniffed under the front door of a house as he passed by, causing him a moments surprise but, soon, he was at the road that ran parallel with the river. He crossed over now, away from the houses and walked along a footpath skirted by a privet hedge. The door of a house on the opposite side of the road opened. An old man looked out, bent down slowly and placed an empty milk bottle on the step. Seeing Tom, he saluted casually with one finger to his cap and turned back into his house, closing the door for the rest of the day. Tom grinned to himself at the thought of the cap being worn inside the house.

"It matches his slippers," he mumbled.

A few metres more and he would be level with his parent's house. The police tape had been removed and from the outside, the property seemed to have been put back into order, a light shone through a gap in the now closed curtains. He crossed back over the road and approached the door, putting his ear to it and listening for a while, but nothing could be heard.

Although he had no cause for concern they were still his parents and their house had been broken into recently, probably because of him. Tapping lightly on the door, he heard a movement coming from inside the living room and the curtains moved. Then a voice called out, "Who is it?"

He recognised the voice of his mother.

"It's Tom."

The door opened and his mother appeared.

"Come in, come in son. How are you? Where have you been since we saw you last and how is Matilda?"

Tom entered the room. It had been tidied up since he last saw it and clearly his parents had returned from the caravan.

"Everything alright?" he asked looking around, "where's Dad?"

"Just gone into town. Yes we're fine, got the house tidy and we went to see your friend at the police station. Strange you know, we couldn't find that anything was missing. We've no idea why the house was trashed like that. What have you been doing with yourself?"

He felt that any lengthy explanation of recent events was not necessary and might only serve to cause concern to his mother, at least his parents were back home now.

"Oh just hanging around with Tilly, you know. I was just walking by and I saw the house, the tapes had been removed, so I guessed that you had returned and I knocked. I'm glad to hear that nothing is missing. I'll call back later when Dads home, see you both, have a cup of tea and a chat, OK?"

"Yes and bring that nice Matilda with you. It's good to see the two of you together again."

Tom was not so sure after all that had gone on recently, but now was not the time for a discussion.

"Sure I will. Tell Dad I called. I'll be in touch."

"Bye son," she called and closed the door as Tom crossed back over and continued along the road.

After fifty metres the hedge thinned and finally ended at a metal gate which led into an area of scrub land. Following the footpath across the middle of it he was soon onto the path alongside the river and turning left made his way towards the rowing club steps. There was no rowing activity at the club today, a weekday, chilly to be on the water and the river was up over the bottom four steps, just the day for maintenance, a coat of paint a smear of grease, he saw a figure in the shed through the Perspex window, the sound of a hammer.

He sat on the top step and looked up and down the chocolate coloured river. Around five hundred metres of straight flow, no bends, ideal for a boat race he thought. To his right was the disused railway bridge and to the left the new road bridge. No anglers today, a few walkers and a runner attempting to beat his best time between the two bridges, stopping at the end of his run, looking at his watch, bending down and spitting into the river.

Good time or not, I wonder? He mused.

The traffic rumbled across the road bridge in both directions, North up to as far as Shrewsbury and South down to the motorway and South Wales.

"Where are they all going?" he whispered, "minding their own businesses, their own lives. People on their way home? An angry wife or husband? He considered Tilly for a moment, off out tonight for a drink or a meal?" and then a thought came to him. All this is happening within a few miles of Hitler's body. "What if the Germans had invaded? Would they be doing the same now? What if the Fuhrer was sitting here along the river? What would he be thinking? Was it worth the deaths of millions of innocent people? Would he even consider it? Why was Adolf like he was?" Tom had had that thought for a while now as soon as it became possible that he was the answer to it all. He remembered the book that was on Joe's table, 'Mein Kampf'. It was a book that he himself had in his collection back at the farm in Australia. He recalled some of the book. Hitler had written that 'he respected his father but loved his mother' and Tom wondered if the abuse that Hitler had suffered in his childhood at the hands of his father, had made him like he was. He remembered also that other members of his family had been mentally unstable and had that transferred to him? One member of the Veit family had been sent to an institution and to the gas chambers in 1940 under the hands of the Nazis. Did Hitler know that, had he sent his own relative to her death? There were reports of inter marriage, requiring special dispensation from the Vatican. Child abuse, mental instability in the family, had this shaped Hitler's character? It was no excuse, far from it, but today, would those circumstances be taken into consideration? Who knows? thought Tom. He was a father and a husband and would certainly be proud of his children, Joe for instance guarding his body with his life? Is he? God I don't know. What would happen if he could be restored to health? No, that mustn't happen, His mind turned back to the matter in hand and he knew that it had to be destroyed, for all these people, for all the people of the world now and to come.

It was a little darker now. He stood up on the steps and picked up a stone that he had just noticed lying beneath his feet and he threw it at a tree branch that was floating by in the river.

"Missed," he sighed. "I hope it's the only thing I'm missing." He looked around. The person in the shed had gone. Let's get on with it he thought and he made his way back across the field to the road and the house.

Chapter 54

It was 18.15, a knock on the door. Tilly answered. Steve and Mick came into the room, took off their coats and placed them on the table.

"I didn't hear a car?" queried Tom

"No we thought we'd walk tonight, hence the coats, getting a bit chilly though."

"Well Tom's been out all afternoon," said Tilly.

"Yes I went down to the river, somewhere to think, make a plan you know."

"And did you make one?" asked Mick.

"Yeah, but before I go into it I just want to be sure that we all know what we are doing, what we are facing here and in particular what will happen afterwards."

"What do you mean?"

"Well you know afterwards when it's all over. Look if we find what we are beginning to expect, what do we do, what do we do with Adolf's body?"

Steve nodded.

"Destroy it," added Mick, "we can't allow it to remain, we have to destroy it."

"Maybe, but first the plan. I guess from what has been said over the last few days that we all know something is going on around us, me in particular. Something heavy. Someone wants me out of the way and we conclude that it must be because of my sessions with Joe, because I can be linked to Major Hamann, the last war and his involvement in it. I seem to be a threat to whoever or whatever is out there, although as I speak now, I don't know for certain what that threat can be or to whom. Clearly I might know something of importance, but only through regression of course and Joe is the key to that, he controls what I can say, OK?"

The others murmured their replies.

"James has spent some time researching what information we were able to give him and, although I think he is after another book out of it, and I don't blame him for that, I have to say that what he has told me follows through logically, do you all agree?"

"Yes."

"So what do we have? At first I thought Steve was after getting rich and so did he, didn't you brother? But that seems to have gone by the wayside."

Steve nodded. "But there may still be something; you know some way we could benefit financially."

His comment was ignored. "Tilly offered me an idea that as Hamann I might be able to tell the world, I presume, where all the escaped Nazis went and who helped them and so on and I think that that could be an issue, but it's not the main issue. In the end, it has to be the idea that is the most unbelievable, what we have to concentrate on is Joe's house and the possibility that Hitler's body is there. We must also take into consideration the fact that Joe could be his son and he is the guardian of the body until it can be brought back to life. Now if we do nothing well, maybe that would be fine, after all perhaps there will never be the ability to bring him back and it remains there forever or at least until Joe dies, then what? Does it just die also? Well I would say no, because there are others who know about it, Steve saw visitors to the house, clearly coming to see Joe or more likely the body and so there would always be a new guardian, agreed?"

"Agreed."

"What about you Mick, do you agree?"

"Yes of course."

"So there is no alternative, it has to be destroyed and we are the ones to do it. Tilly any chance of a drink?"

She nodded and disappeared into the kitchen.

"Tilly once said to me that there may be some powerful friends that we can call upon, any idea what she might have meant?"

The two remained silent.

"You Mick, any idea, you are in intelligence?"

"Sorry mate, I don't think I can help," he replied.

Tom thought his answer a little unconvincing.

"Are you certain?" he persisted as Tilly returned to the room with tumblers of whiskey. "I was just saying that you thought we could have powerful friends."

"Well I just meant, I don't know, perhaps we could ask my Dad, he is in intelligence."

"So is Mick, but he can't help."

"Well then maybe we don't, maybe we have to go along by ourselves." She sat down and took a long drink from her glass. Tom let it go.

"Brother, if you've got some beef with Tilly just forget it for a while will you? I think there are some more important things to worry about at the moment, what's the plan?" said Steve trying to appear diplomatic.

He knew his brother would have a plan, he always, did but would he go for something of this possible magnitude? The risks would be colossal, each person could be in mortal danger, but what was the alternative?

Tom stood up. "OK, after James spoke with me earlier and while we waited for you to come over I've put together an idea that I think will get us forward. I've no guarantee that it will work or any idea as to what will happen if it doesn't or any idea if we shall find anything at all along the lines that Jim has suggested. Also I can't promise that we shall all come through it unscathed. After all as you know Tilly and I and Mom and Dad have already been in the sights of someone and as for the two of us," he glanced at Tilly, "well we could have been eliminated a number of times since I came back to Britain, so bear that in mind as we discuss this."

She had asked to be included; he wanted her to know the score.

"Right," he continued as he picked up a roll of paper from the floor and moving the coats to one side laid it out on the table.

"While we waited for you to come over I went out for a walk and considered a number of alternatives and then I produced a sketch from the local street plan so you can see the area."

He stood alongside the table and held a pencil both for drawing and for pointing out the route.

"You will most likely all be aware of the area but it has to be worth looking at even if you do. This is the road out of the City, to the east," and he commenced to mark the path to be taken.

"The railway bridge that was used the other night is here and Joe's house is just along the road here. Steve said that the house could be easily seen from the bridge and if we need a lookout point then that would probably be the best place."

"You can see the road for some way past the house and again Steve said that the cars he saw all went along the road, around the bend and out of sight before returning. The back of the property has a decent garden which extends to a narrow strip of land and then beyond that we have the river. I think that we can see the back of the house from over the other side of the river if we need to do some field work in advance of the attack."

As he spoke he felt himself taking on more of a military attitude and to the rest of them it seemed a natural thing to do and something that added to the validity of the scheme.

"What we have to do is gain access to the house; we have to find out what's inside. What Joe is hiding and why those visitors came at night. No-one goes to that amount of trouble for no reason, but if Jim's correct then we already understand the reason," he stopped talking and looked at the others.

They remained silent.

"Problem one, we need to decide when we do it. Steve watched the house at night and it was busy. He had visitors, so do we go at night, when it will be dark? No passersby, no neighbours?"

"Think about it though, when we've been to Joe's for the sessions, that's been in the day and it seemed pretty quiet then. I expect you may say that if we were going for the session then Joe would make sure that no-one was about but if what we believe is there, *is there*, then I guess the pressure on him to ensure uninterrupted access would be great. As he saw us at those times it leads me to suspect that during the day there would be no visitors...So I vote we go during the day."

"In the daylight?" questioned Tilly. "Wouldn't we be seen?"

"When I say day, I mean not night," he answered tersely, "but this time of the year it gets dark at around, say, 17.00 hrs but that's well before visiting time," he continued.

"Problem two if we go during the day then using the railway bridge for a lookout could be difficult. Trains could run until around 23.00 hrs and anyone up there could be seen, also from what Steve says it is possible that anyone on the bridge could be seen from the house. What do you think?" he looked over at his brother.

"Well if it's dark, and it should be that time, then you're probably clear but yes, you may be right. I remember that just to one side of the bridge was a clump of bushes and if you were secreted in there then I guess you would not be seen from the passing trains, but as I recall it, if you use the bushes as cover from the railway staff, the position you take up puts you more in line with the rear upstairs windows of the house."

"OK, so we have to decide which is the lesser of two evils with the bridge position.If we have a lookout then we need some form of communication between that person and the attackers. Mick what can you get hold of in this respect?"

"Well, I can get a radio system which will relay to all the others through an earpiece, so everyone can be warned simultaneously, and probably it should be the type where no messages can go the other way. This is so that the attackers, if that's what we call ourselves, are made to remain silent even from each other."

"I understand what you are saying but I'm not sure that I like the idea of having communication only one way."

"Sure but silence in the field is paramount as far as I can see, wasn't that always the case on operations?"

"Right we'll bear that in mind, now what about other equipment. I think we should be as light as possible so all I would expect to be carrying is a personal weapon, what can we get? Anybody?"

"Well I guess that's me again," said Mick, "as I'm still serving, I have my own weapon of course but you'll want a couple more I would expect, perhaps even one for Tilly?"

"No," replied Tom. "I don't want her to have one. I want her only to be involved as a lookout. I don't want her to get caught up in any violence and if we are correct in what we think about this operation then there *will* be violence, so at a distance is the best for her involvement."

He looked at her to get a reaction. She shrugged her shoulders and slowly nodded her head. "OK," she murmured.

"Well these days, the guys are issued with Sig Sauer P226's," Mick continued.

"What about the Walther?"

"Well the Sigs are possibly better. The US navy seals have been using them since 1980 so they must be reliable. They are probably the best option for a number of reasons, particularly as I can easily get hold of them from stock knowing that we probably will need them for only a short time. They are easy to deal with you can carry them easily enough so as to hide the weapon when we first go in."

"We've all been trained to use a weapon like this so I guess it will be a familiar pistol.

I shall use my Walther," Tom replied.

"*Your* Walther? Don't tell me that you managed to get that over from Oz. What about customs?"

"What about customs?"

Mick grinned, "A Walther eh, now that would be ironic."

"What irony?" asked Tom. "I just want the facts on this not a joke or any clever stuff."

"Well you know me I'll do the right thing but I just thought of what we might be doing here. If, as we suspect after all of our investigations or thinking on the subject, we really do find the Fuhrer's frozen body at the house when we get in there and war breaks out, then one result could be the destruction of the body then we could say that we have fulfilled his destiny. Hitler was reported to have shot himself in the bunker and used that very weapon a Walther PPK the standard issue Nazi weapon... ironic or what?"

The silence that followed spoke volumes. The magnitude of the forthcoming episode was colossal and yet each knew that in the end nothing might be known of what was to happen. The possible final destruction of Hitler could occur here in Hereford without the world knowing the truth behind any of the events or the people involved. Probably it was best that way, the war had been over for many years and many people in today's world know nor care anything for it.

Chapter 55

The following day dawned late. A light rain fell over the City and the weather seemed to foretell the next few days' planned events. No wind blew as if to create a silence that would give what the group had to do its very magnitude.

Mick had been instructed to obtain the radio equipment and the weapons and Tom and Tilly would undertake to reconnoitre the area around the house. Mick had a dog, an old white and grey wire haired fox terrier named Paddy and the pair of them would borrow it and take it for a walk along the river. Joe's house backed on to the river and they would be able to see as much as they needed from across the other side.

After a light breakfast the pair began to get ready, clothes suitable for walking in the rain and boots particularly for the anticipated muddy path.

"Are you ready for this?" asked Tom pulling a woollen hat down onto his head.

"Sure," replied Tilly picking up her car keys from the table, "let's get going, we need to collect Mick's dog."

They left the house and drove around the few streets to where Mick was waiting on the step with Paddy who proceeded to bark when he saw the car stop and the passengers get out.

"I saw you coming along the road, here's the dog, he's looking forward to a walk in the rain, I don't think,"

"Fine," replied Tom, "we'll look after him. We plan to drive down to the meadows and walk along on the other side of the river, no-one ever suspects anything about dog walkers and the two of us passing by slowly with an old dog should be able to loiter long enough to see what we need to see, without anyone being too suspicious."

Tilly took the dog lead and returned to the car, opening the door. The animal jumped in readily and scrambled onto the back seat.

"See you," shouted Mick as the car started up and pulled away from the house. The dog quickly stretched out on the back seat.

"Making himself at home eh," said Tom.

Tilly drove her car along the streets and over to the opposite side of the river. She drove onto a housing estate and eventually parked up along a road at a point where there was a path through to the riverbank. Although this was a residential area few people were about. Workers had already left for their places of employment and the rain, although not heavy, was keeping others well inside their houses.

"Well we've got a decent day for it," said a grinning Tom getting out of the passenger side of the car and pulling a reluctant Paddy off the warmth of the seat.

Tilly got out and locked the car and with the lead now on the dog, coats and woolly hats on themselves, they made their way between the houses and onto the wet meadow behind. There was still some way to go until they would reach the place where they would be level with the house on the other side but it was now not a time for idle banter. The river was in flood following a few wet days further up into the hills and it grabbed their attention as they walked. Debris in the form of tree branches and straw washed from the fields swirled along occasionally getting caught in the reeds withered by the season. Tom thought of the man that he had fought on the bridge some days earlier and wondered if he had made it down this far or whether even now his body was entwined within tree roots along the river and perhaps right where they were now walking. Neither spoke, alone with their own thoughts of what life would hold for them both when this was all over.

Eventually the house was opposite them just at a point where a stile had to be crossed from one meadow to another. This would give them the chance to wait a while and get a look across the river over to the rear of the property without anyone being too concerned with what they doing.

The rain was lighter now, a thin mist continued to rise from the surface of the water, even so they could see the rear of the property quite well. Trees seemed to have been cut down at the end of the garden and a small construction of staging had been built into the river. An old metal chair was its only adornment and it was a surprise that it hadn't disappeared during the last flood. The seat clinging to the wooden pier and bedecked with the detritus of the last high water gave the house a neglected look.

As they stopped at the style Tom gripped Tilly's arm and gestured to her. In the distance he had seen another dog walker coming towards them. He was a tall man wearing a large overcoat and with a trilby hat pulled down against the rain obscuring some of his face and although he was wearing boots he seemed rather smartly dressed for this pastime they thought. He arrived at the style his pair of muzzled Rotweiller dogs pulling at their leads anxious to get a sniff at Paddy or even worse considered Tom. Paddy cowered behind Tom's legs trying to get as far away from the other two animals as he possibly could. The man uttered a barely audible "Morning" as they stood to one side allowing him priority at the fence, but with dogs like them this was not the time to dispute rights of way. Their paths crossed and he carried on along the path from where they had just come.

Tom looked after him. "No one ever suspects anything about dog walkers do they?" he whispered. Tilly nodded, understanding the message in the comment.

Still standing at the style he took hold of Tilly's shoulders and positioned her back to the house.

"No time for this Tom," she snapped

"I just need to look in the general direction of the property," he replied, "and with our walker friend just along the way......."

The token embrace took several minutes but that was enough time for him to make a pretty good survey.

The rear of the house was looking as neglected as the river platform, nothing to attract any great attention. The garden reflected the time of the year and probably also the fact that the owner was not a gardener. He could see two large downstairs windows and a door out to the garden, pathways from the front of the house down each side gave access. There were three French windows to the first floor all leading out on to a wrought iron balcony which stretched the length of the building. As he looked he described to his companion what he could see.

"Nothing special Tils," he lingered and gave her a kiss on the cheek. She looked at him.

"So the mood is over can I assume."

"I think so."

She returned the affection but saw that he was still watching the house."What is it Tom?"

"Interesting that, I think. All the curtains are open except for those at the window upstairs on the left."

"So what, it's a dull day, if you don't use a room then why bother?"

"It's an anomaly. You're right why bother, in which case why bother with any of them? You have a look," and he turned Tilly around to face the other way.

"What do you think?"

"You're correct, it is odd and especially as that window doesn't have a curtain anyway, it has a blind."

They were suddenly aware that in the distance the smart man with the dogs was returning towards them.

"OK, let's get back," said Tom, "I think I've seen enough," and they began to make their way back towards where they had parked the car.

In a few minutes they had crossed again with the other man.

"Morning again," Tilly said. Her greeting was returned without any eye contact as he continued in the opposite direction, the dogs again pulling at their leads to get closer to Paddy.

"Bloody serious bloke."

"Hmm," mumbled Tom, "bloody serious dogs as well."

By the time they had arrived back at the car it had almost stopped raining but both of them seemed happy to climb into the vehicle out of the dampness and the dog seemed particularly happy to be inside away from any potential canine danger.

"What do you reckon then?" said Tilly, cleaning the condensation from the windows.

"Well that house is big, I mean large for one person and I guess worth some serious money. Compared to the other properties, it looked pretty standard I suppose and the only thing that caught our attention was that upstairs window and we'll look at that when we get closer around the house later. That's not an issue, we can get inside somewhere like that without much trouble, but that guy who walked by was interesting," he replied. "He was nowhere in sight when we arrived at the river, and was it a coincidence that we met just opposite the house? I don't think so. That'll be something to keep a watch for. Right let's go. I'll tell you what, I think we should have a look around the other side and that will give us the chance to see the bridge also."

Tilly started up the car, curtains twitched at the window of the house outside of which they had parked. A thin cat waited for the car to pull away and then nonchalantly walked across their path. Paddy snored.

Chapter 56

A few minutes later the car was making its way off the housing estate back along the main road and over the river. A juggernaut pulled alongside them as they slowed towards a set of traffic lights on red. Tilly looked over at the vehicle and nudged her companion.

"Not much of a future for them," she said seeing that it was filled with white chickens destined for the local processing factory. The lights changed to green and both vehicles pulled away. As the transporter turned to the left a shower of feathers joined the last of the rain and attached themselves to Tilly's car and to several vehicles in the queue behind.

"What's the future for us do you think?" replied Tom, watching the wipers remove the feathers from the windscreen.

They drove on, the remaining walls that were left of the old City on their right. A few shoppers scurried along in the shelter of the walls. It had started to rain again.

The road had now left the immediate City and they were approaching the railway bridge that had been used by Steve previously and that they expected could be used by Tilly as a watching place. Just before the bridge where the road turned right was a little public garden with a couple of parking spaces in front. She drove into one space and stopped.

"Tom we can leave the car here and walk the rest of the way? We just go round to the right and under the bridge. Steve said there was an access just at that point so I will be able to see where I have to go and the house is only a short distance further on. We can walk past that at the same time, with this rain there shouldn't be too many people about and under the umbrella we are hidden a little bit. Do you think we should leave the dog?"

"Yes, he looks comfortable on the back seat. No reason why we should inflict any more cold and wet on him is there?"

They got out of the car and made their way across the road. This part of town was quiet. The road was one that left the City away into the country and even in the rush hour, traffic was light. All the properties were residential but substantially larger than those where they had previously parked. They were all detached, Victorian houses sitting in their own grounds, many behind tall laurel hedges and having in and out drives. Expensive cars were parked on some of the drives.

"That's something to be aware of," said Tom, "I bet most of the residents are of a certain age or wealth so if we have to come here during the evening as I suggested, they are likely to all be at home. We will need to be careful that no-one sees us."

They walked on, arm in arm and in a few minutes they had arrived at the bridge. The rain gave them the excuse to stop underneath as if sheltering. Tom lowered the umbrella and shook the water from the cover and pointed it towards the steps that led up to the parapet.

"That's your way up. This looks reasonably easy to get to. You can leave the car over the road where we've just parked and make your way here. If you do this just as it's getting dark, you know, little traffic, you should be able to get here without being seen," instructed Tom.

"Yes. Steve said the bridge balcony was low enough for me to see over and I can make my way to a clump of bushes just to one side of the bridge. The trains will still be running at that time but inside the vegetation I should be fine. The drivers won't expect to see anyone and, in any case, they will be approaching the station so my guess is that they will need to concentrate on slowing down at that point, but from there I can see the house," Tilly explained.

"Are you sure you want to do this thing Tils? You know this is likely to be a pretty dangerous effort. I wouldn't want anything to happen to you. I wouldn't want to lose you again. When all this is over….."

"No problem," she interrupted, "nothing's going to happen. You're not going to lose me. In any case what about you? You'll be doing the rough stuff, perhaps I don't want to lose you!!"

She squeezed his arm. "Let's walk up the road now and see what we can see at Joe's." Putting the umbrella back above their heads and arm in arm they left the shelter of the bridge.

Within a few minutes their stroll had brought them outside of the property where Joe lived. They knew that they could not afford to stop here as this might attract attention from anyone looking from inside the house or even watchers from the other houses in the vicinity but their slow pace enabled them both to make a decent observation and of course they would be able to return in a short while.

Passing the house they continued along the road as far as the bend that Steve had mentioned. At this point the road continued away from the City towards the main route to Ledbury. A car came towards them and slowed down at the bend. The driver peered out of the side window at the pair who had stopped and were talking to one another, then he accelerated off towards the City.

"Well what did you see, did you notice anything?" asked Tom.

"I don't think I saw anything more than I could remember from our earlier visits. What about you?"

"I'm not sure… but maybe…, Tils look below the left window when we walk past again. Let me know what you see….what do you think it is that I saw?"

They returned to the bend in the road which had taken them out of sight of the house and stopped walking. The car that had just passed them was parked along the road close to Joe's house.

"Bugger," muttered Tom, "what's he doing there? We'll have to carry on now. If it's a problem then he might be watching us through the rear view mirror."

They walked on. A hundred metres to the house Tom stopped. He bent down pretending to tie a shoe lace. Tilly held the umbrella above him.

"It's moving off," she whispered.

He looked up, the vehicle had started up and was performing a U turn in the road and was returning to them. As the car passed, the driver peered again out of the window, continued around the bend and was away, the sound of the engine dying as he left the area. Tom stood up; they continued along the road, an ordinary couple having a walk on a miserable day in February.

They were now back at the target. Tilly looked carefully below the left hand window of the house as instructed and soon they had passed under the bridge once more and had regained the shelter of the car.

Paddy was still asleep on the back seat, he whimpered and opened his eyes as the door opened but was soon quiet again as it was closed sealing them all off from the elements outside. It was raining more now, the rain drops rattling on the car roof. Tom hoped it would be like this when the group made their visit, bad weather was always an advantage to an operation requiring stealth.

"So what do you reckon it was under the window?"

"Well I think that to me it looked like a door to a cellar. You know one of those that have a pair of doors that lift upwards and you find steps down into the room below," she replied starting the car engine.

"Hmmm."

She drove off the small car park and turned back towards the City.

It was no more than fifteen minutes until they had pulled up outside her house; Steve was already at the property sitting in his car. With the condensation on the inside of the windows and the smoke from his cigarette filling the cabin, he was barely visible.

As they arrived he got out from the vehicle and taking a last draw he threw the nub into the gutter. It sizzled in a puddle for a second and then went out becoming just another piece of litter in the street. Tilly looked at him with a disapproving glance. He shrugged his shoulders and raised his hand as an apology. The front door was opened and they all entered the house.

"Paddy will be alright for a while," said Tom, "he had a good walk but he doesn't like the rain so he's asleep on the back seat.

"OK Steve, what do you know?"

Before he could answer, a rattle on the door at that moment caused the three of them to turn towards it.

"It's only me," came Mick's voice, "let me in will you it's wet out here."

Steve opened the door, taking the opportunity to look out into the street as he did so. Mick entered the house quickly removing his rain spattered coat and cloth cap which he placed on the floor just behind the door. The others saw that he was carrying two plastic shopping bags from a local supermarket and he placed one of them on the table. As it touched the hard surface it made a metallic noise.

"Will these do?" he enquired, as he tipped out the contents revealing three handguns and fifty or so rounds of ammunition which rolled into the middle of the table. Tom nodded slowly, the expression on his face showing the reality of the situation.

Steve took a couple of steps to the table and picked up one of the pieces. It had been some time since he had held a Sig Sauer and he turned it slowly around in his hands, caressing it, stroking the barrel as if it were a valuable work of art.

"An old friend of mine," he grinned and returned it to the table alongside the others.

The three men stood around the table looking at the weaponry for some time and then as if in unison they sat down around the room.

"Remember how to use these then?" asked Mick breaking the silence. "I'm still on active service, so I get regular practice, how about you Tom?"

"Tom's alright," said Steve answering for his brother. "When I was over in Oz, I saw Tom one morning out in his backyard. A couple of ducks or whatever had landed on his pond and he took the head off one at forty feet, first shot."

"It would have to be first shot wouldn't it," Tom replied sarcastically. "You only get one shot if you think about it, miss and they fly away. Yes I remember how to use one although I prefer the Walther, so having gone to all the trouble in bringing it back with me, I'll use that thank you. I shot most days when I was away, target practice mainly, a can on a fence, that sort of thing. I used to imagine it was Steve, I never missed." He looked at his brother, they both grinned eyes narrowing at the same time.

"OK you pair, let's get on with it I know all about that animosity but I also know it's over now." Said Mick as he glanced at Tilly. "Let's get down to business. I've got some other stuff here, radio equipment, map and so on, let's see what the plans are. Tom what did you find out this morning?"

Tom sat forward in his chair and picked up the map. It was a street map of Hereford and he opened it up onto the table, indicating the various reference points as he spoke.

"Tilly and I went for a ride this morning over the river. We parked in a road on the estate and went through to the riverside with the dog. From that side you can see the back of Joe's house and having walked along some way we came level with it, just here." He pointed at the spot where they had encountered the fence. "I wanted to get some idea of the layout and with Paddy alongside us it was what you might expect to see any day along there, dog walkers, so it shouldn't have been too suspicious. I think we saw enough for our information, but we also saw another dog walker and he was a bit of an oddball. The fields were wet, it had been raining for a while and it was still drizzling a bit and this guy came marching along with his animals, a vicious looking pair of Rotweillers. Tilly made the comment that he was hardly dressed for walking in the rain, you know, he looked like he had on a smart suit under an overcoat which reminded me very much of army issue, but not British army."

"Not British, German perhaps?" enquired Mick.

"Well possibly," Tom replied. "His whole demeanour was military, not the usual local in that area. We saw him again as we went back to the car. You know it was as if he was patrolling the fields and of course in the vicinity of the house that we wanted to see. We got back to the car. Mick your dog was really pleased to get inside. Then we decided to go and have a look at the front of the house and on our way there we could get a view of the bridge, you know Tilly's lookout place? The bridge I think is OK. If we arrive just as it's getting dark, she has every chance to access the bridge by the steps without being seen and once she's up there make her way to that clump of shrubs that Steve spotted. If she hides in the thicket then she shouldn't be seen from the house or equally as important, from any passing train, because they are still running at that time."

"Yes I think I will be fine up there," she added, "but what equipment have you liberated for me Mick?"

"Well as I said at the time, when we are at Joe's we need silence so it would be best if we had a system that involves one-way speech. You can speak to us if you see anything, we can all hear what is said, but we won't be tempted to reply. This is what I've borrowed." Mick took a number of ear-pieces from the second bag and began to hand them around.

"This system is pretty easy to handle," he said, "just put the piece in your ear. It's comfortable enough and in any case we will be wearing balaclavas so if there is any activity the pieces shouldn't fall out. Try it and here is the head gear as well."

They all managed to insert the plastic into their ear and Mick passed around a black Balaclava to each one.

"Very fashionable," said Steve, "and warm in the winter.

"Let's hope that's as warm as it gets," said Tilly, as she picked up the handset from the table and handed it to Mick gesturing for him to demonstrate its operation.

"It's pretty easy, Tils, it works by pressing this switch. When it's pressed down there's no sound and this is a safety device really. You can speak when you let it go, so in the field if you are unable to move, you know wounded or whatever, then you can still be heard. Do you understand what I am saying?"

Tilly nodded.

"Alright so far?" said Mick. "Now a couple more things that I think we may find useful."

He reached into the second bag once more. "Well we know the noise that a Sig makes and quiet could be good, so our old standby may come in handy." He held up a number of pieces of wire each piece with a small wooden handle at either end.

"The garrote," he continued, "I appreciate we have to get right up close for this, but that is what we have all trained for over the years, so I trust that's no problem."

The others nodded.

"You never know, it can dispose of an enemy without a sound, except from the victim of course, and so it shouldn't alert anyone else who might be in the property, and also neighbours for that matter."

"Now finally, I've given some thought to what we may find in the house, and I've had to accept that what Tilly's brother said could be right, fantastic but right. If we do find a body in there in some form or another, what do we do about it? There's no mileage in thinking that the world could come to terms with something like that. You know the victims of the war, the supporters of the war, and we are aware that both would dearly love to lay hands on the Fuhrer for very different reasons. So I've brought a grenade each. I think we may have to consider destroying anything remotely connected with him, what do you all say?"

They had all in their own time thought of this eventuality and had separately come to the same conclusion. They nodded solemnly without a word.

"Oh just one other thing I forgot to mention," said Tom during the silence that followed, "when we were at the house just a while back, you know having a look, and we were walking along the road, a car came by and I am sure that the driver was interested in us. What did you think Tils?"

"Yeah, possibly," she conceded

"He seemed to stop outside Joe's place and then came back towards us, having another good look. Well I remembered the registration number. Here it is Steve, can you get your mates to check it out please, as soon as possible?" He handed his brother a piece of paper on which he had written the number. Steve read the number and put the paper in his pocket.

"Any chance of getting it checked now?"

"Well I suppose I could make a phone call now if you think it's important."

"Yes I do. I'd like to know if there are strangers around in the area if we are going ahead with this."

"Fine," said Steve taking his mobile from his pocket and walking into the kitchen."How about a break while he does that? And where's the bottle?"

Chapter 57

Tilly poured everyone a large drink and placed the bottle on the table. The men sipped the whiskey and sat back in their chairs, waiting for Steve to come up with an answer.

"What" they heard him exclaim from inside the kitchen, "there's no such number? What are you talking about? There has to be, all vehicles are registered aren't they?"

The others stared across at the kitchen door as the tone on the mobile indicated that it had been turned off, Steve returned.

"They say that here's no number Tom; could you have got it wrong do you think?"

"No way, I know that the number is correct. What did your man say?" queried Tom.

"Well the number doesn't exist, it's not registered, it must be false."

Tom looked at Mick. "Spooks," he exploded, "bloody spooks, what about that?"

Mick held out his hands and made no comment.

"Hey don't forget that Joe said he had some friends, remember the hospital business?" said Tilly.

"It's just as likely to be *your* powerful friends," he snapped back.

"Don't let's start that again," interrupted Mick, "when are you going to accept that there's nothing going on outside of the four of us?"

"False number plates?" uttered Tom sneeringly.

"It could mean anything, mate. A burglar casing the road, who knows? He saw you, you saw him, he did a runner."

"I don't like it."

"I don't like you having a go at me every so often," said Tilly.

Silence descended on the room, they drank their alcohol.

"OK, I suppose that we should discuss the plan of action next," Tom said, having eventually calmed down from his previous outburst, helped by a further glass of Whiskey. "We had a look from over the river as I have already said and we noticed that there are three French windows at the first floor. One of them had a closed blind to it and so it might be that there was something in the room that the occupants wanted to keep out of sight. You could get to the back garden by paths along each side of the house from the front, so getting round there is not a problem if we have to. Then we went around to the other side and had a look at the front of the place by walking past along the road. I know we have seen it before and of course we've all been inside a few times, but this time we did notice what seemed to be a cellar entrance to one side of the main door, another access point if that was needed. So there are a couple of ways to get in apart from the obvious windows and doors and I think we can do that ok without it being Operation Nimrod all over again."

"Well," said Mick, "you say that, but if we actually were certain of finding Hitler's remains then storming the place would be fine I guess, but as we don't really know what is in there at this point then simple breaking and entering is about the best we can do. What do you think?"

Tom continued, "I think we just need at this time to get inside, after that we work out what is to be done depending on what we find there. That's always the way it went, just be prepared for whatever and if it's a waste of time then we're in and out, no fuss. The only thing we need then is for Joe to be away when we do it and a phone call to him arranging a meet at, say, The Golden Eagle should be enough."

"Do you think so?" queried Tilly.

"No problem," said Tom, "just telling him that I want to discuss my regression will get him there. If he is, what Jimmy thinks he is, then he just couldn't take a chance on not knowing what I have to say, you said that yourself. No he'll be there alright and we will have the time we need to be in and out before he gets back. OK I guess we just now need to prepare, you know the usual rituals that we go through?" He looked at the others they nodded.

Tom's preparation, as with the rest, was something he had had since as long as he could remember. It involved the weapon he would be using at any time during his service with the Special Forces. Apart from the psychological aspect that he employed with his eyes, he was never the most powerful man in the squad and so to him his equipment was of considerable importance. He knew that his pistol brought over from Australia would be sound, in perfect working order, well cleaned and so on, but his ritual involved the rounds. He took out his own ammunition from a sideboard drawer and sat at the table. He inspected each bullet for smoothness and perfect shape and although there was never likely to be a fault, he wanted to satisfy himself in that regard. He held them, caressed them, kissed them and finally warmed the missiles by holding each one tightly in his hands as if in prayer and then he loaded them into his gun. Of course there had been occasions when, in the field, he had needed to reload with some urgency and he was at those times perfectly able to perform this exercise at speed and not surprisingly he had never encountered a problem, but that mattered not, this was his way and he would do it whenever he could.

Steve was a stronger individual whose strategy was to get close to the enemy. Guns made a noise and he was always as silent a killer as he could be. His powerful hands had broken the neck and finished off an enemy many times when approaching from behind at night, but whenever he could he liked to use a wire. Mick had anticipated this and had brought some along and Steve undertook his preparation by inspecting each piece. This he did whilst standing as he could generate more power. The garrotte had to be smooth so it would slide around the neck just below the Adams Apple and strong enough to cut into the neck he used to say. He never explained how that worked against a female, but then he had rarely come up against a female opponent. Many times he had used the wire and many times he had silently removed his victim's head. Mick had produced a small pot of petroleum jelly and Steve used this to lightly grease the length of the wire. He held each grip tightly and pulled, the wire straightened and it seemed to hum with a deep note as Steve's strength generated the force against the thin strip of metal. His face reflected the effort, nostrils flaring, his teeth closed together, as his imaginary victim struggled.

Mick sat quietly in a corner of the room watching the brothers. The same parents and raised the same way in similar circumstances, they had developed very different characters, but he knew that both were perfectly suited to what they did best.

His own ritual was minor in relation to Tom and Steve. He was as powerful a man as the younger brother, short in stature but none the less skilled with his preferred weapon. It was a personal item not drawn from army stock and something that he bought whilst on a trip to the USA. The Bowie knife had a thick blade suddenly tapering to a point and with one sharp edge. He loved this knife. It had a bone handle and an engraving of some unrecognizable animal along the blade which had attracted him to it at first sight when on a visit to Calico, an old silver mining town in California. An old leather faced Indian in buckskins had approached him just outside the town and offered some wares to his group of visitors. At first he had considered this was just some salesman in period dress, typical of the American theme park idea, but Mick had struck up a conversation with the individual and he was very soon aware that he was the genuine article and the knife equally so.

The man asked a paltry sum for the artifact for that was what it was, but Mick doubled it and the deal was done. The seller took out from somewhere within his clothing a leather pouch and offered that with the knife. This time no money passed over but the men shook hands in the kind of contact that spoke of years of friendship although they had met no more than ten minutes earlier.

Mick remembered that meeting and felt that throughout his ownership and use of the knife his life had been guided in some way and all he had to do was reflect on that old man and all was well. The weapon was suited to him and the training he had received concerning its use seemed exactly as it should be. An upward thrust into the rib cage, a twist and then a quick ripping of the knife from the body would cause severe damage and disembowelment of the vital organs.

Each man reflective at this time, not wishing to interfere with another's preparations for conflict, seemed very appropriate for the task ahead. Tilly sat quietly. She had been married to Tom and had then been with his brother for some time, so she knew what they were doing and why it was important to each man.

Soon it was time to put the operation into practice.

"I'll phone Joe," said Tom breaking the silence and he went over to the telephone and picked up the handset.

The number dialed, the ring at the other end loud enough for all to hear. It rang once. "Hello, Joseph here."

Tom considered the speed with which it was answered as if the man had been waiting for the call, or at least a call. His voice sounded different in some way, reverential perhaps, quieter than Tom had remembered and with the use of the full name.

"Hi Joe, this is Tom how are you?"

"Fine thank you and your good self."

"Yes good. Look, is it possible to have another meeting. Since we last spoke I've had a chance to consider what you told me and Tilly's brother has added something to the pot so I want to go a little further with my, erm, Hamann's family. Is that alright?"

"Certainly it is, when?"

"How about this evening at The Golden Eagle. You know have a pint see what else we can look at."

"We can't have a session in public Thomas."

"No I don't need a session at this time, just a chat about what James has said and then we take it from there."

There was silence at the other end of the line. Perhaps Joe was thinking about the request.

"What do you think?" asked Tom.

"Yes that would be fine, just referring to my diary. Can we make it around 5.30?"

"Exactly what I thought," said Tom in as friendly a way as he could muster knowing what was likely to transpire that evening. "See you there then." He returned the handset.

"That was what you wanted to hear wasn't it?" asked Tilly. "He seems to have accommodated us perfectly."

"Too perfectly maybe," he replied. "You know he sounded different somehow and when I asked for the meet it seemed as if he was thinking about it, perhaps having things to do or needing to get back home for something. Maybe a few visitors tonight like you saw when you watched the place Steve?"

"Yes possibly, but they were pretty late at night and we should have done what we have to hopefully before that time and in any case 17.30 hrs at The Eagle keeps him away when we want him to be away. Sounds ok to me, Mick?"

"Yes I guess so. We have to do this sometime so no time like the present. We are all tooled up and ready for it. Let's do it eh? We just have to get Tilly set up with this radio. OK Tils are you ready for this?"

"Sure let's see how it works."

"Right, as I said before, these are the ear pieces, now you guys know how they work, you will have used them many times in the field. Tilly, you will not have one of these because, if you recall this is a one way device. You can transmit but not receive. You saw how to switch it on and off?"

"Yes."

"Now although we will be wearing headgear and so will be covered up, they are powerful enough to work through that and will be fine over the distance that Steve has told me we have to cover.

"As I said, this is a one way system, this will be so that we are not encouraged to speak to you when we will need absolute silence. You can of course speak to us if you see anything or feel we, or you, could have a problem, and that's the point of it all. Your role is very important here as you are our eyes outside when we are inside. You know if Joe or anybody else comes to the house we have to be warned."

"The radio is off all the time provided you have the button pressed down, remember if you release the button, then you can transmit, you just have to speak and we will hear. If it's necessary to switch off then just depress the switch and that cuts you out. I imagine you might do that when a train passes perhaps or maybe it's left on all the time. Whatever you think is appropriate. It's pretty simple you just have to let us know about anything that you see and I mean anything unusual."

"Tilly are you sure you are happy with this?" asked Tom. "This could be dangerous."

She gave him a certain look of determination.

"I know all about that. I want to be involved. After all I've been involved already when they tried to run you off the road, remember? I was in the car with you and consider that I owe them something as well. Let's get this thing tested so we know it works."

She picked up her equipment and left the room, climbing the stairs to the bedroom furthest away and entering it, she closed the door.

"Can you hear me?" she whispered, "can you hear me?"

She quickly returned to the living room. The men nodded as she entered.

"No problem," said Tom.

He knew that when she had made up her mind nothing would change it and in any case he was silently pleased that she would be part of the plan and of his life for the future. Even though there had been some tension between them lately, the closer it became to the finality of what had to be done, the happier he was with their relationship.

"Well that's all the equipment sorted," said Mick. "I guess we just now need to discuss the plan of action. Tom you said that when you looked at the property from rear and front you saw a balcony to the first floor rear and a trapdoor below the front window?"

"Yes that's right. We couldn't see from over the river but generally with houses having a balcony such as that, there will be a fire escape which may be usable. The trap door will go into some sort of a cellar with a second door out of the cellar into the house, so that's two possible entrances. When we visited the house to see Joe in the past, I noticed the front door. Very substantial, possibly two inches thick with locks and bolts, so I wouldn't expect to get in that way."

"Or out if you need a quick exit," added Tilly.

"It's right what you say but I think we are going to aim to exit the way we enter," Tom continued, "and with Joe out of the way, going inside should be no problem. What do you think Steve?"

"In theory it sounds fine as long as there is no-one left in the house when Joe goes for the meet and also, the other thing to consider is what about the guys you saw on the outside, you know, the bloke with the dogs and the man in the car? If either of them have any connection with Joe, then they might be around when we don't want them to be."

"Well if they were of any connection to the situation then they might be around, who knows, but I expect it's going to be similar to the Iranian embassy on a smaller scale, in that we don't know what we shall find until we get in there, not that I was involved in that."

"When was this sort of thing ever easy?" added Steve, "after all that is what we've been trained for at the taxpayer's expense, so we just have to do it."

An uneasy silence descended upon the group. They all understood the risks but there was no backing out now. This had become a crusade, something that they had to do and if James's thoughts on the subject were anywhere near being accurate then they owed it to all the dead of the war and all of the future generations. If Hitler ever returned what would happen?

Outside a nearby church bell chimed indicating that it was 5 o'clock. Joe would be leaving his property for the spurious meeting at The Golden Eagle and by the time they arrived at his house it should be dark enough for the planned entry.

Collecting all of their equipment they left the house at a brisk pace, upbeat about the events that would soon unfold.

Chapter 58

It was dark now and the rain that had been falling earlier in the day had ceased. The wind had changed direction and it seemed a few degrees warmer. They made their way to the car parked just outside the house. Last year's remaining shrivelled leaves from the trees growing up from the pavements outside had collected around the wheels and clouds scudded across the sky occasionally revealing a moon, the light from which supplemented the dull street lamps.

The moon was up early tonight and Steve felt that the intermittent illumination of Joe's garden would be to their advantage. Certainly Tilly would get a better view from the bridge and that could be crucial.

The car started up, a curtain twitched and they were on their way. Slowly pulling out of the street they were quickly onto the ring road. Office workers and shoppers crossed the road every few yards towards the car parks. Coats and hats on against the elements, soon they would be driving home, another day over, unaware that for the occupants of this one vehicle life would never be the same again.

Mick drove relatively slowly, no accidents, no speeding. The last thing he wanted was to be pulled over by an overzealous police officer and then have to explain the hardware and clothes which were in their possession. Leaving the brighter lights around the City centre and along its' walls they made their way to the small parking area just around the corner from the house where Tom and Tilly had parked earlier in the day. It was darker here. What street lights there were, were partially hidden amongst the lower branches of the many trees growing along the road or the evergreen laurels encroaching the footpaths from the various properties. The car parked, they sat for a few moments adjusting to their surroundings peering at the windows of the houses opposite. Would anyone be watching them, this group intent on their purpose? All seemed as quiet as they could have hoped. Little traffic, no pedestrians, curtains closed against the night. A few windows showing lights, they ought to be able to go about their business with little hindrance. The car doors were opened and the four of them exited swiftly, while the door was open a light was showing. Anyone seeing them might well have assumed they were up to no good, an assumption in complete contrast to the purpose of their mission. The door closed they went around to the rear of the vehicle secreting themselves in the shadows. Somewhere in the distance a dog barked.

Tom and Tilly set off first towards the corner of the road where they would next encounter the railway bridge.

Arriving at the bridge they still seemed to be unnoticed by any residents and Tilly prepared to climb the steps up to the track. Tom put his arms around her, kissed her forehead and the two of them started up.

Reaching the top, no train at this time, they made their way to the small clump of bushes which position afforded a view of the house and within which she would be able to crouch down and remain unseen by any passing train crew.

She took her radio from her coat pocket and felt around the device in the dark for the switch. Finding it she pressed down the button and a tiny red light showed, all seemed to be well.

"Good luck," said Tom giving her a squeeze and again kissing her, although with more passion on this occasion. "When this is all over fancy a trip to somewhere nice and warm?"

"Anywhere with you," she whispered.

Tom turned away and made for the steps at the bridge. Descending the steps he found the other two had arrived there. Mick waved an earpiece, and in response all three fitted them and pulled on a Balaclava. Tilly had waited for a short while on the bridge until she calculated that the men had applied the receivers.

Placing the radio close to her mouth she whispered into it, "Hello, please signal if you can hear me."

The signal was to be two flashes of a torch as the men arrived outside the house. A few moments passed no signal.

She repeated the message. This time the torch shone out, contact was made. All that was necessary now was for her indicate any activity she could see in the vicinity, the men would decide if it was a problem.

Chapter 59

The drive of the house was behind an evergreen hedge and once onto it they would not be seen by passersby, the trees blocking out the light from the street lamps. A cloud passed in front of the moon at that very moment immersing the drive with complete darkness.

They peered around the hedge from the footpath, the house seemed empty. Mick held up his hand and the others stopped close behind him.

"Before we go onto the drive," he suggested in hushed tones, "we need to see if the front of the property is clear, you know no-one looking out of the windows. I'll walk past the front first and see what it looks like, then you two come along after, we'll meet just along the road and compare notes."

They gave a thumbs up and Mick slowly walked on and along the road stopping after about thirty metres for the others to catch up.

"Well?" inquired Steve as he and Tom arrived at where Mick had stopped. "Anything there?"

"We'll walk back now," he replied, "have a look down the left hand side. It's dark but that's the point, what can you see in the dark?"

They retraced their steps across the front of the house and stopped again a few yards to the other side.

"Did you see it Steve?" Mick asked.

"Yes I saw it. Just a point of red light for a few seconds then it was gone. I'm not certain but to me it looked as though that was someone drawing on a cigarette what do you think?"

"I guessed you would come to that conclusion being a smoker. I agree there must be a guard or someone around the side. We need to remove him?"

"That's my job."

Steve put his hand inside his coat and removed a piece of wire that Mick had produced earlier He ran his fingers along the metal which he had greased before setting out and holding the metal grip at either end he first pulled it straight. Satisfied with the strength of it he now crossed over his hands making a bow of the wire and slowly began to pull, tightening almost to a knot. Reversing the motion the wire straightened again. He gave a slight grin, eyes narrowing as he nodded his head.

His companions stayed silent during this display and melted into the hedge as he moved off onto the drive but keeping to the shelter of the hedge in front of the house.

He would cross the gravel drive on the opposite side and approach the back garden away from the smoker.

Tom had described the layout to them before they set off and he anticipated a clear path to the back and then along the rear of the property under the balcony.

The drive was covered with gravel. Steve had to tread lightly to minimise the sound, his soft shoes helping his progress.

From the shelter of the front wall a look along the side showed nothing as a problem and he proceeded along towards the back. Looking up he located the balcony and pressed up against the wall slowly moving silently to the other side. His nostrils detected tobacco smoke the closer he got to the end of the building, confirming what he had seen earlier. Now he was at the corner and crouching down peered around it. He held his breath so no sound could be made now and as his eyes adjusted to the darkness he picked out the form of an individual no more than five feet away from him.

It was a man around six feet tall and powerfully built he thought taking account of the additional clothes that might be worn on a February evening in England. The man was casually leaning against the wall of the house as he put the cigarette to his lips and took a deep draw. The cigarette was finished and breathing out languidly the nub was dropped to the ground. It remained glowing for a while on the damp earth. The man watched as the glow diminished and as it ended he straightened up and pulled his coat around his torso.

He looked up to the sky, clouds still passing in front of the moon. This was what Steve had waited for. The action of looking up exposed the man's neck from within the clothes and in a second Steve had stood up and moved behind him. The garotte was quickly over his head and down against the throat. The surprise caused him to react in a way that Steve had expected and the man clutched at the wire trying to pull it away as Steve's strength held it there and the sharpness of the small diameter cut into his neck.

His next action was equally as expected. Overcoming the shock of the attack his obvious training came into effect. Loosening his hold at the metal he attempted to turn taking the wire from the front to the back of his neck and at the same time confronting the attacker. Steve was wise to this and just as quickly moved further around the back of his victim. "Dance macabre," he uttered as he maintained the position. Steve knew his job. He had trained for years with the regiment and had always been the man selected for this work and his colleagues understood that he probably even enjoyed it. His power was superior to that of the guard and the guard now knew it. Unable to confront the attacker his hands clawed again against the wire now cutting deep into his neck. Steve felt a warm liquid ooze over his hands. The man gasped, smoke from his last cigarette on his breath. His knees buckled, strength ebbing from the body he sank to the ground, Steve following him down to the damp earth. The grip was tightened again and again until the thrashing of the body had stopped and still the wire was pulled. The whole grisly action had taken only a few minutes. The man had had no time to deliberately utter a sound and his only noise was the spluttering gurgle of his last breath as it mingled with the blood. Steve took out his pencil torch and looking down at the now lifeless body shone the light on his face. Eyes staring, lips twisted and a deep gash in the throat. He could see the blood spreading along the ground black like oil in the darkness. Careful to avoid it reaching his shoes he loosened the garotte and pulled it from the dead man's neck wiping it and his hands on the man's clothes, he replaced it in his pocket. He opened the overcoat that his victim was wearing to search for a weapon and in doing so exposed the uniform that was being worn. The beam from his torch picked out the shiny emblem, the Totenkopf on the right collar, the uniform of the Schutzstaffel. He had not expected to see a uniform. Was this some military operation? Were there still members of the SS alive? He placed his foot on the man's forehead pulling it backwards the spine showing white against the red flesh in the neck and he looked again at the face of the man, someone around thirty he guessed. "Hmm a guy younger than me," he mused softly to himself, "my Dad always said that a good old un will always be better than a good young un." Standing up again he admired his handiwork for a moment before returning to the others. Pressing himself against the wall and silently passing below the balcony he made his way back along the side of the house and out across the drive on to the road.

"That's one less," he quipped as the others left the cover of the hedge to greet him as he made his way back to where they were waiting.

Tom shook his head silently. His brother was always the sort to enjoy that part of any conflict. Tom knew it was necessary on many occasions and was prepared to play his part but he didn't relish it as much as Steve.

"What happened?" asked Mick.

"The guy was having a quiet smoke but I soon put a stop to that. I always said smoking was bad for your health and now he knows it to be true."

Mick ignored the joke even considering that Steve was himself a smoker and, as was his forte, continued with the business part of the action.

"Where did he come from?" he asked. "Was there any open door to the house or what, did you see a way in from there?"

"As I made my way back out here, I was close to the balcony. I had to creep under it you know. There were steps leading up to the walkway and I think that the way in is through those windows that Tom and Tilly saw, you know the windows with the blind?"

"If there are other guys up there then won't they be wondering what happened to their mate?"

"Well eventually I guess so. I've no idea if there are any others or how many. I think we just need to get on with it now, don't forget Joe will be back sometime. Oh by the way, my man was wearing an SS uniform, *what's* going on here?"

"A uniform? SS? Christ they really mean it don't they, there could be an entire army up there."

Chapter 60

"OK," said Tom, "let's get in there and deal with this. I think we should approach the house from the front to begin with and if that's a problem then get around the back.

He was the first back on to the drive and maintaining as much silence on the gravel as possible, he approached the window under which they had seen a trapdoor. He bent down to inspect the fastening. There was just one large bolt and he slowly began to draw it back. The dampness from the weather had provided some lubrication and very quickly the bolt was withdrawn. Tom slipped his fingers in between the two doors and started to raise them, but they wouldn't move. He adjusted his grip another effort but still no movement.

'Bugger, there must be a bolt or padlock or something on the other side,' he said silently to himself shaking his head. Mick understood.

"They're not going to make it that easy mate."

Tapping Tom on the shoulder he gestured him away from the unyeilding entrance and the pair of them crept across to the front door. Steve had already looked closely at it while the trapdoor had been tried. There was no obvious weakness in the door.

"I had hoped that it might have been left open for us," he joked. "Let's see if we can see anything through the windows."

An inspection of the windows at street level revealed nothing. Each one seemed to have thick curtains which had been pulled tightly across allowing no light to pass through. From the front the residence looked dark and forbidding, empty of people.

"Well if there is a secret in here he's got it well locked away," said Tom, "certainly from this side anyway, let's go around the back."

"There's a secret alright, SS uniform? Follow me," said Steve pointing to the side along which he had made his entrance and exit of the garden. "The body is around the opposite side, do you want to have a look?"

Tom shook his head.

The side of the property was equally well hidden from anyone passing by along the road. An even larger evergreen running the length of the house separated it from next door on one side, and on entering the back garden the hedge continued for a few yards and then was trimmed to a metre in height. It was from this side that Tilly would be watching, so her view into the garden was unhindered, but in spite of what Steve had reported Tom wondered if she would be able to see the front of the house clearly, the approach along the road was clear but the drive, he was not so sure. Too late to worry about that now he thought.

He looked up from the back garden and could just see the dark outline of the railway bridge, could Tilly see them, he wondered? Would she be watching at that moment? The garden was long stretching down to the river and at one time had clearly been well loved. The landscaping had obviously been done in a way that enhanced the view from the house across the water and enabled it to benefit from its position enjoying some thirty metres or so of prime waterfront. That must have been some time ago, thought Tom. The sweeping lawns looked uncared for, even by the standards of February or early spring and the borders had not been tended, left with the withered stalks of last year's flowers. Lengths of grass grew up among the dead sticks still remaining from the summer growth of the now unrecognizable plants. This was no longer a family house, what was its purpose?

Tom had seen this from the opposite river bank and he had memorized the garden layout. "The window that has the blind is at this end," he whispered pointing up to the balcony. "I want to see that first."

"Yes," replied Steve. "If that's where the guy came from then it's most likely to be the way in."

As they moved away from the cover of the laurel into more open ground the clouds, which were continuing their inexorable passage across the sky, moved away from in front of the moon casting a silvery glow onto the wet grass. The men pressed themselves against the house wall, beneath the balcony and with the dark clothes that they were wearing they remained invisible to any neighbours or anyone looking from across the river. Inching their way beneath the balcony towards where the blind covered window was situated all three suddenly stopped. A faint noise increasing in intensity as they approached had become obvious to them and for a moment they stopped and looked at each other questioningly. Tom moved away from the cover afforded by the wall into the open garden and looked around and towards the railway bridge, then he returned to where the others had remained. "Just a train going by. I guess the sound has been picked up by Tilly's radio."

The others nodded.

Arriving below the window they looked up. Steve seemed to sniff the air.

"What's that smell?" he whispered. "Something chemical, a bit like ozone and disinfectant? I didn't notice it when I came here first time."

The others shook their heads. It was not a conventional window but seemed to be two glass doors opening fully onto the balcony. At any other time this would have been ideal for the owners of the property, a doorway allowing access to a pleasant seating area which in summer would be well used with its views over the river, the meadows and hills beyond.

To get to the back of the house they had passed under what seemed to be a fire escape and Steve now turned his attention to it.

"I said there would be something like this," he mumbled quietly, "this is our way up," and he slowly started to climb up the steps. The steps were metal and damp and the cold wet rail slipped through his hand as he made his way up. Mick followed as he turned to look for Tom but he had again moved from the shelter of the house and down the side of the garden to where he could see the bridge. He had detected another noise and was now staring towards the bridge, his eyes straining to see something, anything that would explain the growing sounds which he thought were coming from there. Mick and Steve had also now stopped climbing the steps; they too had begun to hear the muffled sounds.

"Sounds like a dog barking," said Mick, "there are plenty of animals around in this area."

"It's coming from the direction of the bridge," replied Tom, "where Tilly is."

"Probably from that house on the corner," said Steve. "When we left the car I heard the sound of a dog barking from one of the properties there. Either we can hear it from the house or even over the radio, after all we heard the train go by. Come on let's get going up these steps. Joe won't be staying long at The Eagle once he realizes we're not turning up. Tilly will let us know if there's anything going on."

Tom turned back to the fire escape, still some uncertainty in his mind over what he had heard but he knew Steve was right. Joe would be back before long and they needed to be inside and back out again before that.

The soft shoes with which they had equipped themselves enabled them to reach the top of the steps in relative silence and now they were onto the balcony. A metal seat towards the one end was the only adornment and dead leaves from the trees growing in the garden next door huddled against its legs and with the slightest breeze, swirled along the length of the balustrade. Tom looked out over the river. From this height and in the moonlight he could see the fence at which the two of them had halted earlier in the day. He recalled the smart man with the dogs and glanced questioningly towards the bridge. Just shielded now by the hedge growth this close to the house he could see nothing of it but he could hear nothing also. If there was a problem Tilly would have let them know wouldn't she? The strange smell was a little stronger now although no-one could quite put their finger on what it was. They pressed against the wall either side of the glass doors. There was definitely a blind on the other side reaching right down to the floor but now as they were on the same level a small chink of light showed itself at the bottom. It was not possible to see into the room but Mick thought he could see shadows passing along the bottom of the blind, why had a light been left on in this room? They pressed as close as they could to the window and a feint humming noise seemed to come from it.

Mick tapped his ear and then pointed at the window. The others knew what he meant; they nodded to say that they heard it too. He moved away along the balcony gesturing the others to follow.

"There's something in there," he whispered. "The light, that odour coming from inside and the sound, some sort of machinery working. We've got to get in there and soon." He pressed a button on his watch, a dim light lit up the dial. "Nearly six, Joe will have given up by now."

"OK," replied Steve, "let's see. There's no opening latch on the outside of the doors and usually doors open inwards for security. If the guard came from inside here then just maybe they are not totally locked, so that he could get back inside. There's not much room out here for a rush so we need a strong swift push. Two of us can do that with the other at the back. As we push and it opens go to the floor so that the back marker will have a clear view inside and a clear shooting area if necessary. Anyone armed inside will be aiming up at body level so if we are on the floor we will be out of target for a second or so giving us a chance to aim without being shot at.

The back marker will be the target so stay at the side for as much cover as possible the surprise element nearly always does it."

"Nearly?" asked Tom.

"Yeah nearly, provided it opens without much effort, do you want the job?"

"Suits me."

"OK, at my signal," Steve looked up at the sky. A large cloud was beginning to pass over the moon. A few seconds and it would be darker.

"One..Two..Three."

Mick and Steve in unison pushed against the middle the weakest part of the closed doors. A metallic scream sounded, the doors opened and the pair fell to the ground inside the room. In a second they had their guns trained towards the middle of the room, their eyes adjusting to the light.

A man stood to the side of some silver coloured equipment. The unexpected noise and appearance of the intruders to his world caught him off guard but quickly understanding that he was now under attack he regained his composure and drew a revolver from its holster around his waist. Aiming it at the now open doors he managed to get off four or five shots in rapid succession. Steve had guessed correctly, the rounds went above their heads where they might have been had they stood up, passing through the gap and out hissing into the night.

Tom had played his part also and had stood to one side as the deadly missiles passed a foot away. He looked around the door leveling his weapon at the same time and it seemed that simultaneously all the men fired.

The guard recoiled with the force of three rounds hitting him at the same time and his body travelled backwards as if propelled by some invisible hand and smashed against the wall, his body rebounded and crumpled to the floor.

Seeing the now motionless man on the floor, Steve and Mick rose quickly from their prone position, still holding their pistols forward in case of further attack. Tom joined them but no other person was inside and as they removed the balaclavas he approached the body.

"Another SS uniform, young bloke again just like you described the guy outside."

"Yeah," Steve muttered looking around him.

The light in the room came from a substantial chandelier hanging in the centre. Tom recognised the room as being similar to those he had seen downstairs when visiting the house for his sessions. Wood paneling encased the walls and a thick dark blue carpet covered the floor. Expansive and expensive leather armchairs were placed around the sides of the room all facing the fourth wall. A closed glass fronted cabinet filled with bottles of various drinks and glasses stood against the opposite wall and a large book case complete with numerous leather bound volumes completed the furnishings.

But this room was different he considered. In the houses along this road it might be usual to have expensive fittings as standard downstairs but this was upstairs where the bedrooms should be and this was clearly not a bedroom.

Against the far wall was the machinery alongside which the guard had stood, all three men appeared attracted to it as a magnet.

A wide metal, possibly aluminium, tube stood upright reaching some six feet. Rounded at the top, resembling an early space vehicle, there were several cables and pipes attached to one side trailing into a generator from which a continuous low humming noise emanated, an odour in the room reminded them of hospitals. On the wall above the vessel was a portrait of one of the most recognizable men that the world has ever known. A portrait depicting the man in his prime, his uniform immaculate, looking out over his world, a salute to his people. Adolf Hitler. Below the picture a plaque, written on it in a gold script were the words MEINE EHRE HEISST TREUE.

"This is spooky," ventured Tom, "look at the set up of this room. A place where you might stay in relative comfort for a while, a book to read, a drink from the cabinet, a place where you may talk quietly with friends, the reading room of a private club perhaps. At the same time facing that contraption as if it was the centerpiece, and in any case something from the fifties it seems to me."

"Look at it, it's the centre of attention in here," replied Mick, "can you imagine people sitting around doing whatever but facing it all the time, revering it as an altar and the inscription on the plaque, that's the SS motto..My honour is Loyalty. Is this what Joe has been guarding over the years? Steve saw visitors to the house you recall, Is this what they came to see? I have to say it, remember what Jimmy said, frozen bodies and so on. Is this what we have found?"

Chapter 61

The profoundness of the moment caught all of them and for a moment it was as if they too were in reverence of what they saw, what they considered might be in the capsule. The many images of Hitler that have been seen over the years, speaking to the masses, commanding their attention and absolute loyalty came to the mind of each man. The Fuhrer's stentorian voice, his theatrical delivery and compelling body language, it was as if he was there in the room with them. For the first time in his life since he had his dreams, Tom felt a cold shiver run through his body. Gone was the universal hatred of the man, he could now understand why millions worshipped him, he shuddered and turned away. Steve and Mick continued to examine the equipment and its technology but his attention had been caught by something else.

Around the walls of the room hung more pictures, fading photographs in elaborate carved wooden frames, men in uniform. As he approached them he began to see what they were, a gallery of Hitler's men, photographs that he had seen many times before in newspapers, on television, and in books.

As he passed along the line of images he recognised the faces of the people as they looked down on him from history, all with a superior gaze. Himmler, Borman, Hess, Goring and Goebbels, others were familiar although he could not name them. "This whole room is a shrine to the SS and the Fuhrer," he thought to himself. "Why, could James be correct?"

He progressed around the room, inspecting each picture, identifying them, thinking for a moment what he could recall about each one, considering the heinous crimes of which they had all been guilty. As he did so a thought grew in his mind concerning his own part in this. 'If I was hanged for war crimes as Joe said then I'm no better or worse than any of these.'

The idea that he could be within the regime that these pictures represented began to dawn on him; he shook his head.

"I can't believe it," he muttered and he sank down on to one of the armchairs, sitting for several minutes, head in hands. A glance at the others in case they were watching him, thinking the same as he was concerning his role in all of this. They were intent on the machinery. He looked up once more staring at the faces, no one in particular. After a while his gaze settled on a face that appeared to be staring out at him, a face somehow more familiar more personal than the others. Initially it meant nothing to him but as he continued to look it was as if recognition came over him. He felt an unexplained chill, a deep anxiety from within. Who was he looking at and who was looking at him? Slowly rising from the seat, his eyes narrowed. Moving closer he could see a name at the bottom of the photograph, partly obscured by the browning of the paper with age. He blinked and stepped back in surprise, shook his head, "No," he gasped, "It's not possible." Unable to take his eyes from the image he read the name, 'Artur Hamann'. His father was here proudly taking his place within the hierarchy of the Nazi elite and it could be for only one reason. It was true, he now knew, if Hitler was here awaiting rebirth, then it was his father who had made it possible.

Suddenly from behind him he was now aware of some movement. He turned away from the pictures

Steve and Mick were standing now facing the open window, someone was there outside on the balcony.

Tom remained where he stood, out of view of the balcony and whoever was on it. Crouching down now beside one of the armchairs and removing the weapon from his pocket he waited to see what or who was there. From his hiding place he watched as the others moved back into the room. A hand appeared through the opening, holding a pistol, pointing at his comrades, threatening, gesturing. Remaining silent he waited for the person to enter. "Joe," he whispered, "Joe."

"What are you doing here?" Joe rasped in a deep voice very different from the softer tones that he used when dealing with them previously. "What do you want with me, with my house, with my friends?" Although asking the questions it was clear that no answer was realistic, there could be no justification, no possible reason why they were there, no excuse for the body lying in a pool of blood outside in the garden or the body in the room crumpled against the wall, other than the destruction of Joe's world, that which he had revered and must have guarded for years.

They had discovered his secret. It had been hidden here at the house for many years. Something which he had protected, cared for, cherished over the time. An important place that was regularly visited by people who had travelled across the world to be in this room. A place that had been protected by men in SS uniform. Members of the Deaths Head Brigade. There was no way that Joe could allow this to become knowledge outside of this room, they had given him no choice.

From his hiding place behind the armchair, Tom had quickly assessed the situation and he knew that this was only going to end in one way.

He hadn't moved but remained silent, watching, ready to act. Joe was not aware of his presence.

Joe's finger grew taut against the trigger of the weapon, he was going to fire. Raising the gun level with their heads he aimed at the men as if an executioner, the trigger was squeezed.

Tom fired first. Aiming at the hand knowing that a shot to another part of the body could cause a reaction and Joe might fire anywhere. The shot hit the hand, the gun flew from his grasp, he cursed in total surprise. Tom fired again hitting him in the chest. In shock his injured hand went to his chest blood oozing between the fingers. A red hot pain, he looked towards Tom.

"Claus," he shouted in his confusion. "You of all people, you shouldn't be doing this." His voice lowered quickly, eyes questioning becoming soft, sorrowful even as he gazed at the face of the man who had changed from a friend to an enemy.

Joe sank to his knees, blood dripping on to the carpet from the shattered hand and the hole in the chest.

Steve and Mick had drawn their pistols by now and were aiming at Joe, who painfully began to crawl the few feet towards the still humming machinery and leaving a trail of blood across the floor. Reaching it he used the equipment to draw himself slowly up on to his feet and as he did so caressing the tank, draping his body over it in complete adoration of it and its contents.

He looked up at the picture of Hitler; tears began to well up in his eyes and sobbing they mingled with the blood running down the side staining the silver of the container.

He stood there for a little while his now wretching body supported by the tank. He looked around the room at the pictures on the wall taking them in as if he was about to leave a group of friends. He uttered his last words, "Den Tod Geben Und Den Tod Empfangen Leb Wohl, Leb Wohl."

His hand moved slowly, painfully around towards the back of the tank, the men detected a barely audible click.

He stood up unsupported as if to attention and then looked back towards Tom a weak smile on his lips, nodding slowly. Looking back now at the container he raised his head, chest out, arrogant and in a firm voice, "Ein Volk,Ein Reich,Ein Furhrer."

"Out," yelled Mick, "he's blowing up the whole thing. OUT."

The three men made the open window in a fraction of a second. On to the balcony they leapt, down the fire escape and ran towards the river as far as they could go from the house. As they lay on the damp grass the house was slightly above them. They pressed into the soft ground covering their heads with their arms waiting for the explosion that they knew would come.

The initial force from the blast escaped through the open window but over the heads of the three men as they pushed themselves further into the ground. Then the wall of the house opened up as a cave. A yellow flame passed over them with a rush of air and they felt the heat as it sucked the breath from their lungs. The dampness in the air sizzled, the blast so hot that it boiled the moisture around them and singed the hair on the exposed parts of their bodies. The ground buckled and a tide of pulverized furniture, machinery and debris blasted out through the gap in the wall cascading towards them and over their backs into the river. Then another blast which seemed to lift the upper floor of the house into the air the debris falling short of them as it returned to earth. The ruin of the house was now on fire, crackling breaking glass, metal twisting explosions within the bowels of the property.

Getting to their feet, now was the time they had to get away. The way out past the house was impossible.

"Over the fence to next door," shouted Steve, "we can climb over down here and regain the street from this side through this next garden."

People had come out of their houses to see what had happened but within the confusion and the darkness of the strect close to the hedge, the men were invisible. They quickly crossed over to the opposite side of the road and turned for the bridge.

"Why the hell didn't we hear from Tilly, she must have seen Joe come back?" shouted Steve as they ran. Within seconds they had gained the bridge and around the corner to where the car was parked.

Chapter 62

"You two get in the car and drive away, I'm going up onto the bridge," said Tom stopping by the steps that lead up to the parapet. "We'll see you back at the house, this place is going to be swarming any minute."

"No I'm coming with you," replied Mick. "Steve can go. I'm staying."

"Mick, we had no message from her, she *must* have seen Joe come back in his car," Tom shouted as he made the steps to the top of the bridge. Mick was close behind him as they approached the bushes in which she had hidden.

"Tilly," yelled Tom urgently. "Tilly where are you?" There was no reply. He tore at the vegetation in order to make his way into the undergrowth, branches scratching his face and hands, ripping his sleeves as he pulled apart some brambles; there was no sign of her.

"Over here," called Mick, who had gone a little way beyond the place where Tom had been frantically searching. "She's over here, I'm afraid…."

In a second he had reached the spot where Mick was kneeling down alongside the track, what seemed to be a bundle of rags beside him. Grabbing hold of Mick's jacket he pulled him away from the track and stood over the clothes. It was Tilly lying against a rail, arms across her face, her body motionless. He knew she was dead.

Tom knelt down. He moved some clothes to one side. The balaclava was wet, warm sticky blood met his hands as he put them behind the head and lifted it up towards him. Mick stood up and moved a few feet away turning his back on his now distraught friend as he cradled the lifeless form tightly to his chest. The tears flowed mingling with the gore and the soil from along the track, no words were spoken.

The minutes passed. Into the road had driven a police car and two fire appliances and the crowd of people had now grown, all concerned to see what had caused the explosion, the destruction of the house. Blue and yellow lights from the emergency vehicles flashed over the bridge. Tom neither heard nor appreciated any of the commotion. His attention was solely with his own grief. Since his return from Australia he had met Tilly again and in the brief time since then he believed that they had grown together and he had been anticipating a life with her in the future and he was sure that she had reciprocated the affection.

Now it was all over. Destroyed. Taken from him. Why and by whom? How had he become involved in this madness? Even now from over the years of history, Hitler was responsible for the death of innocents.

He had not noticed that Mick had moved a little further away from him and was now speaking on his mobile phone. Tom remained unaware of the animated conversation now taking place. The call ended, Mick put away his phone and returned towards Tom still kneeling by the track.

"She's been shot Mick," he sobbed, "who did this?"

"I don't know, Joe? I don't know. Tom stay here as long as you like. You'll be alright if you remain on the bridge. I've got things to do OK, just trust me. The police have cordoned off the road, no-one will come up here until you are ready."

"Things to do? Trust you? What are you talking about? Tilly's dead," he called, his voice barely audible.

"Just stay there. I'll be back soon."

Mick made his way to the top of the steps and stood there as if waiting for someone. After a few moments Tom heard a motor horn from the street below, Mick ran down the steps. Tom could not see what was happening. Something was going on which he did not understand. Tilly was dead; some-one was going to pay for this. If Mick is involved God help him.

Tom remained on the bridge with Tilly's body. He was talking to her as he held her hand, still warm.

"Tils what have I done to you? I never meant for you be hurt, to be involved in this and now you're dead. Tilly," he called half expecting an answer. "I love you so much and now you've been taken away from me. Why did this have to happen?" The tears flowed. He had been upset of course when she, then his wife, had left him for his brother but the anger he felt at that time was different. He had no tears then and took out his frustration by leaving the country, to get away from the hurt. At that time she was still alive, but this was different. This was final. She was dead. He cried until he could cry no more, until there were no tears left, he had lost all reason.

After some time he stopped crying and began to be aware of what was happening around him.

A gentle rain was falling and he could smell the essence of the railway. Damp oil along the track, wet ashes, gravel smelling of tar, pervaded his senses. Away from the bridge the house was ablaze, leaves on the evergreens in the garden crackled and hissed in the inferno, he could feel the heat up on the bridge. Flashing lights from the emergency services vehicles and from the flames lit up the road. Voices calling, whistles from the chief fireman signaling instructions. Hell must be like this he thought and I've lost my Tilly. He sobbed again.

"Tom, it's Mick, can we come over?" The voice brought back his attention.

We?, he thought to himself, who are we? Perhaps Steve? He didn't want to face Steve at this time. His brother had stolen his wife and now she was dead, it was all his fault, he's to blame. "I'll kill him," he mumbled.

"Tom it's Mick, I'm with two doctors can we come over?"

"Doctors? She's dead, what good are doctors? They can't bring her back, why have you brought doctors?"

"Tom they've come to take Tilly away, we can't let her stay here on this bridge, in the rain, they've come to take her somewhere more comfortable, it has to be done OK?"

The minutes passed, silence, Tom looked up at the sky as if asking for guidance, the rain on his face, then he nodded slowly, sorrowfully. "Yes," he shouted in anguish, "Yes..Yes...Yes," his voice tailing away.

Tom stood up, his hands on the parapet, looking at the commotion in the road. He wouldn't be able to look as the two men took away her body. They approached with considerable efficiency. He noticed their dark overcoats and dark suits beneath. Shoes and leather gloves shining with the wetness from the rain as the light from the flames lit up their appearance. Short cropped hair, young men in their thirties, doctors? Where are the white coats? I'd know what they were if they had on dark glasses he thought, coming back to his senses.

From the top of the bridge his gaze fell on a long limousine parked at the bottom of the steps. A hearse? Certainly not a doctor's car. The windows blacked out but the rear of the vehicle open and the engine running silently, exhaust coming from somewhere underneath. Another man stood by the opening as if on guard. His glance up to the parapet met Tom's, the man immediately turned away.

On the bridge another explosion from the burning house caught the attention of the four men. The doctors ignored it and continued with their work on the body. "Take care of her," Tom urged the men. "Look after her."

Mick was looking at the house.

"What's going on Mick? What's all this about?"

"Let's get it all sorted and tidied up and when we are well away from here, we'll have a talk."

"We'd better, my God we'd better."

"We will. Let's get down from here now so they can help Tilly."

Mick put his hand on Tom's back and guided him to the steps. They were wet and slippery with leaves and moss and Tom held on to the rail tightly as they descended, suddenly unsteady on his feet. Looking back, the men had lifted Tilly and were now carrying her towards the steps and then down to the waiting vehicle.

In the road below the bridge Steve was waiting, he knew what had happened. Tom could see that he too had been crying and why not? He had also been married to Tilly. The brothers embraced silently, too upset to say anything, any animosity between them suddenly a distant memory.

Mick had also reached the road and Tom saw him talk briefly with the car driver who nodded at whatever had been said.

"Let's get to the car and away from here," said Mick as he approached the pair still together in their grief and they followed as he led the way back to where they had parked some time earlier. They would be returning without one of their number.

Mick got to the car first and opened the doors for the others helping them inside before getting into the driver's seat. He turned the key, the engine burst into life and he let out a long silent breath as the wipers cleared the water from the windows.

He turned the steering wheel and they made off towards the City not so busy now, the workers and shoppers were at home away from the weather.

"None of them knows about Tilly," Tom said, "I know they would cry as well if they did."

The others said nothing, there was nothing that could be said now, nothing would ease Tom's pain, only time. It had been just about one hour since they had passed this way out to Joe's house and now on their way back the world had changed. As far as Tom and probably Steve were concerned, not for the better, but for Mick that might well be another story.

Chapter 63

Within a few minutes they were pulling up outside Mick's house. He brought the vehicle to a halt just behind a large black limousine and opened the door to get out and as he did so another large car drew up behind.

Mick nodded to the unseen occupants and opened the back doors of his vehicle to allow his passengers to leave.

The three men crossed the pavement to the front door and Mick quickly opened it ushering the pair inside.

"Let's get these clothes off," said Mick. "Pile them in the corner, I need a drink."

The three of them began to remove their outer clothes. The clothes were wet and smelled of many things all of which they had encountered a short while ago. Blood, oil, tar, smoke but even now Tom detected a faint perfume. He had held Tilly, her lifeless body; she had left a trace of herself on him. They replaced the discarded garments with the items they had left on the floor previously, a small pile remaining in the corner of the room, those belonging to their comrade who had not come back.

Mick had returned to the front door and opened it. Two men entered, they nodded to the room in general and removed their black Trilby hats.

They looked every bit as they should, stereotyped men from the Ministry, thought Tom, but as they never would personally dirty their hands, or be seen at the pointed end, that wouldn't matter.

Sharp suits beneath an obligatory overcoat and highly polished shoes were the order of the day. He considered the men in the silence that followed. Tall, they usually were for some reason, probably ex guards and with short cropped hair. The square expressionless face of the man he took to be in charge seemed to shine. Rain or sweat he wondered or perhaps cologne as a sweet scent permeated the room. The other man was dour, with a slightly broken nose and partially closed left eye but unusually, Tom thought, he sported a short trim beard.

Mick had busied himself in the cupboard at the back of the room and had produced five glasses and a litre bottle of single malt which he proceeded to pour in large measures.

The square faced man shook his head as a glass was offered. "Water will do," he grunted in a sandpaper Scottish accent. Odd thought Steve, Scotsman who doesn't take scotch, as he downed his drink in one go.

"I needed that," he said as he fell down on to the chair facing the still standing men. "Mick, who are these guys?"

"Names are unimportant," butted in the broken nose, his accent gentle, upper-class, clipped, Smith, Jones it matters not. Tom I, we are sorry for your loss, if it could have come out otherwise then we would have wished it so. What went on tonight we had to do either now or in the future. For the loss of one of our number we have arrived at the place for which we have aimed over many years."

"For the loss of one of our number," Tom blurted out rising from his seat, throwing his now empty glass against a wall. "The only person we have lost is my girl, one of our number did you say? What do you mean one of our number? You bastard, who do you think you are. She was one of our number is that what you're saying? I'm not one of you so do you mean your number? She was dispensable do you mean?"

Three steps saw him face to face with the man, his fists clenched, his face distorted in anger. The other man moved quickly between them. Tom felt his unexpected power as he pushed the pair apart.

"No Tom that's not what we are saying. I'm sorry that it came out like that. I fully understand your loss. Words can sometimes convey the wrong meaning. Perhaps I can describe it as being better to arrive at a decision without a reason, the decision may be correct but the reason may not be. Please let us not cause offence by how we say things; it is difficult enough at this time, alright?"

Tom moved back to his chair, he picked a glass from the table not caring whose glass it was and proffered it to Mick who quickly refilled it. Tom sat down and took another draught this time leaving some in the tumbler.

Square face spoke. "Tom you are the most important person here at this time and certainly have been over the last few weeks. You have suffered the greatest loss," he said flashing a glance at Mick, "and so it is to you that the explanation is owed and you have to know the reason why and how we have come to this point. I know that you were surprised at Mr. Cannon's actions on the bridge and so I will hand over to him at this point."

He stood away to the side of the room having motioned for Mick to take over.

"OK Mr. Cannon," said Tom sarcastically, at the same time finishing his drink. "Let's hear what you all seem to know that I don't." He stood up and moved to the table on which Mick had placed the whisky bottle, snatching it up he sat down with it, eyes fixed on him waiting for what was to be said and how it was said.

"OK," commenced Mick with a little hesitancy but a voice clear as one used to addressing or briefing senior officials.

"The story goes back a long way, to the end of the war. Some of it you will know, but please bear with me. The Russian army was now in Berlin and as well as wanting to end the conflict, Hitler was their target, they had been told that he was at the Reichskanzlei. The small group of soldiers arrived there and blasted their way into the bunker, no Hitler. The men were furious; their fortune by way of reward for his capture was gone. What could they do? Amongst the people in the bunker they found one of the Fuhrer's doubles, a man who was used for security purposes, he would do they thought and so he was shot without any compunction, using the weapon that he had on his person, a Walther, the same as Adolf's. Would anyone realize who he really was? Their reward depended on there being no recognition, so the body was burnt and passed off as his and for the next few years, that was that as far as the Russians were concerned."

He looked over at the two men; they nodded for him to continue.

"Well, at the time, the others in the bunker were taken prisoner and eventually handed over to us, the Bolshevics had no use for them and didn't want the trouble, they had other problems. The British authorities at the time, questioned them and one prisoner turned out to be Claus Hamann."

Tom looked up, his face expressionless.

"We knew about Hamann and his connection with Heim and so on and so he was sent for trial and subsequently executed."

Tom remained silent.

"During the trial, presumably in an attempt to save himself, he told us the story about Hitler leaving the bunker with Eva Braun a few days before the soldiers arrived and so we knew, or at least considered, that the Russians had got the wrong man. We kept that to ourselves for future use."

"We needed to find out more and so intelligence was put on to the case," he paused, "Captain Regan."

Tom lifted his eyes towards Mick whose gaze was now directed to the two men, the explanation was at a critical stage and he needed help.

Broken nose continued, "Mr Olive, Tom, *please* listen to what has to be said. It is difficult, I know, the present circumstances are tragic without doubt, but please listen."

"Captain Regan?" shouted Tom standing up, "Captain Regan?" Tilly was named Regan, are you saying…?

"Yes Matilda's father."

Tom moved quickly across the room towards the men, they separated rapidly so he arrived between them, their training ensuring that any attack was now divided. Tom was still capable of causing them serious injury even with this tactic and Steve quickly intervened, holding back his furious brother.

"Tom come away, they're not worth it, let's see the story through first, then if you have to kill them so be it," and he pushed him back from men now obviously concerned for their safety, hands feeling inside their overcoats for weapons.

Mick joined Steve and between them Tom was restrained and he fell down onto the settee.

"Have another drink Tom," said Mick "please let's get this out and then you do what you have to do."

For a few moments they was an uneasy truce amongst them. Tom relaxed a little, glaring at broken nose. A few more minutes, another drink, Mick continued.

"Tom yes, you are correct, it was Tilly's father, he was around twenty years old at the time. Continuing to question Hamann, it was believed that Adolf had gone to Scandinavia, and whilst in custody Hamann had heard of the events with the Uboat and had put two and two together, guessing that the family had now got away as far as South America."

"Ok Tom?" said Steve, "alright if we continue?"

Tom nodded wearily and had another drink.

Mick continued, "No more was forthcoming from the prisoner and you know what happened then. So with the Fuhrer and his family in South America, what could be done? None of the governments over there were friendly, just the opposite, they were obstructive, diplomacy failed, threats and bribery failed, we could make no progress. The years just after the war were a complete loss as far as we were concerned and so other things took priority. Into the fifties, then the sixties, time passed by, still no chance of progress. The Israelis went over there and found nothing, we went over there and found nothing and all the time Hitler, wherever he was, was getting older, we knew we would lose him to old age eventually.

Captain Regan was getting older also, he married, had children, Matilda and James and the pair of them grew up. Tilly met you and married, James went to University and studied history. As children they heard tales of their father's role in the war and James, in particular became interested in Hitler's disappearance, using the story as a basis for his research. He became very good at it and also, with the world changing, more friendly South American governments, technology and so on, he began to find things, stories, information, reports and slowly he built up a picture of what could have happened to Hitler and his family. From time to time, he would discuss his findings with his father and therefore the information was passed on to the government in the form of Military Intelligence."

Mick looked over at the Square faced man and gestured for him to take over the story. "Well as you are MI then I suggest that you carry on where you are involved?" the statement equally as much as a question. Square face nodded and moved to the centre of the room.

Tom looked at him sternly the alcohol beginning to show in his demeanour.

"So when James was giving me all this information, he had already researched it sometime earlier?" he mumbled. "I thought it was all a bit quick, he gave answers to my questions almost as soon as I asked them.

I said that to Tilly at the time, bloody hell, what was going on?"

"Yes that is correct," the other man replied, "and of course it was your involvement that changed the course of our plans. During your marriage you must have told your wife about your experiences with regression and the therapist. She told her father of your belief that you were Hamann and the connection was made through James research. Up to this point we had planned, at an appropriate time, to dispose of Joe and his father's body, which we were now certain was Hitler but we now had a problem, you or Hamann. We know that Adolf died in South America after you were hanged for war crimes, but we did not know what you could be made to say about your past life. We couldn't take the risk that some revelation could implicate the British government in the murder and destruction that was necessary, the Russians wouldn't appreciate it for a second, remember they thought that they had got rid of the Fuhrer years earlier. They would be severely embarrassed if it was proved otherwise and our relations with them are important these days. Joe had a similar problem with you if you think about it. So we had to keep you close, as did he, and be involved, and have you accept some responsibility in what would eventually happen. Your ex-wife pushed this along and persuaded your brother to encourage you to return, subliminally with her as, well, the incentive, and so you returned."

"So all this has been going on for years?"

"Yes, but time was never the issue, Joe was not going to move from his house, he and therefore Hitler's body would always be there."

Tom rose up and moved over to the table, he stood there for a few minutes, hands resting on the piece of furniture as if for some support, and gazing up at the ceiling. He turned to the rest of the room.

"Look there is something here that doesn't add up. You lot are Military Intelligence, you can do anything you like and get away with it. Murder, lie, cheat, whatever, all governments do it all over the world every day, you could have blown up Joe's house and destroyed everything at anytime and called it a gas leak or used some other spurious excuse. Am I right? Eh. And if you can do that, you could have got rid of me easily enough. Out of the way I would be no threat, would I? No more regression, but you say you wanted to implicate me to ensure my silence in case I could say anything in the future to embarrass you or the bloody state. That's crap, what's the real reason, or is none of you men man enough to tell me?"

The four men looked at each other, their faces showing their discomfort, eye brows raised, feet shuffled, hands moved into pockets. Then in unison they turned to the door of the kitchen which had opened and a figure entered the room.

The man was tall, around seventy years old, fit for his age. Grey hair slicked back. His suit was immaculate. Tom even through his alcoholic haze and the passage of time recognised him, Tilly's father, Mr Regan.

"Regan, what are you doing here?" he stuttered, confused by this unexpected appearance of his ex father in law.

Regan moved across the room towards him and he held out a hand to Tom. The handshake was firm and

Tom felt that there was some affection in the way of it as it lingered for a few seconds. He then moved towards the others who quickly and with some deference moved aside as he approached.

"Thomas," he said quietly in his soft southern Irish accent, "you are quite correct to have your doubts. You are owed an explanation and I must be the one to tell you. It is simple really, nothing sinister, in fact just the opposite. These days I am Director General of MI5 and as such have been in command of the organization throughout the time that the situation with you, Hitler, Joe and so on has been current. My predecessor took on the case initially and, much as you say was in favour of a quick destruction of the site, the house, and, I am sad to say, your elimination also. You were considered a threat. I took over the role and the plan of action, but I now brought another element to it, I was your ex father in law and my daughter, my lovely Matilda, your ex-wife. I have never allowed personal matters to influence my decisions before, but now I had to tell her what would happen. Over the years she had come to regret the circumstances of the divorce, no, more than regret, it was seriously effecting her health. She said she had considered suicide, she desperately wanted you back and if you were to be eliminated then whatever happened afterwards would be my fault. Tilly was still in love with you, for some reason now more than ever, absence and so on maybe, I'll never know. But this was my daughter, I couldn't risk losing her over this however much I knew that what I should do was the right thing to do. I was persuaded to let you return, meet her again, rekindle the relationship and possibly the marriage, she said that with the two of you together again, she would ensure that Hamann would never return. I accepted that and so you were spared, if I can use that term, and so here we are."

Tom shook his head, tears filled his eyes, he was clearly upset by this revelation.

"But now she's gone, I have lost her; you didn't foresee that did you?"

"No I did not and I have lost a daughter," Regan sat down, head in hands.

"You bastards, you are all responsible for this, everything is ruined. I'm not going to allow you to get away with this."

"What do you intend to do?" asked Steve with some concern for his brother's state of mind.

"I'm going to get the lot of you for this. I'll tell the world what has gone on here. The Russians can do what they like, anyone can do what they like, you'll all be sorry."

"Tom I'm sorry I was just doing my job," said Mick.

"Yeah, how many Nazis said that at the end of the war?"

"That's unfair," snapped Square face.

"Is it unfair that she's now dead?" Tom shouted back. "And the body?"

"It's done already," intervened Broken Nose, "we've taken away Miss Regan, she had an accident on the railway line. The authorities agree that that is what happened and her family will be informed. The house blew up as a result of, what did you say, a gas leak? Absolutely correct. There have been problems with the utilities in that road for a while," he continued rubbing his fingers together, "just a terrible explosion. The occupant was killed."

"And the others?"

"What others? Our cleaners will deal with anything else on the site, these tragic accidents happen from time to time, elderly man, living on his own, went down to the pub didn't he? Left the gas on, came back, turned on the light, Boom."

He smiled at his light hearted comment, probably the only time he had ever made one, but the sense of it had come home to Steve already. The deed was done and already covered up, what more did he expect from the powers that be.

"But what about Joe?" asked Steve, "I thought that by what he had said to us from time to time that he had help from you people? You know what he had said when he was attacked at his house or when he was in hospital, and wasn't he receiving support when he told you he was chasing Nazis?"

"Certainly not, of course we encouraged him, shall I say, as we needed to stay close to him that was all. What we did for him was solely for our own purposes."

The other suit took over the conversation.

"We will be going now. Mr Cannon is our contact over the next few days. Mr Olive, on behalf of Her Majesty's Government I wish to thank you for your help. I am sorry about your girl friend and also sorry about the way we had to conduct this matter. I think that with time you will see and understand that because of the potential gravity of the situation we could not allow you to know of our motives. It had to be entirely innocent or I have no doubt that Schacht, Ciemny or whatever he called himself would have picked up on the matter. I know that Miss Regan's brother thought that he could have been one of Hitler's children and he may well have been. However he has gone now so we will never know."

Tilly's father said nothing, although head of the Military Intelligence, the loss of his daughter was affecting him in a serious way. He would never have allowed a minion to talk this way in any other circumstances but Broken Nose knew the score. Regan had made a bad call in allowing himself to act this way and make a decision based on emotion, and his daughters emotion at that. He was finished now and his two colleagues knew it.

Tom stood up and placed his long since empty glass on the table. He approached the two men, the effects of the drink now seeming to have passed as he had listened to what had been said and concentrated to understand it.

"Just one problem left then I suppose," stated Tom.

Mick and Steve looked at him questioningly. It seemed as if everything was dealt with however appalling it was. Raw and real now, but after a time they would all resume their lives and the Great Explosion would be no more than an event that happened on a damp February evening, passing from the memory of the good folk of Hereford, a report in a local newspaper gathering dust in someone's garage.

"The problem Mr. Olive?" questioned the younger man. His eyes narrowed as he tried to imagine what could possibly have been omitted from his detailed planning.

"Don't tell me that you have never considered me now that Tilly has gone, my situation in this, what I will do in the future, now that she is no longer here. I may have remained below the parapet with her as my wife, but now? Have you forgotten that I am still Claus Hamann in another time? What if I wish to be regressed again? What if I am able to recall other things relative to the last war involving people who would prefer things to remain hidden, undiscovered or whatever? I remember Joe saying something about possible involvement of the Royal Family, you know German ancestors, The Duke of Windsor and as well as that, important press barons who supported Hitler at this time, no doubt some of those who later would have been given positions in the occupying government and so on. But just as difficult to explain away would be various countries giving Nazis a safe haven after the war, countries such as Ireland or America. Now that would be a big deal wouldn't it?"

Tom remained standing in front of Broken nose and Square face, his eyes taking on their most fearful stare.

"Well I can tell you that we have considered this. We appreciate that what you say could well happen and if your possible future discoveries concerned important people, say in other countries or governments, then as a true patriotic Englishman I have no doubt you would let us know so that we can take the appropriate action if necessary."

"And if it involved the British Government? You know I have been lied to by everyone and just about every day over the last few weeks. I have been used to get to the bottom of a problem not of my making so that the world need not fear the spectre of Adolf Hitler. My life and those of my friends have been put at risk and now the one most dear to me has been killed, and you just clean it up, move on and it never happened, but I think that that is just an excuse, a smoke screen to have me comply and help in the destruction of something that might not exist. Do you know what I really think?"

"You'd better tell us."

"Well I think that it really is to protect vested interests. If I was regressed again I could probably identify some very important individuals, people in authority in Britain today who had an interest in Germany during the war and how embarrassing would that be?" Tom stopped talking for a moment. The look on the faces of the suits spoke to him. Suddenly he understood.

"That's it isn't it? That's what all this is about? You are protecting someone here and now in your government. There is no way that all this could be anything else. The time, the money, it's someone big. Who is it? Tell me who it is."

He voice lowered, "And Tilly she is dead. We made plans and now thanks to you they are all finished. She's dead, *dead*, do you understand?" His voice rising again to a scream.

"Yes I think I do understand," replied the older man. "You can certainly wield some power with what you may know and at some time in the future you may find it useful to divulge what you know. Is that what you are saying?"

"Absolutely right," spat back Tom.

"Then I think that for all concerned, I am going to have to deal with the problem."

His voice lowered as he reached into his coat. He slowly withdrew his hand. It was holding a pistol.

"I'm sorry Mr. Olive, I really am. We had all hoped that it would not come to this. You are now too much of a danger to the stability of Government."

His hand tightened.

"No!" yelled Regan, but it was too late.

The dull click of a silenced barrel. Tom fell backwards, the force from the high powered weapon throwing him across the room and against the wall; a reddening hole glistened in his forehead, eyes staring into the room. He was dead before his body hit the ground. Steve was white, hands to his mouth as he vomited onto the floor, Mick's eyes moistened.

"Christ, what have you done, there was no need for that, we could have dealt with it?" yelled Regan.

Square face shook his head. "Would that be in the same way that you dealt with the situation before? Sir, if I may say so, your ability to deal with problems appears to be compromised. You have been singularly unimpressive during this case, your judgement has been shown to be inadequate, and your daughter has been killed, how would you deal with that? I doubt that you will be permitted to handle any case in the future, but that will not be for me to say."

Calmly the weapon was replaced and the man adjusted his coat against the night air.

He opened the door and stood on the step for a moment looking up at the sky.

"The rain has stopped and the clouds have cleared somewhat," said the younger man. "Bit of a glow in the sky over there," he continued looking in the direction of Joe's house. "Red sky at night, is that what they say in this part of the world?"

He turned back and looked towards the open door. "Goodbye gentlemen, I don't expect that our paths will cross again, certainly I do hope not for all concerned."

They walked out into the street and gestured to the car that had parked up along the road.

The engine burst into life and the vehicle made its way alongside the two men who climbed in, and the car drove away from the house towards the City centre.

Chapter 64

Two weeks had passed. The house explosion in Hereford had made the national news and was reported as an accident.

'Three men killed in gas explosion.

A house in Hereford has blown up due, it is thought, to a gas explosion.

One man has been identified as the property owner, Mr. Joseph Schacht and the others are believed to be his sons who were visiting him from their home in Austria.

It is thought that Mr. Schacht had spent the evening with his sons, at a public house in Hereford City, but had probably left the gas on while he was away from the house. On their return a spark ignited the escaped gas and destroyed the house, killing the three men immediately.

Neighbours said that Mr. Schacht was a quiet elderly man, well respected in the area.

Police said that a few days previously he had been the victim of a mugging outside his house but that the two events were not thought to be connected'.

Square face was in his office in Whitehall and was scanning the morning newspapers. An article caught his attention and he picked up his receiver.

"Send John in here for a moment would you please, there is something I want to show him."

A few minutes later the door to the office opened and Broken nose entered the room.

"You wanted to see me?"

"Yes. There is something in the news that I thought you might like to read," and he handed over the sheet of paper folded so that the report was easily seen.

The younger man read the article out loud.

"The body of a man has been found at a farm situated in the Australian outback. It is believed to be that of Thomas Olive the owner of the farm. He had not been seen for a number of weeks and his post remained uncollected at Radinga Post Office."

"Mr. Olive bought the farm some three years ago having moved to Australia from his home in England."

"It has not been possible to identify the cause of death as the body had been scavenged by Dingoes for what is thought to be several days."

"Although Mr. Olive was divorced and lived alone, he was identified by photographs in the house and a wedding ring that he still wore. His family has been contacted through the British embassy and arrangements made for the body to be returned to England for burial."

He put down the paper on to the desk.

"You shot him in the head; there was no mention of the bullet hole?"

"The local man performed an excellent job with the post mortem."

Square face twisted on his chair to face the window and folded his hands on his lap.

"Please let our friend at Westminster know that it is now finished."

Broken nose left the room and closed the door behind him. The matter was never spoken about again.

END

Lightning Source UK Ltd.
Milton Keynes UK
UKOW051127 030314

227803UK00001B/1/P